DECEIVED

John H. Patterson

Grosvenor House
Publishing Limited

This book is published by
Grosvenor House Publishing Ltd
28-30 High Street, Guildford, Surrey, GU1 3EL.
www.grosvenorhousepublishing.co.uk

A CIP record for this book
is available from the British Library

ISBN 978-1-78148-393-0

Other books by the author :-

"Before The Leaves Fall"

Available through Amazon as a paper back and Kindle e-book.

ACKNOWLEDGEMENTS

Every author needs encouragement and support at some time during their labours. I would like to begin by thanking my wife Elisabeth for her forbearance and understanding whilst I spent many, many hours in front of a computer screen.

Words cannot express my gratitude to my ex colleagues and dear friends Val Thompson and Yvonne Johnson. They have supported me every step of the way with their suggestions, constructive criticisms, corrections and encouragement. Their knowledge of English literature, plot and character development is so much more extensive than I could ever hope to achieve and leaves me embarrassed but forever grateful that they were there to guide me.

As a frustrated amateur historian the period of the Second World War is outside my comfort zone and I am in debt to the authors of the books listed in the bibliography for providing me with information which has set the scene for my second novel.

I would further like to thank my old friend Alan Wright for freeing up time in his busy schedule to edit and proof read my manuscript and offer help where necessary. His erudite comments and suggestions have provided a pragmatic rein in an endeavour to control my fertile imagination. Nevertheless any errors which remain are mine alone.

Finally my thanks go to Laurie Graham, Chairman of the Old Blaydonian Association (Blaydon Secondary-Grammar-Comprehensive School which was established in 1912) for his help in putting me in touch with Jean Young who was a former pupil of the school during the period of my novel and who provided me with valuable historical and anecdotal information.

Auschwitz/Birkenau Gate photograph by the author – 2003 and manipulated in Photoshop.
Front and back cover designs by the author.

FOREWORD

This novel is intended for adult readership. It is a sequel to the author's first book, "Before the Leaves Fall", however, it is also a stand-alone story and readers do not need to be familiar with the first book to enjoy "Deceived".

Actual historical personalities (Heinrich Himmler, Adolf Hitler and others) have a place in the novel as the story unfolds but their involvement and conversations are pure fiction.

Many of the events germane to the story are a matter of historical fact but in some cases their actual time in the chronological sequence of the Second World War has been slightly altered to accommodate the characters as their lives unfold during the novel. This 'slippage' is minimal and in no way detracts from actual events or the flow of the novel.

The main characters are composite and a figment of the author's imagination. They are not meant to reflect real persons and as a consequence any resemblance to anyone alive or dead is purely coincidental.

CHAPTER 1

Katharina 1919

With a heavy, breaking heart Katharina turned away from the horse and trap bearing Robert away before it had even reached the archway leading out of the courtyard. She was not sure whether the nausea that was overtaking her was due to her pregnancy or whether it was the realisation that she would never ever see her young English lover again. She rushed into the nearest toilet and lay there hugging the bowl heaving and sweating. Maria followed her and placing her hand on her shoulder said, "Are you alright Frau Lieper? You go up to your room and lie down and I'll bring up a cold compress."

Generalleutnant Albrecht von Lieper watched the horse and trap out of sight before he turned to follow his wife into the house. Going in through the servants' entrance he bumped into Maria coming out of the kitchen with a bowl of cold water.

"Watch where you're going," he growled. "You stupid Polak."

"Sorry sir," Maria whispered lowering her head and scurrying along the corridor.

"What was the commotion?" Katharina enquired.

"Oh! I bumped into the Generalleutnant and spilt some water on his suit."

"Don't let him intimidate you," Katharina replied placing her hand gently over Maria's. Maria dipped the flannel into the cold water, squeezed out the excess and placed it over Katharina's brow.

"Thank you Maria, that's so soothing. I feel better already."

Although she was only the housekeeper, Maria had become much more than that since Katharina had arrived in 1915. The relationship had initially been strained when Generalleutnant Albrecht von Lieper had commandeered the estate in western Poland as a result of initial military success on the eastern front. Maria and her husband Tamas had either been too old, too stubborn or maybe both to leave when the previous land-owner had fled further eastward in order to avoid the

German army's advance into Russia. Over the years a mutual respect and even friendship had developed.

Katharina was tasked with ensuring that the estate increased its yield and that target production of wheat and barley was transported back to Germany in support of the war effort whilst her husband was at the front. However, with only a pool of young boys and very old men in the village Katharina found the challenge too much for her. Nevertheless, things took an unexpected turn for the better towards the end of 1916. A letter to her husband coincided with his visit to a large prisoner of war camp at Wahn near Cologne. Von Lieper despised the French and had a pathological hatred of eastern Slavs, particularly the Polish and Russians, but he had a grudging admiration for the English and their empire and as such he made enquires at the camp offices about the possibility of any prisoner of war having agricultural experience. Meticulous records directed the Generalleutnant to Robert Charlton who had his own farm back home in County Durham. In no time at all Robert found himself under guard and on a train bound for Poland although he was not party as to his destination.

Katharina had been swept off her feet by the young, dashing, Prussian Junker, Albrecht before the war but very soon after their marriage her relationship with him quickly deteriorated into a cold, loveless one of duty and boredom. The consequences of this for Katharina were that she retreated within herself erecting a wall which allowed for no emotion, cutting her off from the world outside. But more damaging, cutting herself off from her own deep emotional needs and desires which she scarce dared to acknowledge. The births of her two sons had given her a new focus and an outlet for her unfulfilled purpose in life, however, the death of her first-born at the battle of the Marne with Paris almost within touching distance in 1914 plunged her back into a state of despair and isolation from which even her Catholic faith could not extricate her.

It was this sad, distant, withdrawn woman presenting an appearance of disdainful aloofness who received Robert during the bitter eastern winter of 1916. Robert was housed in a converted estate outhouse in the courtyard which showed signs of having previously been a stables or byre. He was immediately intrigued and captivated by the tall, slim figure that approached him. Her finely sculptured chin and cheekbones, proud aquiline nose and skin that reflected an opalescent beauty were revealed when she finally lowered her fur-lined coat hood on their first meeting.

Regular nourishing food and substantial clothes that replaced his filthy, torn remnants of a uniform transformed Robert into the strapping young man he had been before his terrible ordeals on the Western Front. Because of decisions which needed to be made concerning the estate Katharina and Robert formed a working relationship. Over the months she observed his sensitivity and empathic devotion to the land and although 18 years his senior their conversations concerning the crops and harvest became at first more general and later, tentatively more personal. Robert's philosophy that we create our own reality in the here and now and that therefore we can be whoever we want to be affected her deeply and she gradually responded to his insistence that happiness was there for the taking without guilt and that we should seize the moment. This alternative point of view caused Katharina much soul searching and disturbed her deep felt religious faith. In spite of herself she found herself being drawn ever closer and closer to this vibrant young Englishman who challenged and unsettled her so profoundly. Eventually their love was acknowledged and consummated and Katharina had never experienced such emotional freedom and joy in living. Until, that is, when news of the death of her second son in front of Amiens in 1918 reached her. Her new found emotional stability was thrown into complete turmoil. In the immediate aftermath of receiving this news Katharina's mixed emotions found release in insatiable, vertiginous, aggressive, combative sex which forced Robert into reluctant submission. The act gave Katharina vent to expressions of anger, remorse, bitterness, grief and yet a love beyond comprehension. Afterwards, replete, exhausted, they lay together entwined and drifted into a netherworld sleep of oblivion.

The day finally arrived with news that they had both been expecting and dreading. The ending of the war in defeat for Germany left them both to reflect on how changing circumstances would impinge on their relationship. Frau Lieper's husband could be expected to return unannounced at any moment and this reality gave their thoughts for the future a potent urgency. After having been awakened to the enervating possibilities of a life of freedom and joy through love Katharina shrivelled at the thought of returning to a bankrupt sham of a marriage. And yet deep, deep down her Catholic faith, like phantom fish-hook barbs, would not release her and demanded submission to her duty as the church saw it. She could not be persuaded to return to England with Robert although her heart yearned to be with him and as a consequence a deep depression engulfed them both.

Generalleutnant von Lieper did not return until the spring of 1919 and this signalled the moment for Robert's departure. The whole of Europe was in chaos and Robert was told to make his own way to Danzig with the hope of finding a ship bound for England. Within 24 hours of von Lieper's arrival Robert, who was ignorant of the fact that Katharina was carrying his child, was being taken to the nearest main road by Tamas in the horse and trap.

Katharina lay on her bed with a million thoughts going round in her head. Now that Robert had finally gone her immediate problem was how to face life with her erstwhile absent husband with the added complication of her pregnancy with Robert's child. Maria, sensitive to Katharina's dilemma eventually asked calmly, "What do you intend to do Frau Lieper?"

"I don't know Maria. You must think I'm stupid turning my back on a life of certain happiness with Robert in England."

Hesitantly Maria replied, "Yes I do Frau Lieper. I have seen how you have changed since that young man came into your life. These past few months you have been radiant and it was obvious that Robert was absolutely devoted to you. Why not follow your heart and dreams in this time of so much horror and sadness, and with much more to come I think."

"The choice is not that simple Maria. For better or worse I am a married woman I cannot turn my back on Mother Church."

"And for this you would be a martyr? Is your God not a God of love?" Maria asked.

"Yes He is.....but I made a vow in His name and if I break that vow I risk my salvation. So.....my life is with my husband and whilst I shall always cherish my time with Robert, even in adultery, I shall pay my penance."

"What a confused contradiction your life has become."

"Don't you think I know that Maria." Katharina cried in despair. "Why do you think I have been so withdrawn these past few weeks? I have wrestled with my conscience and feared for my mortal soul."

"And what of the child? Will you tell your husband? Will you let him bring it up as his own unknowingly? Would he accept the child if he knew the truth?

"I don't know. I don't know. What should I do? And don't say follow Robert." Katharina answered wearily.

"If you're determined to stay with your husband then there is only one thing you can do and I think you know what that is. It would not be fair for you to unburden your guilt onto others especially your unborn child. You would have to live with the consequences of that, risk losing everything and you would still have your guilt."

"Thank you Maria, I appreciate your honesty and support. I think I'll just lie here for a little longer. Will you please tell Albrecht that I will be down for lunch presently."

Katharina and Albrecht sat opposite one another in the kitchen warmed by the stove. Although the long eastern winter was begrudgingly surrendering to spring there were still patches of snow where the drifts had been the deepest. There was little warmth in the sun as yet and the wind still had a biting chill.

Maria placed bread and cheese on the table. Katharina looked across at her husband. She hardly recognised him after almost four years of absence. She had wondered on many occasions about what their reconciliation would be like. Since his return yesterday he had been moody, taciturn and monosyllabic. Katharina hoped that this was just a temporary aberration of his wartime experiences and that it was not a harbinger of what her future life with him was to be like. He appeared tired and drawn. Where once the three schmitte, duelling, scars on his cheek had been fashionably handsome the pallor of his skin now threw them into ugly relief. He had been proud of his uniform and although the war was over he was still an officer in the Wehrmacht and Katharina was curious as to why he was dressed in a tweed suit. She startled as Albrecht broke the heavy silence between them. "We must leave here straight away and return to Germany. Nowhere is safe, not even the Fatherland but here in Poland we are like wurst between two slices of bread."

"Are we to leave all the work and effort which has gone into the estate over these past years?" She asked quietly.

"You have no idea woman," he growled.

"Then tell me Albrecht, how am I to know or understand cut off here in the middle of nowhere?"

"The whole of Europe is in anarchy," Albrecht pronounced throwing his arms in the air. "Those bastard politicians stabbed us in the back especially the communists and the Jews, always the bloody Jews, and allowed the Allies to dictate an armistice which is an insult to the Fatherland. *Mein Gott* not one foreign soldier set foot on German soil," he yelled. "The Kaiser has been forced to abdicated and flee to Holland leaving Germany in the hands of lily-livered liberals who've formed a National Assembly comprised of opportunists, mongrels and Jews."

"How does that affect us here?" Katharina asked.

"Are you really that stupid?" Albrecht growled. "Since the collapse of pre- war, stable authoritarian rule those on the left and extreme right have fractured into numerous political groups each fighting for control. And I mean fighting. Demobbed soldiers are unemployed and roaming the streets whilst Communist groups are active all over Germany and our neighbour Russia is not just standing back looking on benignly, which is why we must leave here and return to Germany."

"Whatever you say Albrecht," Katharina replied calmly.

"Pack one suitcase and be ready to leave for Ciechanow tomorrow morning..... early. We can get a train from there to Warsaw and on to Berlin. There we can stay in my apartment until things settle down."

They stood up after lunch and putting her hand on Albrecht's arm Katharina said quietly, "Would you like to see what your English prisoner of war achieved whilst he was here?"

"If you insist," Albrecht replied in a bored voice.

They walked beyond what had been the formal garden area before the war to where the fields began, to where Katharina had stood on many occasions watching her lover toiling in the high summer sun. "So, he made a difference, your English farmer." It was more of a rhetorical question than a statement.

"You must have seen the production figures. You know that he did. But it was not what he did, it was more the way that he achieved it. It was almost as if the land knew that he loved it and it responded with increased production." The metaphor did not escape Katharina and she had to stop giving herself away by becoming too animated.

"Perhaps I should have directed him towards my family estate in Prussia instead of setting him free," Albrecht sneered.

Later that evening they lay side by side in bed. Since her chat with Maria Katharina had spent the whole day preoccupied with how she would approach this moment. It was almost impossible to gauge Albrecht's mood. She had to take a chance. It was now or never. She couldn't delay. Turning towards her husband she stroked his cheek. "Was it terrible?" she enquired quietly. "You look so tired and utterly worn out. Here, let me hold you." And she turned towards him cradling his head in her arms and moving her left leg across his lower body. As she stroked his hair she could feel his response against her thigh. Almost immediately he was on top of her and the sex was as perfunctory, quick and loveless as she had remembered it. With a grunt he rolled over and in a very short while was snoring rhythmically. Katharina lay in emotional solitude mourning for her English lover but at the same time consoling herself in the knowledge that it was not unusual for some babies to be born six weeks premature.

Next morning the same horse and cart that had transported Robert away was ready to take Katharina and Albrecht to Ciechanow.

"Look after yourself Maria and I'll write to you as soon as I know where I'll be living, and thank you for everything. I'll miss you and old Tamas. You have been like family to me. Oh....and I solved my dilemma last night." Maria looked slowly into Katharina's eyes and knowingly nodded her head. "May your God go with you Frau Lieper and I hope you have a good life."

Tamas flicked the reins and the horse trotted on through the arch moving from one universe known to another unknown.

Albrecht and Katharina stepped off the train at the Berlin Grunewald Bahnhof just as dusk was falling and transferred to the steam driven urban S-Bahn for their onward journey towards the centre of Berlin.

"Come on," Albrecht urged as he steered her along the pavement. Katharina responded nervously. They weaved their way in and out of the milling, grey, sombre crowd. They appeared to be blocking every road in whichever direction Katharina looked. On entering Wilhelmstrasse Katharina was very aware of an atmosphere pregnant with a heavy, expectant stillness, an electrifying anticipation like she'd experienced before, just prior to a summer thunderstorm. Making their way to the Brandenburger Tor they could hear drums beating and people chanting in the distance. The noise got louder and louder as a large, marching group of shabbily dressed men, some waving red flags and banners approached, the crowd parting in front of them like the Red Sea at Moses' behest. They ebbed, flowed and rippled like a wheat field in a strong breeze.

"I told you these bastard Communists were everywhere," Albrecht said turning to his wife. Just at that moment without any signal or warning absolute chaos erupted. Gunshots were heard and two of the marchers fell to the ground. Panic spread quickly amongst ordinary bystanders who screamed, shouted and ran in all directions bumping into one another in their haste to find shelter from the hail of bullets. From underneath their jackets Katharina saw some of the marching men take out handguns and run for cover. Albrecht with a soldier's instinct grabbed his wife and dragged her into the nearest doorway as bullets zapped and zinged all round them. Crouching in the doorway Katharina could see numerous men in uniform criss-crossing the street running from cover to cover trying to outmanoeuvre the marchers who had now broken ranks and scattered. The pitched battle increased in intensity as flags, banners and bodies littered the street. "Keep your head down," Albrecht shouted as a stray bullet ricocheted and zinged off the wall beside Katharina's head. But it was too late. She screamed as stone fragments and blood splattered her face leaving her momentarily blinded. Minutes later, taking her hands away from her face Katharina saw her husband lying crumpled up in the corner of the doorway. Just as quickly as it had begun there was now only an odd desultory shot to break the silence and Katharina became aware of herself shaking her husband violently and screaming, "Albrecht, Albrecht."

Katharina was released later from the local police barracks after they had been convinced of Albrecht's and her identity and story. It was quite dark now as she made her way alone back towards the Brandenburger Tor. She entered Unter den Linden and walked east for a few hundred yards before turning left into Schadow Strasse and right into Mittel Strasse. She stopped outside a large imposing building, entered and made her way up to the first floor. Putting the key she had recovered from Albrecht's personal affects into the keyhole she turned the stiff mechanism. Stumbling into the apartment she sagged against the closed door behind her letting herself slide down to the floor her body trembling with each breath-gasping sob.

CHAPTER 2

Robert 1919

It felt strange walking through the fields of his farm in his home village of Chepfield in the North West corner of County Durham. Experiences on the Western Front and more recently as a prisoner of war were still fresh in his mind generating a feeling of disorientation, dislocation. His life in Poland for the past two and a half years had, until recently, been Robert's reality, especially his love for Katharina. Knowing that this love was reciprocated but that he would never ever see her again persistently troubled him.

Nevertheless, it had been wonderful to see Rhoda again on his first day back home and subsequently she had brought him up to date with all the happenings in the village. Especially the murder of Margaret, the woman he had previously loved and was the reason for his enlistment in the army a lifetime ago. Apparently, rumour abounded that Margaret had been shot by Joseph Bell, Rhoda's no-good brother, and that he returned to Ireland where he had lived during the war in order to escape his compulsory conscription into the army.

Robert sat down in the meadow on the same spot where four and a half years ago he had first heard about war being declared. He stared out across his beloved Derwent Valley but could only see the view through a floating veil of faint, ghostly, opaque faces that had been his erstwhile dearest friend John James, his brother Norman and all the other friends from the village who would not be returning. At least he was one of the lucky ones and although his experiences would always be a part of him it was time for him to move on. The farm was in remarkably good shape. Whatever else she may have been and done, by having the sense to employ land girls during the war Margaret had ensured that the farm remained productive. He would have to replenish the livestock and there was this year's harvest to plan for. There was much to do and much to be grateful for.

* * * * *

"Sit down Mr. Charlton. Welcome home. It's been a long time. I'd heard that you were back and I expect that you're pleased to be so. I think I know why you're here. I guess you want to get up to date on your farm account," Mr Jopling said shaking hands before sitting back down on his leather chair behind his leather-topped desk. "Would you like a cup of tea?"

"No thank you Mr. Jopling, that's very kind of you but I really want to get on if that's alright with you."

"Of course Mr. Charlton, of course. Well.... really, the situation is just as you left it when you enlisted in 1916, except, I'm afraid that inflation has reduced the real value of your deposit. Miss Black as she was or rather Mrs Forbes-Thompson appears to have kept the farm very productive but of course she couldn't access the farm accounts and I can only guess that she conducted the business on a cash basis. May I ask what your plans are for the future?"

"Well...my immediate concern is to get ready for the harvest. The wheat looks grand and I expect there'll be no shortage of labour to help me get it in. But I would like to build up my livestock again and I've plans to buy some beef and dairy cattle as well as some pigs and a few chickens. At least the army left me my two plough horses Baden and Powell. Do you think that the bank will help me with my cash flow until I can sell the harvest?"

"I'll certainly support your application Robert and I don't see any problem."

"Good, I'll be on my way then," and Robert stood up to leave.

"Oh! There is one more thing Robert," Mr Jopling blurted out as he shuffled through the papers in Robert's file. "I nearly forgot. There's a letter for you. It came a few weeks ago."

Puzzled, Robert turned the envelope over displaying a return address of Braithwaite Associates, Solicitors, 27/30 Northumberland Street, Newcastle-upon-Tyne. Removing the letter Robert read slowly the contents of a very short letter.

Dear Mr. Charlton,
We are acting on behalf of the recently deceased Mrs. Forbes-Thompson and as such we would be pleased if you would get in touch with us as soon as possible.
Yours sincerely,

B. Braithwaite (Solicitor)

Seeing the confusion on Robert's face Mr. Jopling offered, "Forgive me but....you look rather overwhelmed..... I hope it's not bad news Robert."

"No....no....no, I really don't know.....It's a letter from some solicitor firm in Newcastle requesting that I get in touch. Something concerning Margaret, I mean Mrs. Forbes-Thompson. I can't imagine what this is all about."

"Well, it's no good worrying. Look, you can use my telephone, get in touch and arrange and appointment to see them as soon as you can."

"Thanks Mr. Jopling, that's very kind of you."

Rhoda was dressing the display in her shoe and boot store window when she spotted Robert leaving Lloyds Bank. She watched him cross the street and make his way towards the store. Seeing her in the window Robert entered setting the bell situated above the door jingling and jangling with annoying insistence.

"Hello Rhoda, busy I see."

"Yes I am, but not as busy as you I suspect being as you've just been having words with our friendly bank manager Mr. Jopling."

"Your store's too well situated," Robert replied with a laugh. "I guess there's nothing happening in the high street that you don't miss."

"Well...you could say that," Rhoda replied carefully backing out of the window taking care to step down without falling over and upsetting her carefully arranged display. "I hope everything's alright," She continued whilst she straightened her dress and patted everything back into place.

"Yes, thank goodness, everything seems to be in order," and after a moment's reflection he continued, "Look why don't you bring little Annie up to the farm on Sunday morning for dinner? Perhaps I can discuss my plans with you?"

"I've got a better idea," Rhoda responded, "Why don't I come up early and make us a proper Sunday dinner with Yorkshire puddings and all the trimmings. I bet it's a long, long time since you had some good old fashioned home cooking."

"That's a great idea and I can bring you up to date with all the latest."

"Good. That's settled then. I'll see you about ten o' clock and you can look after Annie whilst I get on and make us a feast fit for a returning hero."

"Not so much of the hero thank you very much but I'm looking forward to the feast already."

Just at that moment a customer entered the shop and Robert took it as a signal for his departure. As he closed the door behind him, he called out, "See you on Sunday, Rhoda."

* * * * *

The sun streaming through a gap in the curtains gradually coaxed Robert out of a deep sleep. As full consciousness kick-started his brain Robert realised that he had slept in and that there was much to do before Rhoda and little Annie arrived. He threw the covers back, jumped out of bed and bounded down the stairs and into the kitchen where he resuscitated the range fire and heated some water for his morning ablutions. Sticking a slice of bread on a long brass fork kept beside the range he offered it to the fire and made himself a slice of toast washed down with a steaming mug of tea.

The day before Robert had made his way to the hen coop and from the few remaining birds selected the youngest and plumpest bird. With a skill not forgotten he'd managed to wring its neck and sitting down on a rickety old stool pulled the feathers from the bird which once fully plucked was ready to be hung.

Time seemed to be passing too quickly and panicking Robert dumped his mug in the sink as he made his way quickly towards the pantry. He lifted the bird from a hook behind the pantry door and after removing and setting aside the giblets for gravy rinsed it thoroughly in cold water and laid it down in a basting tray ready for the oven. Vegetables, flour, eggs and milk were placed on the kitchen table at which point Robert decided that a whirlwind spring clean would not come amiss. He was just sitting down when the door opened and little Annie burst shouting, "Look what I've found. Look what I've found outside Uncle Robert." In her hand were a number tail feathers which Robert had just plucked from the hen. "Well...aren't you a clever girl. What are we going to do with them?"

"I don't know," Annie said in a rather disappointed voice.

"I know," Robert replied. "We can make a surprise while mammy's making us a lovely dinner. How's that?"

"Yes, yes, yes," Annie shouted as she danced round the kitchen waving the feathers in the air.

Rhoda, with a large grin stood in the doorway watching the proceedings. She moved to the centre of the kitchen and placed a bag of ingredients for sage and onion stuffing and custard on to the table beside the chicken. Withdrawing a large pin from her best Sunday hat, she removed the hat, replaced the pin and put the hat down on the kitchen table. "Well you've already made a big hit I can see. Why don't you and Annie disappear and leave me to get on and do what I have to do in peace."

"If you're sure," Robert replied.

"It looks like you've done all the hard work already," Rhoda said waving her hand over the prepared vegetables in bowls on the table. "Go on, be off with you both and I'll give you a shout when everything's ready."

Robert took Annie's little hand in his and in a trice they were both hopping and skipping their way towards the barn.

"What are you looking for Uncle Robert?" Annie asked with anticipation.

"I know I've got a piece of cork in here somewhere. I think it's in this corner. Come on, you come and help me find it."

Little Annie didn't really know what she was supposed to be looking for but it was great fun to be down on her hands and knees scrabbling around in the dirt, barley dust and straw.

"Here it is," Robert shouted, and little Annie responded with cries of, "Hoorah, hoorah, hoorah, we've found it, we've found it."

She watched attentively as Robert shaped the large piece of cork into a round bullet shaped object. He pricked some holes in the flat end of the cork with the sharp end of a length of wire. "Now...." He said to Annie, "You take one feather and push it into this hole." With a little help from Robert Annie pushed the feather into one of the holes and stepped back to gauge Robert's response. "Well done," Robert shouted. "Hoorah, I've done it, I've done it." Annie responded clapping her little hands in unbridled glee. More feathers were added to the cork until it had the unmistakable appearance of a very passable shuttlecock. Annie looked at it with a puzzled expression and then looking into Robert's eye she said, "What is it Uncle Robert?"

"Just you wait and you'll see," Robert replied. Casting around the barn Robert found an old, thin fence plank of wood and an old rusting saw. With a few deft saw cuts he fashioned two small bats. Giving one of the bats to Annie he took the shuttlecock in his hand and knocked it into the air. Annie watched it twirling round and round as it fell back to earth.

"Wheeeee," She screeched, as she chased after the shuttle. Bending down, Annie picked up the shuttle and swinging her bat made contact sufficient enough to send the shuttle into the air. "Look, I can do it, I can do it, I can do it just like you Uncle Robert," and she skipped round and round in the barn whilst Robert could not help but be deeply affected by her innocent, infectious giggle. Suddenly their reverie was broken. "It's ready. Come and get it you two. Time for dinner."

Annie grabbed Robert's hand and pulled him along as she skipped and hopped her way across the farmyard towards the kitchen door. "Look mammy. Look what Uncle Robert and me made. It's a shhh... shh...shuckle." Rhoda resisted the impulse to laugh and said, "Well aren't you the clever girl. You'll have to show me how it works after dinner but I think for now you'd better wash your hands after scrambling around in the barn and I think Uncle Robert had better wash his hands too don't you?"

"Yes, yes. Come on Uncle Robert let's wash our hands."

Robert pulled up a kitchen chair and lifted Annie on to it so that she could reach her hands under the tap.

"Come and sit down you two. I hope you don't mind Robert but I've poured you a beer from a bottle I found in the larder."

"Not a bit of it. It's just what the doctor ordered. By but there's a grand smell coming from that range."

The chicken was nicely browned and the flesh came away easily from the bone. The Yorkshire puddings were crisp round the outside and soft in the middle. The roast potatoes were scalding hot, the vegetables not too soft and not too hard and a rich gravy topped it all off.

"That was the best meal I've had in nearly 5 years," Robert opined with genuine satisfaction as he helped Rhoda wash and clear away the dishes and utensils.

"Pleased to be of service," Rhoda replied. "I really enjoyed cooking it. It's a long time since I enjoyed a good Sunday dinner as well. It's a lovely afternoon would you like to go for a walk? You can tell me all about your plans for the future."

"I don't know about that. If I've learnt one thing from the last 5 years it's not to put too much store in the certainty of the future. You never know what's round the corner."

"I think I know that as well as anyone," Rhoda replied, "But you still have to have a plan don't you otherwise your life will simply drift without any meaning. Don't you agree?"

"You're right of course. Come on let's go for that walk whilst the sun's still out."

They walked out towards the top, Long Acre field where the wheat was standing strong and just beginning to turn. Little Annie skipped along singing to herself contented in her own little fantasy world.

"I sometimes feel that I'm living in a parallel world," Robert opened. I don't know which one is my reality, over there, in France and especially Poland or back here in Chepfield. It's as if I've fallen through a mirror and I'm looking back at myself."

"I know what you mean. Over the past few years we've jumped from one reality to another so quickly that we haven't really had time to let go of one world before the other has taken over our lives. It's very disorientating. But I think I've had more time to adjust than you have. And I think that your experiences have had the potential to be more deeply life changing than mine. Little Annie has helped me to anchor my life in the present and with time you'll be at peace with yourself again here on the land."

"Yes I suppose your right. No, I know that you're right but a part of me still doesn't really want to let go. A part of me feels disloyal to those I have shared my life with through love and death. Especially those I'll never see again."

"I can understand that but wouldn't those same people want you to go on with your life, to live their life through proxy and make a success from their sacrifice otherwise it would really all have been in vain."

"You're right, let's not forget, but let's look to the future. Talking of which when I was in the bank Mr. Jopling gave me a letter which apparently had been in my file for some weeks. It turns out that the letter is from a firm of solicitors in Newcastle and concerns Margaret. I can't imagine what it's all about but in any case I'll find out next week 'cause I've made an appointment to see them."

"Well I never," Rhoda responded, "A real life mystery I'll be bound."

"No use wondering, we'll find out soon enough."

They turned to walk back to the farm and it was obvious that little Annie was worn out from her exertions. In one continuous movement Robert bent down and hoisted Annie up onto his broad shoulders. By the time they reached the farm Annie was sagging against Robert's head fast asleep.

"It seems a shame to wake her," Robert said as he carefully placed her in Adams old armchair beside the range.

"Maybe," Rhoda answered, "But if she sleeps much longer she'll be a devil to get to bed tonight. Come on, sit down and I'll make us both a cup of tea."

Robert found this domesticity comforting in its normality and he allowed himself to really relax for the first time since leaving Poland.

CHAPTER 3

Katharina 1919

Darkness could have been the void of unconsciousness but the ache Katharina felt in every muscle as she tried to move informed her that she was still very much in this world. Gingerly manoeuvring herself up into a sitting position but with her back still against the heavy, panelled wooden door for support she tried to scan her surroundings, but her eyes felt as if they were filled with red hot sand. Slowly she got to her feet and carefully made her way to the washroom where she hoped that the water supply was still available. Finding a flannel on the sink she turned the tap and was relieved as the fluid soaked the face cloth. Soothed eyes and refreshed skin helped Katharina towards some orientation. The heavily draped curtains were still open. Daylight had faded and in the deepening gloom she traced her way towards the door again her hands reaching out for support and sliding along each piece of furniture she passed searching for the light switch.

Katharina stood still for some moments. The room was exactly as she remembered it from the last time she was here at the beginning of the war. The heavy, ornately carved, mahogany and walnut furniture suggested a permanence that in her present situation was illusory. The deep piled carpets and rich, red, large patterned brocade suite and chairs seemed a decadent extravagance from another age when compared to the drab, depressed atmosphere which she'd experienced but a few hours previously. Ornaments and photographs crowded on to every horizontal surface rendered an overbearing presence which pressed in on her with suffocating effect. She stood there for how long she didn't know, her breaths coming deeply and slowly. Eventually, gingerly she made her way into the bedroom. That musty smell, which unlived in rooms exude was missing and on pulling back the bed clothes Katharina was relieved to feel that the mattress was not damp and therefore wouldn't need airing or warming.

The kitchen had a lived-in appearance. Further exploration revealed a tin of real coffee which suggested that Albrecht had been familiar with the buoyant black market. More in hope than expectation Katharina filled a kettle with water and she was relieved when the gas ring on the large cooker burped into life.

The hot black coffee seared its way down to the bottom of her stomach and from there the effect of the caffeine switched on nerve endings as it spread around her body. A further search revealed some rather stale biscuits but their bulk was a welcome relief from her now acknowledged hunger. Katharina curled up in one of the large armchairs both hands cupped round the coffee mug. It was obvious to her that Albrecht had stayed here for some time before coming to Poland to collect her. In the circumstances she couldn't decide whether she was angry or relieved.

Equilibrium restored, Katharina made her way to the bedroom. A pressing weight of tiredness bore down on her and being as there was little she could do until the next day she stripped to her underwear, slipped into the large double bed and in spite of persistent fleeting images replaying the events of the last 24 hours she was soon cocooned in a deep sleep.

After the peace and quiet of the estate in Poland, Katharina was awoken early the next morning by the street noise outside her bedroom window. She stretched, got out of bed and made her way to the washroom where she turned on the hot tap more in hope than expectation. To the accompaniment of clattering and banging from the pipework she waited and was eventually rewarded by the sight of steam rising from the hot water pouring into the large cast iron bath. Blue bath salts in a jar on a shelf over the bath may or may not have been past their sell by date but she didn't care as she liberally sprinkled them into the tap stream and watched them bubble up with a luxuriant smell. Basking in the soft, scented water Katharina began to ponder her situation with the realisation that there were certain things, which would need to be put into immediate effect.

There were fresh clothes in the wardrobe, which had remained there since before the war. Fashion had not moved on too much during the last 5 years. The allied blockade during the war had virtually eliminated the import of non-essential goods and as a consequence ordinary people had had to make do and mend. Most of the frivolous clothes she found there would not have been appreciated by the war weary, starved, dowdy people she had seen in Berlin the previous day. Whilst the kettle boiled she hurriedly dressed in the clothes she had discarded the night before. The hot black coffee spurred her into action and with a pencil and paper Katharina jotted down things she must attend to. She could stay on in the apartment but this would only be a short to medium term solution to her predicament. The thought of going to live with Albrecht's extended family in Prussia filled her with horror which only left her with the option of returning to her parents' farm in Bavaria. She knew she would be welcome there.

The train hissed, clanked and buffeted its way slowly out of Berlin Central Bahnhof whilst Katharina tried to make herself comfortable in a window seat. On clearing the suburbs the train reached its cruising speed and settled down to a steady, soporific swaying to and fro. Katharina looked calmly out of the window but her mind was wrestling with the events of the early morning. Had she done everything that needed to be done. Had she omitted any important paperwork or statutory documentation? If she had, she reasoned, it was just too bad. She had sent a telegram to Albrecht's parents with barest details and informing them that she would write to them later. She had also made arrangements to have his body transferred back to Prussia. She didn't know whether or not Albrecht had made a will but she suspected that with property and land to be considered and bearing in mind that there was always the possibility that he might not have returned from the war Albrecht would not have left anything to chance. A further telegram warned her parents to expect her sometime late that evening so she contented herself to sit back and allow the train to whisk her away from one life towards another.

Eventually, entering built up suburbs, the sun played hide and seek with buildings as the train eased its way into Munich Central Bahnhof. Katharina had just enough time to buy a cheese roll and a short length of wurst before her connection to the town of Rosenheim departed. From Rosenheim she would have to take a local bus to Riedering and from there a taxi to her former home near Simsee Lake.

The sky was now ink black and a panoply of stars twinkled with insistent clarity. The taxi navigated its way carefully down narrow, rutted country roads the dim, yellow headlights failing to penetrate the encompassing darkness. Where the land fell away from the road Katharina could glimpse lights from lakeside farms and houses rippling on the surface of the water and reaching out with comforting familiarity.

At long last after a weary day's travelling Katharina's spirits revived as she approached the house of her childhood. The building had always presented a happy, friendly atmosphere. It was not exactly of alpine architectural appearance, missing the ornate and intricate carved external decoration typical of the region but the log structure offered solidarity and a warmth in the colouring of the timber logs. The balcony at first floor level running the length of the front elevation was just as she remembered it although the flower window boxes were devoid of colour. The roof pitched to shed the weight of winter snow. As the taxi crunched to a standstill the front door to the house was flung open and light tumbled out into the cool of the night embracing Katharina in its welcoming glow. Before the taxi had turned round to trace its way back to Riedering Katharina was being embraced by her father and her mother who were now both in their late 60s. "Come inside Katharina," were her mother's first words. "You must be absolutely worn out. It's wonderful to see you after all these years but perhaps not in the happiest of circumstances I suspect." With his arm still around Katharina's shoulder her father continued, "Come inside and sit quietly by the fire for a while. You must feel as if you're still travelling."

"Thank you papa that would be wonderful, I do have a bit of a headache and travel sickness."

"I have some nice hot broth on the cooker ready for you," Katharina's mother shouted through from the kitchen. "Then you can go to bed whenever you like and we'll talk in the morning."

"Thank you mama that would be wonderful."

Katharina left her belongings at the bottom of the stairs and following her father made her way towards the living room. She hesitated for a moment and glanced back at the lonely, sad-looking suitcase.

On entering, Katharina made her way towards a large armchair positioned beside the huge open hearth where a log fire crackled sending sparks up the flue and radiating a welcome warmth into the room. A white ceramic tiled stove with a flu rising up to the ceiling at the other end of the room ensured that there were no draughts or cold areas in the large room which occupied most of the ground floor plan. Katharina felt sure that her face was glowing like a beacon and she fought to stay awake long enough to eat her mother's soup.

Her mother and father sat quietly on a sofa at the other side of the hearth waiting until Katharina finished her supper. "I got your old room ready as soon as I read your telegram so you just go up whenever you want to."

"Thank you mama," Katharina said quietly. "It's so good of you to take me in."

"Nonsense," her father replied, "This is your home. You may be nearly forty years old but you're still our little girl."

"It's been a very eventful and tiring two days and I think I could sleep for a week," Katharina said trying to stifle a huge yawn. There would never be a right or good time to tell her parents of her condition so she thought it probably best to get it out of the way now and give them time to consider the implications.

"I'm pregnant..........."

Otto von Lieper was born on the 5th.of December 1919.

CHAPTER 4

Robert & Rhoda -1920

Robert and Rhoda rushed on to the platform just as the guard was about to blow his whistle and wave his green flag. They entered the carriage and didn't so much sit down as find themselves thrust on to the seat as the train overcame inertia and jerked its way forward with a loud chuff, chuff, chuff, the hiss of high pressure steam and a clanking of chains and buffers. They shuffled to get comfortable and Rhoda rearranged her hat which had been knocked askew in the frantic rush to get on board.

Soon the train was making its way along the claustrophobic, Lintzford section of the River Derwent valley where mature deciduous trees climbed up the sheer sides reaching for the sky. Looking out of the window and in spite of himself Robert couldn't help but recall a similar journey five years earlier when he and Margaret had travelled to Newcastle together with a very similar purpose. On that occasion too, Robert was going to the Marlborough Crescent market to buy livestock for old Adam's farm. Adam had been a surrogate father to the then young farm labourer and when he had died he left the farm to Robert in the hope that he and his live-in niece Margaret would eventually wed and produce a family to continue the farming line. However, this was not to be. Margaret's two-timing philandering with Rhoda's roguish brother was the reason for Robert's early enlistment in to the Durham Light Infantry and his eventual transfer to the trenches on The Somme. Her betrayal and Robert's departure broke old Adam's heart and some say hastened his death.

"We might have been a bit late for the train but at least we've plenty of time to complete the rest of today's business. At least I hope we have," Robert said with relief. "The appointment with the solicitor is not until 11.30 so we can buy the livestock and arrange for transport as soon as we get off the train. The market's only a few minutes' walk from the station. Then we can go and see what this solicitor has to say, have something to eat then take the rest of the afternoon to do some window shopping....if you want?"

"It's all very mysterious," Rhoda replied. "I hope I'm wrong and that I'm not being a Job's comforter. I know it's not right to speak ill of the dead but I'm afraid that anything to do with that woman fills me with foreboding."

"Well, we'll just have to be patient and wait and see." The train slowed now to make its approach towards Newcastle. The green scenery of North West Durham had now given way to a satanic industrial-scape. The track ran parallel to Scotswood Road with a pub on every corner on the left and to the right the black, menacing River Tyne flanked by the two mile long Armstrong Whitworth engineering, shipbuilding and armaments factory which had ensured that there were always enough land and sea borne monsters ready to devour humanity and demand more and more fodder between 1914 and 1918.

Robert helped Rhoda alight from the carriage and together they made their way unseeing through the steam and smoke along the platform and towards the exit. On turning left out of the station and making their way towards Marlborough Crescent Robert couldn't help but stop and look back.

"What are you looking at?" Rhoda asked curiously.

"I never tire of looking at that impressive station entrance with its proud columns giving an air of permanence and power."

"Permanence is not the word I would use." Rhoda replied. "My last memory of the station was the day I said goodbye to John James never to see him again.....but I shouldn't project my hurt and disappointment on to a building."

"Perhaps not," Robert replied thoughtfully, "But we can't help memories resurfacing when we visit places where things have happened to us causing great stress and life changing moments. God knows I've experienced plenty....we can't change the past but I'm determined to try to be more positive about the future."

"Good thinking," Rhoda responded as she linked his arm and they continued briskly up the street.

The market was already in full swing when they arrived. To the uninitiated, auctioneers fired an unintelligible language which appeared to make sense to some of the crowd at least. Rhoda followed Robert as he inspected beef and dairy cows with an expert eye. Next came a few pigs and some chickens.

"Can I make a suggestion," Rhoda offered.

"Of course you can," Robert replied with a laugh. "What do you have in mind?"

"Well.... during the war there was one thing, a few things actually, but the one thing that people missed, especially those with children was milk. It's an excellent source of protein and builds strong bones in little ones. Can I suggest that you consider a strong dairy herd as opposed to a strong beef herd? I think that it would be more consistently profitable." Rhoda waited for Robert's reply.

"Hummm.....you might be right," he said thoughtfully. "But we're not at war now and people do like their roast beef."

"Aye those who can afford it," was Rhoda's terse reply. "This is not really the time or place to discuss this but I'm convinced that there is unfinished business as far as Germany is concerned and this will impact on our economy."

Robert had forgotten how militant and politically astute Rhoda was. Being side tracked now Robert replied, "What! You don't think that there'll be further trouble do you? They were soundly thrashed in the last show."

"That's my point Robert," Rhoda answered warming to her subject. "The terms of the armistice were harsh and I don't want to get into whether or not they were deserved, but the point is, the Versailles Treaty was vindictive, the implications of which we don't yet know but mark my words, Germany will be seething with humiliation and resentment and will be looking to reverse that situation when the time's right."

"My God Rhoda, I thought we fought the war to end all wars and here you are predicting another one."

"The Americans and British are proposing a League of Nations to prevent a future conflict like the last one but Germany is to be excluded. How can that work? The world is war weary at the moment but we cannot afford to leave Germany to fester in isolation. There, that's my sermon for now, so let's get on with your business and then we can enjoy the rest of the day."

"Aye, come on. I've made my selections and on your advice I'll add a few more dairy cattle."

Business completed to both their satisfactions Robert and Rhoda had just enough time to make their way to Braithwaite Associates, solicitors. Northumberland Street was more than just the retail Mecca of the North East. There were a cluster of solicitor practices and banks but it was mainly the shops which drew the large crowds. Rhoda couldn't help but gaze into each shop window they passed with a critical and envious professional eye. Robert, on the other hand, had his head tilted back looking for the name Braithwaite Solicitors above each of the huge, solid entrances squeezed between the large store front windows as they passed. Northumberland Street was the main A1 trunk road from London to Edinburgh which passed right through the centre of Newcastle. As a consequence it was congested with traffic of all descriptions from horse drawn delivery carts to private motors, commercial lorries of various sizes, charabancs and electric trams clanking their way to various city suburbs. At last Robert stopped abruptly outside numbers 27/30 and Rhoda, otherwise occupied, bumped into him. "Oops! Sorry," she said, "I was just wondering what it would be like to be the manageress of one of these extravagant shops or heaven forbid, perhaps even being an owner."

"Come on inside," Robert said with a laugh, "You've changed the world enough this morning already."

"Perhaps I have," she replied and linking Robert's arm again they made their way up the stairs leading to Braithwaite's chambers.

They entered an outer office where the atmosphere was as encompassing and oppressive as any church. The dark, oak panelled walls were lined with large, gilt-framed, sombre oil paintings of gentlemen dressed in formal clothes with high starched white collars whilst others wore the gown and wig of the legal profession. The whole effect was one of intimidation and claustrophobia. Robert gave a little start when a voice in the corner broke the solemnity and said, "Good morning, can I help you?"

"Oh...er, yes, I hope so. I have an appointment with Mr. Braithwaite for 11.30, Mr. Robert Charlton."

"Take a seat Mr. and Mrs. Charlton and I'll see if Mr Braithwaite is ready for you."

A smile passed between Robert and Rhoda as they sat down on two chairs next to a small table topped with two neat piles of magazines about country pursuits and North East businesses.

The door to an inner office opened and the secretary come receptionist said, "Mr Braithwaite will see you now. This way please." She stepped aside and ushered them through, "Mr. and Mrs. Robert Charlton."

Mr. Braithwaite, who was in his middle 50s Robert guessed stood up and extended his hand towards each of them in greeting. "Take a seat please, and don't look so anxious, there's nothing to worry about."

"Actually, it's Robert Charlton and Mrs. Rhoda Horton, a friend and companion." Robert said to allay any confusion.

"Good, good," Mr. Braithwaite continued. "Well, let's get down to business, I'm sure you're wondering what this is all about."

"It is rather out of the blue I must say. I can't think of anything the life ...or death of Margaret Forbes-Thompson has to do with me." Robert suggested.

"Well it appears that she thought otherwise Mr. Charlton. She must have held you in high regard as what I am about to say will inform you."

High regard, Robert thought. We were supposed to be going out together and planning to get wed. The last time I saw her she was fucking Joseph Bell, Rhoda's no-good brother in my own barn. A funny way of showing high regard he remembered bitterly. His reminiscences were cut short as Mr. Braithwaite continued, "Mrs. Forbes-Thompson was a very wealthy and successful Newcastle business woman in her own right even before she married Douglas Forbes-Thompson the wealthy land and mine owner who lives at Forbes Hall out near Hexham. Due to her astute business sense and, how shall I say, her feral cunning, she managed to build up a series of enterprises under the heading of Hadleigh Holdings. The good news is that she left instructions that if anything ever happened to her all her assets were to be bequeathed to you."

Robert sat rooted to the chair not knowing how to react. He couldn't believe what he was hearing and in any case this would have been the farthest thing from his mind. "Whoaaah! This is going to take some time to sink in," he said with a dry throat.

Noting his discomfort and not a little confusion Mr Braithwaite asked, "Would you both like a cup of tea.....sweet tea....it's supposed to be good for shock I believe." He pushed a button under his desk and the secretary appeared promptly. "A cup of tea for Mr. Charlton and Mrs. Horton if you please Mildred."

"Yes sir, right away sir."

"Now that you've had a moment to....take in what I've just told you Mr. Charlton if you don't mind I'll continue and fill in some of the details." Not waiting for Robert's acquiescence Mr. Braithwaite shuffled a few papers and continued. "There are some bank loans but substantially the business is on a firm footing and survived the war without too much financial impact. You'll need to get a good accountant to help you pull together the different strands of Hadleigh Holdings and of course we would be delighted to continue to handle your legal requirements. Mrs. Forbes-Thompson had...how shall I put it ...many business contacts and there may well be some strands to her dealings which have not been committed to paper if you get my meaning. As far as I am aware Hadleigh Holdings owns a warehouse on the quayside behind the central railway station. This is a warehouse for storing imported fruit and vegetables ready for distribution to various retail grocery shops and market stalls. However, as you will see from the books the German submarine blockade during the war had a major effect on imports from the Empire. Wholesale foodstuffs are delivered by lorries owned by Hadleigh Holdings' own transport company which is based at a depot on Scotswood Road nearest the station marshalling yards. Just before her demise Mrs. Forbes-Thompson secured a contract with her husband to transport coal from his pits to local coal merchants. At some time in the near future you might like to contact Douglas Forbes-Thompson with a view to securing this lucrative contract for a few more years. There is a large house in Osborne Road, Jesmond, north of the city centre and a shop in Westgate Road. There is also a fruit and veg stall in the Green Market. Further afield there is a shop in Consett as well as a market stall and a number of rounds in various pit villages in and around Chepfield. One further thing, there's a blue Ford Model 'T' which belongs to the company and which Mrs. Forbes-Thompson used to travel around her various business enterprises, when she was not using her husband's Rolls Royce that is. I believe the vehicle is kept at the lorry depot. I expect that this is not only a shock but is a lot of information to assimilate in one bite. I've prepared a port-folio for you giving you an outline of the extent of the business assets and the financial situation. There are some keys and some other bits and pieces which you can take away with you. I think I've covered everything but if anything else comes to mind I will be in touch with you and it goes without saying that after you've had time to study the paperwork if there is anything, anything at all that we can help you with please do not hesitate to get in touch. We are always willing to help."

Reaching across the desk and taking the manila folder Robert said, "Thank you Mr. Braithwaite. It's going to take some time for all this to sink in. I feel as if I've been hit by a sledge hammer.....I expect I'm going to need a lot of help....initially at least, so it's very likely that you will be hearing from me. Once again, thank you very much and thank you for the cup of tea."

"Think nothing of it Mr. Charlton, that's what we're here for. You have my details in the folder and don't hesitate to telephone if there is anything, anything at all that we can help you with." Standing up he extended a hand to Robert who took the gesture as a signal that business was concluded. Shaking hands with Rhoda Mr. Braithwaite pressed the bell again with his left hand and almost immediately Mildred was at the doorway. "Goodbye and good luck," and turning to his secretary he continued, "Show Mr. Charlton and Mrs. Horton out would you please Mildred."

"Certainly sir," came the crisp efficient reply.

It seemed only seconds before that Robert had been standing outside the solicitor's offices wondering what was to come. The last three-quarters of an hour were a blur and Robert stood on the pavement beside Rhoda, oblivious to people scurrying by and the constant noise of the road traffic, scarce knowing what to say. Rhoda too, for once was also lost for words, but not for long.

"Well....that is a turn up for the books. Who would have thought it? I might have judged her harshly....I suppose that it's to her credit that at least one of her final acts was to look for some redemption. It's no more than you deserve that's what I say."

"Ummm..." was Robert's slow response lost in his own thoughts. Then somewhat pragmatically he continued, "I don't know about you but I could do with getting out of this crowd. Let's find a café and have something to eat. It might give us a little time to gather our thoughts. There's a little place up here in the Haymarket."

In spite of recent events weighing on their minds both Robert and Rhoda surprisingly enjoyed their hot mince pie, peas, bread and butter and lingered over hot cups of strong tea. Robert broke the silence.

"Well....where do we go from here then? It's too much to take in in one go. What the hell am I going to do with Hadleigh Holdings?"

"For now, I think the best policy is to leave it for a few days. Let the dust settle and give yourself time to get over the shock and I think that then you'll be in a better frame of mind to decide what to do. You can't possibly be expected to be in a position to make any decisions right now." After a moment's consideration Robert replied, "You're right of course. I'm too punch drunk at the moment to even think straight."

"I have an idea," Rhoda suggested enthusiastically.

"Not another one," Robert scoffed, "Where do they all come from?"

"Oh shut up you big bully," Rhoda responded digging him playfully on the chest. "Listen.....instead of window shopping as we'd planned, why don't we do some window shopping of a different sort?"

"What do you mean?"

"Well.....we're already here in Newcastle, why don't we take the opportunity to survey your new empire. Get the lie of the land as it were. What is it they say in the army, make a reconnaissance? Jesmond is just up the road. If you think it's a good idea we could catch the tram, take a look at this house on Osborne Road then get the tram back down to the Central Station and visit the transport depot and warehouse. Whatever else she was Margaret was no fool. The transport depot and warehouse are not only close to each other but are ideally situated for rail, river and sea transport. Or..." pausing in thought, Rhoda continued, "Perhaps it was my rogue of a brother who set it all up. How she came by it is anyone's guess but I've got my suspicions. Anyway, that'll probably be enough for one day before catching the train home. You could visit the shop in Westgate Road and the stall in the Green Market on another day. What do you say?"

"It's something practical to do....I think it's a splendid idea.....at least it will give us something real and solid to throw into the mix." Tentatively Robert continued, "I keep finding myself saying 'we' when really all this responsibility is mine but I have to say that if you're willing I'd really like you to share this good fortune with me. You're managerial business experience would be invaluable and even though it was on a smaller scale the process can't be that different. Besides, it's only a couple of hours ago that you were wondering what it would be like to manage or even own one of those swanky shops in Northumberland Street. Now, out of the blue, you have the opportunity to be part of a huge enterprise. Say you'll join me....it makes perfect sense to me."

"It sounds a wonderful idea and my immediate reaction would be to say yes.... but there are a lot of practical things to be taken into consideration. Let's not be too hasty and make promises that we both might not be able to keep in the future. Let's wait and see. Look...here's the tram coming...if we're quick we should be able to catch it."

The tram pulled away from the stop and Robert led the way down the aisle stopping beside the first empty seat. He tilted the seat back so that they were sitting on the wooden slatted seats facing the way that they were going. "I hate travelling backwards," Robert offered. "It's the same on a train. I hate having my back to the engine. I like to know where I'm going not where I've been."

"Really......" Rhoda responded and they both spontaneously burst out laughing.

The large terraced houses sweeping round Osborne Road were a magnificent sight beyond belief after the rows of identical colliery houses in Chepfield. They continued walking up the road trying not to look too much out of place and eventually stopped outside the property belonging to Hadleigh Holdings. There was a short front garden separated from the pavement by a low granite wall topped off with ironwork railings cast in an intricate floral design. The front door was solid looking and was framed by solid pillars supporting a portico. The double fronted windows bowed out into the garden and continued up to the first floor their granite mullioned architecture contributing to the air of grandeur. Skylights suggested that there were further rooms up in the attic, loft area. Robert took a bunch of keys out of the folder, contemplated them, then having made his selection tried the key in the door. The lock was initially stiff but activated smoothly and the door swung open. "That has got to be a good omen," Rhoda suggested, "A door that opens onto the rest of your life."

They stepped into a large panelled hall with doors leading off to left and right. There was an unlived-in musty smell and a thin layer of dust covered the large coat and hat stand and its mirror. A wide staircase with a solid carved mahogany banister reached up to the upper floors. Slowly Robert opened the door to the left and entered what he presumed to be the living room. It was the biggest room Robert had ever seen. The marble fireplace with its mock Inigo Jones carvings dominated the far wall and the carpet, drapes and furniture offered an opulence beyond imagination. The plasterwork on the ceiling was bold yet with delicate detail picked out in gold. "Have you ever seen anything like this before?" Robert breathed.

"Do people actually live in places like this?" Rhoda responded. "I suppose they do because there are many houses like this in the area. So much for equality and a land fit for heroes."

They reverently crossed the hall and entered the other ground floor room. It was a dining room with a large table and chairs taking central attention. Two silver candelabras, one either end of the table, reflected an ambiance of affluence which was affirmed by a large sideboard decorated with other silver ornaments, bowls and picture frames. At the end of the hall was a huge kitchen and laundry come utility area with a garden extending out at the rear. "Look," Robert pointed, "One of the back door window panes has been smashed near the lock. Looks like someone has tried to break in."

"You'll need to get that attended to," Rhoda said, "Can't have the working class riff raff stealing the family silver." When they'd stopped laughing Robert replied, "You're such a tease Rhoda, but you know, this brings it home that this really is the beginning of a whole new life for me....for us....."

The upstairs bedrooms were no less opulent and the bathroom, a luxury neither of them had ever experienced was nearly as big as the whole miner's terraced house Robert had been brought up in in Tees Street, Chepfield. "I feel as if I should be sleeping in the servants' quarters up in the loft," Robert said, "It's.....it's all so grand and beyond all imagination. It's like a fairy tale, this can't be real."

"Better get used to it. The folder in your hands says it's all yours, every brick chair and silver nick knack."

The journey to the Central Station was passed in silence except for the swaying, clanking and screeching of the tram wheels as they negotiated corners and points, each lost in a myriad of thoughts brought about by recent events.

Getting his bearings Robert pointed, "Scotswood Road starts over there behind the Marleborough Crescent bus terminus and the cattle market." Rhoda linked his arm once again and they walked briskly towards where Robert had pointed. Within a short time they stopped outside a double-gated entrance with a weathered board overhead declaring 'Hadleigh Holdings'. Inside was a large compound surrounded by buildings which appeared to be a collection of offices, workshops, garages and storage facilities. Bits of engines and other discarded lorry parts were piled haphazardly in one corner where the ground was stained and saturated by discarded, black engine oil. The blue model 'T' Ford mentioned by Mr. Braithwaite was parked nearby and a group of mechanics were working on two wagons which were tilted over on jack supports obviously being subjected to maintenance or repair.

"It really is real," Robert said turning to Rhoda.

"It certainly looks like it. What do you intend to do now?"

"I've absolutely no idea."

"Can I suggest some more advice?" Rhoda offered calmly.

The question seemed to focus Robert and he replied, "I wish you would."

"Well....my guess is that this depot, this part of the business has been running without proper supervision for some time. I expect that there's a manager here but from my experience of human nature I wouldn't be surprised if he hasn't taken advantage of that situation."

"What! You mean he's probably been on the take?"

"I wouldn't want to go that far without proof but I would guess that things have been allowed to slide a bit. I suggest that you make yourself known to the staff and ask to see the books. That should let them know who the new boss is and that you mean business. It also means that you'll catch them unawares and not give anyone time to cover up any...how shall I say....any mistakes in accounting."

Robert was still in an emotional turmoil but not too much so that he didn't appreciate Rhoda's level headed, cool, clinical assessment of the situation. "I can't tell you how pleased I am that you're here Rhoda. I knew that you'd keep both your feet on the ground and I'm even more convinced that I'm going to need your help and advice in the very near future."

"Perhaps you're right Robert, I can feel myself getting really excited by this whole enterprise. Yes....let's work together and make this whole business a success."

In her new-found enthusiasm Rhoda practically dragged Robert into the building with 'Office' painted above the doorway.

"Can I help you?" a young female whom Robert assumed to be a secretary asked.

"Yes," Robert replied, "I'd like to speak to whoever is in charge."

"Who shall I say you are and can I ask what it's in connection with?"

"My name is Mr. Robert Charlton and my business is with the manager personally."

"If you'll take a seat I'll see if Mr Robson is available," the secretary replied with a scarce disguised irritated sniff.

It was a long ten minutes before the door opened to an inner office. "If you'd like to come this way Mr. Charlton and..........."

"Mrs. Horton," Robert replied finishing off the sentence.

Two uncomfortable high backed dining chairs with tatty, ripped velvet seats were already placed in front of a desk covered with strewn paperwork, an ash tray overflowing with cigarette ends and two mouldy, stained coffee mugs.

"Take a seat," Mr. Robson offered without any deference to accepted courtesy. "I don't normally see people without an appointment but if you can explain your business quickly I should be able to spare you a few minutes between meetings."

Forgetting his previous feelings of doubt and uncertainty, Robert's hackles were up as a consequence of this public face of his new business and his annoyance manifested itself in his being uncharacteristically direct. "I am the new owner of Hadleigh Holdings." He enjoyed the shocked, disbelieving expression on the manager's face. Without waiting he thrust some papers from the folder across the desk towards the manager and continued, "You'll see that these documents are signed and legal. Robert waited a few minutes for the information to sink before continuing, "And if you don't mind I'd like to take a look at all the books, contracts, invoices, receipts, duty rosters, staff list, wage expenditure, everything.....immediately....oh, and I'll be taking them with me." Robert crossed his legs whilst staring directly at Mr. Robson and in spite of himself rather enjoyed his obvious discomfort.

Rhoda observed quietly and assessed Mr. Robson as being very streetwise and this was confirmed by his quick and confident recovery. "Yes sir, of course sir...everything is in order and I'll have the secretary collect them all for you promptly." He shouted through for the secretary to enter and gave her the necessary instructions. A quick knowing look, which would normally have gone unnoticed, passed between them but it didn't escape Rhoda and her penetrating stare into Mr. Robson's eyes informed him that she had seen it.

The pile of cardboard cartons filled with box files and folders took both Robert and Rhoda by surprise and Rhoda whispered, "How are we going to get all of these on to the train?" Robert thought for a moment and then without hesitation turned to Mr. Robson, "Oh, and I'll be having the keys to the automobile outside. I presume that you have been availing yourself of its convenience but I'll be taking it over from now on." Robert held out his hand and Rhoda observed the muscles tighten around the manager's mouth as he fumbled in his pockets searching for the keys.

Turning to the secretary Robert asked, "What's your name?"

"Mary sir," she replied with more contrition and deference than the last time she'd spoken to Robert.

"Well, Mary perhaps you'd like to put all of these cardboard boxes into the back of the blue Ford outside."

"Yes sir, right away sir."

"Can you direct me towards the warehouse down on the quayside please?"

"Certainly sir, you turn right out of here. The road bears right and you then fork left, you can't miss it."

Turning to the shell-shocked manager Robert said, "Carry on for now Mr. Robson. I'll be in touch shortly, and try to get this office tidied up a bit before my next visit."

The office door closed behind them as Robert and Rhoda made their way towards the Ford. "Just one thought, you can drive can't you?" Rhoda prompted.

"Well...sort of," was Robert's response. "I had a go in France so I think I can get by."

"You did a fine job in there. Just like a boss, I'm proud of you. The adventure starts here."

"Yes....well....let's see if the other place is as slip-shod as this one."

The manager of the warehouse enterprise proved much more accommodating, professional and efficient. He conducted Robert and Rhoda on a guided tour of the warehouse yard, storage space, cool rooms, and offices which looked out over the River Tyne and the Swing Bridge. He explained succinctly the processes of import and distribution and willingly produced the books for Robert to take away with him.

"Thank you Mr. Carson, you've been most helpful. I'll return the books to you as soon as I can and I'll be in touch shortly."

After helping Rhoda in to the passenger seat, Robert steered the Ford towards a Shell petrol pump standing near the garage entrance and asked one of the mechanics nearby to fill up the petrol tank. With a crunching of gears and a series of jerks the Ford coughed and rattled its way out of the yard.

"Do you intend to drive all the way back home? What are we going to do about the rail tickets?" Rhoda asked.

"Not a problem," Robert replied cheerfully. "I'll nip into the station, get a refund then telephone the station master at Lintz to let George know that we won't be needing him and that he can drive the horse and trap back to the farm on his own."

CHAPTER 5

Katharina 1923 – 1926

Katharina shot bolt upright in bed as just below her bedroom window two explosions in quick succession rent the night and were followed immediately by Otto's distressed crying coming from the room next door. Hastily pulling on her dressing gown she ran to her son's bedroom. "There, there darling, Mama's here," and putting her arms around four year old Otto she continued, "There's nothing to worry about. You stay here in bed and Mama will go downstairs and see what's happened and don't be frightened."

Katharina became more aware of a commotion as she descended the stairs and made her way to the front door where the light of the front porch pushed outwards only to be swallowed up by the pitch-black night. Standing in the doorway was her father with his hunting shotgun in his hands. "My God Papa, what on earth is going on?" Just at that moment two bullets cracked into the wood log above their heads splattering them with splinters. From the dark night void a voice bellowed, "Stay inside old man. We're too many for you and we don't want to hurt you. Just lower your gun and go inside and we'll be gone in a few minutes."

"You good for nothing bastards this is my farm and we're in the shit just as much as you but I'm not going to let you steal from me and my family." Katharina's father raised his gun again as he spoke. The action brought an immediate response and once again two bullets smacked into the door lintel just above their heads.

"You've been warned once already old man. Get inside if you want to see the morning."

"Come Papa," Katharina implored, dragging her father inside. "Come inside. Whatever it is that they're up to it's not worth your life. Come on."

The reluctant Werner allowed his daughter to drag him back into the house and placing his gun on the table slumped into a chair. Crisis seemingly over for the moment Otto flashed back into her mind and Katharina rushed back upstairs where she saw her mother sitting on Otto's bed with her arms around his shoulders. "There, I told you Mama would be back soon." Turning to her daughter she continued more quietly, "What's going on? Is Werner alright?"

"I don't know.... I mean to say...yes Papa's okay but I don't know what's going on. Stay here with Otto and I'll go back down stairs."

"What was all that about Papa?" Katharina asked with anxiety obvious in her voice.

"Neighbour Rupe in the next farm warned me that this might happen. He had a similar experience last week." The conversation was interrupted by the squeal of one of Werner's pigs followed by the noise of a lorry being driven off up the track. "They took one of his pigs and some sacks of wheat. We'll just have to wait until the morning to see what damage they've done us."

"Who are they?" Katharina asked enquiringly.

"Who knows for sure but I'd bet that they're bloody communists either unemployed or on strike or just lazy scum. Either way they'll probably be from the working class estates in Munich out to steal food."

More conciliatory Katharina continued, "In truth Papa I don't think that we can blame them. We're finding it hard to exist but at least we can grow food here on the farm. The workers are destitute. This inflation will be the ruin of us. I was planning to go to Munich tomorrow to make enquires about Albrecht's war pension. It hasn't been paid for the last few months and I want to know what's happening."

"If that's the case then you'll want to be off early in the morning. I suppose we'd better get off to bed. There's nothing we can do now and I don't expect that our visitors will be back again tonight."

It was a crisp, bitter cold November morning when Katharina walked out of the Munich central railway station. The sky was grey and oppressively low overhead as the first large powdery snowflakes of winter danced on a light breeze. Katharina pulled her coat tight against the cold and set off for the ministry offices dealing with benefits and pensions in Konigsplatz.

She entered the large building with its atmosphere as cold and unwelcoming as the grave. Scruffy, dishevelled flotsam shuffled individually and in small groups searching for the right office or department. Government officers stood at strategic points looking bored and disinterested making no eye contact even with those who had the temerity to ask them for assistance or directions. At last Katharina found the right office and joined a queue which stretched out of the door and down the corridor. One hour later she was pulled back to the present by a loud shout of "Next!"

The bored, flat voice droned on in bureaucratic monotone, "Yes I understand Frau Lieper but the government has suspended your husband's war pension pending a new review of all benefits."

"Yes, but......."

Without looking up from the file in front of him the civil servant continued, "Frau Lieper, you are much better placed than all these people in the queue behind you. You live with your parents on their farm, and you have an allowance from your deceased husband's estate in Prussia."

"Inflation has made this worthless as you well know, there must be something you can do. I gave two sons to the war and for what, this......." Katharina heard herself shouting.

Closing the file and leaning to one side and placing it on an already huge pile the shabby man behind the counter responded again without making any attempt to look Katharina in the face, "Thank you Frau Lieper that will be all. NEXT."

Once again Katharina found herself on the pavement looking at the demoralised resignation etched into the faces of people as they ambled past. She turned into Residenzstrasse and was immediately alerted by the change in the crowd's demeanour and purposeful movement. Looking more intently now she was able to spot numbers of armed soldiers and police lining the roadway and in small groups at alley entrances. She struggled as she tried to make her way in the opposite direction to that of the majority of the crowd in the street. Remembering Berlin four years earlier, it suddenly became clear to her what was going on. The large demonstration with banners unfurled and flapping in the light breeze marched and forced its way towards the Feldherrnhalle beer hall chanting political slogans. Flanking the marchers were determined, uncompromising men dressed in paramilitary, brown shirt uniforms. As they passed Katharina saw the figure of General Ludendorff whom she recognized from newspaper pictures and next to him the unmistakable figure of Adolf Hitler. As the demonstration neared the Feldherrnhalle the crowd surged and Katharina felt herself being propelled in a direction she didn't want to go. Without warning, shots rang out and there were screams as people pushed and were pushed in turn trying to find shelter and safety. Scuffles broke out everywhere as men used cudgels, batons, spade handles, anything that could be used as a weapon fought with police and soldiers. As the crowds gradually dispersed and the street emptied Katharina was able to make her way back to the railway station unmolested and unharmed but shaken by this second experience of the violence that had descended on the German political scene and was a common occurrence in cities throughout the country.

Katharina had never been politically inclined in the past but concern for her son's long term future greatly concerned her and she devoured the papers for news. Significant events seemed to be unfolding almost daily.

* * * * *

Katherina's father rustled his morning paper and turning towards her said, "Can I make a suggestion? I see in the paper here that Hitler is making a speech in Munich next week. Why don't you come with me and just hear what he has to say. All I say is keep an open mind and you will see that I'm right."

Katharina stared into the log fire for a while and then replied in a measured voice, "Okay Papa, I will come with you because I don't want politics to come between us."

Katharina sat down beside her father in the Hofbrauhaus and looked about nervously. There was an excitable hum of expectation in the room that was rapidly filling to capacity. Down the aisles and along the back of the hall were ranks of the SA, Sturm Abteilung, brown-shirted paramilitary that accompanied Hitler wherever he went. Katharina took in the Nazi red banners hanging on the stage emphasizing a black, stark swastika emblazoned in the centre of each one. The echoing armbands on each of the SA members lining the hall made her shudder. She gave a start as the assembled audience suddenly stood up as one and broke into loud, spontaneous cheering and clapping. Down the centre of the hall walked Hitler flanked by four party members. Hitler was introduced by one of the party members and an expectant hush fell over the audience as Hitler made his way to a dais at the front and centre of the stage. He stood there, arms folded on his chest, silent, looking out into the hall, his expressionless eyes seeming to penetrate the thoughts of every individual. Katharina felt she could reach out and touch the tension in the hall as Hitler continued to draw the people to him before he had uttered even a single word. At last, expectation was fulfilled as Hitler started very quietly and deliberately to extol his lowly beginnings, his experiences during the war and his undying love for everything German and the German race as embodied in the Teutonic mythologies of the past and his vision for a greater Germany of pure Aryan blood. At this point four hecklers stood up in various parts of the hall and were immediately pounced on by the nearest brown-shirts. Fists and truncheons soon silenced the bloodied men as those around them made room and chairs were sent scattering across the floor. Very quickly they were overpowered and dragged unceremoniously from the hall. Whilst the rest of the audience were jeering and those nearest the disturbances were helping the brown-shirts Katharina observed Hitler standing as if turned to a pillar of salt, unblinking, impassively watching the exertions of his henchmen.

Peace restored, Hitler continued warming to his subject attacking those he held responsible for Germany's downfall, current economic problems and international inconsequence. He flung his arms about and his voice became a raucous shout that could still be heard whilst his followers cheered every sentence.

The cheers of the audience almost physically lifted the roof as Katharina shrank back into her seat trying to become invisible. Feeding off the crowd in this symbiotic relationship Hitler's voice continued to rise to an apoplectic screech.

Finally the audience erupted in a paroxysm of collective hysteria with shouts of '*Heil Hitler! Heil Hitler!*' whilst Hitler stood statue still except for occasionally dabbing the sweat from his face with a handkerchief.

CHAPTER 6

Robert and Rhoda 1922

Rhoda and Robert sat at his kitchen table surrounded by piles of folders, ledgers, bank statements, files, invoices and receipts.

"Well," Robert said wearily, "You've had time to go through the books as well. What's your impression?"

"I think that they confirm my original gut reaction, or should I say my female intuition. The wholesale warehouse and distribution documents are all in order and the whole enterprise appears to be well managed although I think that there might well be an opportunity for expansion."

"And the haulage depot?" Robert asked inquisitively.

"It is just as we suspected. The manager, what's his name, Mr. Robson, has been....how shall I put it....less than efficient. In fact he's been running the business as his own and moonlighting with our lorries. There's no evidence of close supervision, we don't know where the various lorries are at any particular time and they could even be away from the depot overnight doing God knows what. There's no check on how much fuel is being used and for what purpose. There are huge gaps in expenses, income receipts and invoices so that any fiddles are harder to pin down but make no mistake fiddles there have been."

"So where do we go from here?"

"Mr Robson has to go. The man is a liability not to mention probably a criminal. If he doesn't go quietly we can threaten him with the police. I suspect that some of the drivers and mechanics might also have been aware of what was going on and might even have been taking bribes to keep quiet. I think that the sacking of the man in charge will send out a message that we mean business; especially if we institute rigid checks."

"I agree! I've been giving this a lot of thought. We need to tighten up the office. I don't know about you but my priorities would be to ensure all receipts and invoices are dated and filed. The lorry mileages need to be logged at the start and finish of each day and checked against delivery destinations. I'd like the drivers to keep a log as well. We'll have to design some forms and get them printed. Petrol fill-ups for each lorry needs to be logged and checked against destinations and we need to look at our customers, which is mainly ourselves at the moment, to see whether or not we can rationalise journeys to save time, fuel and money. And, as with the warehouse, as you say, there is room for expansion. We don't just have to deliver coal and fruit and veg. We should look for other business."

"Well, I'm impressed," Rhoda cooed, "You've been busy too. But more to the point it seems as if you want to take over this business and run it properly."

"Yes I do Rhoda. It's a challenge but one that could prove very profitable. The big question is....I couldn't possibly do this on my own. Have you made any final decision about how you see your future? I mean...you have your responsibility at the store. Could you combine both interests? I have the same problem as far as the farm is concerned although I have thought of a solution. Young George is experienced enough now to take the farm over as a manager. I can discuss overall strategy with him and leave him to organise the day to day running of the farm just as old Adam did with me when I started. I suppose your problem is slightly different in that you don't own the store."

"I've been giving it a lot of thought as well, and I believe that this is a God-given chance to make better lives for ourselves. I don't think that I should feel guilty about not wanting to be a pit village boot and shoe store manageress for the rest of my life. I've also stewed over the practicalities. Being as Hadleigh Holdings is centred in Newcastle there is the travel to consider. Little Annie will be starting school soon and I've already approached my auntie who has agreed to look after her whenever I'm not around. I've offered to pay her so she's more than happy. When business demands, it would be convenient to stay over in the house in Jesmond. I think it could all work out very nicely.....I might even have to take driving lessons," Rhoda giggled.

"My....all thought through eh! I can see that you've had sleepless nights as well. So, it's an equal partnership then. I'll contact the solicitor and make it all legal then we can take the world on together."

"Wait a minute," Rhoda interjected, "It's your business alone. I only signed up to help you manage the enterprise. I couldn't possibly...."

Robert quickly jumped in, "Rubbish, it's an equal partnership or nothing. If you don't agree I'll make arrangements immediately to sell off the lot. I'll not hear otherwise."

"Well....if you're sure and if you insist. Sounds wonderful," Rhoda replied. "How could I refuse, we'll make a good team."

"Good, that's settled then." Robert said stretching his arms out to give Rhoda a hug. She moved in close and somehow the expected peck on the cheek morphed into a full kiss which for both of them confirmed the start of something more than just a business partnership.

* * * * *

Having put the Lloyds' Bank manager in the picture Robert climbed into the Ford and chugged his way up Chepfield's main Derwent Street giving a honk as he passed Rhoda's store and startling shoppers nearby. Passing under the railway bridge at the north end of the village just beside the coal drops Robert spotted a lone miner sitting on the shale steps that led from the colliery down into the village. This was unusual in that the men swapping shifts would now either be at home or down the pit. Besides, miners always sat in groups at the corner end with their marras, never alone and certainly never on these steps. As Robert drew closed he noticed that the man was slumped against the steps' handrail post with his head down on his chest. Robert stopped the car and jumped out. "Are you alright marra? Is something wrong? Can I help you?" The miner, still in his filthy pit clothes, lifted his head slowly and Robert was shocked to see a black face streaked with white where tears had collected the coal dust on their sorrowful journey. "What's the matter marra?" Robert repeated, "Is there anything I can do? In that same instant Robert exploded, "My God! Tommy.... Tommy, it is you isn't it? It's Robert, you remember....Robert Charlton. The last time I saw you you were in a field hospital in Albert on the Somme in 1916. For God's sake man what's going on?"

"Robert....it's good to see you," Tommy whispered obviously in some distress. "I'll be alright in a minute. Let me sit here a while and then I'll be okay."

Just then Robert noticed a familiar wet patch above Tommy's right knee and he had an immediate flashback of wounded comrades he'd seen in the trenches. Remembering that Tommy had had his leg amputated as the result of a shrapnel wound he continued, "Is it your leg Tommy, is your leg still giving you trouble after all this time?"

"I don't know what I'm going to do Robert," Tommy sobbed. "I'm at the end of my tether. I can't do pit work anymore. It's just too much for me. The stump's alright when I can rest it but you know what it's like underground and I need the money."

"Come on mate let me help you into the car and I'll take you home."

Tommy leaned heavily on Robert and winced as he made his way into the passenger seat.

"Sorry Robert, I've put blood on your seat…sorry."

"You've got nothing to be sorry about marra, don't you give it another thought. I'll have you home in a jiffy."

As he was driving back through the village a plan was taking shape in Robert's mind. He stopped the car outside Tommy's house in Blyth Street and was pleased to see that the ride had given Tommy time to recover his composure a little.

"Listen Tommy, I've got a proposal for you. This could be a lucky day for both of us. Come and work for me."

"What!" Tommy gasped.

"You're not going back to that pit another day. Hand in your resignation and come and work for me."

"I don't want charity Robert, I couldn't live with myself if I had to rely on charity."

"This isn't charity believe me. You'll be doing me a big favour and you'll be working for your money make no mistake about that."

"What's on your mind," Tommy asked hesitantly.

"Look, as it happens I've just heard that I've inherited a business in Newcastle. It's a big enterprise in fact and I could really do with someone I can trust to help me look after the day to day running. Say you'll do it Tommy. It'll be a big load off my mind. You remember Rhoda, John James' wife….well she's in partnership with me but she'll need help to organise and run our transport depot on Scotswood Road. You'd be working alongside her setting up our new structure and working practices and then when things are all in place you can take over as manager. Does that sound like charity?"

"I don't know what to say," Tommy replied unable to take it all in.

"Say yes then you silly bugger. It's all settled. You hand in your notice as from Friday. I'll pay you from Monday on the understanding that you take as much time off as you need and you start work as soon as you're happy with your leg."

"Thanks Robert, it's a life-saver to me. I don't know how I'll ever be able to repay you. I'll never forget this as long as I live."

"Think nothing of it Tommy, we Geordie veterans must stick together eh! Shake hands on it then and let me know when you're ready and we'll sort out the details and you needn't worry about getting to Newcastle neither because I've just heard that they're starting an omnibus service from here to Rowlands Gill railway station where you can get the train direct to Newcastle."

Robert helped Tommy down from the car and saw him to the back door of the house where he still lived with his parents. Tommy leaned against the wall and waved his hand as Robert got back into the car. "See you later Robert, or should I say boss and I mean it, I'll never forget what you've done for me."

"Think nothing of it Tommy, as I said, it's not charity and I'll work you to the bone if you'll forgive the pun." Robert was pleased to see just the hint of a faint smile drift across Tommy's face. "So long marra. I don't want to see you again until that leg of yours has recovered and is healthy again."

* * * * *

"Do you remember when you first came home, you said that you would take me to see where John James was killed if I wanted to and I said that I wasn't ready yet?"

Rhoda and Robert were holding hands whilst enjoying a cup of tea and sitting on a rickety old bench in the farmhouse south facing garden relaxing in the soporific warmth of an early summer sun. The changes planned for Hadleigh Holdings were well established now and ably managed by Tommy but it was still only occasionally that they could find time in their busy schedules to just sit and enjoy each other's company.

"Yes I do," Robert replied. "Why?"

"I've had a letter from the government saying that there's a grant for war widows to visit France. You book it through a government sponsored travel company and the grant includes travel and overnight hotel expenses. Apparently an Imperial War Graves Commission is in the process of building permanent memorial grave sites. Widows and mothers can be accompanied by another person but they must pay their own expenses."

"Are you saying that you'd like to go?"

"Yes I would….but only if you will come with me."

"I swore when I left Poland that I'd never leave England, or even the north east for that matter, again but if you really want to go then of course I'll go with you. Perhaps we can go after the harvest and ploughing. That would be the best time for me and it'll give us time to make the necessary arrangements.

The journey was long and tedious and Rhoda wondered how John James had summoned up the energy to make it all the way to Newcastle and back with a 48 hour pass on his last leave, the last time she had seen him alive. Eventually they arrived at Kings Cross and caught the underground to Victoria Station where they joined other pilgrims gathered at the entrance to the platform for the boat train to Dover and Calais. When all the travellers were assembled the guide checked them off on his list and conducted them to the reserved carriages.

Clickety clacking their way from Calais towards Amiens Rhoda and Robert sat quietly each occupied by their own thoughts. It was six years now since John James had been killed. The raw pain of grief and anger had long ago subsided but Rhoda was wrestling with feelings of guilt. In travelling to see where John James had been killed was she travelling back in order to try to cling on to a last vestige of the life she had planned with him or, was she travelling to find a final closure that would allow her to move on and make a new life with Robert? She knew that she would never have an all-encompassing passion for Robert in the same way that she'd had for John James, but love Robert she did and she was convinced of that. It was a love by stealth, a love gradually recognized and accepted for its tenderness, safety and comfort. A love, she wondered, whether or not that it was rooted in their mutual love for John James but Rhoda also knew that the way to her future happiness would never accommodate a third person in her relationship with Robert and therein lay her dilemma.

Robert watched the familiar French red-bricked villages and agricultural landscape glide by, a landscape that stirred memories that he thought had been buried deep. The closer the train got to Amiens the more Robert felt himself leaving the present and entering another reality where he was laughing and joking and brewing a cup of lukewarm tea with his comrades in a trench somewhere on the Somme battlefield. He glanced up at Rhoda who seemed equally preoccupied staring out of the carriage window. She was beautiful and he knew that he loved her but he also knew that it would never be the love of sexual passion he'd experienced with Katharina. And there was the guilt, always the guilt that he was being disloyal towards John James, that he was dishonouring their friendship. And yet he also knew that John James would want nothing better for Rhoda than that she should make a new life with his best friend.

At Amiens they made their way to the far side of the station. They were now very tired and there was little animated conversation as people struggled with their luggage up and down bridges over the various tracks until they reached the local train bound for the town of Albert.

It was getting late now and the setting sun was bleeding out along the horizon as the little train pulled into Albert station. Considering how much pounding the town had taken from both sides during the war Robert was surprised to see how much restoration building had taken place. The station was obviously functioning but the marshalling yards and accompanying depots and workshops were still mounds of red bricks and dust. The few walls that were standing were still stained black where fire had belched from windows and doors. Rings of rubble were discernible to those who knew indicating where French navvies had used destroyed buildings to fill in shell holes. The guide led the party like a crocodile of school children towards the Rue Victor-Hugo. Progress slowed as people swivelled their heads to right and left gasping in disbelief. The reconstructed parts of the road threw into stark relief the blackened, burnt out shells of previous houses and shops where jagged walls leaned at precarious angles signalling that danger still lurked for the unwary. Eventually they came to a halt and the guide counted them into the Hotel de la Paix.

The morning mist, retreating from the hollows of the Somme landscape, presaged the beginning of a bright day. There was already warmth in the sun and high lone clouds, like anti-aircraft flak Robert thought, dappled a clear blue sky. The assembled group with their rucksacks and maps crowded round a parked omnibus waiting to climb on board.

Robert steered Rhoda to one side, "I don't know about you but I'd really rather not spend the day with other people. How do you feel about hiring a motor and going where we want to go rather than being herded like a load of sheep?"

"I think that's a splendid idea," Rhoda agreed, "I don't think it's going to be a day for sharing with strangers."

Robert informed the guide, who didn't seem too pleased, and taking Rhoda by the arm guided her towards the town centre. They walked slowly up the street and crossed into the Rue de Bordeaux and on up into the town square which was dominated by the ruin of the Basilica de Notre-Dame de Brebieres. Rhoda stood, stock still, shocked and mesmerised by the extent of the damage. They moved closer and could see the once spectacular interior paintings, frescos and gold leaf decoration through jagged shell holes in the walls. The roof had long ago fallen in. Only the stump of a tower remained.

"There used to be a gilt statue of the Madonna and child on top of the tower but a German shell hit it and it leaned into a horizontal position where the Madonna's arm pointed downwards as if accusing everyone who walked past," Robert said ruefully. "There was a myth that the war would end in the year that the statue fell into the road."

"And did it?" Rhoda asked.

"As a matter of fact it did but the Germans also had a rumour that whoever knocked it down would lose the war."

"Well," Rhoda asked enthralled, "They lost so I suppose that they knocked it down."

"Actually they didn't. They took the town in 1918 and we shelled the tower to stop them using it as an artillery observation point."

"Is nothing sacred in war?" Rhoda opined.

44

They turned away noticing that much restoration work was in progress all around but there were still gaping spaces where the only evidence of buildings was a red brick stain on the ground.

"It's been a long time but I seem to remember that there used to be a garage just up here, round the corner. Knowing the French I expect the owner will have had his business up and running again five minutes after the armistice was signed, we'll just have to wait and see."

Although in a boarded up and dilapidated condition Robert was pleased to see that the garage was still in business. Formalities completed Robert helped Rhoda up into an even more dilapidated 1914 Renault Type EJ. "If you see a shop or market on the way out of town give a shout and we can stop and buy some bread, cheese, tomatoes and some fruit plus a bottle of vin blanc, unless there's anything else you would prefer?"

"No, that sounds....look....stop....there's a shop over there."

Rhoda accompanied Robert in to the little grocers shop and was impressed as Robert in his best pidgin French managed to buy all that they needed for their picnic lunch. Their purchases stored on board Robert turned the Renault towards the main road from Albert towards Bapaume. It was an old Roman road which arrowed its way straight across country rising and falling with the contours of the land. The road was elevated above the farmland which dropped away on both sides to the left and the right forming two shallow but long and wide valleys. About twenty minutes later a road sign indicated the village of La Boiselle and Robert took a right turn down a farm track. He parked the Renault and helped Rhoda alight from the passenger seat. Taking care he and Rhoda stepped up on to the raised edge at the side of the bumpy track. They stopped abruptly and with a sharp intake of breath Rhoda peered down into the most enormous crater beyond imagination. "My God!" she exclaimed, "What's this?"

"This mine was exploded under the German trenches on the first day of the Somme battle. We were behind the lines and a lad sitting in the trench next to me had his leg broken by the shock waves of the explosion shaking the trench side."

Observing the small wooden cross and poppy wreath at the bottom of the crater Rhoda said quietly, "Good God! There must still be sons, husbands fathers and brothers buried down there."

"Aye! Your right," Robert replied, "English as well as German, but mostly German." Robert turned his back to the crater and looked out over the tranquil, newly ploughed farmland where it rose gently northwards towards a plateau. With the last stubborn pockets of morning mist dissipated the sun now breathed life into the countryside and a heat haze shimmered and danced across the horizon. Pointing with his finger Robert continued, "See that white scar, up there, coming over the hill?" Rhoda followed the direction of Robert's arm. "That was the German front line trench. The French farmers haven't wasted any time in filling all the trenches and shell holes in and getting back into production. The chalk under the topsoil was thrown up when the trenches were dug and when they've been filled back in it left the tell-tale marks of where they were."

"Yes, I can see it," Rhoda replied drawing closer to Robert and clinging to his arm tighter than usual.

"At the top of this valley the Germans had an observation balloon which looked like a huge sausage so Geordies being Geordies they nick-named this Sausage Valley. I bet you can't guess what they called the valley over there on the other side of the road? Go on, I'll give you a clue. What goes with sausage?"

"Not gravy," Rhoda replied inquisitively as Robert shook his head. "Not Yorkshire pudding....potatoes....oh no!...it couldn't be...it wouldn't be mash would it?"

"Dead right, sausage and mash. Anything for a bit of humour." Then more seriously Robert continued, "The Northumberland Fusiliers came over there and charged up the valley. It was too far, poor buggers. By the time they got halfway they were knackered and German machine guns from that trench were mowing them down like wheat in front of a harvester. Come on let's get back into the car."

Ignoring the main road Robert turned right towards the villages of Contalmaison and Longueval where he took a sharp left signposted for Martinpuich. Halfway towards the village Robert stopped the car next to a graveyard on the left. Rhoda stood quietly looking at the depressingly pathetic sight of rows of wooden crosses surrounded by a wooden fence.

"This is where we came into the line in the September," Robert gestured. "The trench, you can just make the chalk line out, ran through that corner of the wood behind you."

Rhoda turned and stared in disbelief. "You mean this was a wood?" A huge crater filled with water could be seen where the bottom right-hand corner of the wood had existed. Shell holes, where nature had attempted to heal the wounds and soften their stark appearance, overlapped one another as far as she could see. Slivered tree stumps still screamed of death and utter destruction. The detritus of war which the French farmers hadn't scavenged was evident everywhere, rusted, tangled barbed wire, bent pickets, crates, boxes, shattered timbers and ripped sand bags littered the area and yet the once vile, putrefied ground was now green with grass and saplings were sprouting with new life. They walked on up the road for a while.

"Look at this," Rhoda pointed.

"Don't touch anything," Robert replied promptly. At the north west corner of the wood was a neat stack of mud covered shells of various size and calibre. "I expect that there are thousands of these duds all over the Somme battlefield. They're duds simply because they didn't explode when fired but they're all still fused and dangerous. The farmers'll be ploughing them up for years. I guess they're leaving them for the French bomb disposal people to collect and dispose of them. You might even see a tractor with a steel plate fixed behind the driver to stop them from being killed when their plough hits a buried shell."

"The politicians should be forced to come out here in shame to see the results of their greedy, imperial, capitalist policies."

"Aye," Robert replied with quiet resignation and then pointing Rhoda northwards again continued, "See that single hill in the distance?"

"Over there.....oh yes, I can see it."

"It's called the Butte de Warlencourt. It took us two months to fight our way from here across these fields and up to that hill. Come on back to the car and I'll take you up there."

They reached the main road again and turned right heading towards Bapaume. Passing through the tiny ribbon village of Le Sars Rhoda pointed, "Look, there's that hill up ahead just off to the right of the road. It's huge, it looks weird rising out of flat farmland and just standing there on its own. It can't be natural."

"No it's not," replied Robert, "It's a prehistoric burial mound over 60 feet high. Obviously whoever holds this hill has unrestricted observation for miles around and the Germans occupied it and we wanted it. The whole hill is riddled with tunnels and machine gun nests. The vegetation's grown back but you can still see the white scars marking the trenches and entrances to dug outs."

Robert turned off the main road down a track with the mound on his left, stopped, and once again helped Rhoda down from the passenger seat. They walked further along the track until Robert stopped and then led her into a field. Rhoda stood and waited whilst Roberts appeared to be searching the area for something.

"Over here Rhoda."

Robert was standing on a stretch of chalk which scythed its way across the field. As she approached, Rhoda sensed a change in Robert's demeanour. A surreal feeling that he had retreated to another land, another time.

"The clouds were so low and black that dawn arrived without us noticing," He said quietly to himself. "The rain was so heavy it was washing the sides of the trench in and we were standing thigh deep in liquid mud. We waited and waited and waited for the whistle to go over the top and make a full frontal attack on the Butte. Of course they knew that we were coming....they always did. It was here....this exact spot..... where John James was shot.....I was standing right next to him." Without warning Robert sank to his knees and fell forward onto his forearms his head buried in his hands. Rhoda was taken completely by surprise and by the time she reached him Robert was racked by uncontrollable grief. With tears welling up in her own eyes she fell to her knees beside him and saying nothing placed an arm around him lying her head on Robert's back. Neither of them knew how long they stayed in this position but eventually Robert gained his composure and Rhoda helped him up. She leaned forward and kissed both of Robert's eyes the salt stinging her tongue. They clung tightly together for a little while and holding his hand, Rhoda led Robert back to car saying, "Come away Robert...it's done....it's finished."

Six months later Robert and Rhoda were married and within the year baby Libby was born. Two years later Rupert arrived and the family completed a year later when Rowena was born.

CHAPTER 7

Otto 1933 – 1940

Otto was excited and looking forward to the ceremony. At fourteen years old it marked the point where youths were legally entitled to choose their own faith and beliefs and make them public. But more importantly for Otto, it would also signal the moment he had waited for months, the opportunity for him to apply to join the Hitler Youth. Together with his classmates Kurt, Jurgen and Wilhelm on the committee, Otto had chaired the meetings which had planned the format for the big day. Although a civil ceremony, Otto made sure that the local Hitler Youth district leader was made aware of the ceremony programme and his major influence in bringing about a new format. Here was another positive entry into his *Leistungsbuch*, his Performance Book to add to all those already recorded and which he hoped would ensure his future promotion through the ranks.

Drawing himself up to his full 5 feet 8 inches Otto gazed at his reflection in the full-length mirror in his bedroom. He stood square on, legs slightly apart with his hands on his hips. Otto was tall for his age and well built. The few other classmates who were as tall as him had outgrown themselves and were skinny specimens. Already Otto had well defined muscles over a large frame. He was not exactly blond, more a very fair auburn. His face had an aesthetic symmetry with clear blue-grey eyes and a nose which some might say was a little too large. He liked what he saw and allowed a wry smile to morph slowly over his normally impassive stare. The black, leather lederhosen shorts reflected a clinical matt sheen. His brown shirt was ironed to creases razor sharp. Burnished black shoes flashed highlights and contrasted with the white knee high white stockings. A polished leather strap over the right shoulder was attached to his belt front and back. The crisp neck-tie was held in place by a leather woggle and an Austrian pattern side cap was set at a jaunty angle on his head. And finally the red armband emblazoned with the swastika was unmistakable.

Just for a moment Otto wondered what his mother would say when he went down stairs but he didn't really care. He was determined and ambitious and he had his feet on the ladder.

Katharina was sitting with her mother waiting in the large living room when she was distracted by the noise of leather shoes on the wooden floor. She turned, her blood ran cold leaving her face deathly pale. She gripped the side of the armchair and shouted, "Where did you get those clothes? Go upstairs at once and take them off. Where did you get the money from to buy them, they must have cost a fortune we haven't got."

"I save........"

Katharina's father who had followed him into the room stopped Otto from finishing his sentence. "I bought them for him."

"I thought I told you that I didn't want my son to be tainted by the foul, vile warmongering of that madman Adolf Hitler," she replied with uncontrollable rage and it was in that moment that she noticed her father was sporting a Nazi Party lapel badge on his suit jacket. "You too, is this what you want for your grandson?"

"Yes by God, it is. It's your naivety that's a danger to Germany. Look around you, open your eyes and see what's really happening. The future of Germany lies with the strong youth, like Otto here. You should be proud that he's prepared to stand up for the Fatherland."

"Calm down everyone," Katharina's mother said, "This isn't going to solve anything."

"Hitler talks of freedom but he silences anyone who disagrees with him. Remember the way his SA bullies treated those men at his Munich meeting. If he's prepared to beat up opponents in public what do you think he's going to allow in secret in the concentration camp at Dachau, a few miles from here. Do you really believe his lies that they're simply there for re-education. My God, father, don't you know that a society that burns books ends up burning people. You're not marching for a resurrected Germany, you're marching to oblivion and taking my son with you. I'll never forgive you."

Taking the opportunity of a lull Otto said, "It's really time we went."

"I can't go," Katharina said sobbing.

"You must mother," Otto fired back. "You must. I've arranged it...I'll be the laughing stock of the school if you're not there. My future career will be black listed before it's even got started," he pleaded. And then with deliberate menace in his voice Otto continued, "If you don't come I'll never speak to you again....ever. I mean it, you can't do this to me."

"He's your son Katharina," her father interjected, "Be proud that he wants to help build a better life and a better Germany for us all. He needs your support."

"Alright," she said reluctantly. "I'll support you this time because you're my son and I love you but don't think that I condone what you're doing."

* * * * *

There was a hum of excitement and anticipation in the civic room of Riedering town hall. The stage was decorated with greenery, shrubs and flowers. There was a lectern central on the stage with four seats behind. Four rows of six seats each were arranged in a 'V' two at each side of the stage with the lectern at the centre.

A drum roll at the back of the hall signalled the beginning. The drummers marched down the centre aisle and then peeled off to the right and left of the stage. They were followed in by two rows of twelve youths each including Otto and his classmates who also peeled off to right and left and then mounted the stage and remained standing in front of their seats. There was a further drum roll and the school principal followed by a member of the SA and SS with the Hitler Youth district leader bringing up the rear mounted the stage and took their seats. As one, the twenty-four youths also sat down. Another drum roll and the Hitler Youth leader moved towards the lectern and read a short message of support from The Fuhrer

Following the applause and a further drum roll the SS officer stood up and addressed the meeting. He spoke at length of youth leading a resurgent Germany. A Germany purged. A Fatherland of pure Aryan blood. A strong Germany not afraid to take its place in the world and fight for its right to exist on its own terms.

Katharina sat in silent resignation listening to the regurgitated indoctrination she had heard spouted by Hitler in Munich. She knew now that she was totally alienated from her father and probably her mother who would do whatever her father told her. This she could live with but how was she ever going to be reconciled with the path her son was determined to tread?

A further drum roll curtailed Katharina's melancholy thoughts and glancing at the programme read that it was Otto's turn to make the pledge to the Fatherland on behalf of his classmates.

Relations on the farm were strained during the next few days and Otto was pleased to escape the atmosphere. As he travelled on the train from Riedering to Rosenheim Otto wrestled with his feelings for his mother. He supposed that his mother loved him because that's what mothers did. But if she really loved him why couldn't she see that all he wanted to do was help build a strong and better Germany for all Germans? His respect for her had diminished and he vowed he was even more determined not to let her hold him back, stop him from achieving his destiny as a leading participant in the new Reich.

* * * * *

Otto sat in front of the district Hitler Youth leader. "We've had our eye on you young man. There are many reasons why young men your age want to join the Hitler Youth but there are few with your heartfelt belief in what you're doing, your unconditional support for the Fuhrer, your physique, training and academic ability."

"I've given it a lot of thought and I know where I want to be in… say…five years' time."

"Whoooah! I can see that you're a man in a hurry. You'll be wanting to sit in this seat next week if I'm not careful. Let me give you some advice Otto. Normally at eighteen you would be expected to progress into training for the storm troopers but with the right friends a university education would be a direct passport to the officer class in the SS. I think that should be your future."

* * * * *

The heavy falls of winter snow gave Otto the opportunity to organise his group into gangs for civic labour service. Keeping roads open and ensuring that the old had fuel and food.

"I want you to clear the pavements on both sides," Otto said pointing up and down the main street in Riedering town, "But not outside that shop, that one, that one and that shoe shop."

"Why?" Wilhelm asked.

"Because they're Jewish shops dumkopf." Otto said slapping him across the head as Kurt and Jurgen burst out laughing.

"The Jews can clear up their own premises," Jurgen added slapping Wilhelm across the head again to further hilarity.

As if on cue the owner of the shoe shop came out with a shovel and started to push the snow from outside his store into the road. Otto bent down, picked up a handful of snow and compressed it into a large snowball. Taking careful aim he launched it across the road and it crashed against the shop window glass. The gang collapsed in laughter as the shock of the impact made the old man slip and fall on his backside. Before the remnants of the snowball had even commenced to glide its way down the window a fusillade of snowballs bombarded the shop owner in such numbers that they once again collapsed in laughter as the old Jew scrambled towards the safety of indoors.

Work completed for the day the four friends made their way home. Walking along a country lane Otto announced, "I need a pee, it's this damned cold weather."

"Me too," said Kurt.

"I've got an idea," Jurgen added enthusiastically, "Let's see who can pee the furthest in the snow."

"Good idea. Come on let's get in a line. Dicks out. On the count of three, one, two, three, go."

Bow legged, the boys made their way down the lane leaving four yellow streaks trailing behind them. Otto bent forward and looked to the side. "Where's your dick Wilhelm? Have you had a bit cut off or worse still has it all been cut off? Kurt and Jurgen literally wet their pants laughing.

"No I haven't."

"Well you've got a little dick then," Otto teased cruelly and looking at the others for support added, "From now on your not Wilhelm but Little Willy."

"Little Willy, Little Willy," they all chorused as Wilhelm tried hard to laugh it off and not show how hurt he was by their persistent bullying.

* * * * *

Over the next few months, Otto tried to spend as little time as possible at home. He worked hard at school and when not engaged on his assignments he was attending political sessions at the Hitler Youth and planning programmes for camps, hikes and other physical exploits. He himself was eagerly absorbing information on simple military tactics and small arms training. But what he enjoyed most was organising ambushes and counter marches to coincide with Communist parades in Riedering. These events always ended in violence and Otto wore his cuts and bruises with pride. The district office were more than complimentary when Otto managed to infiltrate a Communist cell in Rosenheim and pass on the names of key personnel for re-education at Dachau. There were always Jewish shops and businesses to be identified, picketed and harassed and synagogues to be daubed with anti-Semitic graffiti.

As recognition for his enthusiastic support for the Party Otto was rewarded in early 1935 with a promotion and authority over six hundred comrades. He continued to work hard and proved ever fertile ground for the extreme policies of the Nazi Party and when news arrived that the annual Party Rally was to take place in Nuremberg in September he set about planning arrangements with enthusiasm. He was working up in his bedroom one evening when he spotted a black Mercedes coming up the drive towards the farmhouse. He had a good idea what it was about and crept out onto the landing so that he could hear what was being said. The car crunched to a halt and two men wearing wide brimmed hats and identical long black leather coats stepped out. Werner put down is newspaper and went to open the door. As soon as the two visitors spotted the party badge in Werner's jacket they saluted, "*Heil Hitler,*" and Werner responded. The two men held up identity papers.

"Does Frau Katharina von Lieper live here?" they enquired.

"Yes she does," replied Werner.

"May we speak with her please," one of the men asked.

"Certainly, what's it about?" her father asked.

"We'd rather discuss this with Frau Lieper if you don't mind," the other man replied.

"You'd better come in then," said Werner showing the two men into the living room.

"This is Katharina," and turning to his daughter he continued, "There are two men to see you Katharina."

One of the men moved over to the fireplace whilst the other held Katharina's attention. "It has come to our attention that you are not particularly enthusiastic about our Fuhrer, Herr Hitler and his policies for a greater Fatherland."

"And what's it got to do with you what I think?" Katharina replied forcibly.

"Quite a lot as it happens Frau von Lieper."

On the mantelpiece was a picture frame with the photograph turned towards the wall. The man standing next to the fireplace made a rather dramatic display of turning the picture round and setting the portrait of Adolf Hitler back down with his face looking out into the room.

Kathcrina's father looked at her and spat out, "I've told you about this before, to leave that picture alone."

"I can't even bear to be in the same room as his picture," Katharina replied with equal vehemence.

The two Gestapo members stood listening intently before one of them interjected, "Frau von Lieper out of respect for your father and son and the service of your husband to the Fatherland we will give you a friendly warning. Keep your thoughts to yourself and show respect for our Fuhrer at all times otherwise......" and he left the remainder of the sentence hanging with intended menace. "Don't make us come out here again. *Heil Hitler.*"

Katharina did not respond. The two Gestapo agents stared at her a little too long before turning and walking out of the house without looking back. Hearing the car making its way back out on to main road Otto crept back into his room.

Katharina moved into the hall and yelled up the stairs, "Otto…. Otto….come down stairs directly." She waited but there was no response. "Otto……" she screamed louder, "Come down here immediately I want to talk to you." When there was still no response Katharina charged up the stairs and flinging Otto's bedroom door open so hard that it crashed back against the wall she made straight for him dragging him away from his desk. Otto was taken by surprise at the strength of his mother and the ferocity of her anger, "How could you do this? How could you denounce even your own mother? Is there nothing you won't do to further your own ends? What sort of animal are you turning into? Is this the true face of that madman's weasel words when he talks about *heimat* and one blood, a *Volksgemeinschaft,* national unity? Is this your great Fatherland where families are torn apart?" She screamed out of control. And then in a more measured and sinister voice Otto's mother continued, "I just hope and pray that one day you'll live to regret what you've done."

Katharina turned and slowly walked into her bedroom. Closing the door she collapsed in a paroxysm of heart wrenching sobs. How different it could all have been if she had followed her heart and gone to England with Robert when he had begged her to.

* * * * *

Otto and fifty specially selected members of his Hitler Youth group were weary from their one hundred and fifty kilometre march from Munich to Nuremberg but their excitement and enthusiasm were re-ignited by an adrenalin rush as they prepared to enter the stadium. Above them was a black, velvet panoply punctured by bright pin pricks of light from far away planets and galaxies which infused areas of the sky with a magical translucence. Along with other Hitler Youth leaders, Otto marshalled his comrades at their assembly point as practised earlier that afternoon. The noise, restless movement and animated conversations heightened an atmosphere already electric with expectation and excitement. At last, the hour of midnight arrived with the blare of bugles and the vibrating pulse of drums. Otto and his friends stiffened up and began to march into the Congress Stadium behind their unit banner. The sight that met him filled Otto with such awe that it nearly brought him to a standstill. They marched down the central roadway past rank upon rank upon rank of SA, SS and Wehrmacht units each with their banners gently flapping in the evening breeze. The torchlight procession was a river of liquid fire pouring its way through the darkness spreading a message of shared brotherhood to the assembled thousands. At a given signal huge cauldrons were ignited around the raised perimeter of the stadium and red and yellow flames flared up to the sky imbuing the huge Nazi eagle behind the rostrum with a phoenix like resurrection. Long red banners with the Nazi swastika in the middle rippled gently. Suddenly, searchlight beams sliced the night forming a white cone reaching up to an apex high in the night sky. And then just as suddenly they were extinguished except for two that arced down and focused on a raised rostrum. Standing at the front and centre of the platform was Adolf Hitler flanked by Baldur von Schirach the leader of the Hitler Youth, Heinrich Himmler and Joseph Goebbels. Projected out of the darkness by the spotlights they appeared to be floating unnaturally, suspended in time and space. The cheers of *"Sieg Heil"* erupted like thunder!!! Although Otto could feel his ears hurting he joined in. Goebbels introduced Hitler to more shouts of *"Sieg Heil"*. Hitler stepped forward and basked in the adulation. He raised his hand in salute and as if at the throw of a switch the multitude responded as one by falling into immediate reverential silence. The Fuhrer stood looking out into the arena and Otto felt as if Hitler could see into his very soul. In his usual dramatic way Hitler began his speech quietly but as he warmed to his subject he became more animated and his rough accented German more strident.

Hitler took half a step back as shouts of *"Heil Hitler"* reverberated round the stadium. He moved forward and once again raised a hand signalling silence. Picking up his theme Hitler worked himself up into a frenzy screaming into the microphone and throwing his arms into the air.

Finally a military band struck up and the crowd of 100,000 sang the national anthem Deutschland, Deutschland uber Alles.

* * * * *

For the next two years Otto continued his studies and more importantly totally immersed himself in the Hitler Youth ethos. He honed his military training and volunteered for the patrol service, hunting down those against the Nazi regime. At weekends and vacations he embarked on labour service putting his experience on the farm to good use by helping with the harvest, digging drainage ditches and road building in the mountain districts. Acting on advice he enrolled at Munich University where, as an undergraduate he studied European languages and German literature. The gathering storm clouds of war finally burst in 1939 when Germany invaded Poland. Otto graduated from Munich University in 1940.

* * * * *

Katharina saw the taxi make its way down the track towards the house and was immediately overtaken by fear and panic. However, she quickly regained her composure when she realized that the Gestapo would have used their own transport and not relied on a local taxi. As she watched through the window a tall, well-built young man dressed in the black menacing uniform of an *SS Leutnant,* got out of the taxi and made his way to the front door. At first the cap with its highly polished black peak hid his face but when he lifted his head to pay off the taxi driver Katharina recognised Otto. She grabbed the window-sill to stop herself sagging to the floor. It had been three years since she had last seen her son and the sight of him in an SS uniform was one that filled her with sorrow and foreboding.

"Hello mother, I've just come to pick up a few of my personal things and I'll be on my way." Otto said as if the last three years hadn't existed.

"Is that all you have to say after all this time?"

"I think we've both said all that needs to be said mother. We both know where we stand."

"Oh!....and where's that Otto? Sending disabled children to be gassed because they're a drain on the public finances. Compulsorily sterilizing people categorised as undesirable according to your warped views. Selecting those to be injected because they don't fit in with the Fuhrer's eugenic master race ideal." Katharina had been determined not to lose her temper but her hatred for what Otto had become overtook her. "It's evil and you're part of it," she screamed.

"Give it a rest mother I've heard it all before. You should be proud that I'm helping to build a pure Aryan Fatherland."

In desperation Katharina lost complete control of herself and yelled, "Then you should start with yourself."

Otto swung round to confront his mother, "What do you mean by that?" he shouted challenging.

"If you want a pure Aryan blood Fatherland then put yourself top of the list for an injection because you're a half breed."

Otto grabbed his mother by the throat, "Liar," he yelled at the top of his voice his face contorted, "What do you mean you bitch?"

"You're only half German," Katharina managed to gasp as Otto's hands fell from her throat, "Your father was English," she yelled almost triumphantly. "Yes, you're half English. Tell that to your Ministry of Racial Hygiene."

"Liar, Liar, Liar," Otto screamed as he turned and slammed the door behind him.

CHAPTER 8

Annie 1927 – 1940

The much needed extension to Hill Top Farm house was finished at last. Little Annie was now eleven years old and not so little any more. Libby was five, Rupert three and baby Rowena two and the original farmhouse had not been built to accommodate such a large family. There was also Rhoda's aunt Jean to consider. When she had initially agreed to baby-sit little Annie, then the other children when Rhoda and Robert were occupied with running their business interests, her husband Stuart was still working at the pit. However he had been killed recently in an accident when there was a roof fall at the coalface and as a consequence Aunt Jean no longer had the right to occupy their miner's cottage. It seemed a sensible solution all round when Jean agreed to move into the farmhouse as resident housekeeper and child minder.

The new extension consisted of pushing the gable end out sixteen feet. This created two extra bedrooms and a bathroom and toilet upstairs and an extra bedroom and playroom come study downstairs. Robert and Rhoda occupied the old master bedroom with Annie and Aunt Jean in the other two bedrooms.

Robert and Rhoda's business, Hadleigh Holdings, and Robert's farm were keeping their heads above water in spite of the current harsh economic climate. The consequences of the previous year's general strike were still reverberating round the country, the government hoping that they had averted what they saw as a possible Communist revolution. Democracy had taken a bashing in Europe in the aftermath of the First World War with revolution fomenting in many countries. Russia already had a Communist Government and Germany, Italy and Spain were leaning heavily towards the right. With housing shortages, unemployment and wage cuts for those lucky enough to be working the British working class was no longer buying into the slogan 'a land fit for heroes' and the miners in particular were still smarting at their treatment by Churchill. None more so than the miners of Chepfield who were first out and last to go back to work during the General Strike in 1926. The strike was bitter and coal miners from the Russian Donbass coalfield sent food parcels to Chepfield earning the village the sobriquet of Little Moscow.

Nevertheless there was much to celebrate in the Charlton household. The crowded living accommodation had been solved. Aunt Jean was a Godsend and although tight, there were no real money worries. But best of all Annie had just been informed that she had won a scholarship to Blaydon Secondary School. The school was well known for its academic excellence and entry was only offered to the brightest pupils in the whole region. There had never been any doubt about Annie's academic potential and from an early age her Junior School teachers had all predicted a successful academic career for her, but nonetheless, the recent acceptance was welcome confirmation although it would involve further financial expense.

Robert had exchanged his old Model 'T' Ford for a smart, used 1924 Morris Cowley Bullnose Tourer in blue and black and it was with unconstrained excitement that in August 1927 Annie climbed into the back behind Robert and Rhoda and set off for Isaac Walton, tailors and outfitters, at Newcastle to buy her new school uniform.

"How do I look in this mummy?" Annie shrieked as she twirled round and round in the store.

"Well if you'll stand still for a minute girl I'll be able to tell you," Rhoda responded, scarce able to contain her smile.

Annie stood as still as she could but still fidgeted from foot to foot. She was wearing a navy blue, pleated gym tunic over a white, long-sleeved cotton blouse with the tunic held in at the waist by a black girdle.

"The tunic's a little too long but I suppose by the time winter comes around you'll have grown into it," Rhoda said, "Besides we can't afford to be buying you a new one every year so we'll have to leave some growing space."

"I'm so excited," Annie said.

"Really, we hadn't noticed," Robert replied.

"Don't be such a tease, "Rhoda said hitting him on the arm.

Two pairs of long, black woollen stockings were added to the bill, as were four pairs of navy blue knickers a navy blue overcoat and a cloth navy blue hat.

"Can I try the summer dress on now please mummy," Annie pleaded heading for the changing cubicle. Rhoda handed in the dress and within seconds Annie skipped out wearing a checked blue and white short-sleeved cotton dress. A tie and a pair of black shining leather shoes completed the ensemble.

"Wow, you've got more kit than I had when I was in full marching order in France," Robert said laughing.

"Don't be silly daddy."

"Right madam, I think we'll get you home before you bankrupt us," Robert said paying the bill.

* * * * *

The first day at school was as exciting as Annie had hoped it would be. She felt really grand being dropped off at the school gates in her dad's car. However she would have to travel on the train from Lintzford to Swalwell and walk the rest of the way along Shibdon Road on those occasions when neither her father nor mother was driving to Newcastle on business.

Annie stood in the girls' playground soaking up the atmosphere and when a whistle blew everyone around her ran to their designated place and lined up in classes. Prefects, with bright silver badges on their tunics, gathered all the new girls together and conducted them to the assembly hall where new boys were already seated on the right hand side having been directed there from the boys' play area. There was a buzz of excited conversations in the hall which gave way to immediate silence as the headmaster Mr. Wilson mounted the stage in full academic dress. He welcomed the pupils and reinforced their academic prowess reminding them to make the most of their privileged opportunities whilst at Blaydon Secondary School. The boys were led out of the hall leaving the girls, prefects and Miss Taylor who had now mounted the steps on to the stage.

"Whilst here girls, you will endeavour to become young ladies of some standing in society. You will conduct yourselves with decorum at all times...decorum girls...when in school uniform either inside the school premises or outside. When you are off the school grounds you will always wear your uniform hat and if you're caught without it there will be an immediate detention. Always remember that whilst in school uniform you are acting as ambassadors and the reputation of the whole school and all of us who work here rests on each one of you sitting out there."

Annie could feel Miss Taylor's eyes looking directly at her and she tried to shrink further into her chair.

"You are all looking very smart in your new uniforms and you will stay that way. One final word on uniform, there will be no bare flesh showing between your stocking tops and your knicker legs. You have been warned." Annie fell foul of this rule on the occasion of her first sports day at Blaydon. "Annie Charlton stand still." Without turning round Annie knew that it was Miss Taylor. "Girls who are taking part in sports ought to know that there are no smiles between stocking tops and knickers." Continuing with her welcoming address Miss Taylor concluded, "Now, I want you each and every one to make the most of your time here. Work hard and play hard and make us proud of you."

For Annie her days at Blaydon School were a journey of never ending joyous discovery and she delighted in soaking up information like a sponge. The range of subjects and the enthusiasm her teachers displayed for each of their own academic specialities inspired her but it was the study of languages that fired her imagination. From an early age Annie had always enjoyed the way that Robert would speak to her in German and Polish and his funny pidgin French and her natural aptitude was quickly recognised at secondary school. She appreciated the logic of Latin and revelled in the romance of French. German was not on the curriculum but such was the gratification in teaching such a gifted pupil that her languages teacher gave her extra lessons during some lunch times and after school.

Eventually, matriculation and an exhibition took Annie to St. Hild's College at Durham University where, in 1937, she graduated with an honours BA in modern languages. The following year Annie's post-graduate work was undertaken at the Sorbonne in Paris. Her sister Libby and brother Rupert were also showing academic promise so in order to ease the financial burden on her mum and dad Annie delighted in earning her own money working in bars and restaurants on the rive gauche. This plunged her into the rich tapestry of Parisian street life and if anything proved more of a finishing school than her academic work at the university. Annie often thought with a smile that her old, refined languages teacher at Blaydon School would die of shock if she could now hear Annie's slang, low French vernacular.

Annie was in danger of becoming a perpetual student. After a brief holiday back home in Chepfield, September 1938 saw her enrolled at Heidelberg University to study German literature and become as proficient at swearing in German as she was in French. However, during her year there the mood in Germany became more menacing, darker and oppressive and Annie was pleased to complete her year the following summer, one month before Germany invaded Poland.

* * * * *

"Eeee, lass, you don't know how pleased we are to see you back home," Annie's mother gasped before she'd even got through the door and put her bags down in the farmhouse kitchen. "We've been so worried reading the newspapers an' all."

Annie's brother and two sisters came running in from the playroom/ study almost knocking her over in their eagerness to welcome her back home followed more slowly by Aunt Jean who was now infirm and leaned heavily on her walking stick. "Careful you lot, Annie's just got in and she's tired. Give her a chance to recover and she'll come and talk to you." Then turning back to Annie she continued, "Come and sit down and have a cup of tea and if you're not too tired you can tell us all about it...we're dying to know what it was like Your dad's in the barn somewhere, I'll give him a shout."

Robert came into the kitchen, took off his dirty boots and nearly squeezed the life out of Annie as he hugged her. "Welcome home pet, we've been so anxious waiting for you. You don't know how good it is to see you and how proud we are of you." Annie heard what her dad was saying but she couldn't help but think that he seemed a little withdrawn and his voice flat and missing its usual timbre.

Robert tried his best to hide his preoccupation and apprehension. Since a letter had arrived bearing a Swiss postage stamp he had been in a state of confusion. Memories long buried don't always stay there and the long shadows of past experiences are always there, waiting to stalk us when we least expect it. The frozen moment that had been forgotten these past few years was in danger of thawing. His life was here and now and he couldn't allow the past to dictate his future.

"Thanks dad, I do know actually and I'll be for ever grateful for what you've done for me."

"Had away lass, come and sit doon and take the weight off your legs."

Annie dropped down into an armchair beside the range and watched as her mother took the kettle off the fire and poured the boiling water into the tea pot which was always at the ready.

"Thanks mum, there's nothing like a good English cup of tea. It's good to be home but I wouldn't have missed the last two years for all the tea in China. I've been so privileged and learnt so much, I'll never ever be able to repay you and dad."

"Get away with you, it's what mums and dads do. As long as it's been what you wanted. At the end of the day if you're happy, we're happy, it's as simple as that."

"Thanks mum." Annie answered warmly and then more seriously continued, "There's going to be war mum, sooner rather than later would be my guess. As I mentioned in my letters there's an aggression in the atmosphere over there. You can almost taste it. The county's split down the middle. There's the Nazi party that's hell bent on creating *lebensraum,* living space, in the east which can only bring them into conflict with Russia despite Hitler's non-aggression pact and ordinary Germans who fear for their lives and are frightened to put up any resistance. Lecturers at the university especially Jewish ones simply disappeared overnight. Rumour had it that they'd been taken away to concentration camps by the Gestapo and *Schutzstaffel,* the SS. The really frightening thing was that this was often at the instigation of the students themselves. The Hitler Youth, insinuated themselves into the student fraternity houses, gradually took them over and fomented anti-Semitic hatred. Those teachers who weren't spirited away had their lives simply rendered untenable and were hounded out of their positions. To offer any resistance was to find yourself either beaten up or denounced to the Gestapo, never to be seen again. Intimidation, fear and aggression were everywhere."

"We have to read between the lines in the newspapers here." Robert ventured. "Everyone can see where this is going and yet the government seems hell bent on appeasement whilst it's as plain as the nose on your face that Hitler is determined to expand German territory."

"Aye," Rhoda added, "I said after the end of the last war that Germany would be seething with resentment and would wait for the first opportunity to avenge their treatment at the Versailles Treaty. Your letters describing what's going on inside Germany were almost unbelievably frightening. You should have come home sooner. As a foreign national you could have found yourself caught up in the street violence." Rhoda said anxiously.

"I was safe really. I kept my views to myself and my fellow students offered me nothing but friendship. There really is an admiration for the English and they see us as Anglo Saxon cousins but there's also an arrogance, especially among my age group, which has been indoctrinated by propaganda from an early age and fuelled by the unhinged evil of Nazi doctrine. Hitler is hell bent on creating a Europe dominated by a German master race and once he's achieved that, in spite of his plea for peace, he'll turn on us."

"I always said that we should have marched to Berlin in 1918," Robert offered flatly.

"But everyone was war weary by then." Rhoda added, "I predicted to your real dad before he even went to France in 1915 that this would happen. The politician's war to end all wars was always an illusion and so it's proved."

"That's true mum, but this is about more than just economics and a place in the sun. This is about clearing other people off the face of the map. Eliminating completely the *untermensch,* sub-humans, as defined by Hitler. This is real inhuman evil mum. No one dare talk about it but Hitler is even murdering his own people. These things can't be kept secret and people know what's going on. Anyone in an institution with a disability, whether mental or physical, is quietly given an injection and the next of kin are being told that they died of pneumonia or some such.

Even fit people with a transferable genetic condition capable of being passed on to their children are being forcibly sterilised. People are being forced to boycott Jewish businesses. The owners are being bought out for well below the market value by Nazi sympathisers. That is if their business hasn't already been smashed up or worse still, set on fire."

"Can't the decent people organise any resistance?" Aunt Jean interjected.

"Auntie, you've no idea how bad it is. I just couldn't express in my letters how dreadful it was, especially for the Jews. You had to be there to experience it....to see it.....to see old men kicked and beaten in the streets with passers-by laughing at their distress. The Gestapo, SA and SS are everywhere threatening imprisonment for the least evidence of dissent. Neighbours are denouncing neighbours, some to settle old scores, but often to carry favour with the regime and deflect suspicion from themselves. To help a Jew is to be beaten up yourself. The war aims for the last war were blurred and often jingoistic to say the least but this coming war is going to be a clear fight between good and evil."

"How can a country with such a high culture in art, music and literature have descended into such evil hatred," Rhoda wondered out loud.

"The sheer evil megalomania of one madman who has tapped into the zeitgeist of a broken and resentful nation." Annie took a sip of her tea and continued, "Remember, I told you vaguely in one of my early letters, I'd only been there a couple of months when one day I was sitting in the common room having a cup of coffee with my fellow students, all German. They were very animated and excitable and when I asked them what was going on they said that they were going hunting that night. "I've never been hunting," I said, "What are you going to hunt?" They fell about laughing for ages and then one of them said, "Jews....of course, why don't you join us? You English are too soft, one day you will wake up and it will be too late." Anyway, later that night, the 9th. of November it was, I'll never forget it, I went down from the university into the town which was heaving with people running around with torches, shouting and chanting "Perish Jews. Out with the Jews." I got carried along by the crowd in the direction of the Jewish Synagogue, and once there I couldn't believe my eyes. They smashed all the windows, broke down the doors and smashed up all the furniture whilst others came out with the Jewish Rolls of Law and other religious artefacts. Then they set fire to it and even prevented the fire-brigade from putting out the flames. There were SA brown shirts, SS and Hitler youth everywhere and even though some bystanders expressed indignation they daren't do anything to stop it. Once the synagogue was well alight they marched through the town smashing the windows of all Jewish shops and businesses. It was well planned, they must have had accurate lists of addresses. It was horrible, people lost all sense of human dignity and behaved like maniacs. Where the owners lived above their shops their flats were broken into, families and furniture both thrown into the street where the men, women and children were beaten. You know mum, there were even schoolchildren being egged on by adults to kick and push old men to the ground. Their furniture and bedding was burnt in the streets and looters vandalised and simply walked away with stock that had been thrown out from the shops. The police just stood by and watched and did nothing. It was absolutely unimaginable, it was like a scene from Dante's Inferno. The next day the Jews had to clean up all the mess themselves and I mean pick up every feather from torn mattresses. Even then the Nazi's weren't satisfied and old men were made to get on their hands and knees and lick pavements clean with their tongues whilst people stood around laughing and mocking."

"I don't know how you could have stayed there after that," Rhoda interrupted.

"I did have second thoughts, but I was determined to experience and learn as much as I could about, what after all, were monumental events. The really, really frightening thing is that what I saw that night was repeated in every single town in Germany. Can you imagine such organised national hatred? Heidelberg is such a beautiful city that it's impossible to imaging such ugliness to be thriving in a city of culture. Anyway, with no Jewish students or lecturers or teachers and now no Jewish businesses Heidelberg ended up being a virtually Jew free city. If this was happening all over Germany then Hitler really is determined to annihilate a whole race."

"It's too horrible to contemplate," Rhoda said putting her arm round Annie's shoulder.

* * * * *

With the news of Hitler's invasion of Poland on 1st. September 1939 a heavy feeling of resignation cast a shroud over the whole country which was echoed in the Charlton household. Two days later the whole family were sitting in the kitchen listening to the radio tuned to the BBC. Everyone sat still, heads down, listening intently to an announcement by the Prime Minister Neville Chamberlain.

"......*British ambassador in Berlin handed the German Government a final note that unless we heard from them by 11 '0' clock that they were prepared to withdraw their troops from Poland a state of war would exist between us."* The Prime Minister didn't need to finish his statement. As his sombre voice droned its way into every home in the country there was no rejoicing such as had been seen in 1914. A generation now knew what a voracious appetite an industrial mechanised war had. *"...I have to tell you now that no undertaking has been received and that consequently this country is at war with Germany."*

"Good God," escaped from Rhoda's lips, "Have we learnt nothing?"

"We have a duty mum. We can't let what's happening in Germany happen in every country in Europe, including this one when he invades. The man is determined to kill millions of innocent people. I can't stand idly by and let that happen. I'll have to do my bit."

"Well, here we go again. Let's finish what we started in 1914 and settle with these bloody Huns once and for all," Robert said with no pleasure.

"Are you alright dad," Annie asked concerned, "You've seemed a bit.....well...distant since I came back."

"Yesss, of course I am, nothing for you to worry about, but this news certainly isn't for rejoicing is it?"

* * * * *

Annie enlisted immediately in the Women's Army Auxiliary Corps but became quickly disillusioned. With Hitler occupied on the eastern front, there was a vacuum in England where nothing much appeared to be happening and which quickly became nicknamed the phoney war. Apart from initial drill exercises Annie found herself occupied as a driver, secretary and a cook. However, once Hitler turned his attention west and invaded Belgium and France the phoney war quickly became a battle for Britain. The evacuation of the British Expeditionary Force from Dunkirk in June 1940 focussed resources and there appeared to be a likelihood of invasion at any time. The German occupation of France was lightening quick, a blitzkrieg which isolated Great Britain from the rest of Europe. The immediate effect of this was that the government had to act fast to organise, coordinate and support isolated resistance movements in France and ensure that reliable intelligence about German troop movements and intentions could be established.

Annie spent a year in the WAACs wondering how she could get more involved when one day a letter arrived for her at her barracks. Initially she scanned the letter with curiosity having no idea who would be writing to her from London. The letter began,

Dear Miss Charlton,
You are invited to attend an interview at the Victoria Hotel,
Northumberland Avenue, London, on Wednesday 11ᵗʰ. December 1940
at 1400 hours. Your commanding officer is aware of this appointment
and arrangements **BUT ON NO ACCOUNT MUST YOU TELL**
ANYONE *ABOUT THIS COMMUNICATION.*
A Travel warrant is included for your convenience. Be prompt.

Vera Atkins,
Assistant Head of Operations.

Annie put the letter down on her bunk and stared at it. She
hadn't the slightest inkling what this interview was about or would
portend but she felt some reassurance in that at least it was signed by
a woman.

On arrival at Kings Cross Railway Station Annie looked at a map
of the London Underground and made her way towards Euston Station
on the Northern Line from where it was only a few stops to Charing
Cross. Annie blinked at the light as she left the station or it might have
been because of the cold wind that was swirling around Trafalgar Square
and funnelling down Northumberland Avenue pushing her along
towards she didn't know what. Sand bags were piled up into protecting
walls at every doorway and the windows of every building she passed
were criss-crossed with tape to eliminate flying shards in the event of a
bomb blast. So many people passed her in uniform that Annie wondered
if the whole of the British armed forces were in London.

She easily found the Victoria Hotel and manoeuvring her way
round the sand bags stepped up to the entrance and opened the door.
The entrance hall was small and rather shabby. The carpet pile had long
disappeared between the front door and the reception desk. Brown and
cream paint and dark, wood clad walls closed in creating a depressingly
claustrophobic atmosphere. In the far corner, opposite the reception
desk and stairs leading to the upper floors, was a low coffee table and
three sorry looking leather arm chairs which had survived many years
of unsympathetic treatment. A newspaper was lowered revealing a
smartly dressed woman sitting at one of the chairs.

"Miss Charlton?"

"Yes."

"I'm Vera Atkins. Thank you for coming." She stood up and
extended her hand.

"Pleased to meet you," Annie answered and before she could
continue, Vera Atkins cut in, "If you'll come this way please Miss
Charlton." Not waiting for a response she led the way towards the stairs

and Annie followed on behind. Half way along the first floor corridor Vera Atkins stopped and tapped gently on a door.

"Come in," a male voice answered quietly.

Vera opened the door and ushered Annie inside. The room was bare and not a bedroom as Annie had expected. In fact it was quite bleak. The only furniture included a desk and three folding chairs. A naked light bulb hung from the ceiling and a blackout screen was drawn at the window. Annie began to feel decidedly uncomfortable and increasingly nervous. Vera motioned Annie to sit on one of the chairs and then took her place beside a man dressed in a rather dowdy civilian suite behind the desk.

"Welcome Miss Charlton, I'm Major Selwyn Jepson, don't let this rather low rent accommodation put you off it's just that it's rather convenient for us. I expect this has come as a bit of a surprise for you and that you're wondering what it's all about. Don't be worried and all will be revealed in good time but first things first. I know it's a bore but before we go any further I must ask you to sign the Official Secrets Act."

Seeing Annie's puzzled look, Vera Atkins reached over a pen for Annie to use. "Don't worry, its standard practice."

Without any warning Selwyn Jepson switched to perfect French and whilst being taken by surprise for a split second Annie responded in her best colloquial Parisian French. He had a file open in front of him and surprised Annie by how much he knew about her already. The interview continued to be quite low key and eventually after about twenty-five minutes he said in English, "Thank you for coming Miss Charlton," as he nodded to Vera who had remained silent throughout. "Would you wait downstairs in the lobby for a few minutes Miss Charlton," Vera said as she opened the door to show Annie out.

"Well, what do you think Vera asked?"

"I think she would be perfect," Selwyn replied. He was an extremely experienced interviewer and an excellent judge of character whose first impressions never let him down. "She speaks French like a native, a very slight hint of an accent but nothing that we can't accommodate. She's bright, confident and level headed. Yes, I think we'll take another look at her, what do you say?"

"I agree entirely, she has an assured presence but not enough to draw attention to herself, if she doesn't wear make-up that is. Yes, I think she's worth another look."

Annie got out of the chair as Vera approached her with a smile.

"Well, Miss Charlton, if we haven't scared you half to death and you've established that we don't bite we'd like to see you again on Friday back here at the same time. I know that you must have a thousand and one questions to ask us but just let the dust settle, enjoy a show or a drink or something and it'll give you time to gather your thoughts. May I remind you that you must tell no one, absolutely no one about where you have been or what you have been doing. We'll let your CO know that you're not AWOL. This really is top secret. Well, will we see you on Friday?"

Friday arrived all too soon and Annie found herself back in the lobby of the Victoria Hotel. The procedure was exactly as before and Vera showed her up into the room on the first floor.

"I'm pleased to say Miss Charlton," Selwyn Jepson opened, "That your loyalty to your country is indisputable and that we don't see you as a security risk."

"I should hope not," Annie replied a little affronted.

Selwyn ignored her reply and continued, "I understand that your experiences in Germany in 1939 polarized your views about this war."

"Yes they did rather," Annie replied, "Hitler is an evil megalomaniac bent on European domination if not world domination and we cannot allow millions of innocent people to be annihilated on his whim of a super Germanic race."

"You've been in the WAACs for the last twelve months but I'm sure that we can find something more suitable to your talents to help the war effort, what do you say?"

"I have to say sir, that I've been bored and felt pretty useless these past few months. I'd welcome the opportunity to do something a bit more active and constructive, not that the army doesn't need cooks and drivers of course."

Selwyn outlined the need for people to work closer with the enemy especially in France and asked if Annie would be prepared to undertake subversive operations which would put her life at risk without exactly specifying what these activities would be. He also made it perfectly clear that there was a strong possibility of not returning.

"No one, except us, will ever know where you are or what you're doing nor must they ever know, especially your family who you will not be able to contact." He waited a few minutes then continued, "I think that you should go away and think seriously about what we've discussed, the full implications of our proposal before making your final decision. I don't need to remind you but I will repeat, whatever your decision you must never tell anyone about these interviews. You must not mention anything to anybody about your decision which you must make of your own volition and independently. You have a lot to think about over the weekend and we'll see you back here on Monday at 1400 hours."

Annie spent a restless weekend turning over and over in her mind what had transpired during the previous week. But she knew in her heart of hearts that there was only one decision which would give her peace of mind. Whenever there was a slight doubt the image of old men being forced to lick the pavement clean whilst being mocked and reviled and kicked hardened her resolve to help rid Europe of this vile, ugly, inhuman contagion that was Nazism.

The interview on Monday was a formality.

"Well do you want to join us," Selwyn asked.

"I've thought long and hard about this over the weekend," Annie said, "But deep down I know that this is what I want to do. So yes, I will join you if you'll have me."

Selwyn stretched out his hand, "Good show, and welcome aboard Miss Charlton. Train hard, you never know when it might save your life. I'll leave you with Miss Atkins who will complete the formalities. I'm sure our paths will cross again so I'll say goodbye for now and good luck." With that, Selwyn put his papers into a battered old briefcase and left the room.

"Now that you're one of us I suppose I should call you Annie from now on," Miss Atkins said smiling, "Please call me Vera. Now, I must arrange for you to be transferred to the First Aid Nursing Yeomanry or the FANYs as they're called and I don't need to tell you that it's a good chat up line for all the soldiers from here to Timbuktu," she said laughing and then continuing, "We commission all our agent recruits into the FANYs as it offers protection under the Geneva Convention."

"So what happens now," Annie asked.

"Return to your unit, and I can't say this too often, remember that you've now signed the Official Secrets Act, and we'll be in touch shortly. Just let me say that you really impressed Major Jepson who's the Recruiting Officer for 'F' Section and I'm confident that you're the sort of person we need. Just so you know I'm 'F' Section's Intelligence Officer and we'll get to know each other much better during your training.

CHAPTER 9

Otto 1939 – 1942

Otto left the house of his childhood in a huge rage. How could she face him with a blatant lie knowing how he felt about the Fatherland and being proud of his Aryan blood? Did she hate her own son that much? She was denying him the meaning of his existence, his very reason for living. What mother would do that to her son? He could feel the anger building inside and feeding on itself. He threw himself inside the waiting taxi and slammed the door on what little remained of his association with his mother. His mood darkened on the journey to Riedering where he was to catch the omnibus to Rosenheim and the train on to Munich. The taxi stopped at the bus depot and the driver got out to take Otto's fare and his bags out of the boot placing them on the ground. Otto drew himself up to attention and saluted, "*Heil Hitler.*" The taxi driver ignored him as he made to climb back into the driving seat. "Salute your Fuhrer you filthy scum," Otto screamed so loud that people stopped and stared. He took his Luger pistol from its holster and waved it in the driver's face, "Salute your Fuhrer you half-wit," Otto screamed.

The taxi driver did as he was told and muttered under his breath as he watched Otto storm off to catch his bus, "*Mein Gott, verschone uns von diesen Nazis.* My God spare us from these Nazis."

Once in Munich, Otto made his way to the train for Berlin where he was to change for Warsaw in order to join his unit. The journey would be twelve hours if there were no hold ups but at least he would have time to have something to eat in Berlin before catching his connection.

* * * * *

Otto had enjoyed his SS training immensely. He graduated from Munich University in June 1940 and because of his connections and excellent record whilst in the Hitler Youth he was accepted immediately for the officer training school. Reichsjugendfuhrer Baldur von Schirach had the ear of Heinrich Himmler and was more than happy to advance his protégé who straight away found himself leaving Munich for Brunswick Castle which was the established SS Officer Cadet School. It was like being in the Hitler Youth again after life in academia and Otto loved every minute of it. His physical strength, athleticism and endurance more than equalled his intellectual ability and Otto, not for the first time, caught the eye of his superiors. He outperformed his fellow year cadets in mobile small-unit tactics, raids, ambushes, weapons training and patrols as well as the theoretical and practical aspects of military planning and logistics. When not engaged in timetabled instruction Otto revelled in skiing, swimming, riding and all manner of track and field sports. His one dilemma was which direction he wanted his SS career to develop. Whilst the aim of the cadet school was to produce flexible, adaptable officers who could undertake a post in any part of the SS there were four areas for Otto to consider, concentration camp duties, a combat unit, the police or the wider SS organisation. In the end he decided to finish his course and let his superiors detail him to wherever they thought his talents would best serve the Reich. After twelve months training Otto passed out as best cadet of the year. It was a proud moment when he was presented with his ceremonial SS officer's dagger and was promoted to *SS Untersturmfuhrer* (Second Lieutenant), on his posting to Warsaw in Poland.

* * * * *

Otto managed to scrounge a lift in a Wehrmacht troop carrier from Warsaw railway station to SS headquarters where he presented himself to the commander of the already established Jewish ghetto Colonel Heinz Auerswald.

"Come in *Leutnant* von Lieper, I've been expecting you. Sit down, sit down, you come highly recommended *Leutnant*. I hope we don't disappoint you," the Colonel gestured with a laugh.

"I'm at your service sir," Otto replied, "I'll do whatever you require of me sir."

"Excellent. The corporal outside will give you details of your billet. Get yourself settled and if you're not too tired after your long journey report back here at 0100 hours and you can join us on a typical patrol. Then tomorrow I'll give you a conducted tour of the Jewish quarter."

"Yes sir, whatever you say sir. I'll report for duty tonight."

The corporal conducted Otto towards a smart apartment building just round the corner from the headquarters.

"Is it always this cold corporal?" Otto asked pulling his coat tight.

"*Mein Gott*, this is mild," the corporal replied, "Just wait until the snows really arrive in January and February your piss freezes before it hits the ground."

"Then I shall have to make sure that I'm not caught short then corporal eh!" Otto replied with a chuckle.

These are your quarters sir, the apartment used to belong to a solicitor. Anyway, he doesn't need it now being as he's over on the other side of the wall," the corporal offered.

"Thank you corporal that will be all for now. *Heil Hitler.*"

"Anything you want or need just let me know sir, *Heil Hitler.*"

"I don't normally take an active part in operations these days, the mountains of paperwork keep me behind my desk but I like to keep my hand in," the Colonel grunted as he levered himself out of his car. "That's the trouble with promotion Otto, it always takes you away from the action and turns you into a paper shuffler. Take my advice and never let your troops lose sight of you behind a pile of files," the Colonel added sagely. Then more seriously he continued, "We've been given information that the little gutter snipes have been popping up in these streets. I've posted men at various vantage points and we can wait in that doorway over there."

Otto followed the Colonel half way down a narrow street and stepped into a doorway hidden in the shadows. It was a freezing cold night and the first dusting of winter snow danced along the cobbled road. Barely half an hour passed when the colonel tapped Otto on the arm with his Luger. Otto drew his pistol as the colonel whispered, "There….do you see…..in the middle of the street. That sewer cover has been pushed up from below just a fraction. Looks like they're on the move tonight."

The movement held Otto's attention and eventually, the sewer cover was raised higher and then slid quietly out onto the road. He held his breath as nothing happened for the next minute or two. Slowly a head appeared, exposing only the forehead and eyes, and rotated three hundred and sixty degrees. After a further minute or two someone emerged slowly from the sewer and staying close to the ground waited until a bundle of some sort was handed out to him. During the next five minutes three other bodies emerged from the city drains each with a bundle tied with rope. Otto watched as the four bodies crawled to the side of the road and then gradually stood up pressing themselves against the buildings for cover.

"We've got them now," the Colonel whispered to Otto, and without waiting ran out from his hiding place shouting, "Stop. Hands up. Stop or I'll shoot."

Seeing that the bodies were not going to comply with the order Otto ran in the opposite direction to the Colonel to get the four people in a crossfire and cut off their escape. They both opened fire at the same time, the sharp crack of shots and the whining of ricochets magnified as the noises echoed back and forth in the narrow street. It was a lifetime of excitement for Otto but in reality only a matter of moments before the four lay dead on the pavement. In the ensuing silence other, echoing shots could be heard from neighbouring streets. The two Germans crossed the street and examined the bodies, Otto kicking them over onto their backs. Surprised Otto exclaimed, "They're children. They can't be any more than eight or ten years old."

"That's right *Leutnant,* they send their children out to do their work for them. I'll show you tomorrow but what these little bastards are doing is sneaking out of the ghetto to sell clothes and any other manufactured goods on the black market. Raw materials, food and medicines are smuggled in the opposite direction. The children are used because they're small enough to crawl through the sewers. They know the consequences but still use their own children for God's sake. Let's go, there won't be any more excitement tonight. Come Otto, I think we deserve a schnapps," the Colonel said slapping Otto on the back, "Welcome to Warsaw."

Passing one of the four guarded entrances in the barbed wire topped wall surrounding the ghetto the Colonel said with some pride, "We have 400,000 Jews in here from all over the city and surrounding district. You'll have noticed that any perimeter building with windows facing outwards has had them bricked up to eliminate escapes." The Colonel's driver steered them round some of the nearest streets of the ghetto where a biting east wind was driving snow into the beginnings of drifts against buildings and gutters. "They live in filth and squalor. See, over there, they can't even be bothered to pick up their own dead no wonder there's Typhus and Cholera."

"Only 399,996 Jews to go Otto, have you got enough bullets?" the Colonel laughed. "This is like a city within a city," the Colonel continued as if nothing had happened. "The Jews have their own council, run their own civic affairs. The council collaborates with us and they even have their own ghetto police but their independence is pure fantasy. The council thinks that they can bargain and discuss with us but they're either stupid or delusional or both. They have schools, soup kitchens, hospitals and pharmacies, even an orchestra, workshops for clothes, boots, household goods you name it and they make it. Of course we don't buy their goods for the full manufacturing rate but they do exchange their pittance of earnings for food and medicines at inflated prices which is why they smuggle things in and out. The problem now is that we're under pressure. These are mainly Polish Jews….but Jews are now being deported east from Germany and we have nowhere to put them. We're also seeing thousands of Romany people. If we get a new shipment of 20,000 that means we have to eliminate 20,000 from the ghetto to make space for them. So no matter how many we get rid of we still have the same number."

"I've heard that gassing has been perfected and is very efficient."

"It is but the numbers are staggering and we need to increase plant and productivity if that's the right phraseology. At the moment it's economic to keep the able-bodied working until they drop. At least they can be replaced. The old and infirm we can do without. Which brings me to your responsibilities Otto. I want you to separate out those who are a useless burden here in the ghetto and arrange for them to be re-settled, if you know what I mean."

"No problem sir, I'll get right on it tomorrow."

Otto proved every bit as efficient as his superiors had predicted. He organised teams of Wehrmacht clerks to sift through thousands of registration documents weeding out those unfit for work. The logistics of organising transport and trains to satellite holding camps in order to accommodate the thousands of Jews in transit to camps such as Treblinka was organised, put into effect and eventually running like clockwork. What did it matter if hundreds died from starvation, freezing or disease on the way to the camps.

* * * * *

Operation Barbarossa, which launched three million Reich soldiers against Russia in June 1941, was an initial success which brought its own problems for the SS Special Purpose Units clearing up those Polish and Russian villages which had been bypassed. There were thousands of POWs, Slavs and Jews and resistance groups to be dealt with. The system was creaking.

A freezing cold afternoon in January 1942 saw the colonel and Otto enjoying a vodka or three when out of the blue the colonel said, "Hard work and enthusiasm have been recognised Otto."

"What are you talking about sir," Otto replied looking puzzled.

"I have new orders for you Otto. Because of your fine efforts here in Warsaw you've been promoted to full Lieutenant, and you're to transfer to Ciechanow north of here. You can read your orders later but apparently fifty per cent of the population of the city of Ciechanow are Jews. Half of the whole city are Jews. Can you believe that?" The Colonel said incredulously. "Anyway, you are to take up your appointment immediately and I doubt if those figures will be the same in a few months' time eh Otto," the Colonel said laughing whilst slapping Otto on the back.

"Thank you sir," Otto replied, "I couldn't have done it without your guidance and support. You must have sent a good report up to headquarters. Thank you again sir I appreciate it."

* * * * *

During the first week of his new appointment Otto spent the time out in the town getting a feeling for the place and watching how the present local German authorities operated. The pre-planned administration of aliens appeared to have been put into effect. Registration and the issue of identity cards and work permits had already been accomplished by an army of clerks and secretarial personnel but he was not impressed by the practical implication. There appeared to be no overall, coordinated plan. Labour details seemed to be haphazard and it was obvious to Otto that a more efficient system would scoop up those members of the population who were either backsliding or hiding.

The following Monday Otto called a meeting with the head of the local German police and other SS personnel.

"Gentlemen, as you know I have spent these last few weeks familiarising myself with the situation here in Ciechanow. Before I acquaint you with my proposals is there anything outstanding that I need to know about?"

The question was met with silence. "Good," Otto continued, "Then I want the following put into immediate effect. The Germanisation of businesses and factories is making progress and Jews over 15 years old, male and female, who have been allocated and hired out for labour must assemble at their appointed place before marching out to their workplace. Women with children may miss work detail on payment of a levy. Any Jews missing these roll calls will be found and shot immediately. I want names and addresses of all over sixty years of age screened from the records plus all those unable to work whether because of illness or physical, or mental infirmity. These are to be eliminated. As you may know, land is being distributed to German settlers and farmers in compliance of the Fuhrer's lebensraum policy and Hitler wants these Polish towns to be refashioned as residential cities according to Germanic style architecture. As a consequence you are to use those Jews who have not yet been able to be allocated meaningful production and put them to immediate effect with the demolition of all Jewish properties in order to widen the streets in preparation for a subsequent rebuilding programme. Owners will be given one hour to salvage their possessions after which if the house is not emptied their goods will be confiscated. The logistics of these orders will be your priority. *Heil Hitler."*

The assembled meeting was left shell-shocked and could only respond with "Heil Hitler," knowing that their new commander meant business and was not to be messed with. On leaving the room Otto approached the nearest NCO secretary.

"What's your name sergeant?"

"Gruner sir, Sergeant Gruner."

"Do you know this area very well Sergeant?"

"Yes sir I have been here for six months."

"Good, tomorrow I want you to pick me up at 0800 hours and we'll take a drive round the district."

Next morning the Sergeant was there as ordered, "Where do you want to go sir?"

"Just drive me round the countryside, I'll know what I'm looking for when I see it so just take me round the farms and fields away from built up areas."

They left the town heading north and very soon Otto spotted a large wood situated in a shallow valley. Seeing Otto making notes in his pocket book the Sergeant offered, "The Poles call that the Red Forest sir."

The Sergeant turned east then south intending to circle back towards Ciechanow. They passed through a small village, Chrzanowek and continued driving through agricultural land towards a hamlet of a few houses called Topolowa. The roads were now narrow and little better than tracks as the driver threaded his way between the fields.

"Stop," Otto demanded, and the Sergeant obeyed slamming on the brakes. "What's that over there," Otto asked pointing to the top of a large country house scarcely visible just peeping through the trees.

"It used to be a large estate but I believe it was divided up into small farms after the last war."

"Can we get closer?"

"I'll try," the driver responded.

After an uncomfortable ride down a narrow track Sergeant Gruner brought the staff car to a halt in a square cobbled courtyard. The detritus of years of neglect was piled up in corners and spilled out into the yard. On the left was a row of derelict outhouses with broken windows, shutters missing and doors hanging on rusted hinges. Some of the wooden shingles had long ago been blown off in severe winters past.

Straight in front was a high, stone wall with gaps where the stone had been broken down but a large archway was still intact. To the right was a large country mansion which looked as if it had seen better days but was still structurally sound. Otto walked through the archway and into what must at one time have been a formal garden. He mounted the wide steps leading to the large front door and kicked it open. Looking round he could see that the structure was still sound and that the roof, although showing signs of some small leaks was also in good repair. The place had a damp atmosphere and musty smell and pieces of broken furniture littered the floors in every room but nevertheless Otto considered that part of it could be made habitable for his purposes for a little while at least. He wandered back to where the car was parked and went in to one of the outhouses which had clearly been a cow byre at some time but had obviously been converted for habitable use. Household rubbish and broken furniture were piled up everywhere. He wandered over to the window facing the courtyard and absent-mindedly ran his fingers through the dirt on the windowsill. As soon as the dirt was dancing on the cold draughts sneaking in through a hole in the glass Otto noticed the carving. He blew the last of the dust away and read the letters carved into the sill. *Robert Charlton 9th. DLI 1916/17/18/19.* There was no doubt in his mind that the name was English. The 9th. obviously referred to a military regiment or division but he didn't know what DLI stood for. The dates, he surmised, probably signified that whoever had carved his name had lived in this room for up to three years. What on earth would an Englishman be doing in Poland twenty-five years ago? Could he have been a prisoner during the last war Otto wondered? It would make a nice little project to find out when he had more free time.

Turning to his driver Otto said pointing further down the track, "Do you think we can drive down to that wood over there or will we get stuck?"

"I can try sir, but we might have to get out part way down and walk the rest."

The sky was closing in as they walked into the wood and explored various pathways which were now a lot narrower than they had originally been. The wood was quite dense and choked with undergrowth. Otto looked up and the first real snowflakes of winter were finding their way through the pine branches and floated, hovered then swayed ever so gently to the ground. Further up the track were some wooden buildings which turned out to be a disused lumber yard. Otto made a thorough inspection and satisfied himself that it could be brought back into a working condition with very little effort or expense. Pleased with himself he turned to Sergeant Gruber, "Thank you Sergeant, you've been very helpful. I think I've found out all I needed to know so take me home before we find ourselves snowed up in this God forsaken hole for the rest of the winter."

Weeks passed and eventually Otto had all the information he had requested including a schedule for the demolition of Jewish houses. The snow continued to fall and Otto needed to press on quickly with his new project. He picked up his telephone and asked his Desk Sergeant to request a meeting with the Chief of Police within the hour.

The Police Chief was shown into Otto's office and asked to sit down.

"Tell me chief, do you know how many Jews over 60 we have in Ciechanow?"

"I have the exact figure in my office as you requested sir, but at a rough guess I would say that there are about two thousand plus those who are unfit for work for one reason or another."

"Good," Otto replied curtly, "I want them all assembled within the ruins of Mazovia Castle tomorrow morning at 0600 hours armed with picks, shovels, spades anything they can use to dig and move earth."

* * * * *

From the back of an army lorry the next morning with a cold, indifferent expression Otto viewed the Jews being assembled. Those who struggled due to age or infirmity were encouraged with the prod of a bayonet or a blow from a rifle butt. The snow was now about four inches deep and many of the people assembled in ranks wore soft canvas shoes or no shoes at all. When all was present and correct Otto gave the order for the gathered Jews to walk north, out of the town. SS and Wehrmacht guards flanked the struggling masses and two lorries followed up the rear. The oldest and those with the greatest infirmities were soon incapable of staying on their feet let alone walk. Legs were numb up to the knees and neighbours struggled to keep their friends upright and moving on. It was very quickly established that those who fell by the wayside were rewarded with a bullet from the nearest guard and left where they fell. No one bothered to count. It didn't matter anyway but Otto guessed that a few hundred had been eliminated on the journey to the Red Forest.

Putting a megaphone to his mouth Otto addressed the assembled Jews, "We need to prepare a defensive position here. If you want to protect your town and your loved ones then we need to dig anti-tank ditches. If you look on the ground you will see that a trench has been marked out. You are to dig this defence barrier as quickly as you can. Your guards will allocate you all to a section of the ditch. Anyone attempting to escape will be shot."

Hands and feet were frozen and progress was slow. Those with soft shoes or no shoes at all swapped their spades and shovels for picks or buckets. Otto walked up and down the length of the ditch offering an encouraging kick or punch when he thought that not enough effort was being expended. The death toll mounted and bodies were left to freeze where they fell. At the end of the first day the group were marched back to the castle, their route lined by the grotesque poses of frozen bodies whose stiff arms pointed heavenwards, fingers beckoning friends to join them under the white shroud of final painless peace.

The castle ruin comprised of four thick walls arranged in a square with round towers at two of the corners. There was no roof but at least the walls provided some little shelter from the biting wind. Once crowded into the castle a watery potato soup was distributed together with a slice of black bread. Some thin blankets were thrown from the backs of the lorries and the town's Jews were left to huddle together for whatever warmth they could find.

This routine continued for the next two days until Otto was satisfied with the depth of the ditch. The covering of snow and a pale, low winter sun bathed the countryside in a cleansing tranquillity, all ugliness embalmed and covered by a blanket of nature's purity. Otto's SS men had been briefed and the assembled Jews were ordered to undress in the wood. Hugging themselves against the cold the first group was pushed, bullied and beaten towards the trench where they were ordered to stand in line along the edge, bent, broken and shivering. Each guard had been allocated fifty rounds and they stood in two ranks each comprising of twenty Wehrmacht and SS personnel. The Jews, some already on their knees waited passively, as did the guards, for the order to fire. When satisfied that everything was in order Otto, who had taken up his elevated place on the back of one of the lorries shouted, "Fire," and the peace and tranquillity of the winter afternoon was shattered by the noise of gunfire. Otto noticed that one of the soldiers near him appeared reluctant to carry out the order. In a rage, he jumped down from the lorry and taking his pistol from its holster stormed up to the young boy. "You will obey your orders soldier or you will end up in the ditch with the rest of the scum....like this," Otto screamed placing his Luger to the head of the Jew in front of the soldier and pressing the trigger. He moved on to the next Jew and placing the gun to the back of his head pressed the trigger again. Blood and brains exploded in all directions landing on Otto's field uniform and face. Turning away, Otto raised his left hand up to his face to flick away the flecks of brain, bone and blood.

The only evidence that over two thousand souls had lived and died here was a dark brown scar left on the ground marked in stark relief by the red spattered snow, a mere razor nick on the face of the earth.

That evening, having showered and changed his uniform Otto was determined to forget the scenes witnessed during the day. Relaxing by a raging fire with a bottle of vodka on the table and a full glass in his right hand his left hand lifted automatically and flicked imaginary specks of brains from his face.

Totalling up the statistics the next day Otto was satisfied that there were now over two thousand less Jews to worry about in Ciechanow. The demolition of slum houses making way for the rebuilding programme was off to a good start. Those who were displaced had to find accommodation with friends or in garden sheds or lofts. Overcrowding, starvation, cold and disease was exacerbated by still more Jews from the surrounding district being displaced to Ciechanow. He contacted the German Government East informing them of his situation and further resettlement plans but was informed that transport was impossible and in any case Treblinka, Sobibor and Majdanek camps were full to capacity. To clear Ciechanow of the remaining Jews except for those who were working and creating profit for the Germans Otto submitted his ideas to higher authority and was given clearance to carry them out.

Further orders were quickly disseminated. The remaining Jews were to bring the lumber mill at Topolowa back into production. The trees in the forest were to be cleared and exchanged for timber already seasoned and barracks were to be built surrounded by a barbed wire fence. Part of the old estate mansion was to be cleared and made habitable for whoever would eventually be made commandant of the new camp. Once finished this satellite camp was to act as a holding camp for all the Jews from Ciechanow pending the final solution at Treblinka and Auschwitz. In the meanwhile arrangements were made for a mobile gas death squad to be based at Topolowa. The camp was well sighted in a hollow surrounded by forest and out of sight.

The Desk Sergeant brought the morning mail into his office as usual. Otto scanned the envelopes and opened first the one that looked the most unusual. It was from SS Headquarters in Berlin and Otto quickly ripped it open with his desk paper knife. He scanned it quickly as was his habit. Re-reading the letter more carefully a second time the implications of the contents sank in.

My Dear Otto,

Adolf Eichmann has recently acquainted me with your exemplary service since your transfer to the East and especially Ciechanow. Your devotion to the Third Reich in general and the Fuhrer in particular continues to give me great satisfaction. The enthusiastic and energetic way in which you fulfil your duties is a shining example to all SS Officers. To further your experience in the service of the Fatherland you are to be transferred to Paris, France with the rank of Captain. You will know that in normal circumstances you have not served the required amount of time as an Obersturmfuhrer before being promoted but when I showed the Fuhrer your service record to date he was absolutely delighted and prepared to intervene personally to make an exception in your case. This is indeed a great honour which you richly deserve. I offer my sincere congratulations

Your duties whilst in Paris will be to help speed up the resettlement of the Jewish population. However, in the initial stages the Fuhrer does not want to give the French any reason for them to organise resistance and destabilise the occupation whilst the Russian situation has yet to be resolved. Therefore only resident Jews who are not registered French citizens will be deported. Arrangements for the remainder are to be decided at a future date.

You are to report to Standartenfuhrer Helmut Knocken, Senior Commander of Security, France, at SS Headquarters in Paris on March 21st at 0900 hours.

Heil Hitler.
Heinrich Himmler.

Otto put the letter down on his desk and allowed himself to bask in the confidence and praise offered by his superiors. He was already looking forward to his posting to Paris, however, his delight was tinged with disappointment in that someone else would see his Ciechanow project through to fruition. Although it was still mid-morning Otto allowed himself a celebratory large shot of vodka and absent-mindedly flicked his left cheek.

CHAPTER 10

Annie 1940 – 1941

The staff car turned off the main road and stopped at a barrier manned by two armed guards. The driver and Annie showed their passes and were waved through. Having become accustomed to Spartan military accommodation over the past twelve months Annie was taken by surprise as she approached Special Training School No.5 (STS5). Instead of the usual War Department nondescript single storey blocks Annie stood at the entrance to Wanborough Manor near Guildford, a sixteenth century Elizabethan Manor house set in its own grounds that had been requisitioned by the Special Operations Executive (S.O.E.). It was built with the red bricks so favoured during that period with three large gables facing the front. At each end of the front elevation two gabled wings extended forwards forming a symmetry that created a three-sided gravel forecourt. The driver retrieved Annie's holdall from the boot of the car and handing it to her gave a smart salute before getting back into the car and disappearing down the drive. Annie turned and walked into the manor through the main entrance. Moving through into a large entrance hall she was greeted by an army clerk who stood quickly to attention and saluted smartly.

"Lieutenant Charlton," he said enquiringly, "We've been expecting you. Take a seat and I'll let them know you're here."

"Thank you," Annie responded.

The Corporal at the desk said something into a telephone and a few minutes later Annie's attention was drawn to a door being opened on the other side of the entrance hall. She was relieved to see the familiar face of Vera Atkins and immediately stood up giving a salute.

"*Bonjour Annie, accueillir au Manoir Wanborough. J'espere que vous avez eu un bon voyage. Toutes les conversations pour le prochain quatre semaines servont dirigees en francais.*"

Annie was not expecting this but immediately responded in perfect French, "Thank you, yes I had a very pleasant journey. Just one thing, how shall I address you whilst I'm in training here?"

"Well...we tend to be a little informal here, but in training use my rank otherwise Vera will do nicely. The Corporal will show you to your room where you can settle in and familiarise yourself with the layout. There will be a briefing at 1800 hours and dinner is at 1900. *Je vous verrai plus tard.*"

"Yes, I'll see you later."

There were already people sitting in the briefing room when Annie walked in. Scanning the room quickly she shuffled along one of the rows of seats and sat beside the only other woman in the room.

"Hello, my name's Annie."

"Hello, I'm Christina I was beginning to think that I was going to be the only woman on the course. My experience of men in the army is that they can be such bigoted pigs."

Annie recognised straight away that Christina was French and responded with a smile. "Well....we'll just have to show them that we're better than them won't we."

When they were all assembled there were eight men, Annie and Christina. At 1800 hours prompt, the door at the back of the room opened. "Atteeention." Conversations stopped immediately and the assembled group stood ramrod erect. An officer walked straight down the centre aisle and mounted a small dais at the front of the room.

"Sit down please.....my name is Major Roger de Wesselow of the Coldstream Guards and don't ask me how, but I'm commander of STS5, 'F' Section, 'F' because you're all proficient in French and familiar with the country and it is behind French lines where you will be expected to operate. On your seats you will have found some papers which outline the routine whilst you're with us and the timetable for special training. You will be prompt at all times...no excuses will be tolerated. You will be assessed twenty-four hours per day. You are never off duty in that respect and French will be spoken at all times. I strongly recommend that you do not enquire too much into each other's past histories. The less you know about each other the less you will reveal under duress. This could save lives....remember that. The next month will be the most intense of your lives to date. You will train hard and what you learn here may one day save your life. If at the end of this initial course you are not selected to go on to the paramilitary training you will return to your unit and this part of your life will be expunged from your memories forever. There is no shame in not being recommended for further training and there will be absolutely no repercussions during the rest of your military careers. In finishing I'd like to say that I am always available for whatever reason or the ladies may wish to approach Captain Atkins. Thank you for listening. Enjoy your dinner and mentally prepare yourselves for tomorrow morning. Always remember, stay focused and keep your mouths shut....thank you."

Next morning at 0700 hours the physical training started with mild, warming up stretching exercises quickly progressing to muscle quivering press-ups and other more violent routines. After a brief warm down and break a cross country in the grounds of the manor was ordered. As Annie sloshed and kicked her way through mud and water she wondered what her old Blaydonian sports mistress would make of her now, especially as there was more than a smile below her knicker line. Annie was in the leading pack but noticed that Christina was starting to lag behind. She was more than please that she had continued with her interest in sport after leaving school and her stamina supported her through the pain barrier. At the finish, Annie was still on her feet but bent over breathing hard whilst most of the others were flat out on the ground gasping and coughing including Christina. After lunch it was into the classroom for the theory of basic map reading.

That evening Annie tapped on the door of the room next to hers and it was opened slowly almost timidly by Christina.

"Are you alright," Annie enquired, "It was tough out there today my legs feel like lead," she lied.

"Come in," Christina said quietly. "You were great today, I hope I can get myself a bit fitter over the next couple of weeks."

"You will," Annie comforted, "There were some blokes out there really struggling and at least you finished which is a fantastic effort for the first day."

"Do you really think so," Christina replied brightening up. Then changing the subject she continued, "Your French is excellent, like a natural born Parisian, where'd you learn to speak French like that?"

Remembering the warning given at the initial briefing and not wishing to give too much away Annie replied, "I've spent a lot of time in Paris and worked in bars and restaurants to pay for my room."

"So that's where you picked up your slang. You'll fit in just like a native when you get back there."

"What about you?" Annie asked.

"We lived in Reims. My father was killed in the first days of the invasion and my mother and little sister left to stay with an aunt in the south of France near Toulouse. I was determined to join the resistance but my mother insisted that I come to England, so here I am, doing my bit to liberate my country."

"It's getting late and we've got another early start in the morning. Get a good night's sleep and don't worry about today, you did just fine. You'll get back over to France and do your bit don't you worry."

"You're so kind Annie, good night...and...thanks."

There was no more time for conversations after that first evening. Every night Annie fell into her bed, eyes closed before she even hit the pillow. Just like in her school days Annie absorbed the training and in spite of the fatigue and pressure she enjoyed every minute. Once the Physical Training instructor was satisfied with their physical endurance there was unarmed combat accompanied by large black and blue bruises. Weapons training with pistols and the Sten sub-machine gun left Annie with raised blisters and broke fingernails when weapons had to be stripped and assembled over and over again until she could do it blindfold to clear a blockage or jammed round.

* * * * *

With a pile of progress files on his desk Major de Wesselow and Vera discussed in turn the merits of progressing each member of the group for further training.

"What about Christina?" The major asked Vera flicking her file open.

"She's a girl with determination and hidden depths," Vera offered. "First impressions are that she's a bit of a timid little mouse but this is to underestimate her inner resolve, adaptability and resourcefulness. Initially her physical fitness and endurance were in doubt but she has toughened up during her month here and her small frame belies her strength."

"So you would recommend her to go forward?" The major asked.

"Yes I would," Vera replied positively. "I think her general shrinking violet demeanour would be an asset. She would not draw attention to herself and could easily be overlooked in a crowd and I think this would be her strength. That and the fact that she's French would in my opinion make her a natural. She has a burning patriotic desire to succeed."

"Okay then...next...what about Annie?"

"Annie is quite the most remarkable young lady we've had here so far. She has a mind like a sponge. But it's not like she simply regurgitates wrote learning, she adapts, improvises and utilizes what she's been taught. I have to say that she's excelled in all areas of the training. There's just one reservation but it's one that we will be able to overcome and not one that should prohibit her from going forward for further training."

"Oh, and what's that?" The major asked looking up from her file.

"I'm sure you haven't missed the fact that she's a striking looking young woman. She's tall, looks athletic and has blonde hair to die for. You can see the attention she attracts whenever she walks into a room and with make-up on she's even more stunning. She's not a woman any man is going to forget in a hurry. Blending into the background is going to be difficult for Annie but I can see situations where she might be able to turn this to her advantage. However, she is sensitive to situations, and aware, and she would not dress or act inappropriately. Nevertheless I think we might have to work on trying to help her to become more anonymous by changing her hairstyle and make-up. Her French is perfect and certainly good enough to fool any German and probably most French nationals as well."

* * * * *

Before she knew it Annie was leaving London on a very early train heading for Glasgow. It was a tiring, tedious journey and she was pleased when the train stopped and she was able to get out. She stood still on the platform for a few seconds feeling slightly dizzy as everything around her seemed to be in motion. There was enough time before her connecting Mallaig train left and she made her way to the station buffet where a bowl of hot Scotch broth, a crusty bun and cup of tea fortified her for the next part of her journey.

The Mallaig train was not quite as crowded as the London train had been and Annie managed to get a seat beside the window. Leaving the urban sprawl of Glasgow and heading north towards Fort William the scenery became more and more rugged. Beyond Fort William deep, dark-brooding lochs looked menacing and yet tranquil and beautifully quiescent at the same time and set Annie wondering if you could always find tranquillity and beauty where there was also darkness and implied malevolence. Was it possible to appreciate the one without the other she pondered? Was it the existence of evil that made the good more empathetically human? Would the exhilaration of light be nothing without the dark preceding it? Was life always destined to exist in an unstable world of contradictions? She supposed that this was the consequence of human freedom which brought with it the responsibility of choice. Staring out of the window as the changing landscape rushed past the thought occurred to Annie that the consideration of these contrasts had never troubled her before. Perhaps the realisation of what she was about to do, the reality of deliberately placing herself in danger for some altruistic ideal was finally beginning to focus her mind. What is it they say? 'You always feel most alive just before death.'

Sea inlets scythed, jagged-deep into the landscape forcing the train to skirt the shoreline in places and clickety clack over steel girder bridges. Further into the west coast highlands the rail-track was forced to follow the path of once glaciated glens and on occasions almost doubled back on itself is it rounded high mountains on either side. Pine trees marched up the mountain sides gradually giving way to more permanent tundra, scree and bare rocky outcrops standing defiantly sentinel. 'I hope I don't have to do any cross-country running here' Annie thought to herself with a shiver.

Eventually the train slowed to a halt at Beasdale Station in the middle of nowhere. Annie couldn't for the life of her think why there would be any reason for a station to exist here. She was the only person on the platform and stood forlorn as the engine hissed and clanked its way further up the glen. Apart from a small waiting room and even smaller ticket office there was not another building in sight. The only sop to civilization was a road which ran parallel to the rail track. Her directions were to leave the station and walk south for half a mile then turn right down a private road towards Arisaig House. By the time Annie reached the driveway in front of a solid granite-grey overpowering mansion a dark laden sky was swallowing the mountaintops and threatening to tumble down enveloping the whole landscape.

Annie pushed the large heavy oak door open and walked inside. As at Wanborough, she was greeted by a receptionist who examined her papers and directed her towards a door with a sign that read common room. She entered a large room and was immediately struck by the array of stags' heads and antlers hanging from the walls. There were large oil paintings of tartan dressed lairds standing on rocky promontories striking proud poses against skies of tumultuous grey-black clouds with shafts of sunlight arrowing down to where lochs washed up against heather. The ceiling was heavy with plaster relief designs and at the far side of the room was a formidable granite fireplace where a log fire crackled, spit and burned fiercely. Legs and arms poked out from high, wing-back leather chairs and heads appeared as Annie closed the door and walked towards a vacant chair near the fire. A shriek made her turn quickly and before she could drop her bag on the floor Christina had her in an embrace kissing her on both cheeks. "I knew you would be here," Christina said with excitement. "They wouldn't give me any information at Wanborough but I knew they wouldn't turn you down. I'm so pleased to see you."

"Christina, it's good to see you too, I wonder what they've got in store for us this time. Judging by the terrain outside it's going to be no picnic."

"We can cope," Christina replied guiding Annie towards the empty chair.

The arrangements were much the same as at Wanborough but very quickly Annie realised that the training was to be much more intense, pushing mental and physical boundaries to the limit. Weapons training was expanded "Tuck that firing arm into the hip," the instructor yelled at Annie. "Don't forget the double-tap system, always fire off two rounds."

Unarmed combat took on a more menacing intent when methods of silent killing were practised using a knife. "Remember it's you or him, you might not get a second chance. Strike quietly and strike hard." The message ringing round and round in Annie's head.

Classroom lectures in explosives presaged practical exercises and the remoteness of the training school now made sense when Annie practised sabotage techniques, laying charges and the demolition of railways and rolling stock donated by the London Midland and Scottish Railway Company. Lectures in the theory of small unit military tactics and manoeuvres were put into practice over and over again during exercises involving setting and responding to ambush and how to storm a house.

Annie had never considered her ability to interpret spatial and visual awareness as a special talent but clearly these traits were fundamental to her languages skill and ability to interpret information from maps. They were also a major influence on her ability to memorise the Morse code and with constant practise she learnt to transmit coded messages quickly and efficiently.

The intensity of the course honed Annie's reflexes and there was now a different dimension to her personality. A primeval, feral instinct of which she had previously been unaware had been awakened, tamed and trained and she felt more alive now than at any other time in her short life.

The first that she knew that Vera Atkins was in the building was when she was summoned to the commandant's office and saw Vera sitting behind the desk.

"Well, Annie, I don't think that it will come as any surprise that we're going to send you to 'finishing school'." Vera saw a hint of a crinkled nose as Annie tried to digest what was now in store for her. "That's what we call the third and final stage of your training. You'll find details of your travel arrangements in this envelope. You're to report to Beaulieu Manor in the New Forest where we'll pull together all that you've learnt in preparation for your work in France."

* * * * *

"Your training is almost completed but what you'll learn over the next few weeks will probably be the most important lessons you'll ever learn. You'll be instructed in how to survive practical day to day life in Nazi-occupied France. Those little insignificant nuances which, in themselves seem unimportant but when displayed in a foreign environment of suspicion can mean the difference between freedom and capture. Things have changed dramatically in France since you were last there as I'm sure you can appreciate. I know you'll apply yourselves as diligently to this final round of your training as you have done to the previous two courses." Vera's welcome was as efficient and professional as usual but there was also a warmth and respect which Annie felt and appreciated. She had come to look on Vera as a surrogate mother these past months. "Here's your timetable, I'll fill in the gaps as and when. Have a look at it and we'll see you all after breakfast."

"Good morning, I'd like to introduce you to Thomas who has just come back from a sojourn in France. Listen carefully and internalise everything he says no matter how trivial. Remember, the devil is in the detail." Vera retired to a chair at the side of the platform as Thomas stood up and moved forward.

"To be timid and unsure is to draw attention to yourself. The secret is to be alert and confident whilst outwardly appearing to be going about your daily routine. The hardships of occupation are really beginning to affect life in France especially in the cities. Be aware that in restaurants certain foods and drinks may only be available on particular days, check the menu before you sit down and you won't draw attention to yourself by ordering something unavailable, a dead give-away. Watch and learn. Remember the French do not place their knives and forks on their plates when they've finished their meal nor do they sip their soup from the side of the spoon. Forget these tiny details and any Gestapo officer at the next table will be asking to see your papers. You must blend in and make sure that you don't look conspicuous in any respect. If you are stopped for any reason and asked to show your papers never ever volunteer any more information than you're asked for. Even the most mundane things that we take for granted are unavailable in France, except perhaps on the black market, and make-up is one of them. Clothes are now worn out and shabby as are leather shoes. There is no polish so don't draw attention to your footwear. Any woman seen in Paris or any other big city wearing bright lipstick, nylons, smart clothes and shoes is immediately recognized as a German officer's tart and collaborator. I presume you will be given your cover stories soon and you must live that story. Ensure that your activities and routine fit in with your cover. If stopped, try to tell the truth as far as possible. Apart from your cover story do not lie or invent or you will very soon become entangled in a web of lies which will become obvious to any interrogating Gestapo officer worth his salt. I have no doubt that you will be given every opportunity to practice these activities as well as spotting someone who is following you and how to lose them. Vera has helped design this course to give you the best possible chance of survival and I wish you all good luck."

The next few weeks were the most intensive and especially mentally tiring that Annie had experienced so far. It seemed that the more she learnt the more she realised she didn't know. There were military uniforms, insignia and ranks to remember. Different security departments had different jurisdiction especially in Vichy France. Various types of interrogation were described and all the while she had to practice sending Morse code until she was proficient at twenty words per minute. Codes and security check systems had to be learnt including the use of 'bluff' checks to be revealed under torture and 'true' checks never to be revealed as well as knowledge of atmospherics, wavelengths and jamming. If captured, Annie was told to resist torture for as long as possible but in the event for at least forty eight hours which would give her comrades enough time to close down any cell and scatter to safety. Annie could feel the tension as the increasing information with which she was being bombarded became the reality of what she was about to become and do.

Four weeks since arriving at Beaulieu Manor and Annie was summoned to Vera's office.

"Good morning Annie, take a seat. How have you found this last leg of your training?"

"Good morning Ma'am. I'm not sure, it seems one step forward and two back."

"Don't worry, that's not unusual you've had much to assimilate. I can assure you that we've seen you grow into your new situation with skill, enthusiasm and confidence. You're on the last lap and I'd like to talk to you about your cover story. All the paper work has been put in hand to support your new identity and by the time we drop you into France your details will have been placed in the records of the Sorbonne, just in case someone checks up on you. We are also arranging a job for you in the Municipal offices of the Fifth Arrondissement. Your name is Annette Hugo and you were born in the French colony of Algeria where your mother died in childbirth. You were brought up by a number of different Algerian women and that will account for any detectable accent. Your father was a minor civil servant in Algiers and never re-married after your mother's death. Algiers was your home right up until the time you entered the Sorbonne to read German, French,

French and German literature and philosophy. Whilst there your father died of a heart attack leaving you financially secure enough to finish your degree and make your permanent home in Paris. You'll find all the minute details, places and dates relating to Annette's life in this dossier. Read and imprint these details on your heart as if your life depended on them because believe me, it does. Now we need to decide on a code name for you. Have you given it any thought?"

"I have actually," Annie replied. "I thought I might use 'Grace' if that's suitable?"

"It's as good as any, what made you choose 'Grace'?"

"Grace Darling was the daughter of a lighthouse keeper on the Farne Islands off the Northumberland coast. In 1838 she rowed out in an open coble to rescue five passengers on the Forfarshire which broke in two and foundered in a storm. She's always been a heroine of mine and, I hope, an inspiration."

"Okay, I want you to spend the next week going over what we've covered during the last month but most of all I want you to become Annette Hugo and we will test you. That'll be all for now Annie."

One week later, Annie was summoned again to Vera's office.

"Well, we think you're ready for a dummy run. You'll find all the details in this envelope but in a nutshell, late this afternoon you'll be driven in an enclosed lorry to somewhere along the south coast. You'll be dropped off in the dark without a compass or map. You'll have with you a radio, an empty pistol and four dummy explosive charges. Radio frequencies etc. are all in the envelope and are to be memorised. Your mission is to lay the explosive charges on the radar aerial at Branscombe. When this is accomplished you'll radio the code 'London Bridge' which will indicate that you've been successful and that the tower has been demolished. Afterwards you're to make your way undetected back here. You have forty eight hours from dropping off to complete your task. Good luck and I'll see you when you get back, hopefully not in a police car."

Annie stood in the hallway looking at the envelope with anxiety and excitement jostling for emotional priority. Where the hell was Branscombe? The whole panoply of over three months of training flooded her mind all at once with effective paralytic impotence. Minutes later, sitting on her bed Annie's heart stopped pounding and she made a successful, conscious effort to control her heightened state of anticipation. Cold logic took over and Annie reasoned that any place ending in 'combe' had to be somewhere in the West Country, Devon or Cornwall perhaps. If her target was to be a radar aerial then it would have to be situated somewhere on the channel coast. A broad plan was being formulated in her mind as her clothes, gun, radio and dummy explosives arrived at her room. Annie felt confident about the mission but her only worry was the radio she had to carry which was in a suitcase weighing over thirty pounds. Lugging such a heavy suitcase would slow her up and limit her options for improvisation.

*****

Before she knew it Annie was being tossed about in the back of an army lorry with its canvas flaps securely tied down. She tried to remember left and right turns but it was useless and she gave up after ten minutes. Four hours later the lorry stopped and the canvas cover flung back. It was pitch black and a chill wind quickly dispelled any warmth which had previously existed in the back of the lorry.

"Down you get Ma'am," a Corporal said extending his hand to help her with the heavy suitcase. "Good luck Ma'am," he continued as he climbed back into the lorry and it disappeared into blackness, lights extinguished. The only evidence of it having ever existed being the receding growl of the engine which was also eventually swallowed up by the night. Her isolation was complete. Annie stood for some minutes trying to get her bearings. She was standing on a track where vehicles had churned up two channels with their tyres forming a raised hump in the middle. Looking around Annie could make out an undulating featureless landscape. Venturing to the side of the track to keep her feet dry Annie fell over and was pleased when her landing was somehow cushioned. Feeling around, the cause of her fall became apparent and her soft landing was by courtesy of clumps of heather. 'Okay you buggers,' she said to herself, 'you've dropped me in the middle of Dartmoor, I guess, but I'm not yet sure of which compass point yet.'

She got to her feet and waited until she was fully acclimatised to the darkness. Thin fluffy clouds drifted across the sky tantalisingly revealing the stars which make up The Plough. Taking a line from the end two stars Annie plotted the North Star. Secured her shoulder bag and keeping the North Star on her left Annie picked up the suitcase and started to walk. All roads lead to somewhere and she knew that sooner or later she would find her bearings. There was a choice of walking in the mud-filled tracks, in the wet heather with the chance of a sprained or worse, broken ankle or down the bumpy centre of the track. She chose the latter and whilst there was still the chance of a turned ankle at least her feet were dry and warm. An hour and a half later a hint of dawn squinted over the horizon and was quickly followed by gashes of light escaping from a fractured clouds in front of Annie confirming that she was heading east. The bleakness of the plains in all directions became ever more evident as fingers of light reached out across the sky. Heather and gorse were now gradually giving way to grassland and in the near distance in a hollow Annie spotted a farmhouse with outbuildings. Sticking to the hedgerows and creeping up behind the barn her worst fears were realised when two farm dogs sensing her presence started to bark. With heart pounding she slipped into the barn through a side door hoping that if the farmer had been disturbed he would assume the presence of a fox for being the reason setting his dogs off. Annie sat down on a straw bale pleased to divest herself of the heavy radio. Thinking ahead she guessed that the aerial compound would be surrounded by some sort of wire fence and that she would need some wire cutters and something to secure the explosive charges to the aerial stanchions. It was just about light enough now to assist Annie in her search and she was lucky enough to find a pair of wire cutters hanging near the door together with a roll of twine and a knife. She quickly stowed these in her shoulder bag and silently sneaked out through the side door and back into the chilled air. Ten minutes later she was walking on a narrow metalled road heading east. Whilst she had not come across a village or hamlet, cottages were becoming more evident of civilization. The road twisted and turned and was edged with steep banks topped by hedges. Continuing along the lane Annie was alerted to what she thought was the sound of an engine from a commercial vehicle rather than a car coming up behind her and she decided to take a chance.

The lorry driver shouted down from his cab, "Are you alright miss? Can I help you?"

"Yes please," Annie shouted over the noise of the engine. "Can you give me a lift?"

"Where do you want to go to miss?"

"Where are you going?" Annie asked.

"I'm taking this milk to the dairy in Exeter if that's any good?"

"That would be wonderful, thank you so much," Annie answered throwing her suitcase up into the warm cab.

Annie waited for it and after a few minutes the inevitable question came. "What's a pretty young lady like you doing out this early in the morning miles from anywhere?"

"Well...my boyfriend and I were supposed to be having a holiday before he was shipped overseas but we had a massive row and I forced him to stop the car. He drove off in a temper and here I am. I didn't realise I was so far from civilization."

"Well don't worry miss we'll soon have you in Exeter."

After a while Annie continued, "We were supposed to rent a cottage near Branscombe. He might have gone on there, do you happen to know where it is?"

"Aye, it's the other side of Exeter, between Sidmouth and Seaton. You can get the bus from Exeter to Seaton and ask the driver to put you off at the stop for Erston. Bransombe is further along the road and off to the right towards the coast."

People were already making their way to work when Annie got down from the lorry cab. "Thank you," she said, "You've saved my life."

"Think nothing of it miss, hope you manage to patch things up with your boyfriend. Cheerio."

The first thing Annie wanted to do was ditch the heavy radio so she made her way to the railway station and put the suitcase and her shoulder bag in a left luggage locker. A mug of tea and hot buttered toast in the station buffet revived her, which was just as well being as she had long day and night in front her and only a few shillings left in her handbag. Leaving St. Thomas Station Annie sauntered along Aphington Street and on towards the shopping area of Fore Street. Shops were just opening for business and she stopped outside a newsagents come souvenir come tourist information shop. Annie wasn't surprised that she couldn't see in the window what she was looking for so she pushed the door open and walked inside accompanied by the friendly tinkle of a bell.

"Can I help you miss?" the smiling lady behind the counter said.

"I don't suppose you happen to have any maps of the area do you?" Annie enquired.

"Oh dearie me! No miss. We had to remove them all from the shelves because of the war you know."

"I thought as much," Annie responded trying to sound as disappointed as possible. "It's just that my fiancé and I were supposed to be spending a short holiday in a cottage near Branscombe. We had a massive row in the car and he drove off leaving me stranded. I was hoping that he had gone on to the cottage and that I might be able to make my own way there." Annie finished with a sob.

"Just you wait here a minute miss and I'll see what I can do." There were sounds of rummaging in the back storeroom and eventually the assistant emerged with a small, paper-backed guidebook. "I'm afraid this is all we've got," and flicking through the pages she continued, "but there are some maps of nature walks and cliff walks." She held the book up and pointed at one page, "There you are dearie, this one shows the coast walk at Branscombe."

"Thank you, it's just what I'm looking for, how much?"

"That'll be one and sixpence miss, thank you. I hope you find your fiancé."

Annie was just about to leave the shop when she stopped and turned, "You don't happen to have a local bus timetable do you?" she enquired.

"As a matter of fact you're in luck, yes I do have one or two left. I shall have to get some more not that there's that many tourists around these days."

Pulling her coat tight round her against the unwelcome caresses of a biting, cold wind Annie made her way to the bus station knowing that she needed to carry out a reconnaissance of the radar site before her night mission. Her plan was to find the best approach and escape routes giving her as much cover as possible as well as looking for a suitable place to hide. The guidebook gave general locations but was not detailed enough for Annie's purpose so she would have to fill in the missing information by relying on guesstimation. She boarded the Seaton bus and asked to be put off at the turning for Branscombe village. A heavy sky pressed down squeezing the colour out of everything and leaving in its place a grey, depressing monotone world. Annie sat back as the bus progressed through agricultural land and past numerous dense coppices. Road signs had been removed because of war department restrictions but with the aid of the guidebook Annie knew that she was heading east on the A3052. The town of Sidford was left behind and once again the landscape comprised of fields, coppices and woods. After three or four miles Annie switched from repose into a high state of alert. All of a sudden the bus was passing numerous military buildings all fenced in. Just over the brow of a hill Annie could see the top of a radio mast. Her instincts told her that this must be her target but it was some distance from the village of Branscombe. Not only that but where Annie had envisioned an isolated mast with a control room at its base this was a large military installation.

At the next junction Annie called for the bus driver to stop. This was going to be a lot tougher than she'd imagined. She had no idea of the complex layout but she was certain that there would be a lot of military personnel inside. Walking back along the road would have made her too conspicuous so Annie waited until the bus was out of sight and then climbed over a gate into a field. Using the hedges and trees for cover Annie approached as near to the fence as cover would permit. She worked her way round the perimeter to try to find her safest point of entry near the mast. Using the plain note pages in the back of her guidebook Annie tried to sketch and name the locations of each of the buildings. Each time she moved to a new position she lay still watching and recording. There were two long buildings which she guessed were barracks. Another building appeared to be the main administration centre and next to that was what she decided was the officers' quarters.

The more Annie reconnoitred the more formidable her task seemed. The military hardware buildings looked solid and blast-proof. One in particular stood out from the rest. There were steps at the side leading up to a lozenge-shaped base which itself sat on concrete stilts. On this site was a tall concrete block with the mast situated on the top. Annie guessed this was the transmitter/receiver operations block. To the side was a secondary control room and a generator room. Annie lay formulating a plan and then worked her way back to the main road and waited for a return bus to Exeter.

Collecting her radio and shoulder bag from the left luggage locker Annie was drawn to the smell of a fish and chip shop. She had been so preoccupied with going over her plan again and again that she hadn't realized just how hungry she was. Taking her purse out and counting her change she reckoned that she just had enough left to buy some fish and chips to take out and buy a bus ticket back to Weston, the nearest stop to the radar station. After that she would just have to rely on her wits to get her back to Hampshire.

The last bus to Seaton was almost empty. It was pitch black outside and because of the blackout regulations there was little illumination either inside or outside the bus. Annie got off the bus at Weston just before the complex, not too far to walk but not close enough to be conspicuous. She climbed over a fence and keeping to the hedgerows made her way towards the large wood which bordered the base. Fortunately there was little undergrowth to hinder her and keeping to the edge Annie made her way round to the north-east side of the wood. There she found a tree with a large root complex and pushing her radio and handbag under one of the roots covered them with her raincoat, brush and leaves. It was now very cold and Annie's breath hung in the air like speech bubbles in a comic cartoon. Rubbing her hands in the dirt Annie smeared her cheeks and forehead. Already her feet were soaking wet and cold as she hunkered down at the tree line facing the complex. She knew that there were guards at the entrance but that afternoon she had not seen any evidence of patrols inside the perimeter fence. Because of the blackout regulations there were no lights visible. She could just make out the silhouettes of the various buildings and having memorised her building layout sketch, keeping low and using scrub bushes for cover, Annie made her way to that part of the fence nearest the operations block. A clearing of twenty-five yards had been created all-round the fence and Annie had to crawl forward on her stomach until she touched the wire. Once there she stopped, held her breath and listened. The only sound was the rhythmic thump, thump, thump, phut, phut, phut of a diesel engine coming from the generator building. Taking the cutters from her shoulder bag Annie commenced to cut a small, hinged flap of wire at ground level. Leaving the cutters there and pushing the flap open she crawled through and worked her way towards the transmitter mast. Just as she reached the building voices could be heard approaching and Annie, standing up pressing herself against one of the concrete stilts had to slowly move round keeping the support between herself and the two soldiers deep in conversation. They mounted the stairs at the side of the building and entered the control room. Annie waited some minutes just in case the two men had been the relief and that their comrades would be making their way back to the barracks. Slowly, Annie climbed the stairs up on to the platform. With her back to the wall she worked her way round the building until she reached the rain drainpipe she'd spotted that afternoon. After giving the pipe a tug to make sure that it was secure Annie started to climb. At the top there was a significant roof overhang. Taking off her shoulder bag Annie swung it up on to the roof and followed it by scrambling over the ledge. Remembering her training that the human eye is sensitive to the horizontal and therefore you never ever rise up and make a silhouette, Annie continued to crawl on her stomach towards the mast. Reaching into her bag she took out the four charges and one by one, using the twine she'd found in the farm barn, she tied them to the base of each of the mast's four stanchions. After placing a dummy detonator in each of the explosives she crawled back to the drainpipe and silently made her way back down to ground level.

Retrieving her radio and handbag Annie wanted to get as far away as quickly as possible. With the radar complex now behind her Annie decided that she'd take a chance walking along the road. The fields were too wet and muddy making progress difficult and slow. Her feet were now thoroughly chilled and every footstep made her wince. Pulling some grass up from the side of the road she tried to remove as much of the camouflage from her face as she could before finishing off with her handkerchief. She also wiped as much mud off her shoes as she could in order to make herself look presentable to anyone she met. Likewise she rubbed her slacks and jacket with her handkerchief which afterwards she deposited in her shoulder bag. She hoped that the raincoat would cover the worst of the mud stains on her clothes. There was another wood about a mile and a half along the road and Annie set off walking as quickly as she could. On reaching the wood Annie opened her suitcase and reeled out the seventy feet of aerial along a string of branches. She quickly tuned in to her home frequency and although her fingers were cold she tapped out the code 'London Bridge'.

With no money left for public transport the only way Annie was going to make her deadline at Beaulieu Park was to rely on hitch hiking, her cover story being that she was returning to her army unit after visiting her fiancé in the area. As the morning sun began to pour colour and warmth back into the landscape Annie secured her first lift of many and was thankful when she saw the large front door to the manor beckoning.

After being debriefed, Annie had a welcome hot meal and an even more welcome soak in a hot bath, her feet hurting now more than ever. At long last after two nights without sleep Annie glided under the bed covers and curled up into a deep foetal sleep.

CHAPTER 11

Annie/Grace 1941 – 1942

A violent dream woke Annie from a deep sleep or at least she thought that it had. It was pitch black and she had no idea what time it was. Except that now she was awake the nightmare continued with a vivid reality. She was being pulled out of bed and forced, half walking, half dragged, along corridors and down stairs by two men in German uniforms. Eventually she was flung into a murky, cold, damp room. Someone pulled her to her feet and forced her to sit on a straight-backed chair which was situated in the centre of the room. From the surrounding gloom, all of a sudden a desk lamp was shone in her face. Annie screwed up her eyes to escape the blinding light.

"*Quel est votre nom?* What is your name?" A question was barked from behind the light.

Before she had time to answer Annie was slapped across the face and the question was repeated. "*Quel est votre nom?*"

Annie caught her breath in shock and replied meekly, "Annette.... Annette Hugo."

"Liar, your name is Annie Charlton and you are a member of SOE."

"My name is Annette Hugo."

"Where were you last night? What is your name? What were you doing in Devon?"

Questions continued to be fired in rapid, staccato succession not giving Annie the opportunity to answer any of them. Time ceased to exist and Annie guessed she must have passed out because she was being revived on the floor by having a bucket of cold water thrown over her. Cold wet pyjamas clung like a second skin sending her body into uncontrollable quivering.

"If you can't stay on your chair then you obviously don't want it. Stand up."

Annie was harshly pulled up from the stone floor and almost fell to the ground again when the rough hands released her.

"Stand behind the chair." The voice barked at her again.

Annie shuffled round behind the chair and put her hands on the back to steady herself.

"Now lift it above your head..... Higher, you bitch.... higher."

From somewhere within, a determined resolve surfaced and Annie gradually took control over her body's responses. She spread her feet for balance and slowly raised the chair straight above her head.

"What is your name?" The questions were fired at her once again.

"Annette Hugo," Annie managed to gasp as she was once again doused by a bucketful of ice-cold water. Under the assault she lowered the chair when a sharp searing pain in her back sent her crashing to her knees.

"Get up bitch...you were not given permission to lower the chair...higher...higher."

In spite of her physical strength and powers of endurance, two nights without sleep and unknown hours of abuse were beginning to have a debilitating and disorientating effect on Annie. With her head now sagging on to her chest and her will determined not to give in to the screaming pain in her body the next bucket of water sent her sprawling across the floor. Coughing and spluttering she was once again roughly hauled back onto the chair. Repeated periods of consciousness and unconsciousness left Annie disorientated, time having ceased to have any meaning. Somewhere in the distance Annie heard a soft voice saying in English, "Thank you. That will be all Lieutenant Charlton. I expect you could use a nice cup of tea now, eh?"

"Yes sir, thank you sir" Annie managed to whisper in English.

"Noooo," the harsh voice barked back at her again in French, "You have just signed your death warrant. Take her back to her room."

The two Gestapo guards supported Annie back to her room and closed the door as they left. Annie stood swaying unsteadily and then sat on the side of her bed before she fell down. After a few minutes, she didn't know how many, Annie staggered to the bathroom where she took off her wet pyjamas and dried herself with a soft warm towel. With the towel wrapped around her still shivering body Annie noticed that it was dark outside and her bedside alarm clock read 10-o'clock. She had been questioned non-stop for approximately twenty-four hours she surmised. The towel trailed on to the floor and naked, Annie crawled into her bed and fell into a painful, restless sleep.

"How do you feel this morning?" Vera asked Annie with concern after knocking and entering Annie's room.

Annie struggled to sit up and lean against her headboard but with the effort she involuntarily let out a sharp cry as a searing pain shot down her back. "A bit washed out actually Ma'am." Annie replied with an attempt at trench humour. "My lip's swollen and cut inside and I've got a terrible pain in my back." And recalling recent events Annie continued, "I'm sorry Ma'am, I'm afraid I let you down yesterday."

"Actually it wasn't yesterday but the day before as well." Vera sat on the side of the bed waiting for this information sink in. "You have nothing to reproach yourself for Annie. You completed your assignment with flying colours and I have to say that Branscombe Radar Establishment are stepping up their security systems after they found their wire cut and four charges tied to their mast. I think there would have been some red faces after my phone call to them. As for your interrogation, you lasted forty-eight hours not twenty-four, of continuous questions and harsh treatment. This was a magnificent effort let down in the end by an understandable slip when you were tricked at your lowest ebb. Don't be too harsh on yourself but remember the experience and it won't happen again. We'll have the M.O. give you a once over and if he agrees then I think you're entitled to some R and R, rest and recuperation. Have Christmas and the New Year with your family and we'll see what 1942 has in store when you return in January. The first thing on your agenda will be your parachute training at Ringway near Manchester but more of that later. For now I'll organise your relevant paperwork and travel warrants."

"Thank you Ma'am, I could kick myself for allowing myself to be tricked so easily."

"Not so easily Annie...you'd been without sleep for four nights, two nights and days of torture. It's no wonder you were disorientated. This exercise was about as harsh as it could have been because we knew how good you were and wanted to test you to the ultimate. You did more than expected and now have another shot in your locker. Have a good break and we'll see you back here in January."

* * * * *

"How was your parachute training?" Vera asked once Annie had settled herself in to a chair in Vera's office.

"It was fantastic," Annie enthused. "The drops were a sensation like nothing else I've ever experienced, so exhilarating."

"Good, I'm pleased. Except....and I hope this doesn't disappoint you, there's been a change of plan. On this occasion you'll not be parachuted in to France. You'll be flown in because there's someone we need to fly out urgently on the return flight.

Now....as for your real assignment....it's not just going to be about supporting resistance groups and sabotage, although you will be involved in that. What we want from you is something more....long term and potentially more dangerous. We want you to get as close as you can to the German centre of administration in France and report back their overall, planned strategy and anything else which you think would be of value to the war effort whilst also drip-feeding false information back in to their system. I know this sounds a bit nebulous but we think that your talents would best suit in close proximity with the enemy. Make no mistake this will be a cat and mouse game potentially much more dangerous than blowing up a few troop trains or bridges. Be ready to move at a minute's notice. As soon as the met. people give us a satisfactory weather report you'll be off."

* * * * *

At the end of January 1942 Annie found herself in a staff car driving through the entrance to Tangmere airfield in Sussex and straight onto the runway. The Lysander was already warming up on the runway when Annie climbed out of the car. The familiar figure of Vera approached Annie and gave her a hug, kissing her on both cheeks, "Good luck and we'll see you when you get back."

"Thanks Vera, thanks for all that you've done for me and I'll try not to let you down."

"You won't do that Annette. Here, I've got a little going away present for you but you mustn't open it until you're airborne. I hope you like it and you never know, it might come in handy sometime. You might want to take this with you as well."

"What is it?" Annette asked.

"We offer it to all agents," Vera answered almost apologetically, "It's a cyanide tablet."

Annette climbed on board, the door slammed closed, the engines revved, the whole fuselage vibrating and rocking the little plane shot forwards as the brakes were released. Once airborne the pilot set course for Rouen keeping the Lysander low beneath the German radar. Annette put her hand in her pocket and pulled out Vera's present. She stuffed the unidentifiable brown paper under her seat and gasped as she realised that she was holding a gold compact. There seemed a finality in the gesture and Annette found herself wiping a tear from her eye.

It seemed no time at all before the co-pilot was coming back to give Annette her final details.

"We're nearly there. We're landing you on a rural plateau to the east of Rouen. When we land we'll heave the supplies straight out of the door, you'll jump down and our returning passenger will climb aboard and we'll be off before you can say 'ITMA'."

The Lysander skimmed the treetops and quickly dropped into the torch identified clearing the frozen clumps of grass making the landing an uncomfortable, bumpy experience. Annette stood up and immediately overbalanced as the plane swung round ready 180 degrees for a quick take-off. Three large canvass holdalls were thrown from the door followed immediately by Annie who jumped down from the step ladder and was almost knocked to the ground by a dark clothed figure who quickly scrambled up the steps and dived in through the door which was closed immediately and the plane was airborne again within seconds. From the edge of the field eight figures ran towards Annette. Two grabbed the Sten gun delivery, two the ammunition and explosives and two the medical and food rations. The remaining two resistance personnel approached Annette and told her to follow them as quickly as possible. "The Germans will be here in a few minutes. *Rapid, rapid si les Allemands nous ont entendus ils serant ici quelques minutes.*"

Annette picked up her radio suitcase and holdall and followed the shadowy figures as they dispersed from the field. The six members of the resistance who were carrying the shipment quickly disappeared into the countryside leaving the remaining two to accompany Annie to a safe house. They moved quickly and silently along tracks through coppices and woods keeping close to any natural cover. Without warning the leader of the trio stopped and put his hand up, "Shhhhh." They all heard the drone of lorry engines at the same time and dived to the ground as a convoy of three Wehrmacht troop carriers passed along a nearby road heading in the direction of the landing site. Once they'd passed the three moved on with more urgency. The engines stopped and Annette could hear in the distance a German officer barking out orders for the patrol to spread out and keep their eyes open. The Frenchmen obviously knew the area like the back of their hands and they eventually approached a car hidden under branches in a copse well away from any main roads. Driving quickly but not recklessly the car was ultimately steered down a long sunken road leading to an isolated farm and outbuildings. The car was parked in a barn beside a tractor. The driver of the car jumped out and climbed onto the tractor, started the engine and threw the tractor into gear with a grating clunk and a jerk and proceeded to pull three large straw bales revealing a trap door in the floor. The other Frenchmen lifted the trap door and beckoned Annie to climb down a ladder. They quickly disappeared down the hole and closed the door behind them. Annie imagined her tomb being sealed as the noise of the tractor pushing the straw bales back over the trap door reverberated round their hiding place.

The Frenchmen introduced himself as he switched on an electric light, "Now we can relax, my name is David and up top is Pierre. This is his farm." They shook hands and Annette introduced herself simply as Grace. "If the Boche come looking for us here tonight," David continued, "We'll be safe. They've been here once or twice before on routine searches but haven't found anything yet."

Grace guessed that the room they were in was about ten by twelve feet. The walls, ceiling and floor were boarded out with fence planks. Two wooden framed bunk beds stood against opposites walls whilst a table and three chairs completed the furniture. Four Sten guns together with boxes of ammunition and hand grenades were stacked in one corner and in the other corner was a cupboard for crockery, cutlery and assorted pots and pans and tinned food. A Primus stove and oil heater stood on a concrete slab under the steps leading down from the surface. Grace thankfully noticed a ventilation flue which, she imagined, exited somewhere at the back of the barn.

She was brought up to date about the current resistance situation and in return she gave little away other than she needed to get to Paris.

"I expect you could eat some soup," David said opening a tin of vegetable soup and lighting the primus stove.

"Thank you, that would be kind but just a little, I'm not too hungry. I had a good meal before I left England. The condemned man's last meal I thought."

"I don't think so," David replied with a smile. "If you can, sleep for the rest of the night and we'll get you to the railway station in Rouen tomorrow."

The next morning Pierre and David inspected Grace's clothes for authenticity and gave her their approval. She wore a black skirt and matching jacket, white silk blouse and had a black wool overcoat. Her hat was not really a beret but had that lean to one side in a rather Breton style. The shoes were of black leather, clean but scuffed and definitely of a worn appearance. Her long blonde hair had been cut short before leaving England and there was only the faintest hint of light make-up.

It was mid-morning by the time Grace had finished her breakfast in the farm kitchen and Pierre put her luggage in the boot of the battered 1934 black Citroen Traction Avant. She said goodbye to David and climbed into the passenger seat where the leather stitching was split in places. The engine rocked into life and they were soon heading west towards Rouen.

"I know where most of the permanent road-blocks are," Pierre said, "And can usually avoid them but the bastards have a habit of throwing up temporary ones at different sites."

Pierre stayed on minor roads twisting and turning but this became more difficult the closer they got towards the city.

"Damn, I guessed we wouldn't get through without at least one stop."

Ahead of them was a counterbalanced red and white pole across the road. Two Wehrmacht soldiers sat on a motorcycle at the side of the road one of them in a side-car with a machine gun mounted on the front. Two other soldiers stood by the barrier their machine-pistols slung on leather straps over their shoulders, the barrels pointing towards Pierre and Grace as the car glided to a halt. One of the soldiers moved towards the driver's door.

"Step out of the car." Pierre was ordered.

The second soldier approached Grace.

"Papers," the order was snapped and Annie handed her documents out through the car window.

The first soldier was already scrutinising Pierre's papers.

"Where are you going?"

"I'm going to catch the train for Paris."

"Open the boot," the soldier demanded wagging the gun barrel towards the back of the car. His French was minimal but his intent was obvious.

Getting out of the car Grace allowed her skirt to ride up over her knees. She smiled at the distracted soldier and said, "There's just my old suitcase and holdall in there."

The two soldiers on the motorcycle sat menacingly quiet staring at the car, smoke drifting up as they dragged slowly and deliberately on their cigarettes. Grace stood still. Her hand was on the pistol in her coat pocket wondering what their chances were if the young guard opened the suitcase. He rummaged around in the boot and then pointed to the suitcase where the buttoned cuff of a white blouse was dangling out of the case lid. "You look as if you packed in a hurry mademoiselle," the soldier said quizzically pointing at the escaping blouse sleeve with the barrel of his gun.

"Not really," Annie replied with a forced laugh. "A girl can't have too many clothes." Bending down she flicked the catch nearest the silk cuff, eased the battered, soft leather lid just enough and pushed the cuff back inside. "I think I've overloaded my case," she giggled.

"Why are you going to Paris?" He persisted.

"I'm starting a new job there," Grace replied confidently, "I have employment papers here if you want to see them."

"That won't be necessary," he replied, and leaning on the car roof with his gun pointing at Pierre asked, "Are you going to Paris as well?"

"No I'm just taking her to the station. I'll probably be coming back this way in about an hour."

The soldiers handed back their identity papers and nodded to a comrade to lift the barrier.

"Well done Grace," Pierre said, "That was a close shave. You never know how these bastards are going to react."

Rouen Rive Droite Railway Station was a mêlée of mostly military personnel. Grace made her way to the ticket counter and purchased her single ticket to Paris. The adrenalin from her encounter at the check-point was still coursing through her body and she had to admit that she felt a certain frisson as she negotiated her way onto the train and a German officer helped her with her suitcase up on to the luggage rack. The journey to Paris through a washed-out winter countryside passed without incident although the German officer who had helped her with her luggage tried to engage Grace in conversation and when he finally realised that she was not interested he gave up.

Two hours later the train pulled into the Paris Gare Saint Lazare. Grace consulted the metro map and made her way down to the platform and waited for the underground train to take her to Chatelet where she would need to change to another line for the two-stop ride to St. Michel in the Sixth Arrondissement. The Sorbonne was situated on the border between the Fifth and Sixth Arrondissements and Grace had had doubts about returning to an area where she had lived. On the one hand she was very familiar with the region but on the other it was only three years since she was last here and having worked in various bars there was always the off chance that she might bump into someone who would recognise her. It was a chance she was just going to have to accommodate.

Emerging from the metro station just as a light dusting of snow was being blown along the street and pavements Grace was instantly reminded of her carefree student days. It felt like coming home, except it wasn't. Parisians going about their business looked dour and miserable and appeared deliberately to avoid looking at each other. Clothes, on close inspection were dowdy and there was a depressing, intangible atmosphere she could almost touch and which contrasted with her memory of Paris as the City of Light. The only laughter appeared to come from groups of sightseeing German soldiers and officers with their Leica cameras dangling round their necks. Red and white banners with the black swastika in the middle hung from public buildings and military transports seemed to be driving in all directions. She bought a newspaper and knowing of a small hotel nearby made her way down the Boulevard de Saint Michel for two blocks then turned left into the Rue des Ecoles. Halfway down the street she stopped outside the Hotel du Commerce then went in through the main entrance.

The receptionist looked her up and down and from behind a cloud of cigarette smoke said, "Yes, can I help you?"

"I'd like a room for the night please," Annie replied, "Maybe two nights but I'll just pay for one now."

With little deference to a friendly welcome or even good manners the receptionist pushed a piece of paper over the desk towards Grace. "Fill this in...identity card." He copied the details of Annie's card and handed it back together with the key to room 14. "Up the stairs and on the left." Annie was not surprised when the receptionist made no attempt to carry her bags or conduct her to the room. She let herself into the room and flopped into a chair beside the dressing table. There was a single bed with a washbasin in one corner. A towel, which had once been white, hung on a rail beside the basin. The chair she was sitting on and the dressing table completed the furnishings apart from a battered wardrobe with a block of wood under one corner where previously a carved ball foot had been. It was Thursday and she was due to start work the following Monday so ideally she wanted to find a flat or bedsit as soon as possible and give herself the weekend to familiarise herself with a Paris that she no longer recognised. The room was too depressing to stay in so Annette decided to find a café, have a cup of coffee and scan the paper for accommodation to let. She knew of a little place called Le Chat Noir on the Rue Saint Jacques and within minutes was sitting at a table with a cup of ersatz coffee whose taste defied description. Scanning the paper she found three possible lets and persuaded the café owner to let her use his telephone to make arrangements to view. One thing in her favour was that the number of students at the Sorbonne had diminished since the war and as a consequence there was a greater choice of cheap accommodation than there would have been otherwise. It was now late afternoon and Annette found herself beginning to relax and realising that she was quite hungry she ordered a bowl of soup. Remembering to sip from the front of the spoon the soup fortified Annette as she watch the surreal world unfolding in the streets around her.

The following morning the first two rooms Annie viewed were unsuitable being either too small, too dirty or too expensive. Arriving at the third choice in a narrow street, the Rue de Chantiers off the Rue des Fosses St. Bernard she met the landlord who took her up to the top floor of the building. He opened the door and Annette knew immediately it was just what she was looking for although she didn't want to appear too keen. There was a reasonably sized living room which had a warm welcoming appearance. A kitchen area had been built into one of the corners. The window opened up and gave a view across roofs and a forest of chimneys. The bedroom was small but big enough to accommodate a double bed and to the side was a bathroom and toilet. It was perfect for her needs. As expected the rent was more than she could afford but with some hard bargaining she managed to reduce it to a more manageable amount. By now, unfortunately, it was too late for her to check out of the hotel and besides her tenancy wouldn't begin until Saturday so Annie had to resign herself to another night in her dismal hotel room. She paid a deposit and her first month's rent and put the key to her new life in her handbag.Saturday began in a spirit of optimism. Annie arranged her few belongings in her new flat and explored the immediate area for shops which could supply her with food and domestic needs. What she was not prepared for was the absolute lack of quantity of food in the shops, even with rationing, and the lack of range or choice. Having had the foresight to take her holdall with her, Annie managed to buy some basic rations and household commodities at inflated prices. The reality of life in occupied Paris was beginning to dent her optimism. That afternoon she timed her walk to the Municipal building so that she ensured that she would not be late on her first day on Monday.

Her first transmission was due that evening and after curfew she removed the few clothes she had placed on top of the radio in the suitcase. It was quite dark now and taking the aerial wire, Annie opened the window and climbed out on to the roof. Having noticed the day before the number of utilities wires which were suspended across the roofs, Annie had considered that one more wire would not look suspicious. This would save her having to deploy the aerial every time she wanted to use the radio and more importantly in an emergency she would not have to panic in dismantling it if there was a raid. Making her way out along the roof Annie trailed the wire behind her until she was sure of the maximum length. She wrapped it around existing wires leaving enough slack at the window to connect with her set. This end could easily be thrown over the party wall in an emergency and would not be seen from the window. At the same time as she'd noticed the wires the previous day Annie had also noticed that two of the coping stones on top of the building outer wall were loose. Making sure that nothing fell into the street below, she wiggled the stones backwards and forwards until eventually the first one slid at an angle against the roof like a mini lean-to. It was heavier than she'd anticipated and had to use all of her strength to stop it crashing on to the roof tiles. She manoeuvred the second stone similarly making it overlap the first. Hoisting the suitcase up on to the roof Annie could just slide it under the coping stones and was pleased that it could be hidden out of sight from the window and that it would be protected from the weather.

Bringing it back indoors Annie connected the aerial and composed herself before her appointed 'sked', schedule. Knowing that the longer she was transmitting the easier it would be for the Germans to triangulate her position she wanted to ensure that she was completely ready.

The listening station at Grendon acknowledged her first transmission and Annie quickly dismantled the aerial from the radio and stacked it behind the copings on the roof. Half an hour later she was tucked up in her new bed her mind replaying the events of the last few days like a movie in fast motion. She decided that she would use Sunday to take it easy and re-familiarising herself with the area and maybe take a walk in the Jardin des Plantes before presenting herself for work on Monday.

CHAPTER 12

Annie/Annette and Otto 1942

Annie presented her letter of introduction to the receptionist who, scanning the paper, picked up the phone on her desk. "Someone will be with you in a minute," she said with a smile.

She had scarce time to admire the magnificent large marble entrance when she gave a little start as someone behind her said, "You must be Annette Hugo. Welcome to our Municipal Building, I hope you'll be very happy here." The code was slipped smoothly into the conversation, "I see you admire our Napoleonic architecture."

"The architecture, yes, but not the man," Annette replied with the correct response. A quick eye contact between the two women signified a silent mutual understanding.

"Come along then, I'll introduce you to your new colleagues. I'm Collette the department manager and it's my job to keep all you girls under control," she said laughing. "You can call me Collette, we tend to be friendly and informal here."

Annette immediately warmed to Collette. She was middle aged and dressed in a rather frumpy style, her hair tightly held in a bun at the back of her head. Heavy, brown, flat-soled shoes, thick brown woollen stockings and rimless spectacles completed the homely schoolmistress appearance.

They had already climbed the wide marble steps and were clip, clopping along a long corridor as Collette continued, "We tend not to specialise in the department, whatever needs to be done is shared out and if there's a panic or overload, well, it's all hands to the pump and we help each other out. This is partly because most of the previous male personnel joined the military and because our administrative overlords of course are now the Germans, but generally speaking as long as we work within their framework we're pretty much left to get on with the job unsupervised. Our responsibilities are quite broad. Sometimes you'll be making 'on site' visits outside and writing reports when you get back to the office. We're responsible for all the municipal buildings, roads and parks. We also keep records of rented accommodation and population movement." At this point Collette stopped outside a door labelled Municipal Administration and before going in whispered to Annette, "I am your only contact. Trust no-one, absolutely no-one except through personal introduction by me, collaborators and informants are everywhere."

There were six desks in the room arranged in two ranks of three, five of which were already occupied and a vacant sixth to which Annette was directed. There was a side office with the name Collette Bezier, Manager, on the door. As they moved into the room some of the girls were typing whilst others were busy at filing cabinets. Annette registered immediately that there were two senior workers, about the same age as Collette and three other girls all under the age of thirty she guessed. They all stopped what they were doing and turned towards Collette as she introduced the newcomer. "This is Annette, she's coming to help take some of the workload off you all so make her welcome. Beatrice, show her the ropes and would you please be responsible for seeing to it that Annette is familiarized with her responsibilities."

Annette spent the next few days shadowing Beatrice and getting to know the routine and system. Brigit worked at the desk in front of Annette and Marianne, working at the desk next to Annette, introduced herself and quickly adopted a mentoring role. She was a pretty dark-haired girl slightly younger than Annette. She had an open, friendly and fun-loving personality to the point of being a bit scatty which Annette quickly discovered belied her efficiency and work output. Nevertheless Annette was sure that in any given situation she would be prone to being innocently indiscreet.

* * * * *

Over the next two months Annette's life settled into a routine. At the office menial filing and general secretarial jobs were gradually being replaced with more responsibility. Lunch usually consisted of bread and cheese and was eaten at her desk but as the weather improved Annette accompanied the other girls to the municipal building garden quad where snowdrops and crocuses were just beginning to welcome early spring. Some evenings after work Annette would go to the cinema or simply enjoy a walk along the Seine making sure that she was back home before the curfew.

Magically, it seemed to happen overnight, there was warmth in the sun. Tulips and daffodils filled the parks and tree buds burst into blossom in the boulevards. This was the April in Paris that Annette remembered although not filled with the optimism of her last visit to the city. One Friday Marianne leaned over her desk and said to Annette, "What are you doing after work?"

"Nothing in particular," Annette answered, "Why?"

"Well usually at the end of each week we go to a bar for a glass or two of wine and maybe something to eat. With a bit of luck," she winked, "We might even be able to persuade some German officer to pay for it. We think that you're now one of the girls so we'd like you to join us. What do you say?"

"Thank you, that's very kind of you, I'd love to join you."

Half an hour later the four young women were seated round a table basking in the spring sunshine. Marianne and the others were quickly becoming quite merry but Annette, whilst enjoying the relaxation encouraged by her glass of Sancerre, was being more circumspect. The more they drank the louder Annette's companions became, ribald comments about the various men, French and German passing by resulted in fits of giggling. The table next to them became vacant and was immediately occupied by four SS Officers. How unfortunate Annette thought that her chair should be the one that faced their table. The SS Captain ordered two bottles of wine in perfect French whilst his comrades were engaged in their own humorous conversation. It was obvious to Annette that they were the focus of the young Lieutenants' adolescent attention seeking behaviour. Huddled comments brought laughter and none too surreptitious glances in their direction. The Captain, Annette noticed, sat a little apart. From first glance she registered that he was extremely handsome. She guessed that he was about six feet tall with an athletic physique. His face demonstrated an assurance and authority with a square set jaw and a nose which some could say might just have been a little too large. Even at the distance between them his eyes were unmistakably a piercing blue and his hair, although not Aryan blond was fair. It seemed inevitable that their eyes would meet and Annette looked quickly away but she knew instinctively that he also had registered the contact. In her peripheral vision she noticed the Captain call the waiter over and whisper something to him. A few minutes later the waiter returned with a bottle of wine and placed it on their table to whoops of delight from Marianne and the others. This was the signal for the young officers to turn their chairs round and engage the girls in conversation. The captain sat still, staring at Annette. He lifted his left hand to his face and flicked his cheek before raising the glass in his right hand in salute. Annette leaned over the table, "Sorry girls but I'm going to have to leave you. It's been fun."

"Don't go yet Annette, there's hours before curfew and the party's just starting." Marianne pleaded.

"Don't mind me, enjoy yourselves and I'll see you on Monday."

Annette got up slowly to leave the table aware that the captain was still staring at her. She walked slowly down the street feeling his eyes boring into her back.

During their Monday bread and cheese lunch the girls were full of their exploits with the German officers the previous Friday. Annette had the distinct feeling that Marianne was the ringleader and that the other two were more wary of being branded collaborators. As the deprivations of occupation were really taking their toll now, resistance was stiffening and those seen fraternizing were shunned and condemned.

"That Captain, Otto was his name I think, was really smitten by you Annette. He asked a few questions about you after you left. We couldn't tell him much but I got the impression that you'll be seeing more of him in the very near future," Marianne took delight in telling Annette.

Her mind drifted away from the idle chatter and focussed on whether or not this might be the opportunity she had been waiting for. Clearly, if she encouraged the attentions of this SS Captain then she would surely be branded a collaborator. If she was to be ostracised then she would just have to endure the taunts, insults and even worse the exclusion and isolation as the price for a higher purpose. As her mind was feverishly considering different possibilities Annette, for a moment, allowed herself the dalliance of considering other possibilities with the very handsome Otto. But she immediately dismissed this fantasy on the grounds that involving emotions in what was potentially a highly charged situation would be distracting, foolhardy and dangerous in the extreme and would surely sabotage her prime objective or even worse. Pillow talk could lead to carelessness. Could she really balance the two? And yet she may have to adopt the roll of a Nazi tart in order to gain his confidence and in that scenario how far was she prepared to go?

"What do you think?" Marianne was saying prodding Annette back to the present.

"Oh....sorry, what were you saying? Sorry, I was miles away," Annette answered.

"I was asking whether or not you'd like to go back to that café on Friday?"

"I suppose we could," Annette answered not wishing to sound too keen. "You probably noticed that I don't drink a lot but....yes....let's go, we've got to do something to keep our spirits up haven't we?"

* * * * *

Annette pretended not to see the same four officers cross the street and head for the café. Her three colleagues were, frivolously, three glasses of wine into not caring either way. Two couples at the nearest table to Annette's were left in no doubt that they were expected to vacate their seats. Without any invitation, the officers immediately moved their table and chairs closer to Annette's and flamboyantly ordered two bottles of wine.

"We wondered if you would be here," one of the officers asked in barely adequate French.

"I bet that you knew we would be," Marianne answered with a giggle seemingly oblivious to the looks of disgust on the faces of the other customers. It was quite obvious to Annette that the officers had had a drink prior to joining them although she was uncertain about Otto. Either he was sober or he carried his drink well. One of the younger officers jumped up and putting his Leica camera up to his eye shouted, "Let's have a happy group photo," and as the remaining officers leant inwards the girls picked up their drinks and laughed into the camera. Annette managed to make sure that her wine glass was between her face and the lens. However she was later caught off guard when the Lieutenant surreptitiously managed to catch her and the captain together in one shot. Once again Otto sat a little apart from his comrades and although courteous and relaxed, appeared completely in control of himself, aloof even. Leaning towards Annette and without waiting for a reply he said in perfect French, "Permit me to top up your glass. Do you drink your Sancerre because of patriotic reasons?" He continued.

"I drink it because it is my preference," Annette responded dryly.

"What about our German wines?" Otto continued, "Have you tried them?"

"Yes, I have." Annette answered offering no more information.

Otto allowed her answer to hang undeveloped for a few seconds.

"And....." he answered encouragingly.

Looking directly at Otto, Annette replied, "I find both the Rhein Später Jareszeitwein and the Neckar Valley wines too sweet. In fact I find all German wines too obvious and superficial."

"That's a very honest and forthright opinion.....or...... perhaps it's a veiled metaphor?" Otto countered.

"I'm sure I don't know what you mean," Annette replied, "I was just making an observation in response to your question."

Otto was not sure whether or not she was deliberately sparring with him or was just being pragmatic. Either way she was confirming his first impressions of her. Apart from being physically striking and beautiful, there was a quiet confidence and intelligence not shared by her flighty friends. Whilst he was pondering, Annette stood up to leave.

"Thanks for the drinks girls, I know it's early, but I'm afraid I'm going to have to go."

"Ohhh....stay a little longer, you seem to be having quite a conversation," Marianne pleaded.

"Enjoy the rest of your weekend and I'll see you Monday, au revoir."

Annette swung her bag over her shoulder and without a backward glance walked slowly away from the café. She got no further than ten yards when she heard Otto's voice calling, "Mademoiselle." She pretended not to hear and continued walking. Next time the voice was closer and called, "Annette, wait." She stood still and Otto was immediately beside her.

"Thank you," he said. "Let me apologise. I'm sorry for the behaviour of my officers. They know no different. They're little better than ignorant thugs but I have to work with them."

"Not your *Nietzche Ubermenschen*, Nietzche Supermen then," Annette risked saying.

"You know the work of our philosopher. I'm even more impressed," Otto answered with a laugh. "You don't shrink from speaking your mind do you? But please, I am also forgetting my own manners. We have not been formally introduced," he continued clicking his heels, "I am Captain Otto von Lieper of the Waffen SS at your service."

"And what service would that be Captain?"

"Whatever mademoiselle requires," came the reply.

"Well," Annette continued not sure whether this conversation was going where she wanted it to, "This is my country and you are here uninvited so how would it be if I said to go home?"

"Ah, if only I could," Otto lied. "The war has overtaken us all and placed us in a situation we might otherwise have wished to avoid. I'm afraid I have to bow to higher authority and do what I am ordered."

They continued to walk towards the River Seine. Annette knew that she might not get another chance like this. Otto presented her with an ideal opportunity, if handled correctly, to get close to the Nazi inner administration. Her obvious antagonism had been a risky barb to hook Otto but she needed to proceed softly, softly to reel him in. She had rightly calculated that his intellect and arrogance would respond to her challenge and indeed he had enjoyed their initial sparring.

"Look," Annette said rather contritely, "We might have got off to a misunderstanding. I'm sorry, I suppose it's the deprivations and drabness of the war which is affecting us all and making us irritable."

"And she speaks perfect German, is there no end to your talents? Of course....I agree with you about the war" Otto replied, "But it doesn't have to be like that. You're very beautiful and in the very short time we've been together I can tell that you're extremely intelligent and I've really enjoyed our banter. I don't get much opportunity to engage in challenging conversation. Let's forget the war, start again as friends but only if you promise not to stop needling me as that would rob your personality of a trait which makes you so attractive."

"Agreed," Annette responded laughing.

They were now walking along the left bank, Quai de Montebello, opposite the Notre Dame Cathedral when Otto turned to Annette saying, "We've been so busy analysing our five minute relationship that I have completely forgotten how to treat a lady. I'm guessing that you haven't eaten since lunchtime and that that wouldn't have been very appetising. Let me take you for a proper meal as a symbolic gesture to our....partial.... cessation of hostilities and the beginning of a beautiful friendship."

* * * * *

Annette waited until it was dark. She switched the lights off in her living room. Climbing onto a chair and leaning out of the window strained to slide the radio suitcase out from under its hiding place behind the coping stones on the roof. Taking extra care she climbed out on to the roof to retrieve the hidden end of the aerial wire. Dragging the end of the aerial in through the window she connected it up to the radio and quickly established contact with Grendon informing them that she had made a contact and to await further developments.

Their meetings became more frequent and Annette was actually beginning to look forward to them. Otto was always polite and attentive and she knew instinctively that he would move their relation-ship on to a different level given the slightest encouragement but she did wonder how long she could maintain this pretence without rousing his suspicion.

Some weeks later, Otto was summoned to a series of meetings in Gestapo Headquarters at number 84, Avenue Foch by Theodor Dannecker who was the SS officer in command of the German police in France. Otto was introduced to the other members of these meetings including Rene Bousquet, secretary-general of the national police, Helmut Knochen of the SS, Emile Hennequin, the head of the Paris police and representatives of the SNCF, the French railway service. Dannecker opened the inaugural meeting.

"Gentlemen, there are 150,000 Jews in Paris alone, 64,000 of them foreigners. We have been charged with the task of beginning the resettlement of Jews in France. Otto, this was the reason Himmler personally sanctioned your transfer here from Poland. We know what you have achieved in the east and we wish to make use of your experience in this major project. The organisation and details we'll leave entirely up to you as long as you keep us informed and up to date as to your progress. The actual round-up and transportation of the Jews will be carried out by the French police and with the complicit knowledge of the French Vichy Government. Only Jews between the ages of 16 and 50 of non-French citizenship are to be resettled with the exception of those women who are pregnant or breast-feeding infants."

* * * * *

The usual repartee between Annette and Otto was missing that evening at dinner.

"You're very quiet Otto, is something wrong?"

"No not really," he replied, "I've just got something on my mind."

"Well, it seems to be troubling you. Would you like to tell me about it?"

"You must promise not to tell another living soul. I have to plan the resettlement of all non-French Jews from Paris in to work camps. I should be pleased that the Reich has confidence in my ability but it's a huge project. These Jews are renegades from all over Europe and must be accounted for and put to work."

"Surely you must know where all of these people are." Annette probed.

"Of course we have files classified and colour coded according to profession, nationality etc. but it's still a major undertaking. Please forgive me for being pre-occupied....it's extremely ungallant of me when in the company of the most beautiful woman in Paris. See all the other officers looking at me with envy."

Ignoring his flattery Annette continued. "Please don't think I'm being too presumptuous but may I make a suggestion?"

"Please do." Otto replied intrigued.

"Well.....in the municipal building we have street plans and large scale drawings of various areas even individual buildings. It should be possible to extend your colour code system to as many categories as you require and then transfer them on to the various street plans. In that way you would know instantly the occupancy down to the detail of what number and category of person lived in each house and apartment. You would be able to see at a glance the demographic concentrations and where to place your road blocks and transports."

Otto sat silent for a while considering what Annette had said and then with a smile on his face reached across the table and held her hands. "That is incredible, it's brilliant," he exploded in obvious delight. "Why didn't I think of that? But I've got an even better idea, why don't you come and work with me as my personal, civilian secretary and help me put this plan together. As I said this is a huge undertaking and will require a lot of personnel, you could help me coordinate and check the progress of our administrative staff. With your fluent German you'll also be invaluable as an interpreter. Please say yes and that way I'll get to see you every day and not just evenings sometimes during the week. You'll have all the protection and documentation you need. You needn't worry about the curfew and I'll see to it that you're well recompensed."

Without wishing to appear too eager Annette responded, "Well....."

"Please say yes Annette, we'd make a good team. I just know it."

"Well.....you'll have to let me work out my resignation at the municipal offices."

Word spread that Annette was leaving to work for the SS. She was aware of a different atmosphere as she walked down the corridor and through various offices. Annette wasn't sure whether or not she simply projected her feelings onto those around her but what she was certain of was that she definitely attracted attention. Trying to read the meanings behind the faces of those she passed proved unproductive and futile. Was that contempt or was it fear? Was it jealousy or admiration? The one thing that did reflect back to her was the deference to her potential power and influence as the result of becoming Otto's confident. She said her goodbyes to the girls in her office and commenced working for Otto the following Monday.

* * * * *

After weeks of meetings and planning the date was set for the round-up to start on 16th. July. Annette now had firm information on which to act. She made contact with Collette and they arranged to meet in the Jardin des Plantes on the Quai Saint Bernard next to the Seine.

"Thank you for meeting me Collette. I need your help. The Germans, or rather the French police under the authority of the Germans, are going to make a massive round-up of foreign Jews in Paris on 16th. and 17th. July. I suspect....no...I'm sure that this is just the beginning and that French nationals will be on the hit list soon after. I've left all the details wrapped in this newspaper which I'll leave on the bench when

I go. I want you to inform as many of the resistance as you can so that they can pass the information on to the Jewish communities in the hope that as many as possible can escape before they're lifted. If you can tell me the names of some trustworthy Rabbis I'll approach them with the information as well. We need to emphasise the urgency Collette because the Germans also intend soon to sweep Vichy France in the south so there will be nowhere safe."

"I will, but be very careful Annette, it's a dangerous game you're playing. The Germans may be bastards but they're not fools."

* * * * *

At 4.00a.m. on the 16th. July Annette and Otto sat in his staff car watching the programme unfold. The police arrived in lorries and buses and immediately spread out entering buildings and apartments making as much noise as possible. Truncheons and batons rapped on doors and the inhabitants were dragged out, many of the older, slower people were encouraged by the same batons. As Annette sat watching coldly, loud speakers repeated over and over again, 'You may only take one blanket, one sweater, one pair of shoes and two shirts.'

Crowds of bewildered Jews were herded into waiting buses and Annette was inwardly shocked at the high percentage of women and children in the queues and who also felt the weight of the Gendarmes' truncheons. Inspections at other sites in the city proved that the meticulous planning for Operation Vent Printanier, Operation Spring Breeze, was running like clockwork. Otto leaned forward and spoke to his driver, "Take us to the Velodrome d'Hiver near the Eiffel Tower."

Annette knew the velodrome intimately as she'd spent many happy hours there roller-skating whilst she'd been at the Sorbonne. She spoke quietly, "I'm still not convinced that the Vel' d'Hiv is the best place to concentrate 13,000 people Otto. There are only a few working toilets and one cold water tap."

"You worry too much Annette. There was a change of plan at the very last minute and 7,000 have already gone straight to the intermediate camps so there will only be 7,500 people in the velodrome. Your humanitarian suggestions have been accommodated and the Red Cross and a few doctors and nurses are in attendance with water and food. Besides they will only be here for a short time whilst we make sure that we have not rounded up anyone by mistake and they will be away to temporary resettlement camps at Drancy, Beaune-la-Rolande and Pithiviers within a very short time."

Annette sat quietly as convoys of buses disgorged their shambling passengers who were organised into lines at the velodrome entrances.

The velodrome had a glass roof which had been painted dark blue to avoid attracting allied bomber navigators. As a consequence, the next day temperatures inside the velodrome soared and numerous people died from exhaustion and dehydration.

"Well done Annette, a smooth operation because of your enthusiastic contribution. This will not go unnoticed or unrewarded I promise you. I have a lot of loose ends to tie up but I think you deserve to play truant and take the rest of the day off to do whatever takes your fancy. Here, take this and buy yourself a nice dress. I've a feeling that you may be needing one soon. I'll drop you off wherever you want on my way back to headquarters," And he leaned towards her kissing her on the cheek.

Later that night Annette sat in her small apartment drinking a glass of wine and looking at the black evening dress hanging up on the back of the door. Depressingly she wondered if this was her thirty pieces of silver. She reasoned that the round-up would have taken place whether or not she had been involved. By insinuating herself, at considerable personal risk, at the centre of Nazi planning hadn't she been able to save the lives of countless Jews by passing on details of the raid? It was time for her sked and with practised efficiency she had the radio connected and was transmitting within minutes. Through the window Annette could hear the regular mournful wail of klaxons rending the mid-summer night tranquillity. She listened with nervous anticipation but was relieved when the tone changed signalling that they had passed and moved on to another district.

On the first morning back at work after the Operation Vent Printanier Annette entered the SS Headquarters building and made her way to Otto's office and knocked on his door.

"Ahhh, come in Annette, sit down. After our success at the Vel'd'Hiv our assignment has been expanded. Some individuals managed to spring the trap though and this makes me wonder if they'd been tipped off. It seems that it's impossible to keep anything completely secret and water tight here in Paris." His ice-blue eyes looked directly into Annette's soft brown eyes and she went cold inside. She wondered if he suspected her and was playing her for his warped amusement. However she was too far in now to try to opt out without confirming any suspicions he might have. She would just have to continue to bluff it out.

Otto continued, "Probably some patriotic gendarme passed details on to his resistance friends. We shall never know. Nevertheless 13,000 less Jews in Paris is a good start. You have become the headquarters' sweetheart and I'm the most envied officer in the building. Now....I've boosted your ego enough today so down to work. Our Jewish round-up formula for Paris is to be rolled out across all the large cities and districts in France so for the rest of this year we will be travelling round making sure that all administrative centres are prepared for the resettlement of all Jews in France including French nationals.

CHAPTER 13

Annette 1942

The rain and sleet continued to buffet Annette's attic apartment window as she made radio contact with her home partner at the listening station at Grendon. She passed on information about the Germans' plans to transfer troops in to the previously unoccupied area of Vichy France. She had previously made contact with Collette and made sure that the information would be made known to the resistance. The proposed troop movements would have major implications for the resistance groups working in mid and southern France and also for any future Allies' plans for the invasion of Europe. Annette had got into the habit of holding one of the ear- pieces of her headset to one ear rather than place the earphones over her head thus covering both ears. She was just signing off when she heard the familiar sound of German klaxons echoing through the streets below. It was a most unnerving sound and Annette grew more and more anxious as the sound grew louder and louder except on this occasion there was no Doppler shift and the radio detection van squealed to a stop outside her apartment block. Immediately everything seemed to be happening at once. Annette moved quickly. Extinguishing the light she crossed the room and threw the window open taking care that the wind didn't smash it against the wall. Sleet and rain like hot needles stung her face and eyes as she wrestled to slide the radio suitcase out of sight under the displaced coping-stones on the roof. Fortunately the wind was in the right direction as she threw the radio end of the aerial over the roof party wall. At the same time in the street below she could hear the arrival of other lorries and the ominous sound of boots as they struck a staccato clatter on the cobbled street. The sound of loud barked orders flying up on the wind assaulted her ears and was accompanied by rifle butts hammering on apartment doors below as well as the thunder of hobnails on the marble stair treads. She quickly closed the window but the tell-tale wet patches where the rain had leached in were far too obvious. Quickly, with a towel Annette wiped the rain spots from the window sill, glass and surrounding casement frames. She filled a basin with water and placing it on the table beside the window, ripped off her blouse and dipped her head into the water making sure that her hair was soaking wet and that she had splashed water from the bowl all over the floor. The noises from the floors below became louder and more threatening as the soldiers scrambled up the stairs, landing by landing. "*Öffnen Sie die Tür, kommen jetzt aus. Öffnen Sie die Tür*," the soldiers shouted and screamed over one another whilst battering down apartment doors. "Open the door. Come out now, open the door."

Annette knew that they had reached her landing and she went to open the door when it burst open sending her crashing across the room. Two burly soldiers burst in kicking the door off the only hinge that remained holding it to the frame splintering and shattering the wood in the process.

"I have papers," Annette shouted. "I work for the SS, for Captain Otto von Lieper. Let me show you my papers."

The two soldiers, one each side, grabbed her by the arms, lifted her bodily from the floor and threw her towards the doorway. "I have my papers in my handbag," Annette gasped as she half turned to retrieve her bag. The blow of a rifle butt between the shoulder blades sent her crashing out on to the landing where the banister prevented her from tumbling down a flight of stairs. Her assailants pounced immediately and without waiting for Annette to get to her feet dragged her down the flights of stairs, out into the cold wet night and threw her into one of the waiting lorries. A sharp pain made Annette cry out involuntarily as her shin-bone hit the sharp metal lip protecting the wooden floorboards at the back of the lorry. At least the canvas cover gave some protection against the weather and as Annette became accustomed to the gloom she recognised male and female neighbours from her block in various states of shock and terror. Some were sitting on the side benches comforting friends and relatives whilst others were curled up lying and groaning on the floor.

The sound of klaxons bounced back and forth in the narrow street with shrill intent as the driver gunned the engine, dropped the clutch and everyone overbalanced jerking backwards as the lorry set off at great speed. People kept their heads down, looking at the floor avoiding eye contact and retreating in to their own nightmares and fears. It was not too long before the convoy came to a screeching halt. The canvas cover was thrown back and the lorry tailboard unbolted and hinged down with a clattering fatality. "*Aus, aus,*" the guards shouted, pulling young and old out of the lorry not caring who fell prone onto the cobbled wet

124

street that was Avenue Foch. Once again Annette felt the blow of a rifle butt as she staggered through a doorway that she recognized as Gestapo Headquarters. She had scarce time to catch her breath before once again she was dragged by the arms down a series of steps, the atmosphere becoming damp and colder with each downward flight. Attractive chandeliers had now given way to functional, bulkhead lamps fastened to the sweating ceiling and barely illuminating with a depressing, dull yellow glow. A heavy door was kicked open and Annette was flung fiercely into the cell. The metallic bang of the closing door seemed to resonate with every nerve in Annette's body. Lying on the floor she could hear the grating sounds up and down the long corridor of rusty steel bolts alternatively being withdrawn and locked and heavy steel doors clanging against stone walls like the hammers of hell. Gingerly manoeuvring herself into a sitting position Annette surveyed her surroundings. Illuminated by one dim bulb she registered that she was in a windowless cell of about twelve feet square. A wooden framed single bunk leaned precariously against the wall opposite the door. The thin mattress was filthy and stained, Annette guessed, with blood, urine and faeces. Now sitting on the bunk the cold began to seep into her bones and realising that she was without her blouse she wrapped the single threadbare blanket around her shoulders and drew her knees up to her chin. In the corner beside the door was an empty bucket.

Time was now meaningless and Annette was unable to discern how long she'd sat there before she was startled back to the present by the sound of her door being opened. Once again she was manhandled along the corridor and dragged into what she ascertained was an interrogation room. She was pushed into a chair and her hands and feet immediately tied to the chair arms and legs. A single light bulb hung from the ceiling. The two guards stood either side of her and Annette could just about make out the shape of a third man seated behind a desk, his rimless spectacle lenses reflecting the dull yellow light like the candle-lit eyes of Halloween pumpkin lanterns she had carved on the farm at home. An unnaturally long silence became threatening, intimidating and oppressive but Annette was prepared for this psychological pressure and it gave her time to gather her thoughts and steel herself for what was to come.

"What is your name?" The voice from behind the desk asked in French coldly and deliberately.

"My name is Annette Hugo and....."

A violent punch to the side of her head cut Annette's sentence short by sending her crashing sideways on to the floor. The chair was quickly hauled upright. Annette gripped the arms of the chair and tried to stay focused even though her left temple throbbed where it had cracked down on the stone floor and her right ear was ringing from the blow.

"What is your name?" The question was repeated and before Annette could answer the voice continued, "Where did you hide your radio?"

"I have no radio." Annette managed to gasp before another fist blow sent her crashing to the floor in the opposite direction this time.

"Who is your contact?"

"What is your real name?"

"Tell us where you have hidden your radio."

"What is your name?"

Annette lost count of the number of blows but as each one sent her crashing to the floor she became more resolute and stubborn.

"Take her back to her cell so that she has time to remember." The voice ordered.

Annette was dragged back to her cell and thrown in through the door. Time was punctuated by screams of fear and pain as numerous doors up and down the corridor were slammed open and closed and the various prisoners submitted to beatings and torture. Annette listened intently as the guards' footsteps continually approached and retreated past her door until once again they stopped outside her cell.

The whole process of questions and beatings was repeated and repeated without Annette giving away any information.

"Where is your blouse?" The voice asked with quiet, slow menace.

Annette was not expecting this line of questioning but answered honestly, "I took it off to wash my hair."

"You're a very striking woman Mademoiselle Hugo." The voice continued. Annette shivered internally as she consciously realised for the first time that her fulsome breasts were bulging out from the top and sides of her silk petticoat. "I think I might let my guards amuse themselves for a while as a diversion from their work. What do you say?"

Defiantly, Annette answered strongly, "Either you have found my papers and you know who I am or you have not bothered to find out. Either way it is you who should be concerned not me."

At that response the voice screamed, "Take the whore back to her cell and let her contemplate her part in rest and recuperation for personnel of the occupation forces."

Annette lost count of the number of times she was taken to the interrogation room, questioned, beaten then returned to her cell. Sleep was impossible. When other prisoners' screams didn't keep her awake the guards ensured that she was deprived of the opportunity to sleep by opening her cell door and prodding her awake. Half-conscious she was dragged yet again for the umpteenth time back to the interrogation room. She was tied to the chair once again.

"Where is your radio and who is your contact?" The voice repeated.

"Annette Hugo and if you have searched my apartment you will know that I have no radio."

"You are trying my patience Mademoiselle Hugo, if that is your name. You have brought this upon yourself and you can cause it to stop whenever you want." Turning to his two henchmen the voice continued, "Tie them to her hands." Leering at Annette he continued, "We have other….how shall we say….more intimate places where we can put these but for now this is just a sample."

The clips were fastened to Annette's hands and she saw the two wires disappearing into the gloom. A stick wrapped in leather was thrust into her mouth.

"Bite on this." Her interrogator said, "We don't want you to bite your tongue off now do we? We want you to be able to talk."

Annette could remember nothing beyond the clunk of an electrical power switch being thrown. The voltage was increased up to the point where she could scream no more. Her whole body stiffened and jerked uncontrollably until the power was turned off. When consciousness returned Annette was back in her cell her muscles quivering with cold and shock and her head pounding with a pain she had never experienced before.

Otto was late arriving at his office and noticing that Annette was not at her desk asked the Corporal where she was.

"I don't know sir," came the reply. "She hasn't been seen this morning sir and I don't think that she has turned up for work today."

Annette had never ever missed a day at work since she had become his civilian assistant and fearing that she might be unwell Otto called for his car to be brought round to the front of the headquarters building. He had never been inside Annette's apartment but he knew where she lived and pointed his driver in the direction of the Rue de Chantiers on the left bank of the Seine. The driver pulled up outside Annette's apartment block and Otto got out. He looked around and noticing two Wehrmacht soldiers on guard outside the main entrance he approached them directly. The soldiers jumped to attention and ignoring their formality Otto demanded, "What's going on here soldier?"

"All the residents have been arrested sir on order of the Gestapo sir."

"Oh! And why is that?" Otto replied quickly.

"I'm not sure sir but...I think that the radio detection van has been monitoring this area for some time and picked up a signal from the building last night."

Otto bounded up the stairs and on reaching the top floor was furious when he was confronted by Annette's door lying in the middle of her living room and the whole apartment looking like a disaster area. Picking up her handbag and seeing that her SS sponsored identification papers were still inside Otto's anger exploded in a screamed expletive. "Fucking ignorant pigs." Turning, he ran down the stairs so quickly that more than once he stumbled and crashed into the wall when the stairs turned at right angles on each landing fuelling his anger even more. He rushed out into the street knocking over one of the soldiers and sending his rifle skidding and bouncing across the road. "Gestapo Headquarters." He yelled at his driver, "And don't fucking stop for anyone or anything."

Kicking the car door open and shearing the doorstop strap in the process Otto ran full tilt up the steps and in to Gestapo Headquarters. The clerk behind a desk in the entrance hall was about to approach Otto but quickly backed away under the full onslaught of his out-of-control anger. "Don't you fucking dare ask to see my papers," Otto yelled at the top of his voice. Everyone in the vestibule froze as did the people on their way up and down the wide marble staircase leading to an upper gallery where stony faces peered down to get a better view of the commotion. "Which room is that bastard *Krimminalkommisar* Schleicher in?" Otto yelled at the clerk. "I asked you a fucking question you idiot...which fucking room?" The last three words shouted with such force that Otto could feel his voice crack.

"Room 42 on the first floor sir."

By the time the timid reply had been uttered Otto was halfway up the stairs. A quick look right and left and Otto followed the numbers on the doors to room 42 with a brass name plate *Krimminalkommisar* Schleicher screwed to the dark mahogany wood. In one swift movement he turned the handle and with his shoulder to the door forced it open sending it crashing back against the wall. More in shock than in controlled authority Schleicher stood up behind his desk and shouted, "Who do you think you are bursting into my office, I'll have you arrested?"

"Sit down you worthless piece of shit," Otto yelled approaching the desk. "You come under the authority of the SS and if there's any arresting to do I'll do it."

"You have no authority in here." Schleicher countered without conviction.

Otto ignored this and continued, "What have you done with Annette Hugo? You arrested her last night. If she's not brought here immediately from your dungeons I'll have you transferred to the Wehrmacht and on your way to the Russian Front before you can shit yourself. Do I make myself clear? You fucking idiot she has SS papers in her handbag and your illiterate, ignorant scum didn't even have the sense to look at them." Otto's anger had now taken complete control and the *Krimminalkommisar* shrank back not wishing to provoke any unpredictable violent outcome. Picking up the outside line phone Otto again screamed," Get her up here now or I'll phone Herr Himmler and you'll be out of here within the hour. Well!!! Fucking do it." And he slammed the phone back down on the rest.

Schleicher picked up the internal phone and ordered whoever was on the other end of the line to have Annette brought up straight away to his office. Otto paced backwards and forwards like a caged animal until he eventually turned and saw Annette supported by two soldiers in the open doorway. He gasped and would never have recognized her had he not known that it was her. Rushing forward he pushed the two guards out of the way and gathered Annette up in his arms. Turning to Schleicher, Otto hissed with cool, deliberate icy clarity, "As sure as I'm carrying this young woman you'll be carrying a rifle on the Russian Front before this week is out." And he was true to his word, but the irony of the situation didn't seem to register with Otto.

All eyes were on Otto. Everyone was motionless as he descended the staircase except for those who were between him and the front door and these people, military and civilian, moved quietly and fearfully aside. Once outside Otto placed Annette's limp body in the back of the car and climbed in beside her. Placing a rug over her exposed body Otto directed his driver to take them to his hotel carefully avoiding any potholes in the roadway.

Annette winced and moaned softly as Otto placed her gently on the large bed. He rang for a medical officer to attend immediately and returned to sit on the bed beside Annette. Blood from the wounds on her face had congealed trapping her blonde hair in areas of scabbed matt. Saliva and bloodstains traced their way down her chin, neck and on to the upper curve of her right breast. Both eyes were swollen and closed, her knuckles grazed and one of her legs had a gash which exposed her shin bone. Black and blue bruises were evident everywhere. Compassion and anger in equal measure assailed Otto. 'I hope the Russians give that bastard Schleicher a bit of his own medicine,' Otto thought. Moving into the bathroom he filled a glass with warm water and taking his face flannel returned to Annette. He dipped the flannel in the water and very gently began to bathe Annette's face and tried to tease the strands of matted hair from the dried blood. She moaned quietly. With tears forming in the corner of each eye Otto said softly, "Sorry my darling. The doctor will be here soon." Annette opened her eyes to mere slits and whispered, "Otto." Before drifting off into unconsciousness.

The doctor examined Annette and declared that no bones were broken. Given time the cuts would heal and the bruises would fade away. A stitch in her split lip might leave a small scar but it was too soon to say.

"I think the best thing for the moment," the doctor said pragmatically, "Is for the young lady to sleep. She is bound to be in shock and a good long sleep will give her mind and body some time to accommodate the trauma. I've given her an injection which should knock her out for up to 36 hours. I'll leave some sleeping tablets with you in case she needs them and some strong painkillers for when she wakes up. When she's ready let her have a soak in the bath, bathe her wounds with this disinfectant and rub some of this salve into the exposed cuts and grazes to prevent infection. She'll feel stiff and it will take time for the bruising to dissipate from her muscles but my guess is that she should make a complete recovery in a few weeks."

"Thank you Herr Doctor," Otto said showing him out of the room.

"Pleased to be of service Captain, if you think you need me again please do not hesitate to call. Good day."

Otto removed Annette's shoes, socks and skirt. He wasn't sure whether to go any further his coyness and embarrassment being a new and unfamiliar experience. Her petticoat was soiled and blood-stained and Otto decided that to get rid of it might make Annette feel better when she eventually came round. His anger resurfaced when he saw the huge bruises on her back left by the rifle-butt blows but gradually subsided as he stood looking at Annette lying peacefully in her brassiere and camisole knickers. Looking beyond the cuts, abrasions and bruises Otto was filled with desire. In spite of her injuries she was even more beautiful than he had realised. Her frumpy occupation clothes had hidden a figure which was beautifully proportioned. Her legs were toned, long and with a symmetry that was shapely without an excess of fat. Her hips were gently rounded emphasising a flat stomach which flowed into a ribcage supporting perfectly formed breasts whose inviting weight allowed them to swell and spill sideways out from her brassiere.

Otto hadn't noticed that evening was drawing in and that after his day of emotional turmoil he was now feeling depleted and tired. He poured himself a glass of schnapps and downed it in one gulp. He poured a second and placed it on a low table. Turning an armchair round he sank down into its enveloping softness without taking his eyes off Annette. Stretching out his right arm Otto lifted up the rim-filled glass and flicking his cheek with his left hand threw his head back and let the schnapps sear its way down his throat.

How long he sat there Otto didn't know and cared less. It was now quite dark outside as he stepped out of his uniform and hung it up in the wardrobe. Wearing nothing but his vest and underpants he climbed onto the bed and slid under the clean white sheets. He leaned over and gently pulled the other end of the bedclothes over Annette's broken body. Otto slid his arm under her neck and cradled her head against his chest whilst gently stroking the strands of blonde hair which were not sticking to her scalp.

CHAPTER 14

Annette and Otto 1943

It took Annette longer than anticipated to get over her ordeal at the hands of the Gestapo. Spring had quickly morphed into summer and the warmth of the Paris sunshine was having an ameliorative effect on torn and strained muscles. Her body may have been battered but it was healing and any psychological scars had been eradicated in a renewed determination to help bring down the evil Nazi regime.

Otto could not have been more attentive, often neglecting his duties. Annette found that she missed his company when he was not with her and looked forward with impatience to their next meeting. The dichotomy of these two emotional responses troubled Annette but she accommodated it, superficially at least, by resolving to believe that there was good and bad in all situations and all people and admitting to herself that her feelings towards Otto at a personal level was not incompatible with her hatred of the political system he represented.

For Otto too, recent events had been a revelation. Never in his life had he acknowledged or even recognised a caring side to his personality. His whole life and existence was one of duty to Hitler and the Fatherland and to rid Germany of any virulence affecting the purity of his nation. And yet there was his mother's parting shot that his father was English and not German which was an itch that never quite went away no matter how often he scratched it. The rounding up of Jews throughout France was proceeding like clockwork due to his unrelenting will and organization but he was beginning to feel that life in Paris was making him soft, that he was being diverted from his sole purpose and that...yes....perhaps Annette was becoming a major influence and diversion to his fore-sworn loyalty to Hitler. But he could have both couldn't he?

"I have something for you," Otto said as they sat in the sunshine outside a bar in the Place du Parvis Notre Dame enjoying a glass of wine.

"Well…two things actually." And reaching into the top pocket of his uniform he took out a small brown envelope and presented it to Annette.

"What is it?" Annette asked with excitement.

"Open it and see." Otto replied with a smile.

Annette carefully opened the envelope and eased out three small photographs. She stared at them with mixed emotions. The first was a picture taken months ago of four German SS officers and four girls sitting at a café table drinking wine. Annette recognised that she was in the photo even though her glass was held in such a position as to hide her face. On the back was written Paris 1942. She remembered that one of the officers had been waving his Leica camera around taking tourist snapshots but she had not realised that at some stage he had caught her and Otto in conversation. The second photo clearly showed her sitting next to Otto and although her face had the hint of a serious frown it was obvious that Otto was enjoying her company. She turned the photo over and on the back she read, Annette and Otto Paris 1942. She smiled at Otto but inwardly felt uncomfortable about being recorded in this compromising situation. The third photo was one of Otto, head and shoulders, by himself. He was dressed in his black SS dress uniform, wearing his shiny black peaked cap and Annette had to admit that he looked incredibly dashing and handsome staring out of the picture with assurance and pride and not a little arrogance. Again she turned the photo over and read, To Annette, All my Love, Otto. 1943.

"Thank you Otto, I shall treasure these memories."

"I hope they will not just represent memories," Otto responded in a hurt voice and Annette was not sure whether or not he was mocking her.

"And now for my second surprise," Otto continued, taking another larger envelope from his pocket.

Again Annette opened the envelope slowly not knowing what to expect this time. She read the enclosed card and was rendered speechless.

"Well…." Otto prompted impatiently.

"I can't believe it," Annette gasped. "Not even in a thousand year Reich."

"Are you trying to tease me, you minx?" Otto responded.

"Yes, of course I am." Annette answered laughing. "And succeeding. I was trying to unlock some German humour. Who are you going to take as your guest?" She enquired.

"As if you didn't know. You really are in a coquettish mood today aren't you?" Otto said leaning back on his chair.

"No…I'm just happy." Annette answered placing her hand on his.

She looked again at the card and read out loud, 'SS *Oberstgruppenfuhrer Heinrich Himmler requests the company of SS Hauptsturmfuhrer Otto von Lieper and guest to attend a performance of Das Rheingold by Richard Wagner at Bayreuth on Saturday 31ˢᵗ. July 1943. Dinner with The Fuhrer will follow the performance.*

"Do you think you'll be fit enough to travel?" Otto asked concerned.

"Wild horses wouldn't keep me away. I'm so thrilled, thank you Otto. I'm looking forward to it already."

Her obvious frisson of excitement at having some time away with Otto masked a deeper recognition of the possibilities with which this new development presented her. London must know of this new situation. In spite of diversions her main mission must remain on track.

* * * * *

It was late afternoon before Otto and Annette were ushered into their Bayreuth hotel suite and their overnight bags deposited on the luggage stands at the bottom of a large king size bed. Otto tipped the old porter who touched his forelock. "I hope your stay is a pleasant one sir. If there is anything more I can do for you please ring. *"Heil Hitler."*

The journey had been tedious and they both collapsed into easy chairs for a few minutes respite before freshening up and going down to the restaurant for a light tea. Annette was just finishing her cake as Otto pushed his chair back and stood up. "Excuse me dear but I just have to check something with reception. I'll be back in two minutes."

A little later Otto unlocked the door to their suite and stepped aside as Annette entered. "We don't have a lot of time," Annette said, "And I could really do with a bath before I change into something suitable for tonight."

"I could do with a bath myself," Otto replied. "But you go first. I know how long you ladies like to spend making yourselves beautiful for us mere men."

"Pig," Annette responded as she walked through into the bedroom in order to access the bathroom. She opened her valise and was just about to make her way towards the bathroom door when her attention was caught by a large parcel on the bed. "What's this on the bed?" she shouted through to Otto.

"I don't know. I can't see from in here." Then standing in the doorway he continued, "You'd better open it to find out."

Annette opened the large cardboard box and peeled the tissue paper back carefully. "Ooooooh! Otto you're a complete devil," she screamed. She ran into his arms, kissed him then ran straight back to her present. She lifted the creation up to her shoulders and twirled round the room. "It's absolutely stunning," Annette cooed. "It must have cost you a fortune Otto. You're much too indulgent but it is rather beautiful."

"Nothing's too good for my Parisian beauty," Otto replied.

Annette knew that many of the Paris fashion houses had closed down with the coming of the war and the designers moved to America. As if Otto could read her mind he said, "There are still original dresses to be bought if you know where to look and have the money. This is a Jean Desses original evening gown and I have it on good authority that it was made with your name on it." Otto teased.

Minutes later Annette was bathing in hot water in a large bath overflowing with the now unheard of luxury of perfumed, foam bubbles imagining how she would look in her new gown. Otto sat on the toilet seat with a glass of whisky in his hand watching her with a faintly recognisable lecherous smile on his face.

"Here let me wash your back," Otto offered putting his whisky down, "And your front," he added.

"Not a chance," Annette responded laughing. "If I let you anywhere near me neither of us will be ready in time and I don't think your Fuhrer would appreciate your excuse do you?"

"Perhaps not," Otto acquiesced with a laugh.

Otto climbed into the bath recently vacated by Annette whilst she floated through into the bedroom wrapped in a huge, down-soft bath towel. The anticipated minute arrived when at last she stepped into her evening gown. It was made from the most delicate cornflower blue silk chiffon. The strapless sheath was diagonally ruched and draped releasing into a floating panel at the right waist. The bodice was lightly boned emphasising the swell of her breasts. The diagonal lie of the fabric allowed for flexibility, drape-ability and accentuated her body lines, the soft drapes clinging to her curves.

Annette was not impressed by the exterior architecture of the Wagner Bayreuth Festspielhaus with its late nineteenth century façade ornamentation of undecorated bricks. The interior too was disappointingly plain. The auditorium was shaped like a horse-shoe, the seats arranged in a single steeply-shaped wedge with no galleries or boxes but the unmistakable hum of excitement and anticipation filled the auditorium. Most of the men were in officer uniform but civilians and party members were also evident. Wounded and recuperating ordinary Wehrmacht soldiers filled the first three rows and Annette wondered how they would receive nearly four hours of Wagner. The extravagance of silk and jewellery displayed by the ladies shocked Annette by its ostentatious disregard for not only the suffering of people in the occupied countries but the ordinary German citizens too who were also suffering the deprivations of the protracted war. She touched the fabric of her own creation and felt more than a little hypocritical. With a certain proprietorial pride Otto didn't miss the aside admiring glances of his fellow officers and their women guests and neither did Annette. Large Nazi banners hanging either side of the proscenium arch reinforced a stark simplicity emphasising the political one state, one people.

Eventually the tension in the auditorium was released when Hitler finally arrived. Shouts of "*Sieg Heil*" reverberated in the hall hurting her ears which apparently had suffered some as yet, undetermined damage as a result of the repeated punches suffered during her night of torture. Hitler walked down to the fourth row and stood smiling waving with his right hand soaking up the palpable adoration. On his left shoulder and slightly behind was his female companion Eva Braun. Also with him, Annette recognized a coterie of Nazi officials including Himmler, Hermann Göring, Goebbels and Adolf Eichmann. Eventually Hitler sat down followed by everyone else in the auditorium. Apart from some occasional restless shuffling and coughing the audience waited in quiet anticipation. Annette wondered why people who are perfectly healthy suddenly developed the most infuriating coughs as soon as they entered a theatre or concert hall.

The conductor raised his baton and the timeless chord of 'E' flat major, at first almost inaudible, weaved and rippled its way through the orchestra gradually increasing in volume as the curtain was slowly raised. In the dark she reached for Otto's hand. "This is incredible," she whispered, "I can feel the hairs on the back of my neck standing up." The stage set was magnificent in its simplicity and reality was at once suspended at the bottom of the Rhine. "I've never seen you glowing with such excitement and anticipation," Otto whispered in her ear and she squeezed his hand in silent response. Dark blue lighting created the illusion of a deep, mysterious, underwater world where the river currents were represented by waves of light rippling and travelling over the rocks and across the stage. Rhine-maidens suspended on invisible wires swam gracefully before alighting on the rocks and beginning their teasing, torment and eventual lament when Albrecht the dwarf snatched their gold whilst vowing to pay the price by forswearing love.

Breaker columns with Corinthian carved tops placed at intervals up the sides of the auditorium were not just there for visual affect. The pillars and spaces behind them created an acoustic atmosphere and echo of sound which completely enveloped Annette. She whispered to Otto, "Can you feel my hand vibrating? It's incredible, it's as if the whole sound is emanating from inside me, is part of me, is me." Annette was transported to a nether world of Gods, love, hate, deceit and power. She recognised the archetypal manifestations of the human psyche as they unfolded during the performance and captured so dramatically in the music and libretto. "Wagner really is a genius," she whispered once again to Otto. "Doesn't his understanding of the human personality, presented in such a dramatic production, just leave you breathless?" she asked Otto not really expecting or wanting a reply.

The scene of Wotan's descent through the Rhine and into the Nibelheim underworld of dwarfs held Annette in enthral. "If you don't release my hand I'll never be able to hold a sword again," Otto whispered and smiled as he released her white knuckled fingers from their vice-like grip on his hand. The stage set of dark rocky caverns where the red glows of numerous forges and the advancing and retreating of unified rhythmic hammering on real anvils created an evil, malevolent atmosphere. It was here that the Rhine-maidens' gold was to be forged into a ring symbolic of the human consciousness and libido to be used for what nefarious means? The overwhelming power and portent of the scene left Annette breathless and clinging to Otto's arm.

At the climax Wotan, Fricka his wife and Freia his daughter crossed the mountains on a rainbow bridge and enter the Gods' fortress of Valhalla to a crashing, orchestral crescendo which almost had Annette leaping to her feet cheering. She was not the only one to have been affected in this way for even before the last chord died away the whole audience was on its feet cheering and clapping. As the adulation died away Otto was about to join the throng making its way to the exit, Annette grabbed his hand and pulled him back down into his seat. "Let me sit here for a while please. I'm so completely overcome so totally overawed I can't think or move yet. I need a couple of minutes to come back down to earth."

"So! We Germans are good at something then." He teased.

"Ah, time to get your own back is it?" Annette responded.

"Come on you she devil," Otto said pulling her out of her seat, "We mustn't be late at the hotel. The Fuhrer would never forget nor forgive."

The gathering before dinner was getting into its stride when Otto ushered Annette into the reception room. He caught Himmler's eye and was beckoned over.

"Otto my boy, thank you for coming."

"Not at all Herr Himmler, I was delighted by your invitation."

"My pleasure Otto. A little enough reward for the work you have been doing in France. And I think I can guess who your guest is."

"Yes sir, may I present my assistant Mademoiselle Annette Hugo."

"Good evening my dear." Himmler said clicking his heels and extending his hand. "I've heard a lot about you and the Fatherland owes you a debt for the enthusiastic support you have given our rising star Otto here. I've kept The Fuhrer informed of your work together and he would like to meet you. This way if you please."

Otto squeezed Annette's hand and followed Himmler across the room to where the Fuhrer was joking with his henchmen. Himmler waited for an opportune moment to catch Hitler's attention.

"Mein Fuhrer, may I introduce Captain Otto von Lieper and his French assistant Mademoiselle Annette Hugo."

Hitler turned towards Annette and for some seconds stared at her unblinking and without saying anything. Annette went cold inside and was sure that Hitler was searching her very soul, divining every secret and thought she'd ever had. She had never felt so naked or vulnerable. After what seemed like an eternity he eventually said, "Germany is grateful for your support and help Mademoiselle Hugo. Tell me, what do you think about our Wagner? Do you think the gold stealing dwarfs will come to a deserved end?"

Annette was immediately on her guard. She knew the implication of the question. She daren't give away the least hint of her hatred of anti-Semitism and she wondered if the question was a deliberately leading one to test her loyalty to the Nazi ideal. She couldn't say that power was there for all to use either for good or evil or that the evil dwarf Albrecht was a symbolic projection of everyone's dark thoughts and ambitions. The implication would not be lost and it would be disastrous.

"Yes....I think you are right Mein Fuhrer....they will.

I'd just like to say one more thing Mein Fuhrer," Annette continued hoping that her calculated obsequious sycophancy would not be too obvious, "and I hope that you do not consider me too presumptuous, but the whole of Germany can see that your heart has its reasons, in Wagnerian terms to rejuvenate the Fatherland with a burning energy." Annette could swear that she detected Hitler's chest swell just a little and his usually veiled eyes give a fleeting access to his pathological absorption with his own power and omnipotence.

"And do you see our Wotan as the Norse God Odin, symbol of our Germanic burning energy, rebirth and rejuvenation?" he asked fixing Annette with his hypnotic stare.

Annette's survival instincts were on high alert and she knew she had to pick her words carefully. "Wotan was not born wise," she said thoughtfully. "He acquired his understanding by searching for it and drinking from the fountain of wisdom for which he paid the price with the loss of one eye. A wisdom and understanding that gives the individual knowledge of himself as indeed you have yourself Mein Fuhrer and others can sense and feel it. Germania lives it."

"I have never considered this psychology but I can feel that you understand my destiny and love and unity with the people of the Fatherland. Thank you for being so forthright. You are a remarkable young woman and Germany will thank you for your zeal. I hope that von Lieper appreciates your support. We may talk again, in Berlin perhaps. Good night mademoiselle."

Anxiety stalked Annette in that she was anxious that she hadn't stepped over the mark this time. She had not been truthful in her interpretation of Wotan's search for self and she prayed that Hitler was not familiar with Carl Jung's work on the personality. How could she tell Hitler that becoming the individual who really is himself is not done by becoming egocentric since the ego is not, as it tends to seem, the centre of the personality and Hitler was a prime example of an individual driven by an uncontrolled ego. Annette was brought back from her private thoughts by Otto's voice in her ear.

"How many other facets are there to your diamond-bright personality?" Otto whispered as they joined the small, select group following Hitler into the dining room.

It was well known that Hitler never went to bed before two or three-o' clock in the morning. Midnight was too late for Annette to eat a large meal and she picked at her veal and pushed the vegetables around her plate. Hitler too appeared to eat and drink very little. At last Hitler stood up followed by his entourage and made his way towards the exit. The rest of the diners stood and saluted, "*Sieg Heil.*"

Himmler split off from the group, approached Otto and whispered in his ear. "Could I have a quiet word in confidence Otto?"

"Of course sir." Otto replied and turning to Annette said, "Would you excuse me for a few minutes Annette. Here are the keys to our room and I'll join you in a short while."

"Of course Otto." Annette replied quietly touching his hand with a stroking movement as she took the keys.

They both watched her leave the room and Himmler conspiratorially pulled Otto out of earshot of the few remaining guests.

"I'll get straight to the point. What are your intentions towards this Frenchwoman? I can see why she provides you with a diversion. She's beautiful, very intelligent and obviously supports the Fuhrer but she's French. You have a great career ahead of you Otto and it has given me satisfaction to mentor and support your zeal but anything beyond a dalliance with this creature will do your future irreparable damage. You have committed yourself totally and relentlessly to Hitler and the Party but it has been noted that there is one area where…perhaps your duty to the Fatherland has been lacking."

"*Mein Gott.*" Otto gasped, for God's sake I had no idea, tell me what it is."

"You are a pure Aryan specimen Otto and we need more men like you to serve the Fatherland. We need to provide the next generation to continue the work of the Fuhrer, to consolidate and expand our thousand year Reich. You need sons Otto and you need a good German wife to provide them." Himmler waited quietly for his advice to sink in.

Before he'd met Annette, Otto would have accepted this aspect of his duty without hesitation. He knew that his life's purpose had taken on another dimension as a result of his developing relationship with Annette but to admit this would banish him to obscurity. Yet he had to tell Himmler what he wanted to hear, and make it convincing. "You're right Herr Himmler. I've been so pre-occupied with my Jewish resettlement programmes that I haven't even given this matter any thought at all. Now that you mention it I can see that I have been negligent in my complete service of the Fatherland."

"Good, I'm pleased to hear it, I thought that there would be a logical explanation. I said as much to Hitler over dinner and he understood but expects the situation to be rectified as soon as possible."

"Of course Herr Himmler."

"Listen Otto....I have a niece, Sieglinde, in Berlin who is a fine German Mädchen. She has completed all the Party motherhood and Hausfrau courses with flying colours and the family have been most anxious for her to meet the ideal Aryan man to ensure the continued purity of our German race and culture. I can think of no one more suited to this task than you dear Otto. She's an outdoor girl with a complexion as fresh as morning dew and a fine physical body. I think you should meet her. I'll arrange something in Berlin and let you know. I don't think I'm letting any secrets out of the bag when I tell you that I can predict a further promotion and a new posting for you. I have to fly back to Berlin now with the Fuhrer. *Auf Wiedersehen Otto.*"

"*Auf Wiedersehen* and thank you Herr Himmler for all your personal interest and support."

"Think nothing of it. I'll arrange something and be in touch later."

Why did life have to be so complicated Otto considered with annoyance. He picked up a bottle of champagne and two glass flutes from a side table and made his way towards the stairs. Things were so much simpler when all he had to do was shoot and gas Jews, Poles and Gypsies. If he wanted his career to move forward then there was no way he could ignore his obligations towards Himmler and the Nazi Party ethnic purity demographic. Perhaps this Sieglinde might be very attractive and personable but considering the graduates of the Party Hausfrau programme that he had met in the past he was not hopeful. Most of them were fitness fanatics with muscles to match any soldier, culturally ignorant, narrow minded and unable to articulate any intelligent conversation that didn't concern *Kinder, Küche* but not necessarily *Kirche,* children, kitchen and church. Perhaps he could have Sieglinde in Berlin and Annette in Paris but Himmler's Gestapo spies were everywhere and besides, what would he do after the war? Otto was conscious that he was very irritated and that his planned denouement to the evening was in danger of being spoilt. Perhaps the champagne might help to get it back on track.

Annette was just coming out of the bathroom as Otto entered the room. "How beautiful you are," Otto said, "And so knowledgeable. I'm the luckiest man in the world. You even had the Fuhrer eating out of your hand. How could anyone not fall in love with you?"

Otto popped the cork and poured two glasses of champagne. He handed one to Annette and led her towards the sofa. "I think we've earned a nightcap don't you? We've done our duty this evening and deserve the rest of the night to ourselves." His other unexpected duty re-surfaced into Otto's consciousness and he had to fight to suppress the recently presented implications. He flicked his left cheek and raised his glass saying, "A toast I think. To us."

"To us," Annette responded. She tipped the glass up a little too far and as the bubbles danced along her taste buds she coughed and spluttered. After catching her breath she continued, "Why do you do that?"

"Do what?" Otto replied.

"You know....flick an imaginary fly from your left cheek."

"I didn't know that I did," Otto replied.

"Is something troubling you Otto? Is it me? I've noticed you doing it before and it always seems to happen when you're upset, annoyed or irritated. Have I upset you in some way Otto? Please tell me if I have."

"Of course you haven't my darling. You're the best thing that's ever happened to me."

"Is that before or after Herr Hitler?" Annette teased.

"You really are a provocative devil aren't you," Otto said dragging her up off the sofa. Putting both their glasses down on the bedside table Otto took Annette in his arms and kissed her urgently full on the lips at the same time loosening her dress bodice. He stepped back and with both hands folded down the bodice to Annette's waist releasing her firm, full breasts. He bent down and circled her left nipple with his tongue before drawing it into his mouth. She felt her nipple grow stiff sending urgent rippling sensations to her groin. He switched his attention to her other breast and Annette gasped involuntarily pressing her hips hard against Otto.

Annette too was in turmoil. It had always been obvious to her that this was the way the evening was going to end even as she had initially read the invitation all those weeks ago. And so she had the answer to her question. Yes, she was prepared to prostitute herself in support of her country's war effort, but it no longer felt like that. A personal need, desire had overtaken her and she wanted to possess him and be possessed in return.

They hurriedly undressed each other and collapsed onto the bed in their mutual urgency. Annette was swollen and wet to the extent that her virginity offered no resistance as Otto plunged into her. Their gasping synchronized, both rushed towards that release which was now impossible to deny. Afterwards, for some minutes they both lay quietly as their bodies relaxed and breathing returned to normal. They turned their heads to look at each other and burst out laughing. "I love you Otto von Lieper," Annette whispered.

"I love you too Annette Hugo," Otto replied. "I've waited so long for this moment."

"I know, me too," Annette responded and then more seriously she continued, "I only hope that our two nations don't pull us apart."

"I won't let that happen," Otto said with confidence and then his recent conversation with Himmler came rushing back into his head again. At that moment he felt that he was no longer in a position to determine his own future.

Annette too was struggling to come to terms with what had just happened. What future was there for them regardless of who won the war or who lost? The thought was immediately dismissed from her mind by the sensation of something cold being trickled over her breasts and down to her naval. She turned sharply to see Otto with the bottle of champagne in his hands. "You monster," she squealed, as Otto climbed on top of her and commenced licking the wine from her body. The contrast between the cold liquid and Otto's warm tongue once again had Annette's nipples and groin responding. They kissed, the champagne dribbling out between their lips. Otto entered her again, this time more slowly, more deliberately. Annette couldn't resist the desire to hold him with her hand, to pull him deep inside her, to fulfil the yearning, to fill the tumescent space that eagerly demanded a connection. At the guiding touch of her hand, Otto moaned as her warmth gradually encircled him. The rhythm was slow at first. Gradually, neither knew where one body ended and the other began as their passion increased to an all-consuming tension unrealised the first time round. Lost in time and space they both eventually collapsed in a loud lung explosive exhalation. Annette was unaware of the weight of Otto on top of her as they lay entwined their heavy breathing slowly becoming normal and the sensation of his gradually shrinking away from her leaving her sad and empty.

Lying there in post-coital repose half way between consciousness and sleep, more pragmatic thoughts invaded Annette's mind. 'You stupid girl. What if you've got yourself pregnant? Your whole training and mission will be for nothing. How could you let yourself be carried away like this? Stupid, stupid, stupid.' She did a quick calculation and decided that she was not in the fertile period of her monthly cycle. Or at least she hoped she wasn't. She resolved to keep a closer account in her diary of her monthly visitor. Her mind was now working overtime. Weren't British soldiers given access to prophylactics? She was sure they were and thought that the German Army would be the same. She decided to wait for the right moment and would approach Otto with this solution to her problem. Otto himself could do without the complication of a pregnant secretary/mistress she reasoned. Although in the circumstance he would probably get himself transferred or dump her or both. Either way the situation had to be avoided.

CHAPTER 15

Otto and Ziggy 1943

On return from their trip to Bayreuth Annette was surprised and delighted to see that her apartment had been redecorated and cosmetic damage done during the raid had been repaired. Otto really was a thoughtful darling she mused. He tried his best to persuade her to move into the hotel with him. For obvious reasons she declined his offer, but they reached a mutual compromise whereby she would stay over with him two or three times a week when they could make uninterrupted love whenever the mood took them which was often. Annette was now in even more of a quandary. She was not only having to protect two identities, her own personal life as Annie Charlton and her persona as Annette Hugo, a French national working for the resistance but now a third as the willing lover of a German SS Officer with connections at the highest level. Otto too was having to reconcile but mostly compartmentalise his all-consuming and fanatical devotion to the Nazi regime with his unforeseen love for a beautiful French woman who disturbed him deeply. The fact that he would have to face a choice thrust upon him by his superiors filled him with much anxiety and trepidation.

Otto and Annette found themselves working harder now than they had been at any time previously. Jews were now being hunted mercilessly all over Europe and sent to concentration work and extermination camps mainly in Germany and Poland. Annette's initial acquaintance with this racial cleansing during *Operation Vent Printanier,* Operation Spring Breeze, twelve months earlier in the summer of 1942 when Jews had been rounded up and assembled in the Paris Vel.d.Hiv, had involved only those Jews who did not have French citizenship. However the net was now been cast wider and all Jews were being resettled for either work or extermination but usually both. Being at the centre of these French operations allowed Annette to pass on a constant catalogue of information via her contact Collette and thereby forewarn Jewish enclaves and communities of impending sweeps.

Since the humiliating defeat of the Germans at Stalingrad in the winter of 1942 the Russian war machine was grinding slowly westward towards Germany with relentless brutality and barbarity. There was a tangible sense in France that the tide of the war was turning. The consequence of this was that the initial timid, small-time and uncoordinated attacks by French resistance fighters were hardening and becoming more organised and overt and the Germans could no longer give them a low priority. Resistance cells were now being pursued relentlessly. Those captured were tortured and murdered, especially in Vichy France. Maquis resistance fighters were pursued viciously by the Malice, a paramilitary police organization comprising of fellow countrymen. The Maquisards were supplied with arms and equipment by air-drop from England but they also used stolen German arms especially MP 40 sub-machine guns which, they joked, were as common as hookers on the streets of Paris and got about as much action. At the moment, more worrying for the Germans was that resistance in the east was reaching unacceptable proportions with large groups of Jewish and Polish resistance fighters causing massive disruption behind the German lines whilst the Russians continued to advance. In the autumn of 1943 everyone knew that an Allied invasion of mainland Europe, opening up a second front, was coming. It was only the where and when that was unknown.

The French railway system was beginning to creak under the stress of demands for troop movements as well as shipping thousands of Jews to the east. Hitler's defensive system, the Atlantic Wall which stretched for 1,670 miles from Norway in the north to the Spanish/French border in the south was a monster devouring more and more time, resources and personnel and was requiring a massive transport infrastructure to deliver 17 million cubic metres of concrete and 1.2 million tonnes of steel in the Normandy, Brittany and Pas de Calais regions alone to feed its construction. The Atlantic Wall was not a wall in the sense that Hadrian's Wall in the north of England was a defensive system stretching right across the country in one continuous structure. Rather it had begun as a number of separate bunker and gun emplacements to protect the U-boat pens at Brest, La Rochelle, St. Nazaire and Lorient facing England across the English Channel. As the war dragged on and the knowledge that the Allies were left with no alternative but to attempt an invasion of mainland Europe Hitler insisted that the defensive shield be strengthened and Field Marshall Erwin Rommel was directed to take command of Army Group 'B' for the defence of Normandy. The formidable protective shield of Hitler's fortress Europe now consisted of pillboxes, machine-gun posts, massive bunkers and gun emplacements, mines and anti-tank traps on the beaches and hidden by high tides. Inland too, defences were strengthened in order to forestall parachute incursions.

French collaboration was there for all to see and involved civic authorities as well as commercial industries. Civil engineering companies were growing very rich by accepting contracts to build the fortress Europe defences with the use of slave labour. Annette kept London informed of these developments and the companies involved. But, she thought, what else could they do? Everyone needed to work to live and besides these same companies would be needed to reconstruct the country after the war so she guessed little action being taken against them when the war was over.

Annette had maintained her contacts with representatives of the French railway service the SNCF and her privileged position allowed her to pass on information to the resistance about train routes, deliveries and times as well as relaying information to London about troop movements and dispositions. There was an infectious neuroticism abroad which seemed to be affecting occupied and occupiers alike in hyper-activity.

Annette looked up as Otto approached her desk with a piece of paper in his hand. "I've been summoned to Berlin," he said in a serious tone.

"What's it about?" Annette enquired.

"I don't know," Otto lied, "But it must be important."

"I suppose I've been expecting this for some time. I can't ignore it."

"You've been in Paris for a long time now and I had a premonition that a new posting wouldn't be long in coming. When do you have to go?"

"I have to catch the morning train and I've no idea when I'll be back or even if I'll be back."

Annette moved round from behind her desk and threw her arms around Otto. "I've been dreading this moment for so long Otto, I don't want to lose you."

"Nor I you," Otto whispered into her ear. "I'll let you know as soon as I have any concrete news. Come and have dinner with me at the hotel this evening, I want to make love to you all night."

Annette immediately felt those involuntary tingling, rippling sensations that presaged a moist, swelling reaction. A need which demanded immediate satisfaction but in the circumstances left her with an urgent, uncomfortable, unresolved desire.

In spite of an expensive dinner washed down with her favourite Sancerre wine the meal was passed in a sombre mood. Otto knew that if he did return to Paris it would only be to hand over to his successor.

They made their way up to Otto's room each lost in their own thoughts, fears, anxieties and hopes. As soon as the door was closed behind them they were in each other's arms, then tearing off each other's clothes as carelessly and quickly as possible. Otto picked Annette up intending to carry her to the bed but she locked her legs around his waist. Taking him in her hand she forced him inside her Otto taking her weight with his hands under her thrusting bottom. Locked in a mutual headlong rush towards a climax they bit and scratched and squeezed. It was a combative embrace such that neither had experienced before and the release was so explosive that they both collapsed on to the carpet sweating, panting and eventually laughing.

"You're incredible," Otto whispered.

"And you've obviously taken your physical training sessions very seriously," she giggled.

They bathed together, made love together and eventually fell asleep entwined together.

* * * * *

The train slowed as it approached Frankfurt suburbs. Otto stared in disbelief at the scale of the destruction he witnessed through the carriage window. Railway tracks in the marshalling yards, some with sleepers still attached, pointed upwards in twisted agony as if some giant had ripped them up and tied them in knots leaving them looking, against the grey-smoke sky, like the black striated lines of some dissident, decadent, modern art. Bomb craters were everywhere as were freight wagons, which had been thrown up in the air and scattered at random like so many children's dice. Some reduced to blackened steel skeletons whilst others, still smouldered, spread acrid smoke on a light breeze. Shuffling labourers were everywhere collecting dead bodies and shovelling debris into craters. A pall of smoke drifted over the city buildings both industrial and residential. After Paris the scale of the destruction left Otto shocked and angry. Building after building was no more than a heap of rubble and those walls which remained standing bore the blackened scorch marks of intensive heat. Gable ends and roof timbers, which had not yet collapsed inwards, were exposed, naked, pointing accusingly towards the sky and still burning.

The train picked its way into Frankfurt station which itself had been badly damaged. Otto collected his overnight valise, stepped down from the carriage and made his way round piles of debris making every effort not to turn his ankle on rubbish yet to be collected. He approached a porter, "*Heil Hitler,*" and waited for a response.

The shell-shocked porter turned a vacant staring visage towards Otto, mumbled something and raised his right hand. "Where can I get the connection to Berlin?" Otto demanded.

"It usually leaves platform three but you'll have to go over there and ask if it has been redirected. You can see the place is a mess after yet another night raid. I don't know why those RAF pilots don't take lodgings here."

"Watch your mouth," Otto shouted, "Defeatist talk like that can get you into a lot of trouble with the Gestapo."

Because of the blackout, the streets of Berlin appeared bleak and featureless as Otto made his way through the exit of Anhalter Station. It had taken him a weary twelve hours to reach Berlin from Paris and he was beginning to wish that he'd taken the sleeper the night before. But a familiar stirring reminded him that he wouldn't have had a night of passion with Annette had he left immediately. His first priority now was to find an hotel, get a good night's sleep and ring Himmler in the morning to confirm the time of his visit.

Breakfast consisted of an unappetising selection of cold meats of indeterminate origin and bread rolls that looked as if they had been made with sawdust. His meeting with Himmler was scheduled for that afternoon so after breakfast Otto decided to fill in the time sightseeing. As he walked around it was obvious that so far, Berlin had escaped the massive air raids suffered by other German industrial cities. There were a few bombed out buildings but nothing on the scale of Frankfurt. The city was thronged with military and civilian personnel and the traffic incessant but no one seemed to be smiling as they hurried about their business. He was now in Potsdamer Strasse. Looking at his watch he was surprised to see that it was approaching noon already and after his meagre breakfast Otto was looking forward to a decent lunch. On his left he could see the distinctive cupola roof of the Weinhaus Huth. To his right was the famous Café Josty once the haunt of writers, artists, politicians and members of the international society. Apparently the café had changed names a few times recently and was now known as the Kaffee Potsdamer Platz.

The meal was satisfactory, the wine very welcome and the bill extortionate. Disgusted Otto made his way towards the Brandenburger Gate where he boarded the electric S-Bahn for Steglitz Zehlendorf. Himmler had a large house in the Dahlem district of Berlin courtesy of the Party. He left the train at Sundgauer Strasse and made his way to Dahlemer Weg where he eventually stopped outside Himmler's impressive mansion house. Making his way through the large front garden Otto reached the main entrance and rang the doorbell He was admitted by a maidservant and shown into an immaculately and expensively furnished lounge.

Before he even had time to sit down Himmler entered the room. *"Heil Hitler."*

"Heil Hitler." Otto responded.

"It's good to see you again Otto my boy," Himmler continued gesturing Otto to sit down. "How was the journey?"

"Tedious." Otto replied. "I think I'll take the sleeper in future."

"Probably wise." Himmler agreed. "Time's short so I'll get straight to the point. You know why you're here but first the good news....well... the first piece of good news. Your promotion has been agreed by the Fuhrer. Congratulations Major. But of course along with your promotion comes extra responsibility and I'm counting on you Otto to continue your efficient wrestling with the Jewish question. The situation in the east is giving cause for concern and we need someone to help bring back some stability and order. I expect rumours and lies have filtered west but the fact remains that there have been some difficulties, which I'm sure, would respond to your attention. I don't know what you've heard but the facts are that significant pockets of Jews are increasingly becoming a security risk and need to be eliminated as quickly as possible. In January this year an uprising of Jews in your old haunt of Warsaw had to be resisted but there is no doubt that their limited success encouraged them. During a Ghetto round-up in April the Jews again resisted. We know that they called on the Polish nationalist resistance to help them but were refused. SS Units finally crushed them killing to the best of our knowledge, 7,000 Jews in street fighting and another 6,000 in burning buildings. I ordered the Ghetto to be razed to the ground, all cellars and sewers to be filled in and bricked up. In fact all Ghettos in the east are to be eliminated and part of your duty will be to see that this is accomplished. As the numbers of Jews are reduced in the Ghettos you will see to it that the camps at Subibor, Belzac and Treblinka are wound down. There was even an attempted resistance at Auschwitz during the summer. Apparently, French resistance and Polish communist underground people together with other groups in the camp rebelled and had to be resisted by SS reinforcements. The Russians are making progress westwards and the Fuhrer wants all evidence of the camps to be eradicated and this also falls within your command. So...you see Otto...there is much work to do and I know that I can depend on you to play your part."

"I shall look forward to it Herr Himmler."

"Not so formal Otto, we're more or less off duty here so please call me Heinrich. Now...may I suggest a timetable for the remainder of your stay here in Berlin?"

"I shall be only too pleased to fit in with your arrangements sir." Otto replied knowing that he would feel uncomfortable using Himmler's Christian name.

"I propose that I phone ahead to my personal tailor and warn him to expect you later this afternoon. He can measure you up for your new uniform and will have it ready before you return to Paris to formally hand over to your successor. When you've finished at the tailors come back here because I've arranged a dinner in your honour this evening for 7.30pm and I'll introduce you to my delightful niece Sieglinde. Don't worry about an hotel, you must stay here this evening then tomorrow we can check your *Ahnentafel,* family tree, and make sure that your 'Marriage Certificate' is all in order although I'm sure that there will be no problem being as I personally shall endorse it. How does that sound?"

"Perfect," Otto lied.

* * * * *

The maid admitted Otto and immediately conducted him upstairs to a bedroom. His valise had already been placed on a chair and opening the door to an en suite side room she said, "Herr Himmler thought that you might like to freshen up before you come down to dinner sir."

"Thank you," Otto replied, "That will be all."

There was already a small gathering in the lounge when Otto entered.

"Come in my boy," Himmler said jovially whilst gesturing with his arm. "First things first, what can I offer you to drink? A schapps or a vodka perhaps to get you in the mood for your new posting."

"A schnapps would be fine," Otto replied.

"Let me introduce you Otto. This is my wife Margarete, Marga, and the apple of my eye my fourteen year old daughter Gudrun, my little *Puppi.*

Otto clicked his heels, kissed Marga on the hand and much to the delight of both Himmler and his daughter greeted Gudrun in exactly the same fashion.

"Marga lives in the country now but we get together occasionally for special functions."

This may be true but Otto knew that because of Himmler's affair with his secretary and fathering two children with her Margarete had left him in 1940 but there had been no divorce.

"My elder brother Gebhard Ludwig, his wife Hilda and their beautiful daughter Sieglinde."

"Call me Ziggy, everybody does. Sieglinde's such a mouthful and so formal don't you think?"

Just as the introductions were completed the maid entered the room announcing that dinner was ready. Otto offered his arm to Ziggy and escorted her into the dining room.

Otto's first impression of Sieglinde was that her looks were inoffensive. Her dress was a shapeless shift design but even so it was obvious to Otto that there were no feminine curves from waist to hips beneath the fabric panels. Her blonde hair was plaited and rolled into buns either side of her head whilst her breasts were ample in a matronly fashion rather than holding out the promise of sexual delights. That she would make excellent marital and maternal fodder Otto had no doubt. For all that she walked lightly and had an obvious athleticism about her.

"Are you looking forward to your new posting?" Ziggy asked Otto during the soup course.

"Yes I am," Otto answered with obvious enthusiasm in his voice.

"And do you think the Russians will continue to roll westwards towards the Fatherland?"

Otto had not been prepared for this level of conversation from Ziggy and was surprised by her understanding of the current situation in the east.

"Once we have eliminated all the Jews and Polish resistance behind our lines that will release more than enough men and hardware to deal with the Red Army."

"Oh I do hope so Otto," she continued.

Himmler turning towards Otto whispered, "I said to Gebhard here that you two were well matched Otto." Then smiling he continued loudly, "But enough of this heavy conversation, is the wine to your liking Otto?"

Otto picked up his glass, swirled the golden liquid round and looking at it proclaimed, "It's German."

There was silence for a few seconds whilst his simple reply was being digested then everyone burst out laughing. But Otto was not laughing inwardly. Annette's comment about German wines being too obvious and superficial reverberated around his head. He felt confused, disloyal and guilty that he hadn't given her a thought during his conversation with Ziggy.

Dinner finished the group made their way back to the lounge. The heat of the day still hung breathless and Himmler opened the French windows allowing the scent of roses to permeate the room. Turning to Ziggy he said, "Why don't you show Otto the garden Ziggy the camellias have been magnificent this year."

Otto followed her out into the huge garden at the rear of the house. Sheltered and protected by trees and shrubs it was impossible not to imagine that they were deep in the countryside instead of in a popular urban area of Berlin. Even though he had been brought up on a farm Otto was no gardener but he did appreciate the colours and smells of a well-tended garden. The paths meandered through so many different species of plants, bushes and shrubs some of which he recognised but didn't know their names. Japonica he recognised and rhododendrons and luxuriant fuchsias in different colour combinations. Ziggy and Otto sauntered along one path which navigated round a border which contained a luscious floral range of blue hues including campanula, delphiniums, agapanthus and geraniums. The scent was intoxicating.

Once they were out of sight and earshot Himmler turned to his brother and said, "Well, what do you think?"

"I think he'll do very well. He reminds me of myself when I was his age. You've chosen well brother. What's your opinion Hilda?" Gebhard asked his wife. "He's very handsome. I should think that he could have the pick of the girls and our Ziggy should be well satisfied. I got the impression during dinner that she was infatuated. But what about Otto, he didn't give much away. A bit deep I thought. But I can't wait to have blond grandchildren."

"Oh Hilda," Himmler said, "You women are all the same. Don't worry about Otto, he's as solid as a rock and very well thought of at the highest level. He knows where his duty lies and they make the perfect Aryan couple....so it's settled then....we get them married as soon as possible."

The sound of tinkling water offered the possibility of some cool respite from the heat. They sat on a bench in an alcove beside a large water feature where three bronze nymphs clinging to a tree stump spouted water from their mouths into the pond.

"You know why you're here?" Ziggy asked. Before Otto could reply she continued, "I'm sorry, I feel so embarrassed. I know that we're expected to do our duty for the Fatherland and I don't really have a problem with that but I would not want you to feel trapped and to end up hating me or yourself for that matter."

"I must confess that I didn't know what to expect. I've met a number of potential Reich mothers and they have all depressed me with their one-dimensional personalities. But I have to say Ziggy and I hope you don't think that I'm being condescending I've really enjoyed your company and conversation."

"You mean I'm not a retard then?" Ziggy challenged.

"Far from it," Otto replied laughing. "I mean we'll be able to have intelligent discussions when we're not too busy working to ensure the future continuity of the Aryan race."

"So you see it as potentially work do you?" She continued to needle.

"I can't believe I just said that," Otto replied with contrition. "No I didn't mean that, what I meant was…."

"I know what you meant Otto…..but be honest with me, do you see us having a future together?"

"Honestly…..if I have to do my duty for the Fuhrer I can think of no one I'd rather do it with than you. I don't mean that to sound dismissive and business-like. I like you, I really do and I think that we could make a happy family together. What about you?"

"Honestly…." She deliberately copied him, "I have met one or two animals in black uniforms and you make a refreshing change. You're successful, educated, very, very handsome and what girl wouldn't be flattered by your attentions. I say yes. Let's surprise the oldies indoors and give them our good news."

The next morning Himmler's family bid their goodbyes. Otto unselfconsciously kissed Ziggy on both cheeks saying, "Until next week."

"Yes," Ziggy replied, "I can't wait."

They stood watching the taxi out of sight, Ziggy leaning out of the window waving vigorously.

Turning to Otto, Himmler said, "I'm absolutely delighted for you my boy. Gebhard and Helga are equally thrilled and give you their blessing. Now let's get the paperwork out of the way then you can return to Paris to clear your desk before coming back for your wedding and new challenges in the east. Exciting times for you eh?"

"Indeed sir. I've brought all my documents with me in anticipation. I hope I've got everything."

"As efficient as ever Otto."

Otto opened a side pocket in his valise and took out a file. Opening it he placed a piece of paper on the table. "This is my family tree. You can trace it back two hundred years. Prussian Junkers on my father's side and Bavarian farmers on my mother's side, all pure German blood. My last SS medical report is here and I hope sir that you will give me a political reference. It might be a bit out of date now but I've also brought my Hitler Jungend Leistungbuch as continuing proof of my devotion to the Party."

"That's not in doubt Otto."

"I've also got passport head and shoulders and full-length photographs. I think that's everything."

"Everything is in order as is Ziggy's application. I'll order both sets of details be entered in the SS Clan Book, you're marriage certificate will be registered and the happy event can take place as soon as you get back here from Paris."

Otto slept fitfully on the overnight sleeper train back to Paris. A short while ago his life and career were mapped out clearly and he felt the luxury of being in control of his own destiny. Then unexpectedly Annette happened and whilst this new dimension in his life was welcome and could be accommodated the happenings of the last two days had created a complication that was beyond his control leaving him frustrated and angry. Lying awake listening to the wheels clacking their way along the track his mind played over and over again different scenarios as he considered various options and their possible outcomes. There were too many imponderables, too many unpredictable events which would yet shape his future. Being pragmatic, marriage to Ziggy was not negotiable. He would have to keep this fact secret from Annette and his posting to the east would solve this problem for the foreseeable future. Any further difficulties or problems would have to be dealt with as and when they occurred. The thought of lying to Annette troubled him but he convinced himself that because of his love for her it was the best thing to do in the circumstances.

It was late morning by the time Otto arrived at his office. Annette looked up as he entered and it was all she could do to stop herself from running across the room and throwing herself into his arms. Otto saw the spontaneous projection of her love and his heart skipped a beat. He kissed her demurely on each cheek the physical effort of constraint almost killing him in the process.

"Oh I've missed you so much." Annette whispered breathlessly.

"Me too," replied Otto meaning it. "Let's talk later. Take the rest of the day off and I'll meet you at the hotel for dinner. I have a lot to do here and not much time to do it in."

"Does that mean that you're posting has been confirmed?" She asked quietly.

"I'm afraid it does but we'll discuss it tonight." Otto kissed her on the cheek again then quickly disappeared into the corridor.

The atmosphere at dinner was flat and subdued. Each had secrets that they could not reveal and which impinged on their relationship begging the question as to whether their relationship was real or just a fantasy. Could they really enjoy or even expect true love when key elements of their relationship were based on lies and deceit. And yet when they were alone to consummate their love the feelings and emotions were real enough at the time. Can there ever be such a thing as guilty love? The oxymoron had Annette confused. Surely true love is open, free, honest, safe and spiritually enhancing not closed, fettered, dishonest, unsafe and emotionally diminishing she wondered as she sipped her wine and looked at Otto over the rim of her glass. She had encouraged the relationship for one reason only and had then discovered that human emotion cannot always be bridled. Guilt was eating away at Otto too. He was lying and deceiving Annette and she deserved better than that. She loved him and had given herself to him and yet he was prepared sacrifice her on the altar of political dogma and personal self-important gain. Twelve months ago he would have looked her in the eye without any regret about his deception but somehow she had become a splinter that refused to be plucked out, could not be ignored and focussed all attention.

Dinner finished they made their way up to the bedroom where they made love slowly, languidly and controlled as if each wanted to cling to the other for as long as possible, afraid that the climax might signal the end of something more than just the release of a physical tension.

"When are you leaving?" Annette asked quietly her head resting on Otto's chest.

"I'm catching the sleeper to Berlin tomorrow night," he replied breathing in the scent of her tousled hair.

"And then you're heading for the eastern front," she enquired.

"Yes, as we suspected, that is where I'm being posted. There is much to do there if the Russians are to be stopped."

"Do you believe that Germany can still win the war Otto? Since Stalingrad the Russian war machine seems limitless and the Allies are massing for an assault on the mainland sooner rather than later. Can Germany really sustain a war on two fronts?"

"Apart from one or two setbacks, granted, but the Fuhrer has outmanoeuvred the Allies so far and will continue to do so."

"I know what you will be doing in the east Otto. I have helped you round up French Jews but I did this thinking that they were being resettled for labour purposes. I am being honest with you when I say that I have been disturbed by rumours which have been spread west about what is really happening in the camps in Poland, Silesia and Czechoslovakia."

"These people are the enemies of Germany and as in all wars enemies must be eliminated. There must be no new generations left to continue or renew revenge wars in the future. There must be peace, surely you can see this."

"I am worried for us. I am worried for you Otto.

"I will come back for you." Otto said stroking her right breast. He was not sure he believed this but it was what he knew she wanted to hear.

"Have a care Otto. Whoever fights monsters should be on their guard that in the process he does not become a monster himself. I know that you're overwhelmed by the national dream of a master race and that any attempt to question this will be a lonely and frightening place to be. But no price is too high to pay for the privilege of owning your own soul, of owning yourself. All human beings are ends in themselves, don't use them as a means to your own end. Promise me my love that you will think on these words when you are out there doing your duty for the Fatherland. If you gaze long enough into the abyss, the abyss will gaze back into you.

CHAPTER 16

Annette 1943

They made love with a desperation borne out of their impending loss. Their sweating bodies still entwined Annette whispered, "Come back to me Otto."

Stroking her breast Otto replied, "Whatever happens I will always come back for you. You must remember that. I love you." As soon as he'd said it Otto was overtaken by the guilt of his deception. So much depended on the outcome of the war. Whether Germany won or lost he knew that Annette would be there for him. Either way he would have to keep her ignorant of his service record in the east. He was certain that deep down she didn't approve of the methods the party was using to create a pure German Race and lebensraum in the east. Then there was the complication of Ziggy. If Germany won how was he ever going to reconcile his marriage with his love for Annette? Even if Germany lost the war he would still be married. The thought of telling Annette the truth never entered his head. Being pragmatic and a fatalist Otto resolved to believe that something would turn up and that things had a way of working out.

Annette knew what Otto's posting to the eastern front entailed. She knew what his mission was and she asked herself how she could love such a brute. How could she lie in the arms of someone complicit in the deaths of thousands of innocent people and yet there was something intangible which drew her to him. A sensitivity of which he himself was unaware and which she believed she could touch. She shivered.

"Are you cold my dear?" Otto asked concerned.

"No, I think someone has just walked over my grave."

"Your grave! My goodness… how serious…well…we'll just have to try and bring you back to life won't we?"

It was mid-morning before they eventually dressed to face the day.

"I'd dearly love to spend my last day with you but I'm afraid I'm going to have to be occupied with official business all day. I have a lot to do before I catch the sleeper for Berlin tonight."

"What about me?" Annette asked with concern. "What will become of me whilst you're in the east?"

"I've given that a lot of thought," Otto replied. "I did wonder about you coming east with me but that's not a place for a woman and anyway I don't think I would have been given permission. Besides, since the Russians held Stalingrad at the beginning of the year they've been advancing west slowly but surely and I wouldn't want you falling into the hands of those animals. I did consider an apartment in Berlin but recent developments have made that impossible as well." Otto couldn't elaborate on what those recent developments were and he hoped that Annette wouldn't ask. "All things considered I think it might be best if you stay on here in Paris. I'll ask my ex comrades to look out for you so at least you'll know that you'll be safe. If you want, I'll arrange for you to continue your work at SS Headquarters as an interpreter come secretary come consultant. That way you'll earn decent money and should be able to have a better standard of living than other Parisians."

"Would it be possible for me to just work part-time? I don't think I could bear to look at your desk every day with someone else sitting there," she lied. "I haven't seen my cousins in Rouen and Clermont in Vichy for years and I'd like to spend some time with them whilst you're away. Do you think you could spare some time to arrange for me to have documentation to travel anywhere outside Paris without being harassed by the Gestapo? I know it's an imposition when you've got so much else on your mind at the moment."

"Consider it done sweetheart. Now I really must be going. I don't know what time I'll be finished at headquarters so can you be at the Gare de l'Est for 22.15 to see me off?"

"Of course I can."

They embraced and kissed deeply and longingly. "Until tonight," Annette whispered.

"Until tonight," Otto replied. He turned quickly leaving Annette standing alone in the hotel room her head whirling with a myriad thoughts.

Back at her apartment Annette took a calculated risk and sent a short message to her contact in Grendon to the affect that she was going to meet up with her original contact cell in Rouen and could they relay the message for her.

The rest of that day passed slowly. Annette sauntered along the left bank of the river, crossed over the Pont Saint-Michel and made her way towards their favourite cafe on the Parvis Notre-Dame. She ordered a cassis and sat watching the world go by. The shortages of occupation were now having a severe effect on Parisians. It had been a while since Annette had had the time to notice such things and she was shocked by the appearance of ordinary people as they walked past, some eyeing her with ill-disguised contempt. Clothes were shapeless and shabbier than she remembered. Shoes were scuffed and although there had been attempts to clean them it was obvious that they were not going to last much longer. Faces were gaunt and sallow from the lack of nutrition and Annette felt a pang of guilt.

A quick changing palette of varying shades of pink, red, yellow and orange dappled the sky as the sun fell with alarming speed towards the horizon causing the shadow of the Eiffel Tower to creep with menace up and down buildings and across pavements and boulevards. Making her way towards the Gare de l'Est Annette suddenly realised that the time between the present and her glass of cassis near Notre-Dame earlier that afternoon was a complete fog. She couldn't remember where she'd been or what she had done to fill in the time. Her mind was a blank. Approaching the station entrance her temporary amnesia was overtaken by a pounding in her chest. She felt that her heart was about to burst. Her head felt as if it was expanding fit to explode and her ears buzzed like a swarm of hornets. Although the ambient temperature was still pleasantly warm her hands were icy cold and she had to consciously instruct her legs to keep her upright and move forward one after the other. Even though the hour was late the station was busy mostly with German military the curfew keeping civilian Parisians off the streets. She looked at the departure board and made her way towards the Berlin sleeper train which was standing like a huge black, malevolent, mechanical dragon, panting, hissing, spitting and spewing smoke across the platform. Cylinders violently vented jets of steam into the atmosphere. Where the shaded electric lights imbued the cloud with a fluorescent ghostly glow a dark amorphous shadow gradually coalesced into the unmistakable silhouette of Otto. She rushed towards him flinging her arms around him and burying her head on his chest. "Otto," she said, "I'm going to miss you so much....more than you'll ever know."

"I know. I'll miss you too. I'll try to write but if you don't receive any letters it doesn't mean that I've stopped loving you. You must know that I'll be occupied with my duties."

"I understand. I love you, you know that but let me say something and promise me that you'll give it some thought."

"Oh dear, this sounds very serious."

"Well......I suppose it is in a way but just promise me that you'll think about where your duty lies and what your real duty is. Look into your heart and ask have you really made your choice of duty by free will? I mean.....have you really thought about what the responsibilities of your duty entail and is your duty to yourself and your conscience or is it to another authority? I suppose what I'm saying is, duty can be a concept created by superior authority to trick us into falling in line with their will. Demanding a sense of duty is a subtle, psychological device to control people and bend them to another's will."

Annette knew that Otto was no fool and she realised that she should beware of forcing him into making a choice between her and Adolf Hitler although this was the seed she was trying to plant. Stretching the credibility of Otto's love for her and that she was treading on dangerous ground by challenging his submission to the will of the Party and Adolf Hitler during his formative years. Perhaps she had gone too far and was laying herself open to suspicion as anti-Nazi. And yet her motives were to hook, to try to touch that spark of humanity which she sensed, knew for sure lay dormant like a seed waiting for the spring warmth and rain to bring it to flower. Having risked precipitating the first drops Annette moved on to lighten the conversation.

"Let me know where you are and I'll write to you but I expect that you'll be moving around a lot so my mail may not catch up with you but remember that you'll always be in my thoughts and prayers. Look after yourself and come back to me."

Reaching into the inside of his tunic Otto pulled out a leather wallet and extended it to Annette. "Here, before I forget, are your travel documents and all the authorisation you'll need whilst I'm away. You should have no trouble. I've informed my successor and if by any chance there is a problem contact him and he'll vouch for you." He framed her face with the palms of both hands and drew her lips towards his. How long the embrace lasted Annette couldn't tell but the emptiness she felt when they finally broke apart opened a potent chasm between them.

"I must go," Otto said quietly.

"I love you Otto. Oh...here...I nearly forgot. I've bought a little present for you. Open it on the train and think of me every time you use it and always remember what I've said....if you give love you'll receive it but if you give hatred you'll receive that in return and it will eat you up. Look into the abyss my darling and it will look back at you and destroy you. Don't let that happen to you Otto, I love you too much."

"I love you too," Otto replied. "And thank you for the present. Whatever it is I shall keep it with me always."

He showed his papers to the guard at the gate, turned and walked down the steam and smoke shrouded platform gradually dissolving into a nebulous, dark, shapeless shadow which floated away from her and all too quickly ceased to exist.

In a cacophony of noise the train shunted and clanked its departure into the unknown. Annette stood, rooted, staring at her future disappearing into the gloom. She shivered, turned and walked slowly out of the station where she was immediately challenged by two Gestapo officers. She showed them her papers and they backed off sullenly, partially in undisguised contempt but also because they had been deprived of another victim.

The next morning Annette made contact with Collette in the park. "I'm leaving Paris for a little while," Annette informed her, "So don't be alarmed if I'm out of circulation for a while. Otto has finally left for the eastern front so I'm taking the opportunity to join my original cell. For obvious reasons I won't tell you where."

"Be careful Annette, the Germans are very jumpy at the moment. They know that an invasion is coming sometime. The resistance is becoming more adventurous and this is really pissing them off so keep your wits about you. *Bon chance.*"

"Thanks Collette. *Je te verrai plus tard et prendre soin,* I'll see you later and take care."

They kissed on both cheeks and Annette watched as Collette made her way back to her office.

* * * * *

The train to Rouen was so crowded with soldiers that it had the ambience of a troop transport rather than that of a normal civilian train. Annette managed to secure a window seat but the rest of the compartment was jammed with soldiers whose rifles, kit bags and bayonets became entangled resulting in curses, blasphemies, much pushing and shoving and bad-tempered scuffles. Except for two male civilians who kept their heads down and made no attempt to make eye contact with their fellow passengers. It was a boring stop, start kind of journey and even the passing countryside couldn't relieve the tedium. She was aware that the nearest group of soldiers had been eyeing her up for some time and their sexist, ribald comments amused her, especially when one of the group, egged on by his comrades, eventually plucked up the courage to address her in his schoolboy French. *"Qu'est-qu' une jollie fille comme vous... errr....emmm...fait voyager sur....son propre? Ou allez-vous?"* "What's a pretty girl like you doing travelling on her own? Where are you going?"

"Je vais a Rouen pour voir mon cousin. Ou allez-vous?" "I'm going to Rouen to see my cousin. Where are you going?" Annette replied pleasantly and it amused her to hear the young soldier struggle to make himself understood especially as his comrades were feeding

him chat-up lines in German and enjoying his naïve attempts to gain her attention.

"If your cousin is as pretty as you I have a friend who would love to meet her."

"I don't think that you or your friend have enough time. You look as if you've got other things to occupy you. Where did you say you were going?" Annette asked casually.

"I've no idea," the young soldier replied. "We're being transferred to a place called Caen wherever that is....but it's got to be better than fucking Poland," the young soldier spat out.

"Oh!...I thought you Germans were keen to be in the east," Annette said smiling.

"Believe me, it's a shit hole. The Poles are filthy scum and the Russians are like hordes of vermin swarming all over the place. And the women are ugly hags not chic like you." The conversation was proving difficult for his level of French and he interjected German here and there.

"So...the fighting is tough out there."

"You could say that. You shoot one Russian and ten more pop up. So I need a beautiful girl to take my mind off it."

"I think that the peaceful Normandy countryside will do that for you," Annette said calmly. To keep the conversation going so that she could pump the young soldier for information Annette used some basic German but not enough and not in a precise grammatical way that would reveal her fluency.

"I don't think so," he continued. "I don't know what's up but there's a lot of movement at the moment towards the coast so I don't expect any rest which is why I think that you could help me relax."

"I don't think that you would have the stamina for what you have in mind after your efforts in Poland," she replied in German much to the raucous amusement of his comrades. At this the young soldier visibly shrank in embarrassment as his comrades waved their crooked little fingers at him. Annette was left to complete the journey unmolested although from that moment on some of the whispered comments she overheard were less than complimentary.

Pierre was waiting for her as she exited the gate from the platform. They embraced briefly and kissed each other's cheeks. "Welcome back to Rouen Grace," Pierre said using Annette's code name. "David is waiting in the car outside. Let's not waste time as the gendarmes and Gestapo are stepping up security in the region."

They walked purposefully out of the station and crossed the square heading in the direction of the old Citroen parked in the shadow of a narrow alleyway. Annette climbed in to the back seat, leaned forward and shook hands with David who was seated behind the steering wheel. "Good to see you again Grace," David said. The engine coughed into life and he steered carefully out into the city traffic. "We managed to avoid any road blocks on the way here so we'll take the same route back to the farm," David suggested. As predicted the journey was without incident although there were a lot of military vehicles on the move.

"The Germans are putting a lot of effort into strengthening their Atlantic defences," Pierre said seriously. "They're obviously expecting the invasion but my guess is that they don't know where or when. But they're certainly moving in a lot of matériel and personnel. We've got wind of a shipment of munitions being trained through here for the coast so if you're up for a bit of fun you're welcome to join us tomorrow night."

"That's what I've come for," Grace replied. "I hope my time in Paris hasn't turned me soft. For obvious reasons I can't tell you what my orders were but I've missed the excitement of practical, hands on contact."

"Well…I hope we don't actually have any hands on contact but I can certainly guarantee some excitement," David volunteered. "There's been a huge increase in traffic and we've been very busy lately trying to disrupt their transports." They finished bringing Grace up to date with their recent missions just as they entered the farmyard. After a much appreciated evening meal Grace settled down in the bunker hidden in the farm yard barn and eventually drifted into a restless sleep.

Twenty four hours later Grace was crouching down making her way along a hedgerow together with Pierre, David and six other local resistance fighters. The field had been harvested and they were careful not to give their presence away by standing on and snapping the dry brittle stubble. Pierre knew the area like the back of his hand and had planned their route avoiding known road blocks and check points. What he could not guarantee was their luck as regards chance, unscheduled patrols which were becoming more frequent.

"We have to cross the road here," Pierre whispered. "We'll cross individually, the rest providing covering fire if necessary." Grace crouched down in the ditch her Sten gun aimed up the road. David lay beside her looking down the road in the opposite direction. "Go," Pierre whispered as he waved Bernard, the first one across the road. Grace was next, keeping low she ran across the road, jumped into the ditch and immediately took up a defensive covering position for the rest of the group. It was a warm night and the ground was firm. Visibility was limited but only so long as the restless clouds covered the full moon. The group needed to scan the skies as well as their surroundings on those occasions when they had to cross open ground. Single file they walked carefully through a dense wood. Pierre stopped suddenly, raised his hand. The small group crouched down and Grace imagined that her deep breathing could be heard all over the wood. German voices and laughter could be heard over towards the right where a road block had been set up on a narrow road running through the wood. Grace listened to the guards' conversation about their last leave in Rouen. Pierre lifted his hand in to the air and directed his palm towards the left indicating a route avoiding contact with the Germans. Ten minutes later they reached the edge of the wood. There were fifty yards of flat clear scrub land ahead of them before it sloped upwards forming an embankment along which ran a railway line.

"The track starts to run downhill from here all the way towards the coast," Pierre whispered to the assembled group. "About five hundred yards from here it makes a turn to the left and that's where we'll give them a big surprise." Turning to Bernard who worked for the railway company he continued, "You're sure the maintenance shed is just down here."

"It was yesterday when I was at work," Bernard replied sarcastically. "The tools are all there and I was last to leave making sure that the door padlock looked as if it was locked."

"Good," Pierre answered, "Then let's use the edge of the wood for cover as far as we can."

The group edged its way parallel to the track and eventually stopped, the maintenance shed clearly visible across the open ground. There were two railway sidings and other small workshop buildings on the site. Derelict wagons rotted and rusted against buffers with the black, oily, coal dirty detritus of rail transport lying abandoned everywhere. Bernard now led the group towards the shed. He unhooked the padlock and they slipped inside leaving two of the group outside to keep watch. Knowing exactly where the tools were kept Bernard handed out four huge spanners and the steel tubes necessary to give extra torque to the spanners. In the darkness of the cabin and in his haste to lift the spanners out of the tool box other tools were displaced with a loud metallic clattering. The group stood frozen, holding their collective breath and listening for the sound of German voices. When no challenge materialised they retreated down the embankment and made their way towards the bend in the track.

Once in position Bernard directed four of the group towards a section of the track on the outside of the bend whilst the remainder took up sentry positions. The four placed their Sten guns on the ground within easy reach and offered the spanners up to the bolts holding the rail fish-plates in place and slipped the steel tubes onto the ends of the spanner handles. Leaning on the tubes with all their strength the four men grunted and gasped quietly as the bolts, one by one gave way, were unscrewed and removed.

"Why are you not using an explosive charge?" Grace whispered to Pierre.

"We resorted to this method of sabotage when we ran out of explosives," Pierre responded. "Besides, loosening a section of rail is fool proof and works every time. With an explosive charge there's always the possibility of a misfire. Not only that but with a charge we have to wait until the train arrives before we can press the plunger and that means that we're still close to the scene when the Germans respond with search parties. This way we can leave the rail loose a long time before the train arrives and we can be miles away before all hell breaks loose."

With the fish-plates removed guaranteeing a derailment the party returned the tools to the shed. Bernard locked the padlock and the group returned to their original assembly point making sure to avoid the previously contacted check-point. The group shook hands and split up each making his way home before the early light of dawn made their progress more hazardous than necessary.

Back at the farm the continuous blare of klaxons echoing around the countryside signalled that their night's mission had been a success. Hidden in the farm bunker Grace could hear German soldiers searching the barn above her head and although she was certain that she wouldn't be detected the anxiety she felt gave her an adrenalin rush which translated into a feral instinct for self-preservation. She waited quietly her Sten gun pointing up towards the bunker trap door in the ceiling. After what seemed like hours but in actual fact was no more than fifteen minutes Grace heard officers shouting, recalling their men and the sound of lorries making their way out of the farm yard and onto the road away from the farm.

Subsequent radio contact with Grendon relayed to Grace London's urgent need for information about German progress with their Atlantic defences on the Normandy coast. Grace needed no elaboration about what was required in terms of troop positions and movements, positions and types of bunkers and ordnance and coastal and beach defences in general. It was a dangerous mission and given the jumpiness that the Germans were displaying at present, one that would need careful planning and Grace discussed the feasibility of her proposed plan with Pierre who agreed to help.

Once again Grace found herself sitting beside Pierre in the front of his battered Citroen except this time the rear seats were occupied by a bicycle and not fellow resistance fighters. They entered Rouen without any trouble their prepared cover story being that Pierre, being a farmer in the region, needed to see his bank manager. Pierre parked in a side road near the railway station and helped Grace manoeuvre the bicycle out of the back of the Citroen. They embraced and kissed on both cheeks.

"Good luck," Pierre said with obvious concern. "Don't take any silly chances. You'll be away for a while but contact me as soon as you get back to Rouen and I'll arrange for you to be picked up." He kissed her once more on the cheek and saying, "God go with you," quickly climbed back into the car.

"You look after yourself too. Don't try to win the war all by yourself. The end is definitely coming and you want to be there to celebrate."

Grace looked on as Pierre graunched a resisting first gear into engagement and the black Citroen lurched out into the main road traffic. Suddenly feeling alone and isolated after the close camaraderie she'd experienced during their recent resistance missions against railways, communication centres, telegraph exchanges and storage depots, Annette wheeled her bicycle across the road and entered the station. She arranged for her bicycle to be put in the guards' van at the rear of the train and bought an open return ticket to Deauville on the Normandy coast.

Late summer had slipped and crept away without Annette consciously registering the fact. As a wind off the sea blew down the streets of Deauville its chilling effect shocked her into realising that autumn had suddenly arrived overnight. She pedalled away from the station towards the sea front conscious of the pistol in her coat pocket rhythmically knocking against her thigh. A determined military presence was obvious the closer Annette got to the beach and she turned off the main road and began a search for an anonymous hotel in the narrow streets between the Rue Victor Hugot and the Boulevard Eugene Cornuche. Releasing her valise from the rear pannier frame and removing her over-night bag from the handlebar basket Annette left her bicycle in the courtyard. She registered into the small hotel for one night and surrendered her identity card to the scruffy, monosyllabic concierge. "Room three, up the stairs, on the left." The lighted cigarette stub bobbed up and down on his bottom lip as his growl broke into a hawking smoker's cough.

She put her valise and bag on the single bed and surveyed her surroundings. At best it could be described as basic. Where a carpet pile still remained it looked greasy and was ingrained with years of dirt. In the doorway, beside the bed and in front of the sink Hessian backing threads poked through holes scuffed by the tread of countless guests. Red flocked wallpaper was peeling away from the walls where they met the ceiling revealing stained, damp patches and the smell from the wash basin plumbing couldn't be ignored. At least the bed linen was clean even if the blanket edges were frayed and dangling down touching the floor. Annette decided to find somewhere to eat and then do a reconnaissance of the harbour area. She found a small café in the Rue de la Mer and sat at a table in the window. The young waitress brought her some vegetable soup and a glass of red wine. Whilst enjoying the hot broth Annette gazed out of the window with a professional eye noting everything of military importance.

The whole of the sea front was fenced off the only access being through specific guarded gates. The scene appeared chaotic and manic as a constant stream of commercial lorries delivered building materials and covered military wagons delivered what she surmised were armaments. Having finished her meal Annette walked west along the left-hand side of the Boulevard Eugene Cornuche. The other side of the road was off limits because of the boundary fence which made it impossible for her to see what was going on in the various industrial storage depots, warehouses and fabrication factories. The whole area between the boulevard and the beach and promenade was a hive of activity both civil and military.

The evening was closing in fast and Annette decided that it was time to retrace her steps back to the hotel before curfew. She entered the hotel, approached the desk and asked the concierge for her key. No one else would have registered his quick glance and nod towards a man sitting in the corner of reception reading a newspaper but Annette was immediately on the alert. She heard the rustle of the paper behind her whilst at the same time a voice said coldly, *"Bon soir Mademoiselle Hugo."*

Annette turned round slowly to see a man, about forty years old, in a long grey raincoat and wearing a trilby hat sitting in the shadows. He was looking down at an identity card in his hand.

"Do I know you?" Annette asked calmly.

"I ask the questions, you answer them," came the flat, emotionless reply.

"You are a long way from home Mademoiselle. What is your business here?"

"Not that it's any business of yours but I'm here on a cycling holiday." Annette answered steadily.

Reaching into his coat pocket the man withdrew a small leather folder and flicking it open revealed that he was a member of the Gestapo. "Everything in this town is my business," he replied with a proprietorial sneer. "It's a strange time of year to be taking a holiday." Standing up and approaching Annette the Gestapo officer continued, "Perhaps you'd better come with me and explain what this….holiday of yours entails."

Annette knew that most Gestapo officers were bullies, thugs of low intelligence with the mentality of petty officialdom. The one thing they did understand was authority and their place in the hierarchy of things and in this instance she decided that attack would be her best form of defence.

Rummaging in her handbag and taking out a folded card she handed it to the officer. Switching to her impeccable German Annette took the man by surprise, raised her voice and expressing annoyance continued, "Perhaps you'd better take a look at this before you decide to take anyone anywhere." She stared straight at the man and knew that she had the better of him when she detected the merest hint of defeat register in an almost imperceptible twitch of his eyes. Waiting a few minutes and letting the full effect of her personal SS sponsored identity card impact on the officer she continued, "Now….unless you want me to contact SS headquarters in Paris with your name and rank I suggest that you let me get on with my well-earned holiday without petty Gestapo interference." Whereupon Annette drew herself up to her full, imposing height swung her right hand in to the air and shouted, *"Heil Hitler."*

The Gestapo officer was thrown completely into a turmoil and like the automaton that he was gave the Nazi salute and responded with a loud *"Heil Hitler."*

"Make sure you know who you're threatening next time," Annette continued showing no weakness. "Now get out and leave me alone to enjoy my official leave of absence."

The atmosphere in the lobby was electric and his attempt to apologise was ignored by Annette who turned round to go up the stairs. Realising his blunder the Gestapo officer slunk out of the hotel. The collaborating concierge failed to meet Annette's stare and shuffled some papers pretending to be doing some administration.

"A bread roll for breakfast please and I'm sure that you can find some real coffee for me," she said to him as she mounted the stairs.

"Oui Mademoiselle avec plaisir," came the obsequious reply and Annette smiled to herself as she put the key in her bedroom door lock.

With Deauville at her back Annette was enjoying the freedom and solitude of cycling west along the coast. The wind had dropped, the sun was shining and there was a clean, freshness which made Annette feel good to be alive. She had scrutinised her map of the Normandy coast the previous night, and memorised her route to Carbourg before returning the map to its hiding place at the bottom of her valise. To be caught with a map in this region was not something she cared to contemplate. In her handlebar basket she had two, well-thumbed books on the fauna and birds of the area. Her prepared cover story was that she was a keen ornithologist and was on holiday whilst her fiancé was away on the eastern front. However the various birds were code for the different types of defences she was hoping to identify. Large sea birds, gulls, indicated large twelve or fifteen inch naval guns. Smaller birds of magpie size indicated eighty eight millimetre artillery and similar whilst blackbirds and thrushes represented machine gun nests and finally tits, sparrows, robins indicated positions of trenches and troop bunkers with mortars and hand weapons. She would mark these positions on her map each evening.

Cabourg was approximately fifteen miles from Deauville. Annette knew that the coastal road would need to be negotiated with care. The route was well built up and the military presence everywhere. The towns of Villers-sur-Mer and Houlgate could present her with opportunities to be stopped and searched. A little further inland the area was less densely populated with hamlets and farms separated by woods, copses and agricultural land. Annette left the main road and continued her journey through the countryside. Reaching the top of an incline she stopped to catch her breath. Lifting her bicycle up she negotiated her way through the hedge and found a discrete hollow where she could lie down undetected from the road. Taking out her small binoculars she panned the coastline. With a sharp intake of breath she was stunned by the extent of construction being undertaken. Bunkers, machine gun nests, batteries, depots and trench systems from east to west as far as she could see. Workers, like a colony of ants, swarmed the sites. Making a mental note of the positions of what she'd seen Annette hauled her bicycle back on to the road and continued her way westwards.

The road was not as quiet as Annette had expected as civilian and Wehrmacht lorries overtook her sometimes accompanied by wolf whistles and obscene shouts from the back of troop transports. Highly alert now Annette noted that these lorries diverted into fields and woods where the construction of pill boxes and machine gun posts were being erected and camouflaged. It became obvious that a second line of defence was also being constructed with a clear firing line towards the coast.

Without further incident Annette reached Cabourg and as at Deauville she searched out a discrete hotel. Fortified by an evening meal Annette set about transferring her stored information onto her map. It was obvious that the Atlantic defences were going to be a formidable obstacle to any planned seaborne landing.

The programme for the next day was the same as that for the previous. Annette set out for Arromanches on the coast, another ride of approximately fifteen miles. Her legs ached a little initially but she soon got into a rhythm and made good progress. Free-wheeling downhill she rounded a corner and immediately spotted a road block in front of her. It was obvious to her that they too had spotted her and it was too late for her to do anything but ride towards them and try to bluff it out. Two guards were standing either end of the barrier and a third sat in the side-car of a motorcycle polishing his machine gun with a rag. One of the guards stepped into the middle of the road and held up his hand. Annette braked to a halt.

Annette made the opening gambit with confidence, "Good morning officer, it's a nice day."

"Good morning mademoiselle. Papers please," the soldier said pleasantly enough. Annette detected straight away that by his accent he was not German. She handed over her identity card and the travel document Otto had given her. He walked over to his corporal and showed him the papers. They talked quietly but Annette couldn't hear what they were saying. After a few moments he returned to Annette asking, "Where are you travelling to and for what purpose?" Annette repeated her cover story and the young soldier seemed satisfied. With a smile he lifted the barrier and in that moment Annette thought that there might be an opportunity to glean some useful information. Taking a bottle of Calvados she'd bought that morning in Cabourg from her basket she handed it to the young soldier. "It must be boring standing here day after day," she said, "Here, take a swig from this." The soldier looked over towards the corporal who nodded approval. The soldier unscrewed the top and took a good swallow. Wiping the back of his hand across his mouth he handed the bottle back to Annette who pretended to take a drink then passed it on to the corporal who in turn walked over to the soldier sitting on the motorbike. Annette engaged the young soldier in conversation. "You're not German are you?" She asked.

"No I'm Polish," came the reply.

This caught Annette completely by surprise but she showed no emotion to the information. "Really, you're kidding me. What's a Pole doing in the Wehrmacht?" She asked trying to be as innocent as possible.

"It was a choice between being worked to death in a concentration camp or joining the German army. What would you do?" Lowering his voice he continued. "Besides, there are a lot of us Poles in the area and if an invasion does land in Europe we intend to desert and join the Allies."

Annette retrieved her bottle, placed it in her basket and got on her bicycle. Waving goodbye she shouted, "You boys be careful."

Later that night and using all the skills she'd learnt during her training Annette approached the cliff tops just outside Arromanches. Avoiding guards who were carelessly talking in loud voices she approached as close as she could to a massive battery. Noting the geography of the emplacement it was a position of massive strength with all calibres of armament, trench systems and troop bunkers. She crawled back inland from the coast and carefully found her way back to her hotel without detection.

The final leg of her reconnaissance trip the next day took her to Grandcamp-Le-Bains where further evidence of construction and troop concentrations were noted. Pleased with the success of her fact finding tour Annette boarded the train from Carentan to Rouen where she contacted Pierre who picked her up and took her back to the farm.

The following night, together with four more resistance fighters, Annette and Pierre prepared the landing site by knocking a straight line of wooden posts into the earth with muffled mallets. The last post off-set to indicate the wind direction at ground level. Torches were placed on top of the posts ready to be switched on then the six of them retreated to the hedged seclusion of one corner of the field. The cold damp mist hung like a fluffed up cotton wool shroud and circled malevolently chilling fingers and silently insinuating itself into stiff limbs until Annette had to consciously stop herself from shivering. The waiting became intense. A pick-up or drop-off were always times of exposure to danger. There was a hazy full moon and visibility was intermittent. Annette was conscious that the light breeze was from the south blowing any early engine noise away from them with the possibility that the plane might overfly their position before being heard. Any circular sweep would take up precious minutes increasing the chance of enemy detection.

"There!" Annette whispered. "Did you hear something?"

"No," Pierre answered, "I can't hear a thing."

The group strained their ears, "There, there it is again," Annette whispered more urgently this time. The distinctive drone of the single engine advancing and retreating in response to the precociousness of the wind. The group rushed out each person running to their allotted post switching on their torch. The drone of the Lysander engine was now constant and getting louder as Annette fumbled with frozen fingers to flash her recognition code. Her relief was instant when the correct response was flashed back to her. The matte black machine hung in the air like some pre-historic pterodactyl silhouetted against the cold silver light of the moon. The plane circled once allowing the pilot to assess the wind direction and then instantly dropped over the tree tops and bumped down in to the field. The tail swung round and the door was flung open.

Remembering her training Annette approached the aircraft from the right. Any attempt to reach the plane from the left would have been met with gunfire from the cockpit and the plane would have taken off instantly. Cases of arms, ammunition, explosives and luxuries like coffee and cigarettes were quickly thrown out onto the ground followed quickly by another SOE agent.

"Merde alors," Annette said as she rushed past the new operative.

"Merde alors," he responded and was out of sight, swallowed up by the ground mist in seconds. Annette quickly climbed up the fixed ladder. The pilot was already revving for take-off before the door was closed behind her.

CHAPTER 17

Otto and Ziggy 1943

Otto exited Anhalter Railway Station and stood transfixed. He couldn't comprehend the change which met his eyes since his last visit. A number of the buildings in front of him were either smoking, smouldering ruins or completely burnt out shells their fire-blackened, jagged walls reaching up into the sky in silent supplication and painful, agonising lament. He made his way down Potsdamer Strasse in bewildering disbelief. How could the Fuhrer have allowed this to happen to the capital city of the Third Reich? Motor traffic was tripping its precarious way down the road weaving in and out of piles of stones, bricks and rubble where they had collapsed into the street.

Staring in numb despair Otto's eyes were drawn to a first floor apartment where the front wall had been blown out to display the residents' privacy to all voyeurs. Bedroom intimacy embarrassingly exposed as a stained double mattress drooped limply hanging in space and the double bed precariously balanced at a drunken angle on shattered, ruptured wooden joists a metaphor for the owners' disintegrating lives. A tattered, torn bed sheet flapped like a flag of surrender. Intimate personal lives and belongings to be picked over and rifled through by family and strangers alike.

Civilians with shovels and buckets scrambled over the fallen masonry like so many ants trying to repair their damaged nest. For as far as he could see down the street Hausfraus with brooms were intent on keeping the pavements clean and clear of obstructions. He watched an old man carrying a hand shovel and bucket shuffling along on the other side of the road. He was dressed in a shapeless, dowdy suit and battered trilby the colours of which Otto could not discern under the veneer of plaster, brick dust and the layers of memories of nights of terror in some dark, airless cellar.

Most were bent double as if succumbing to the metaphorical exertion of trying to hold up their city's crumbling buildings. Passing the

Brandenburg Gate Otto was relieved to see that the S-Bahn for the Dahlem district was still operating although his journey to Himmler's house was eventually interrupted by rail tracks which had been torn up and a collapsed building which had brought down the electrified wires. Together with other passengers, Otto was forced to leave the tram and walk the rest of the way. There was less evidence of air raid damage in the suburbs and Otto's anger began to subside as he walked down Dahlemer Weg with its affluent mansions on either side of the road.

The doorbell was answered by Himmler himself. "Come in Otto, we've been expecting you. How was your journey? Not too tedious I hope."

"Hello Sir. No, not too tedious. I slept most of the way but I see you've had a visit from the RAF."

"Yes, they're being a bit of a nuisance off and on at the moment but Göring tells me that the Luftwaffe will soon have them swatted from the skies. But enough of the war for now. We have much more important matters to attend to today, eh! I expect that you'd like to freshen up after your journey. You can have the same room you had on your last visit and it's far enough away from Ziggy's room. Mustn't see the bride before the big moment eh.....we don't want to tempt bad luck do we? As a small wedding present from me I've left a brand new dress uniform in your new rank of Sturmbannfuhrer, Major, on the bed." Slapping Otto on the back Himmler continued, "When you've changed come down into the garden to meet the rest of the family and have a good stiff schnapps to steady your nerves."

"Thank you sir....what can I say....you've been too kind already."

"Nonsense my boy, The Reich needs men like you and this is my way of saying thank you for your enthusiastic support. Now get up those stairs, get changed and we'll commence this celebration in style. Everything's ready and we're just waiting for the two stars."

Otto stood by the window in his room looking down into the garden at the assembled guests. Heinrich was being the good host and circulating talking to groups of people Otto didn't know. He recognized Himmler's wife Marga and their daughter Gudrun and his brother, Gebhard Ludwig with his wife Hilda, his future father and mother-in-law. An imitation altar had been set up on the lawn with rows of chairs facing it. A bronze eagle statue and photograph of Adolf Hitler stood on the altar flanked by bouquets of flowers. Between the ranks of chairs and the altar was a large wrought iron arch decorated with large blooms and green foliage. A red carpet led from the house, across the lawn and up to the altar.

Otto sagged against the deep blue velvet drapes in the window recess. What am I doing here he thought? I could be in Paris in the arms of Annette. It's her I should be contemplating marrying not some brood mare chosen for me by the state. Who the hell am I? Did I ever consider that my middle name would be deceit? What am I? Do I control myself, my own destiny even, or have I surrendered every last drop of self-determination to the Nazi Party? Where do I end and where does the Nazi Party begin? Are we really one and the same he pondered? The thought that he should even contemplate considering these things had never ever entered his head before. The doubt he felt was unsettling and uncomfortable. His fist clenched the curtains as a rising anger quickly overwhelmed all other thoughts and emotions. Turning away from the window Otto caught a glimpse of someone staring at him from that mystical shadow world which exists on the other side of the mirror. Caught off guard for a fleeting moment, suspended in an unresolved reality Otto snapped back and was immediately admiring the tall, handsome, athletic figure staring back at him the black, crisp uniform projecting a larger than life aspect which dominated the room. Otto drew himself up stiffly to his full height, pulled his jacket down getting rid of any unwanted creases, flicked his cheek with his left hand clicked his heels together and closed the bedroom door behind him.

Schnapps was replaced with champagne and suddenly amidst much back-slapping and poor-taste jokes the world suddenly appeared a better place. Time was suspended in a perpetual round of introductions and aching cheeks from too much forced smiling. Suddenly from somewhere in the crowd a lone voice shouted *"Heil Hitler"* followed by everyone raising their right arms and echoing, *"Heil Hitler."*

Himmler was suddenly beside Otto ushering him towards the altar whilst all the other guests made their way to the rows of seats. A bugle fanfare split the air and everyone turned round to see Sieglinde and her father stepping out of the house and onto the red carpet. Tentatively, Otto also turned round and was surprised by his reaction. Ziggy appeared quite stunning, statuesque even. She was not as overtly beautiful as Annette but her features were even and flawless and her make-up did an excellent job of appearing to thin out her rounded cheeks. She was wearing a cream, silk dress cut on the bias and which fell straight to the ground from just under her ample bust. Otto remembered that she had a full figure but given her height the dress was well chosen to disguise the fact. Her long blonde hair had been woven into plaits and coiled into two circles one either side of her head in traditional German style. As Ziggy and her father approached she looked quite radiant and Otto commiserated himself with the thought that he could have done a lot worse.

"We are here today to witness SS Sturmbannfuhrer Otto von Lieper and Frauline Sieglinde Himmler offer their vows of marriage to one another and to reaffirm their loyalty to the Fuhrer, Herr Hitler and The Reich." Himmler officiated over the brief, civic ceremony and closed the proceedings by saying, "I offer the newly-weds bread and salt as the symbols of life. All of us present can see what fine examples of Germania these two young people make. We wish them a long, happy and productive marriage. The future of the Fatherland is in their hands. I give you Herr Otto und Frau Ziggy von Lieper." And turning to Otto continued, "You may kiss the bride now."

Amidst much hand clapping and cheering, Otto turned towards Ziggy who moved in closer, sensually moulding herself between his outstretched arms, her kiss with soft, open, wet lips imparting a sensation which took him completely by surprise. With unanticipated reluctance Otto released Ziggy as a second bugle fanfare ripped through the air and from nowhere ten SS officers formed a guard of honour, their ceremonial daggers raised to form a tunnel through which the newly-weds walked arm in arm whilst the guests showered them with rose petals.

"Welcome to the family Otto," Gebhard Ludwig Himmler said pumping Otto's hand up and down. "We couldn't have wished better for our little girl could we Hilda?"

"Our daughter is a very lucky girl Otto. If she doesn't come up to your expectation let us know and we'll sort her out for you," Ziggy's mother said as she laughed and kissed Otto on the cheek. Gebhard Ludwig led Otto over to a table where bottles of champagne stood in iced buckets. Hilda turned towards her daughter and continued, "I expect you to make this marriage more than just a duty Ziggy. You make a fine looking couple and he's so handsome as well as being marked for high office in The Party."

"I know mother, trust me, I can tell that there's a connection between us. We'll be very happy together believe me. Now, where's that champagne?"

"I know it probably doesn't affect you just yet," Gebhard continued as he poured himself and Otto another flute of champagne, "But don't you worry about finding somewhere to live. Brother Heinrich and I have decided to combine a wedding gift and there'll be a house for you to come back to when this war's over."

"What can I say?" Otto responded. "It's very generous of you sir.... of both of you....you're spoiling us....we're very lucky. Thank you sir I really appreciate what you're doing for us."

"Think nothing of it Otto....nothing's too good for our Ziggy and I can tell that you'll be very happy together...oh and by the way, it's Gebhard from now on." They broke off their conversation as Heinrich approached with something in his hand. "This came for you Otto," and he handed Otto a telegram. Otto put his drink down on the table and slowly took the envelope from Heinrich knowing that in these days a telegram was usually the harbinger of bad news. But it couldn't be that. His parents and grandparents were all dead. It couldn't be from Annette for she had no idea where he was. His thoughts were brought to an abrupt end as Heinrich interjected cheerfully, "Come on then Otto.... open it....we're all curious to know what it says."

Otto slipped his forefinger into the envelope and split it open. Slowly removing the paper and scanning the contents the look of anxiety was replaced immediately by one of excitement as he read out loud, "Congratulations on your wedding. The Fatherland is grateful for your service and devotion to duty." It was signed by Adolf Hitler.

"Well done Otto, the Fuhrer is taking a personal interest in your well-being. What more does a man want? You have a beautiful bride waiting for you and the personal support and praise of our Fuhrer, surely this is more than one man can stand."

"Stop teasing Heinrich," Hilda scolded. "What a fantastic day this has turned out to be. We couldn't have wished for anything better."

"Here, here. Come on the buffet's been set out, let's soak up some of this alcohol."

With the party in full swing Heinrich invited Otto into the lounge. "I hope you don't mind Otto but I've booked you and Ziggy a room at the Adlon Hotel near the Brandenburg Gate for tonight. I've put a staff car at your disposal for your remaining time in Berlin. It's waiting for you outside whenever you're ready."

"Thank you, however can I repay your kindness? It's been the most wonderful day."

"Think nothing of it dear boy. But now down to business before you set off." And handing Otto a large brown envelope he continued, "These are your detailed orders. You can read them later but in short I have the feeling that some camp commandants are stealing from the Reich by embezzling money off the top when hiring Jews out for labour to factories. Plus, consignments of dental gold have been turning up on the black market here in Germany and it could only have come from the camps. I'd also like you to assess the military situation at the front. I'm not sure we can trust the Wehrmacht's opinion. I sometimes think that they have their own agenda which conflicts with Hitler's. What's the status of the Red army and do we have the strength to hold them or force them back. It's a wide brief, I know, but you'll have my complete authority to demand whatever it takes. I know I can trust you to deliver a comprehensive report and that it will take you into next year but remember it is vital and you are to report to me only. Do you understand? The report is for mine and Hitler's eyes only."

"You have my word that I'll do my utmost sir."

"Enough said then. Now.....isn't it time that you whisked that beautiful bride of yours away for some time on your own?" Heinrich concluded as he ushered Otto back outside.

The garden was now in shadow and noticeably cooler but the exotic scent of roses still hung heavy in the air as Otto approached Ziggy who was engaged in animated conversation. He made his polite excuses as he put his arm around Ziggy's waist and steered her away from her friends. Otto was surprised by his reaction to the feel of Ziggy's yielding but firm flesh under her dress.

"We should leave now," He whispered to Ziggy. "I'm sorry but I have orders to entrain for Poland tomorrow so we'll only have a few hours together before I have to leave you on your own."

"Well then....we'd better see to it that we make the most of what time we have," Ziggy responded squeezing his hand.

They said their goodbyes to the assembled crowd outside Himmler's house and climbed into the waiting car. They waved their hands out of the car windows until it turned a corner and their family and guests were out of sight. Ziggy snuggled up to Otto on the rear seat and putting her head on his chest exhaled a long contented sigh whilst the car made its way towards Berlin's most celebrated hotel.

* * * * *

A bottle of champagne had been left in an ice bucket on one of the bedside tables and Ziggy shouted, "Oooooohhh! "As Otto popped the cork. He'd had enough to drink but it was something to do to hide the awkwardness he felt at being alone with Ziggy. It had all happened too fast, out of his control.

"Here's to us." She said, raising her glass to Otto.

"To us." He responded.

Ziggy tipped the glass up too far and bubbles exploded in her mouth effervescing their way down her nose. Coughing and spluttering Otto rushed his handkerchief up to her face and dabbed her mouth and chin. He could feel her warm sweet breath as her soft enveloping lips closed on his. Otto put his arms around her and without having to physically draw her to him Ziggy once again smoothly moulded her body to his. She opened her eyes and smiled a mischievous smile at Otto's immediate response against her thigh. "Undo the buttons," she said breathlessly into his ear. Like a teenage virgin, his fingers trembled and fumbled their way down her back until the smooth silk dress whispered its way onto the floor as she stepped back. Otto was overwhelmed by how radiant Ziggy looked. Her long blonde hair was now tumbling down over her shoulders and nestling in curls on her full, round breasts whose large, light pink nipples thrust forwards. Her waist, wide but in proportion, round but firm, swelled out into fecund hips and strong, shapely legs. Any remaining unfamiliarity or nervousness was quickly overtaken by lust as they pulled, dragged and tore what remained of their clothes from each other. Seeing Otto standing naked triggered an instant response in Ziggy who knew instinctively that the wetness between her legs was not perspiration. She felt swollen, heavy, engorged and yet empty with a violently urgent need to be filled, to grasp to draw all life into her.

As if responding to a starting gun they rushed towards each other crushing lips against teeth, tongues probing mouths. With no deference to finesse or sensitivity Otto pushed Ziggy onto the bed and her legs were spread even before he fell on top of her. No hands were needed as he plunged into her unhindered. No need for foreplay, delicate teasing, exploring each other's bodies just abandoned desire expressed in a rush for self-gratification with thrusting, grasping bodies, breathless gasps and grunts, the slap, squelch and slurp of wild, urgent, primeval sex.

Later, sweating, satisfied, satiated, Otto slipped away from Ziggy with his right leg and arm still resting across her body.

"I knew it would be like that the first time I saw you. It was even more fantastic than in my imagination." Ziggy whispered breathlessly. Otto stroked the back of his hand across and under her breast feeling it roll, rise and fall back again pinning his fingers to her chest and she moaned gently. "That will be my first investment in the *Mutterehrenkreuz*, Mother's Cross of Honour," Ziggy continued. "Only seven more children to go and I will be awarded the First Class Gold Medal. But let's settle for a four or five kinder bronze for now."

"Do you really believe that you're pregnant already?" Otto asked propping himself up on one elbow.

"How could I not be after that?" Ziggy replied laughing. "A woman knows."

"Is that all I am to you then.....a stud to sire for a brooding mare?" Otto fired back with annoyance conveniently forgetting that he had deceitfully married her to secure his military and personal advancement.

"How can you say that Otto, I'm just teasing you? But you can't blame me for being broody as you put it....we'll have been married just twenty four hours when tomorrow morning you'll be off to the eastern front and who knows when I'll see you again. It doesn't matter how long it takes for us to have children but what does matter is that we can look forward to days and nights like this trying." The tension subsided and Otto reached across to pick up his champagne accidentally spilling some across Ziggy's breast. "Ooooh that's cold," she squealed, whilst involuntarily jerking her arms up knocking Otto's hand and spilling more of the bubbly liquid. In one movement Otto deposited the flute back on to the bedside cabinet lowering his face into the deep cleavage between Ziggy's breasts. Immediately his tongue was unsuccessfully trying to catch the rivulets of champagne. Ziggy's response was instant with a low quiet moan as she pushed both breasts together either side of Otto's face. Extricating himself Otto reached for the champagne bottle, took a mouthful of the fizzing liquid and locked his lips around the nearest nipple whilst at the same time massaging her other nipple with an ice cube he'd retrieved from the ice bucket. The sensations of the cold champagne then Otto's warm, teasing tongue and the ice cube caused Ziggy's nipples to become rigid and expand sending involuntary, rippling sensations infusing the centre of her building excitement with an urgent demand for release.

When it arrived, Ziggy's orgasm was accompanied by a long loud scream and uncontrollable muscular spasms from which, when he was eventually released, left Otto gasping for air. Grasping, clutching and jerking ceased, Otto was content to allow himself to lie enfolded in the luxurious maternal sanctuary of warm soft flesh. Ziggy revelled in the weight of Otto above her and with her legs still around his she was reluctant to allow him to leave her naked and void.

Eventually, Otto made his way to the washroom followed by Ziggy. The night had drawn in unnoticed and making their way back to the bed they straightened the sheets and cuddled up, Ziggy manoeuvring her bottom into Otto's groin like two spoons in a drawer. Otto stretched his right arm across Ziggy holding as much of her right breast as he could.

"Good night husband," Ziggy whispered.

"*Heil Hitler,*" Otto responded with a smile from behind her back.

The next morning Ziggy woke lying on her left side to feel the stirring of Otto's morning erection pressing with insistence against her. She was not sure whether Otto was awake or not but the thought that he might still be asleep appealed to the devilish side of her nature. And besides, if he was asleep he wouldn't be for very much longer. She lifted her right leg, bent forward and reaching back between her legs guided Otto into her. Initial movements were gentle and slow but she could feel Otto's increasing girth fill her. Fingers teasing her nipples and squeezing her breasts informed Ziggy that Otto was now very much awake as he altered position slightly to drive deeper still inside her. Once again their joint rhythm was synchronised in a rising crescendo to end in yet another exhausting climax.

"*Heil Hitler,*" Ziggy whispered, giggling, as Otto rolled out of bed and walked slowly towards the washroom. He sank down into the invigorating hot water which filled the bath. Within minutes he was joined by Ziggy displacing water all over the bathroom floor in the process.

"You will be careful won't you Otto. I've heard a lot about the eastern front and none of it good. The Ivans are animals who are torturing, murdering, slaughtering and raping anyone in their path whether they be soldiers, resistance, or civilians and even their own escaped prisoners of war so I've heard. I want more nights like last night."

"I don't expect to be doing much fighting," Otto replied flatly. "My orders are to gather information for your Uncle Heinrich. I'll be travelling behind the lines and don't expect to see an Ivan, except in a concentration camp, let alone engage him in fighting." Otto soaped Ziggy's breasts and continued, "Don't you worry. Go back home and wait for me and I'll come back to you just as soon as duties allow."

The staff car put at their disposal was waiting at the entrance to the hotel as previously arranged. There had been no RAF raid the previous night which had allowed workmen to attempt to patch up the city's disrupted transport and services. Ziggy and Otto sat in silence as the large, black Mercedes manoeuvred its way along the Tiergarten and on through the Wilmersdorf and Charlottenburg districts until they finally alighted in the district of Grunewald not far from Dahlem where twenty-four hours before they had become man and wife. It was clear that summer was dying as boulevard tree leaves were beginning to take on their autumn hues.

They approached Grunewald Station when without warning Otto ordered the driver to stop. He grabbed Ziggy's arm and helping her out of the car continued to guide her under a railway bridge. "Where are we going?" Ziggy asked surprised, "The station entrance is further up the road."

"I just need to check something out," Otto replied matter of factly.

"It's a dirty marshalling yard for goodness sake," Ziggy answered in exasperation, trying hard not to soil her cream coloured shoes with oil and coal dust.

"There," Otto pointed, "Gleis Siebzehn (Track 17)."

Ziggy followed the direction of Otto's outstretched arm. Ignoring the scattered ranks of industrial rail wagons littering the numerous rail sidings her attention was focussed on a train of cargo wagons at the far end of the complex. Standing beside the wagons was a long queue of people. As they approached closer to the monochrome, amorphous mass of people individuals became more apparent. The woman nearest to them stood close beside a boy who was clearly her son, her head tilted forward looking at the ground. A patterned but faded headscarf rested on her eyebrows and was knotted behind her head. Beneath the folded line of the scarf her sunken eyes were lifeless and unblinking. A black overcoat with large military style collars reached down to her ankles where oversized shoes anchored her to the ground. Her son, probably about ten years old wore a wool cap which had slipped slightly to one side so that the long peak almost covered his right eye. His pale, blank, expressionless face staring unseeing, uncomprehending. A shapeless jacket with a prominent yellow Star of David stitched to the lapel hung from his shoulders pulled out of shape by the weight of his right hand in the pocket. His left arm reached across to his mother and his hand was held in his mother's left hand her right arm resting round his shoulders. Oversize baggy trousers ended just below his knees to reveal spindly white legs terminating in scruffy shoes whose unfastened laces lay like worms on the black, dusty ground. Old men and women, children and mothers with babies. Very few young men were evident.

"Are they what I think they are?" Ziggy asked.

"Yes," Otto replied. "Jews" he spat out flicking his left cheek.

"They look rather pathetic ambling slowly in line like that." Ziggy added.

"At least there's fewer of them now than there used to be. This whole marshalling yard used to be filled with thousands of them waiting to be shipped off to the east. Those you see over there are the last few hundreds remaining in Germany. Soon Germany will have eradicated the whole race from our soil and in a little while longer we'll have rid the whole of Europe of their presence."

Ziggy linked her arm through Otto's and clung on tightly.

Just when Otto decided he'd seen enough three lorries snarled, rattled and bumped across the yard coming to a halt beside the already assembled queue. Wehrmacht soldiers ran to the rear of each lorry throwing back the canvas flaps shouting, "Aus, aus." Bodies jumped, fell, tumbled and were dragged out of the lorries and forced to join the end of the line. Those who were too slow or infirm to do as they were ordered were kicked, prodded with bayonets and beaten with rifle butts.

Things appeared to be under control as Otto and Ziggy turned away but they were attracted by a commotion beside the third lorry. One of the soldiers yelling, "Stop or I'll shoot" was joined by his comrades and the crack of rifle fire split the air. A youth had broken free and was running and leaping over the railway tracks away from the queue. In his haste to put as much distance and freight wagons between himself and the soldiers the young boy was unaware that he was heading straight towards Otto and Ziggy. Once he looked up and saw them he skidded to a stop, his arms flailing in the air, his head glancing quickly round, wide eyes looking for an escape route. Otto was just about to release his Luger from its holster but was beaten to it as Ziggy had already withdrawn a small Beretta M1935 automatic from her handbag. In one smooth efficient movement she levelled the gun and fired two shots in quick succession. The youth fell instantly, unmoving.

"You have more than one talent then," Otto said enquiringly with a wry smile.

"Oh, you haven't experienced half of them yet," Ziggy replied conspiratorially.

They watched dispassionately as soldiers hustled two Jews to drag the dead body away and throw it into one of the wagons. Turning to go back to the main road, Ziggy looked at Otto and continued, "I wonder if I can get a refund on his train ticket," and they both emerged from the tunnel arms linked and laughing.

The main station entrance was modelled on a castle gate. They passed through the doorway and after scrutinising the departure board walked towards the platform where his train for Warsaw was waiting. They stopped at the gate whilst Otto's papers were checked.

"I'll miss you so much,"Ziggy said almost whispering. "I've known you for such a short time and yet I feel as if I've known you all my life."

"I'll miss you too," Otto responded trying to sound as sincere as Ziggy.

"I'll write to you as soon as you let me know where you are."

Instantly Otto had a feeling of déjà vu and he struggled to hide his confusion. Were his feelings for Ziggy simply ones of convenience and lust? And what of Annette? Was beautiful love just a deceitful lie after all?

To Otto's relief the railway guard shouted the final call relieving him of having to continue the pretence. "I must go," he said, taking Ziggy in his arms. "I might be too busy to write so don't be alarmed if you don't hear from me." He walked through the gate and onto the platform. Ziggy's eyes followed him into the billowing smoke and hissing steam, a scene more like Armageddon she thought, than a scheduled train departure.

The train clanked and then jerked just as Otto found his berth. Annette was still on his mind and he was just about to put his valise onto the luggage rack when he remembered the present she'd given him when he'd left Paris. He rummaged in his bag and pulled out the small package. The carriage rocked and swayed and wheels squealed on steel track as it negotiated the multiple points leaving the station and he had to brace himself from overbalancing. Once seated, Otto ripped off the brown paper to find the parcel gift wrapped with a card stuck to it. Tearing the card off he read, 'My love, always, A.' He put the card in his pocket and teased the shimmering golden paper from its contents. In his hands was an exquisite silver brandy flask. Around the flask were thin leather straps arranged in a cruciform so that the flask could be fastened to a belt. At the top and placed over the stopper were three small, silver cups inside one another and held in place by a leather strap locked down by a press stud. Engraved on the front was a proud stag elliptically framed by the branches of large bushes. He turned it over and read on the back in German,

Trink mich in Liebe und nie Ager.

Meine Liebe immer und ewig.

Annette.

Drink me in love and never in anger.

My love always and forever.

Annette.

Otto removed the stopper and put the flask to his nose. The distinctive aroma of French Cognac alerted his taste buds. He poured some of the contents into one of the small cups. Reading the engraving once again he threw the brandy down his neck and spiralled into deep depression.

CHAPTER 18

Annie 1943 – 1944

Annette was unexpectedly thrown forwards then backwards in her seat as the Lysander came to an abrupt halt below the control tower. The pilot cut the engine and said over the intercom, "Terminus, last stop for Tangmere, Sussex." Annette opened the door and climbed backwards down the ladder fixed to the side of the aircraft.

"Welcome home Ma'am."

On hearing English spoken Annette was immediately on her guard. Her instinct for personal survival was finely honed and it took her a good few seconds to adjust to the unfamiliar surroundings of home.

"I'm your driver Ma'am. Orders to take you up to London I have," the corporal said, holding open the rear door of a W.D. black Humber.

"Thank you corporal," Annette responded weakly as she sank into the soft luxury of the cracked, black leather seat. The heat inside the car moulded itself round her like a soft, soporific inducing comfort blanket protecting her against the cold outside and it was not long before Annette fell into a deep sleep.

"We're here Ma'am," the corporal said looking back from the driver's seat. Annette woke with a start and immediately her hand reached automatically for the pistol in her coat pocket. She relaxed as the corporal continued, "Sorry to startle you Ma'am but we're here, Orchard Court, Portman Square. I believe you're expected. Allow me," he said enthusiastically getting out of the car and opening the rear door for Annette.

"Thank you corporal."

"That's all right Ma'am, my pleasure….all in a day's work. Good night then Ma'am or maybe I should say good morning."

Annette stood in front of the entrance to one of the Special Operations Executive (SOE) many offices in the Baker Street area of London. She turned to look up at a white slashed sky, the harbinger of a cold dawn creeping into the empty city streets. Negotiating the maze of walled sand bags she entered the building and made her way towards a reception desk manned by a young lance corporal. "Good morning Ma'am, name please."

"Annette Hu......sorry, Lieutenant Annie Charlton."

"You're expected Ma'am, up the stairs and first door on the left marked office 'F'."

Annie walked slowly up the wide marble staircase, found office 'F' immediately and knocked gently on the door.

"Come in." A female voice filtered through the oak door.

Annie walked in and was relieved to see the familiar faces of Vera Atkins and Captain Selwyn Jepson as they levered themselves out of brown leather arm chairs. A fire was burning brightly in an ornate Adams design marble fireplace. Annie could tell from experience of her home life on the farm at the north end of the mining village of Chepfield in County Durham that the colour of the flames and the drawing of the fire was communicating a cold frosty atmosphere outside. The image conjured up of cosy nights sitting by the coal fire in the farmhouse during the severe northern winters seemed like a lifetime away, a different world, an alien, fantasy existence. Captain Jepson gestured towards a third chair placed in front of the fire. "Welcome home Lieutenant Charlton."

"Welcome home Annie," Vera added with warm sincerity. "We're so pleased to see you back safe and sound. Sit down and get warmed through, winter's on its way I think. Would you like a cup of tea?"

"If I may, I'd love a cup of real coffee instead of the ground acorn ersatz stuff they're drinking in France these days.....with the added luxury of one sugar lump if I'm not being too presumptuous."

"Not at all," Vera responded and turning towards Captain Jepson continued, "I'll see to that Selwyn."

"We just wanted to welcome you back straight away...... informally as it were.....you understand. It must feel strangely disorientating for you, so the programme is that we'll take you to a safe house in Montague Mansions just off Baker Street, about five minutes from here and leave you to have a good night's sleep or at least what's left of the night."

Vera re-entered the room. "Here's your coffee Annie, just as you ordered." She said quietly with a soft smile on her face.

Selwyn waited until Annie had sampled her thick, sweet coffee then continued, "Write up your report and we'll collect you and bring you back here for your debrief at 1300 hours. We're anxious, eager even to hear what you have to say."

"You've done exceedingly well Annie, you've fulfilled and more, the expectation we placed on you. Have a well-earned rest and we'll see you again in a few hours."

Annie luxuriated in the feel of a soft mattress and clean, white linen sheets. In no time at all she was fast asleep. There was no room for ghosts or jumbled memories to disturb her slumber. Total shut down.

All too soon she was startled awake by a young girl in a WAAC's uniform carrying a tray with a plate of bacon and fried eggs, toast and a pot of tea. "Sorry to disturb you Ma'am but I had orders to wake you at 1000 hours if you weren't already awake."

"That's all right," Annie responded stretching and yawning. "Just put it over there."

"Whilst you're having breakfast and a bath I'll bring you a typewriter for your report Ma'am. I'll come to collect you at 1230hours and accompany you to Orchard Court. If you need me for anything else just pick up the phone and it will get straight through to me. If that will be all Ma'am I'll leave you to enjoy your breakfast."

"Thank you," Annie replied, "Bacon and eggs, ooooh! It's like a banquet. Do you know how long it is since I've had a breakfast like this? Don't ask, but thank you anyway."

"You're welcome Ma'am."

After breakfast Annie sank into a deep hot bath and lay relaxing until the water cooled to tepid warm. Brisk towelling down stimulated the circulation teasing and tingling her skin to a pink glow. Returning to the bedroom she immediately noticed a clean uniform on the bed and a typewriter and paper on the dressing table. Feeling rejuvenated and ready to face whatever the day had to throw at her Annie dressed quickly and then began to rummage in her bag for her maps and notes. She scrolled some paper into the Remington, interlocked her fingers and cracked the joints to loosen them and began click clacking the information which had been filed away in note books and in the back of her head. For a while she was back in France, flashbacks as vivid as reality itself. Eventually she sat back and stared at the last nine months of her life reduced to a number of foolscap pages. Leaning back on her chair Annie rotated her cramped shoulders then got up to stretch her legs but was diverted by a knock on the door.

Seeing Annie in uniform the young WAAC saluted smartly then said, "I've come to accompany you to Orchard Court Ma'am."

"Okay, just let me gather my things together and I'll meet you downstairs.

Ten minutes later Annie found herself being ushered into the same room she had been in only hours earlier.

"Let me present Major General Colin Gubbins. He's Deputy Director of SOE. Captain Jepson you already know," Vera gestured introducing the personnel in the room.

Captain Jepson commenced the meeting. "We'll read your report later Lieutenant Charlton but for now give us a verbal outline. I generally find that what is presented in this way is often the uppermost important information in the agent's mind and the emphasis of this sometimes gets lost in the detail of a written report. In your own time."

Annie was clear and concise in her telling of what had transpired since she dropped into France. Her work with the Rouen resistance group. Her contacts in Paris and how she had managed her prime objective of securing a contact within the upper echelons of the occupation forces in Paris. She related how she had been arrested and beaten by the Gestapo in a radio sweep and how her target, SS Hauptmann Otto von Lieper rescued her, a significant indication of his trust in her identity. Her involvement in the Paris Jewish, Vel'd'Hiv Round-up and warning Jews of impending arrests in Paris and other major cities through the resistance network was listened to intently and there were significant glances between those listening in the room when Annie mentioned her introduction to and conversation with Adolf Hitler. She also mentioned the number of failed attempts to assassinate Hitler the significance of this being that Germany was beginning to feel the strain of total war and that the Wehrmacht High Command and Hitler and his political party supported by the SS were no longer in harmony on future military strategy. Suspicion and conspiracy were eating away at the heart of The Reich and this lack of trust was significant in the mission her contact von Lieper had been given by Himmler, in effect, to spy on the Wehrmacht forces in the east and report back to Himmler and Hitler only. The Russians in the east were giving cause for major concern and the date of the impending allies' invasion of the European mainland was a thorn in Hitler's side with the probability of having to fight on two fronts. They knew that it was coming but not where or when. "The Germans in the west are very jumpy," Annie continued to relate. "And the resistance is having a hard time trying to stay one step ahead."

"What about your reconnaissance to Normandy?" Major General Gubbins spoke for the first time.

"With your permission sir," Annie stood up and spread her map of Normandy on the table. The small group gathered round and Annie continued. "I cycled from Deauville along the cost as far as Grandcamp-le-Bains, here. I used bird watching as my cover and documents supplied by von Lieper ensured that the Gestapo and Wehrmacht Feld Gendarmerie were kept off my back."

"You must have really impressed him," Vera interjected looking straight into Annie's eyes both women knowing what didn't need to be said.

Relieved to be able to divert her eyes back to the map Annie continued, "I used a system of bird size to illustrate the size and position of armaments and redoubts. As you can see here and here, casemates of large naval guns and here, here and here 88mms, machine guns and mortars. I've marked their positions clearly and I think that what you can see emerging are two main lines of defence interspersed with interlocking strong points each supported by the other's fire giving defence in depth. Where the beaches shelve gently into the sea, particularly here at Arromanches, steel girders are being welded together for positioning as tank traps. I wouldn't be surprised if they're not arranged to funnel any landing armament into killing zones. There was something else which puzzled me. They were sinking posts into the beach at a particular height so that they are covered at high tide. I learned that mines were to be placed on top of each post. Otto....I mean, von Lieper thinks that some of the high command in the west think that Normandy is the site for a landing but the word is that Hitler is convinced that any landing there will be a feint and that the main attack will come at Calais. As a consequence Hitler is determined to build up his heavy armament and panzers in the Calais region. One further bit of information that might be useful. I spoke to some Wehrmacht soldiers at a road block who were in fact Polish. They said that there were a number of Poles in the area. They'd chosen to join the German army rather than rot in a concentration camp but they told me that it was their intention to desert to the allies when they eventually landed. The resistance continues to disrupt the deliveries of materiel, guns, ammunition etc. and building materials in an effort to slow down the construction of the Atlantic Wall as Hitler has called his defence. The Germans are being ruthless in reprisals. That's my general overview sir but there is more detailed information in my written report. Is there anything else you need to know now sir?"

"If.....Otto....did you call him...von Lieper has been transferred to the east where does that leave you in terms of your contact with the Germans in Paris?" Vera asked.

"I was introduced to von Lieper's successor and the agreement was that I would continue to work at SS Headquarters part-time as a translator and general secretary. But I also said that I intended to take a long holiday visiting relatives near Claremont-Ferrand and possibly Algiers which fits in with my cover identity. This way my prolonged absence will not be viewed with suspicion and I've secured my flat as a base by paying rent in advance. By the time I left von Lieper had been promoted to Major and he secured all the clearance and travel documents I would need."

"You seem to have all bases covered Lieutenant Charlton," Gubbins suggested.

"I certainly hope so sir," Annie replied.

"How would you feel about going back?" Gubbins asked without any beating about the bush.

"Yes sir, certainly sir if there's a job for me to do."

"We've been working on something, an idea, just waiting for the right person to come along. Vera suggested that you might be that person and now that I've met you and heard your report I'm more convinced than ever that with your contacts we might just pull it off. We still have a lot of details to finalise but can I take it in principle that you'll come aboard?"

"Of course sir if you think I'm up to it."

"Good show." Gubbins stood up, collected his hat, coat and briefcase and made his way towards the door, turned and said, "That's settled then," before disappearing out into the corridor.

"Well done Annie," Vera said laying her hand on her shoulder. "I think you're due some well-earned leave and then perhaps you might like to join us at Beaulieu and give the benefit of your recent experience to our new recruits."

Annie returned to Montague Mansions and found the young WAAC girl who managed to rustle up some beans on toast and a mug of cocoa putting them on a table in a small breakfast room. Afterwards she went up to her room to find her suitcase and personal belongings which had been left behind at Beaulieu when she'd gone over to France. The nights were drawing in and mindful of the blackout and without putting the light on Annie peered through the net curtains out into the street below. Only the occasional car passed by. There were few people about and those that were either wore a military uniform or the city uniform of dark suit, dark overcoat, bowler hat, umbrella and briefcase. A frost-hazed moon harassed by the occasional passing cloud shed a pallid light reducing everything to flat opaque monochrome like an under-developed black and white photograph. A good night for a drop she thought. Drawing the blackout and floral curtains Annie flopped onto the bed with a deep sigh reflecting her struggle to come to terms with the contrasting situations the last 24 hours had thrown at her. A quick wash and change into her pyjamas and Annie was soon tucked up in bed but the deep sleep of earlier proved more elusive this time. Her mind darted hither and thither never settling long before further images, expectations, plans, memories like wraiths twisted and entwined, forming and reforming as smoke in a whirlwind. Predictably her thoughts turned to Otto. Was he thinking of her she wondered? Would her new proposed assignment give her the opportunity to see him again?

What foul murderous operations was he planning or involved in and how could she really love him knowing what he was doing. Annie tossed and turned until the sheets were crumpled and uncomfortable and she had a splitting headache. Taking a couple of aspirins she settle down once more watching as the second hand on her travel clock tick, tick, ticked her gradually towards unconsciousness.

Next day with her bank book in her shoulder bag Annie visited the nearest Lloyds branch and was surprised how much her untouched pay had accrued. Some new civilian clothes was the order of the day and she surprised herself by how much she enjoyed sauntering along Oxford Street through theatre-land and out into The Strand fingering and trying on clothes in shops and department stores but it was the number of clothes coupons required which restricted her purchases rather than the inflated prices.

Annie carried in her head the recent memories and images the impact war was having on French civilians but here in London the more physical reminders of the war were to be seen everywhere. The different uniforms of allies and commonwealth countries, some of their owners enjoying an interlude of sightseeing whilst others were going about more pressing business. Traffic was incessant. Rolls of barbed wire at strategic sites, sand bags protecting building entrances, windows criss-crossed with sticky tape to prevent flying glass causing injury during bomber raids and barrage balloons hanging suspended in the sky like huge trunk-less elephants. The frequent evidence of bomb damaged buildings seemed all the more shocking because of the randomness, the unpredictable horror of it, the luck, the split second difference between life and death.

The sound of music approached and receded on a light breeze as Annie made her way down The Strand. The nearer she got to Trafalgar Square the louder and more persistent the music became. On the terrace in front of the National Gallery was a military band their bright uniforms and polished instruments adding a hint of forced festivity in a drab cityscape. In spite of the flat grey sky people, well wrapped up against the slight chill, sat on seats around Nelson's Column listening to patriotic tunes and medleys of popular songs. Annie sat listening for a while contrasting the apparent optimism of the audience with the resignation and dower existence of Parisians. She wondered if the people around her realised how their lives would have been now if the RAF had not won superiority in the air in 1940 and prevented Hitler from realising his plans for invasion.

A rumbling stomach reminded Annie that she had eaten nothing since breakfast. She left Trafalgar Square and made her way to The Strand Lyons Corner House restaurant. The luncheon menu was finished so Annie was forced to choose from the more restricted tea options. Nevertheless she gave her order to the waitress choosing fried codling and chips, bread and margarine, a cup of tea and fruit tart to finish with. There were only four other tables occupied. Food rationing was having an impact on commercial enterprises as well as on normal families. The rich could always find ways to subvert any restrictions whether it be through the black market or otherwise and many establishments found ways round the rules to accommodate their wealthy clientele. The majority of ordinary Londoners had taken to eating in the British Restaurants, feeding centres set up by the Ministry of Food and run by local authorities where a substantial meal could be purchased for nine pence. Other, more upmarket restaurants were limited to a meal of three courses only and a maximum price of five shillings. This was way out of Annie's price range but the extra she paid at Lyons Corner House was worth it to avoid the institutional atmosphere of the feeding centres with their hundreds and hundreds of queuing customers.

Fortified by her fish and chips Annie retraced her steps towards Trafalgar Square and turned right into Charing Cross Road. Entering Leicester Square she was drawn to the north east corner where the neoclassical frontage with its Corinthian columns decorating the upper façade of the Garrick Theatre caught her attention. Idle curiosity got the better of her and she stopped to see what was showing. The idea of escaping the war if only for an hour or two was difficult to resist and seeing a comedy farce appealed to her. Because of the blitz audiences at London theatres had diminished and Annie had no problem buying a ticket at the box office. She was a little too early for the performance and stood on the pavement considering her options. The noise and laughter coming from a nearby pub might just put her in the mood for her evening's entertainment so she decided to cross the road and push her way into the pub. The place was crowded and her parcels kept getting snagged on people's legs. The fuggy atmosphere was thick with cigarette smoke which caught the back of her throat bringing on a fit of coughing, her eyes involuntarily watering. A badly out of tune piano was being thumped by a corporal of the Royal Engineers as people standing round sang, 'My old man said follow the van. And don't dilly dally on the way,' whilst his comrades slopped beer out of their glasses and leaned against one another for support. She elbowed her way towards a thick heavy mahogany, Victorian bar and ordered half a pint of bitter. Annie was aware that she was attracting a lot of attention but guessed that her lieutenant uniform was protection enough against unwanted advances.

The comedy, "She Follows Me About," which was staged by Bill Travers was all that Annie could wish for in a typically English farce.

A harried vicar had to cope with the hilarious attentions of a group of WAAFs (Women's Auxiliary Air Force) not to mention the complications of a bogus bishop. All the stereotypes were present, the trousers down round ankles and people running in and out of rooms and up and down stairs. In spite of herself Annie giggled and laughed with the rest of the audience. In what seemed like no time at all she was standing for the national anthem. On her way out she picked up a flyer for the next production which was to be Graham Greene's "Brighton Rock" and dropped it into one of her carrier bags.

Annie had not anticipated staying out this late and on leaving the theatre she shivered as the uninvited cold damp caressed her. She hurried towards Leicester Square tube station and descended to the platform for the blue Piccadilly Line to take her one stop to Piccadilly Circus where she would transfer to the Bakerloo Line for Baker Street. The atmosphere was heavy with the warm musty smell of human bodies as strangers and families arranged their bedding on the platform for another night of safety from the Luftwaffe. The push of warm air from the tunnel signalled the arrival of the train and Annie stepped over blanket bundles trying hard not to stand on hands or faces. Back in her room Annie appraised her purchases and congratulated herself on a successful day.

There were only so many theatres, museums, art galleries, parks and shops and Annie was becoming bored. A creeping anaesthesia numbing her brain. She approached Vera and was immediately transferred to Beaulieu where she began to feel alive again. She brushed up on her French and German and even began to learn some Polish. She gave lectures and took part in training exercises just to keep her fit and alert.

* * * * *

January 1944 found Annie back at Beaulieu after her Christmas leave. The farm at Chepfield though was soon just a mirage, a time out of time, an existence within the pages of a fairy-tale book. After an overnight journey from London Annie had taken the train from Newcastle to Rowlands Gill where she caught the omnibus for Chepfield. The driver dropped her off at the entrance to the cart track which wound its way up the hill towards the farm. She looked fondly at the carved wooden sign, 'Hill Top Farm' nailed to the gate post the white paint having flaked off a long time ago. It was a cold morning and the frosted leaves crunched beneath her shoes. Ruts where lorries had churned up the mud into two parallel tracks were frozen solid and Annie had to tread carefully to ensure that she didn't turn her ankle. She stopped and looked across the Derwent Valley which was swaddled in fluffy, cotton-wool mist. Columns of smoke from the chimneys of hundreds of colliery houses arranged in parallel street after street stood sentinel as if propping up the sky. The hills on either side of the valley strained up to touch an overburdened grey sky. You would never know that there was a war on. The air was crisp and cold and felt fresh in her lungs as she breathed in deeply, a hint of sulphur from the hundreds of domestic coal fires down in the village reinforcing that she was home. The exhaled breath floating, expanding, now dissipating to vanish into the stillness of the moment. It was a welcome change to be un-assailed by the smells of war in London, gas from bomb damaged pipes, and open sewers, cordite seeping out from craters and smoke hanging funereal over burnt out buildings. Annie crossed the farmyard and opened the door which led into the farmhouse kitchen. Her mother, Rhoda, was bending over the range stirring a pot of her famous rich broth. Hearing the door open she half turned expecting to see Robert. Still bent over Rhoda instantly dropped the ladle. "Eeeh! Our Annie, shut the door lass it's freezing out there. Ha'way in. Come here and let me give you a hug. Why didn't you say you were coming? Your father would have picked you up at the station. Ha'way and sit by the fire. Would you like a cup of tea? It seems like years since we last saw you." The quick-fire questions of nervous excitement continued in an unabated torrent. "How've you been love? How long can you stay? When are you going back? Libby, Rowena," Rhoda shouted, "Guess who's just walked in. Come on, hurry up and say Merry Christmas to your sister."

The stairs creaked and rumbled like drum-fire as two pairs of legs thumped their way down, across the hall and into the kitchen. The three sisters hugged each other and danced bouncing up and down around the kitchen table.

"Sit yourselves down and get this broth inside you. It'll put hairs on your chests and help keep the cold out. You girls no doubt have a lot to talk about, I'll catch up with the news later. Annie, I'll light a fire in your old room the place is like a morgue it'll help get the bed aired ready for tonight. Then when you're ready you can change out of that uniform and forget about the war for a while."

"Thanks mam. It's good to be home."

"It's just a pity our Rupert couldn't be here. Somewhere in the Mediterranean so I believe but according to his last letter he's fit and well."

Late afternoon and darkness was already rubbing out the country-side. The noise of a car engine whining and snorting interrupted the girls' chatter before the dim yellow cats eyes' glow of masked headlights could be seen prowling down the cart track. The car coughed and sighed to a halt and seconds later the back door opened. Robert took in the scene at once as Annie rushed forward into his arms.

"Daddy!"

"Annie, it's wonderful to see you love. We've missed you so much."

"I've missed you too daddy....all of you. At least I'm home for the holidays so let's make this the best Christmas ever.

It was over too quickly. The enveloping warmth of family love, the presents, the silly games, the carol singing round the piano, the afternoon walks in Chepfield Forrest where the conifers stood straight and confident and the leaf-stripped branches of oaks, beech and sycamore scratched the snow laden sky. The continuing family tradition of Christmas pudding with silver three-penny pieces wrapped in grease proof paper hidden in the mix, a surprise which always caused excitement when Annie, her sisters and brother were little. The mummers who called at the farm one freezing night to present their performance in costume of bold Sir John, his family curse and the slaying of the dragon all in rhyming verse.

All too soon Annie said her tearful goodbyes and got into the car with her father. The journey was one of suffocating silence. Waiting on the platform at the Central Station in Newcastle Robert spoke quietly, "Try to write to us Annie, you know, to let us know that you're really okay. We don't know what you're doing or where you are. I suppose you've got your reasons. We get your field post cards every now and then but they're so impersonal. I know from experience in the last show that it's not what they say, more what they don't say. Your mother doesn't say anything but I know that deep down she worries especially after losing your real dad in the last war."

"I'll try dad.....but I can't say too much....it's all....sort of hush, hush, but I'll try, promise."

* * * * *

Annie sat in a window seat and as the train approached her Alma Mater she had time to gaze out at the magnificent structure of Durham Cathedral when the train slowed down to traverse the high viaduct which skirted the city. Little did she know that her thoughts were exactly those of her father's, John James, when he was returning to the trenches from his last leave with her mother the year she was born in 1916? Perched on top of a volcanic plug above the medieval streets gave the cathedral and castle the appearance of permanence, the mature trees reaching up the bank side from the river as if in sublime supplication, a timelessness which anchored her to her proud, northern roots.

Frustration gnawed at Annie as January gave way to February and March. Being honest with herself Annie accepted that the weather had not been conducive to operations but still the routine at Beaulieu was beginning to pall. Eventually on the week beginning Monday 22nd. March Annie was asked to report to Vera Atkins' office.

"Ah! There you are Annie, come in. I've had notification that you're required at Portman Square, London ASAP. I'll be in on the meeting so we might as well drive up there together so pack your things whilst I order a car."

"Do you know what it's about? Well…I mean…we both know it's about my next mission but can you give me any more details?" Annie asked trying to keep her curiosity in check.

"I'm afraid not Annie. The details of this operation have been decided way above my head, at the highest level. I've a general idea but I think it's best we wait for Major General Gubbins to brief you directly. I'll meet you downstairs in about fifteen minutes."

"Well, here we all are again," Gubbins opened after the initial formalities. "I know that your raison d'être is secrecy but I must impress upon you that this is most top secret…from Churchill himself. If we can pull this off we will probably shorten the war and save thousands of lives in the process. We've been planning this for months, covering every eventuality in detail. We know that the Germans are expecting the allies to invade mainland Europe sometime this year but they don't know where or when. In a nutshell we want to convince Hitler beyond any doubt that the invasion will take place in the Calais region. That's going to be your job Lieutenant Charlton. Where the actual landing will take place doesn't concern us here but it is vital that we try to persuade Hitler to concentrate his main forces in the wrong area in order to give the assault troops the best possible chance to establish and hold a beachhead." Without waiting for any questions or comments Gubbins continued. "Our plan is to place a dead body dressed in RAF bomber flying gear and open parachute as if he has just bailed out, somewhere in France. In a pocket will be his wallet and these photographs." Gubbins passed two black and white sea-side snaps to Annie. The corners were creased and the photos obviously well thumbed. "What do you see?" He asked. Annie held the two snaps up together.

"In this one a pretty girl sitting on the gunwale of a boat," Annie said slowly scrutinising the pictures. "A bit saucy, her dress has blown up showing a bit too much thigh and suspender. Or maybe it was intended. In the second one she's posing leaning against the same boat one elbow on the gunwale with her hand in her Rita Hayworth lookalike hair, again, the top of her dress unbuttoned just a little bit too far. I guess they're the sort of lover's photos that a soldier would keep with him whilst away from home." She turned them over and read on the back of each the same message 'All my love and come home safe, Clare.'

"Now look a little closer," Gubbins pressed.

Taking her time and picking up a magnifying glass from the desk nearby Annie continued. "The lettering on the side is badly weathered, the paint's nearly all peeled off but....wait a minute..... yes.....the name of the boat is Southern Belle....Dover."

"And beyond?" Gubbins nudged.

Annie took her time and moved the glass over each of the snapshots in turn. "My God....it isn't is it.....is that Churchill....and....and.... Eisenhower? It can't be surely." Although the figures were facing away from the camera one of the men had the unmistakable hunched shoulders of Churchill. He was wearing a dark suit and his characteristic bowler hat. He had one hand on the second person's shoulder whilst his other arm was outstretched pointing towards the harbour with a huge cigar between his fingers. Following the direction of Churchill's arm further into the photograph Annie now saw what looked like rows and rows of landing craft lashed together and covered with camouflage nets. The second man was dressed in an USA uniform with the distinctive cap of a high ranking officer and appeared to have the clean-cut profile of Eisenhower. Further scrutiny of the two photographs revealed a convoy of Jeeps and three military cars flying pennants which were undecipherable parked up and attended by armed personnel with white cliffs fading into the sky in the background.

"Okay," Gubbins said business-like. "The two gentlemen are doppelgängers good enough to fool the Germans I think. The landing craft are made from wood and canvas and are decoys. From air reconnaissance suspicious enough to convince the Nazis that we are going to use the shortest distance across the channel."

"It's brilliant," Jepson interjected. "Who would think that two lovers' photographs would have captured, unintended, Churchill and Eisenhower inspecting the progress of preparations for Operation Overlord? Understated and quite brilliant. I suppose this is where Annie comes in?"

"Yes, it's up to Lieutenant Charlton how she does it but we want those photographs in the hands of the German High Command in Berlin as soon as possible." Turning towards Annie he added more gravely, "You do realise that if you're rumbled it's absolutely imperative that you do not reveal the truth about these photos. Under no circumstances are you to admit that this is the biggest hoax of the war."

"I understand the full implications of what you're saying sir," Annie said quietly but firmly.

"Good. The plan is that Lieutenant Charlton will land in France with the body already dressed. Her Rouen cell has already been contacted. Just before landing a squadron of Mosquitoes will attack Dieppe one of them will sweep wide round Rouen igniting a smoke flare feigning damage which would account for the parachute body on the ground in the area. Lieutenant Charlton is to keep the wallet and the rest is up to her." Turning to Annie he continued, "We're dependant on the weather and the procurement of a fresh body. The body's injuries will reflect those of flak wounds and facial features will be virtually unrecognisable. Identity of the flyer and your own up to date papers and cover story are all in place. So you're to go direct to RAF Tangmere from here and be on twenty-four hour alert pending favourable weather and a suitable body coming together at the same time. Are there any questions............? No. good. I cannot impress on you Lieutenant Charlton how important this mission is to the war effort. We're very grateful to you and wish you God speed. I'll say au revoir then and leave the three of you to iron out any last domestic arrangements."

CHAPTER 19

Otto 1943 – 1944

Otto's mood was as flat as the featureless countryside through which he was travelling. The progress of the war could be traced by the increasing amount of destruction witnessed as the ruins of towns and villages scrolled past the carriage window. A vast wasteland reminiscent of a landscape stripped and left naked after the march of a swarm of locusts. The journey was tedious and constantly being interrupted as the train was shunted into sidings to allow troop trains and freight trains with flat-bed trucks carrying pristine new tanks and artillery to thunder towards the eastern front. In the opposite direction came trains of dirty, bloody and broken soldiers on their way to hospitals in Germany.

Wearily Otto lifted his valise down from the luggage rack as the train entered Warsaw in a series of balance threatening jolts and jerks. He made his way to the station exit unhindered and stood on the pavement looking up at a depressingly heavy sky threatening to hammer down on standing buildings and ruins alike without compromise. Taking a deep breath and exhaling loudly he was distracted by a young corporal approaching him.

"*Heil Hitler. Sturmbannfuhrer von Lieper* sir?"

"*Heil Hitler,*" Otto responded, "Who wants to know?"

"Corporal Blucher sir. I'm your assigned driver and this is your kubelwagen for as long as you need it sir. I have orders to take you directly to Colonel Heinz Auerswald. If you'd care to step in sir," the corporal continued opening the kubelwagen passenger door for Otto.

"Thank you corporal."

The corporal drove briskly through the city where the heavy, solid buildings pressed down on the ground with weary fatigue whilst Otto gazed on in disgust at the shabby and shaggy Polish civilians as they shambled along the littered streets. The scenery became more familiar as the corporal brought the kubelwagen to a stop outside the city's SS occupation headquarters.

Otto passed through into the entrance hall and, although he knew the way, on enquiry was immediately directed towards the colonel's office. He knocked firmly on the door and waited for an invite to enter.

A loud "come" was the response and Otto pushed the door open and walked through. The room was much as he remembered it from his last posting in Warsaw. The drapes seemed to sag with a little more dirt, the carpet appeared a little more stained and the furniture in need of some restoration. However, armchairs and a long low table in front of the fireplace were just as they were the day he left.

Rising unsteadily from one of the chairs and raising a glass the colonel slurred, "Otto, my man, I've been expecting you, it's good to see a familiar face after all this time." Looking dishevelled with his jacket undone and his shirt top button loosened he continued, "*Willkommen in der Arschloch sein kann der Welt,* welcome to the arsehole of the world. A little different from Paris I would guess."

"Yes indeed colonel," Otto replied noting that the colonel was showing the stress of life in the east.

"Heinz, Otto, it's Heinz we have history, Ja? But the war has been kind to you Otto, a major now in such a short time and me still stuck in this shit-hole. But I'm forgetting my manners Otto, a schnapps and I think I'll join you." Heinz poured two generous measures and they both took large slugs. Heinz topped up the glasses and they both sat down in front of the fire.

"Sooo, to what do I owe this pleasure?" Heinz asked smiling. "I was given notice of your transfer but no details."

Otto showed only his authorization from Himmler and Heinz continued, "So you really are heading for the top and one of the family now so I've been told." There was no malice in Heinz's last utterance and Otto replied, "You have to ride your luck when it comes along Heinz. I've made no secret of the fact that I'm ambitious but you must know that I don't forget old friends." And he raised his glass, "*Gute gesundheit,* good health."

"Good health. So you're on a fact finding mission eh!" The wily colonel looked straight at Otto whose face remained impassive. Pulling himself together and taking on a more serious demeanour Heinz continued, "I'll be honest with you Otto....and I love the Fatherland as much as you do....but from my experience this eastern front is a tinder box. The Ivans are gathering their forces and my guess is that when they think they're strong enough they'll attack west and I don't think we'll be able to hold them. They're like fucking weeds, for every one you

pluck up ten more grow. We may have rolled over Poland and further
east and worked a few of them to death in the process but take my
word for it there are thousands of Poles in the cities and especially in
the forests and countryside just waiting for the right moment to mount
a coordinated uprising. We try to flush the resistance out but as soon
as we destroy one secret camp they move on to another. That's no
way to fight a war Otto." Heinz lifted his glass, drained his schnapps
and fell silent for a few minutes. Otto waited.

"I suppose you heard about the uprisings shortly after you left
us what seems like years ago for Paris," Heinz asked wearily. "In this
last one the Waffen-SS with some limited help from the Wehrmacht
tried to clear the ghetto in April this year but by this time the Jews
knew that their fate was not to be transported to work camps. We didn't
really have the resources to attack every single apartment block and
alleyway in the filthy rabbit warren and as soon as we entered the gates
we were met with small arms fire, hand grenades and petrol bombs. Our
casualties were slight but it took us a month to flush them out. Himmler
was furious. He sent General Juergen Stroop who ordered the great
synagogue to be blown up and those ghetto buildings that had been
destroyed by fire to be razed to the ground and be replaced by a Warsaw
concentration camp in the city. We pumped water into underground
bunkers and fished for drowned rats, we put flame-throwers into the
cellars and had roasted rats then we put smoke bombs down the sewers
and had smoked rats."

"Quite a Polish smorgasbord Heinz," Otto interjected with a smile.

"Ha….ha, ha, ha, ha, ha, you haven't lost your edge Otto. I thought
you might have gone soft in gay Paris. Thirteen thousand Jews of the fifty
thousand remaining in the ghetto were killed. Even the fucking women
and children were lobbing hidden grenades after having surrendered.
Those we hunted down and captured were transported to Treblinka and
Majdanek, seven thousands of them I think. All together this year we
have culled 300,000 from the ghetto but there are still hundreds hidden
in cellars, sewers and secret blockhouses. Unfortunately it's a fact of life
that we still need some of these Jews to work for our economy. I suppose
you've also heard about the….how shall I put this, the reversal at Kursk.
Field Marshall von Kluge and Field Marshall von Manstein planned a
pincer attack on the Russians' salient but somehow they got wind of it
and we got rather mauled. Thousands of tanks stretched across the
plains and most of them Russian. If you want my serious assessment
Otto I think that was our last throw of the dice in the east. The initiative
is with them and they can only start to roll us back all the way to
Germany. We no longer have the resources to mount a serious offensive.
The Wehrmacht knows this but I've heard that Hitler flies into a rage

whenever one of his generals suggests this so everyone keeps quiet. It's like Stalingrad all over again. That's the route to ruin. I'm still a loyal German Otto and I'll do my duty but I fear that after Kursk the war is lost and the allies haven't even landed on the coast of France yet."

Otto appraised Heinz in silence for a few minutes then asked, "In short then Heinz, what is your overall assessment of the situation in the east?"

"As I see it Otto, we're fighting two wars. The first a conventional one against the Russians and losing, the other a guerrilla war behind the lines against Jewish insurrection and polish resistance. We estimate that there are 45,000 Polish troops across the country and 400,000 resistance troops. A formidable number. The second is taking resources away from the first...without massive reinforcements it's unsustainable."

"Thank's for being frank Heinz. I think I'll turn in now, it's been a long day."

"Of course Otto. I've arranged for you to have your old room in the hotel down the street. I'll have Blucher take you there. He should have stored your gear and made sure that everything is in order. So I'll say good night Otto and welcome to hell."

"Good night Heinz."

The next morning Otto met with Heinz again. "I'm going to be spending a lot of time away from Warsaw Heinz although this will be my base. I'm going to visit the camps in order to compile an overall assessment of the Jewish situation so I expect to be away for some time. We've actually cleared a lot of Jews from the various ghettos and Himmler is beginning to wind down some of them but I need first-hand information. So with your permission Heinz I'll be on my way and I'll see you when I see you."

"Goodbye Otto and be careful. Get Blucher to select two good privates from his platoon to go with you as a body guard and arm yourself with a machine-pistol just to be on the safe side."

"Thanks Heinz I'll do that, Auf Wiedersehen."

"Take me to the ghetto," Otto said to Corporal Blucher climbing into the kubelwagen. As they drove down the ghetto streets Otto was astounded at the scale of the destruction meted out by General Stroop. Where once fashionable apartment blocks had existed and latterly turned into ghetto slums not a stone was left standing on another. "I've seen enough Blucher, let's go."

"Yes sir," He cheerfully replied.

Turning round and making their way towards the exit the kubelwagen plunged into a large pothole which Blucher had only seen at the last minute. The vehicle pitched violently throwing Otto against the steel interior. "Sorry sir," Blucher offered shamefacedly. "It won't happen again."

"It had better bloody not Blucher otherwise I'll be looking for another driver."

As a result of the jolt Otto's hip flask clanged against the metal door and Otto put has hand down to release it from his belt. Removing the small cups he lifted the flask to his lips and took a long pull of brandy. Fastening the cups back with the press stud Otto glimpsed the engraved inscription written by Annette. He read it and looked around at the desolation and for a moment, just a fleeting moment, a moment as instant as the snap of a bullet zapping passed an ear he felt the merest twinge of remorse. He flicked his left cheek and fastened the flask back onto his belt.

* * * * *

"Come in, come in Otto," Heinz gestured. "A successful tour I hope. I've just got hold of a bottle of superb Vodka, here try it. Just the thing for a weary traveller."

"Thanks Heinz, yes a useful trip."

They slouched down in the easy chairs in Heinz's office, put the glasses to their lips and threw their heads back.

"Good, Ja? Here let me top you up."

"Tell me Heinz," Otto said quizzically, "You fought in the last war didn't you?"

"That's a strange question Otto. Yes I did and a bloody affair it was too but at least you knew who and where your enemy was. I suppose in that respect it was a cleaner war than this one. Why do you want to know?"

"Oh....no particular reason. It's just that last time when I was here in an old farm house up near Ciechanow someone had left some words carved into a window sill and they intrigued me. They read Robert Charlton 9th DLI and then some dates 1916/17/18/19. Robert Charlton sounds English and I assume that 9th DLI is a regiment. Do you know what DLI stands for?"

"The British raise their armies locally in the different counties which lend their names to the regiments formed. The 9th stands for the 9th battalion and DLI stands for the Durham Light Infantry. County Durham is a coal mining area in the north of England and as you can imagine the men were as hard as nails. Bloody tough and good soldiers, I know because we fought them on the Somme in 1916 at Martinpuich and The Butte de Warlencourt. Your father Generalleutnent Albrecht von Lieper fought there too and was wounded I believe. I can only guess that this Robert Charlton was an English POW and that he had been sent to work on the farm and that the dates refer to the time he spent there. Three years….a long time………Are you alright Otto…..you've gone as white as a ghost?" Here, have another vodka."

Otto took the drink with thanks and knocked it back in one and held his glass out for another flicking his left cheek at the same time.

"Probably just weary and I haven't had a lot to eat. I'll be alright once this gets into my bloodstream. If you don't mind Heinz I'll go to my room and get my head down."

"Of course Otto. Goodnight and I'll see you in the morning. Here, take the rest of the bottle with you, you look as if you need it."

Otto took the proffered bottle, nodded then made his way back to his quarters.

"Gott verdammt Sie Mutter. Gott damn der Krieg. Gott verdammt. God damn you mother. God damn the war. God damn you all," he screamed at the top of his voice.

The present ceased to mean anything to him and he was living inside his head. His mind was in a turmoil. The facts were almost beyond circumstantial now and in his heart of hearts he knew for sure that his mother, having lived on the estate at Ciechanow whilst her husband was away fighting on the western front, had been telling him the truth about his real father. No matter how much he tried to push the fact down into his subconscious the more it resisted and resurfaced to mock and torment him. He flopped down into an easy chair and poured himself a large vodka. His father might be English but he didn't know him and he didn't feel English whatever that meant. How could his mother have been such a whore as to sleep with the enemy of Germany. He could feel his anger taking over again but a little voice in his head kept repeating, 'What about Annette? What about Annette? Are you not doing exactly the same thing that you're accusing your mother of?' Otto threw the glass into the fireplace with such force that glass slivers flew across the room. Standing up he swept everything off his dressing table and kicked the stool over breaking one of the legs.

"Gott verdammt Mutter." he yelled again.

Eventually collapsing back into the chair his anger dissipated by his recent rant. The cold, analytical side of his nature once again began to take control and Otto resolved that the only way to maintain the integrity of his persona was to be even more German than the rest. There must be no weaknesses, physical or emotional, no cracks which could be misconstrued as anything less than truly Aryan.

The next morning Otto was just about to step into his kubelwagen when a switchboard operator ran out from the SS Headquarters shouting.

"Major. Major von Lieper sir, you're wanted urgently on the telephone from Berlin."

Picking up the phone Otto answered with some trepidation. "Hello, Major Otto von Lieper speaking."

"Hello Otto, Heinrich here. Listen Otto, there's been a slight change of plan. Nothing to worry about but I think this will help you with part of your assignment. A friend of mine, SS Judge, Konrad Morgen has been very successful in uncovering evidence of corruption in the administration of camps here in Germany. I thought that he would be a good ally in your work so I've arranged for you to meet him and his team at police headquarters in the centre of the Polish town of Auschwitz in two days where you can plan your strategy. Ziggy sends her love by the way. Bye Otto and good luck."

"I'll catch the first available train. Tell Ziggy I'm missing her and hope to see her soon. Bye Reichsfuhrer." Otto replaced the phone on its hook wondering if he really did miss Ziggy. He certainly hadn't given her much thought since leaving Berlin.

* * * * *

Otto left the Auschwitz railway station and made his way to the town hall. The atmosphere was pungent with the smell of death. Once inside he was shown into an office where Konrad Morgen was waiting.

"*Heil Hitler.*"

"*Heil Hitler,* major. Would you like a cup of coffee before we start?"

"Thank you. That would be very agreeable," Otto replied formally.

"This is going to be a complex and long investigation Otto, if I may call you Otto, call me Konrad. We're going to be working closely together so there's no point in being formal." Otto nodded in agreement and Konrad continued, "Neither of us has been here before I think but I'm informed that Auschwitz is a huge complex of 20,000 acres. There are three main camps and forty-five satellite camps in the immediate area servicing the IG Farben chemical plant, Krupp armament industry and Siemens-Schuckert. We're talking about thousands of prisoner workers here so there's ample opportunity for anyone to defraud the Party at so many levels. If you agree, I've found that the best strategy in these cases is to approach the industries first and check their accounts then compare those figures with the books in the camps."

"That seems logical to me," Otto replied, "When do we start?"

"No time like the present. I'll brief my teams of accountants and we can start with IG Farben tomorrow morning then move on to Krupp and Siemens."

* * * * *

The director of IG Farben, Carl Krauch, was cooperative and after a guided tour of the plant where they were manufacturing Buna, a synthetic substitute for rubber, the accounts were made available for scrutiny. "We rely on the camp for our labour and have 83,000 prisoner workers here representing 46% of the workforce. You'll see from our accounts with the SS that we pay 5 Marks per hour for skilled labour and 4 Marks per hour for non-skilled labour. I hope you know what an undertaking you're letting yourselves in for gentlemen. If there's anything we can do or any help you need just let me know. Your audit could take weeks," the director said.

This proved to be the case but with their investigation completed and armed with their findings Otto made an appointment to see the Auschwitz commandant Rudolf Höss. The next morning Otto and Konrad arrived at the imposing wrought iron gates with the words *Arbeit Macht Frei,* Freedom through work, attached to an archway over the entrance. They were expected and the guard directed them to the administration building. This part of the camp had been a barracks for the Polish army with block after identical block of red brick buildings in regimented rows but was now being used to house political and criminal prisoners. A double electrified fence surrounded the complex with watch towers and search lights at intervals.

A corporal in the outer office announced their arrival as he opened the door to Höss' office. "SS Sturmbannfuhrer Otto von Lieper and SS Judge Konrad Morgen, Obersturmbannfuhrer, lieutenant colonel."

"Come in gentlemen, coffee for our guests Franz. Sit please and tell me your business."

Although outranked Otto showed his orders and authorization direct from Himmler which obviously impressed Commandant Höss. "That's not a problem Sturmbannfuhrer, perhaps you would like a tour of our complex and I can explain our system to you."

"You read how many acres this site and its satellite camps cover but it doesn't really strike you how huge it is until you actually see it." Otto said after the tour.

"Yes indeed, it's as complex as a small city to run. Well, gentlemen, if that's all you wish to see may I suggest that we return to Auschwitz." They walked back to the entrance. "If you're not doing anything this evening gentlemen may I invite you to dinner? I'd be happy to introduce you to my wife and five delightful children."

The audit was a huge undertaking given that the camp was so huge and its organization so complex. However armed with figures from the various industrial plants Konrad's experienced accountants found evidence of embezzlement in spite of double book keeping and other accounting subterfuge. At a simple level accounts showed that labour was being sold at 4 Marks for skilled labour and 3 Marks for unskilled labour whilst the industries were paying respectively 5 and 4 Marks per hour. Taking into account that thousands of inmates were being hired out by the SS every day this was a huge sum of money which was being creamed off the top. Further to this they discovered that the number of inmates registered for labour in the camp records was far below the actual number delivered and being paid for by the industries. These ghost workers netting a handsome profit. No doubt gold from extracted teeth from corpses and melted down into ingots was also being syphoned off but this was difficult to prove.

The same practices were discovered at Majdanek camp and others. Himmler was delighted with Otto's progress and Rudolf Höss was eventually removed from his post but others were not so lucky and ended up in concentration camps themselves.

*****

After a break back in Warsaw, together with his driver Corporal Blucher and the two privates Otto was once again on a train travelling east and the next few weeks were spent visiting one monotonous camp after another interrupted by tedious, slow, interminable train and kubelwagen journeys in bitter, freezing conditions. Although the best of food was reserved for the SS, Christmas dinner with the luxury of traditional goose was celebrated without cheer and the new year greeted with less than enthusiasm and the fact finding mission continued for another two months. Otto returned to Warsaw at the beginning of March to write his initial report and, unexpectedly, to respond to letters from his wife Ziggy. Her letters expressed the usual wartime sentiment about missing him and what she would do to him on his return. Air raids over Berlin were becoming more frequent and effective and food was terribly expensive but still available to her. Not wanting to go to the trouble of writing and posting a letter Otto picked up the phone and instructed the switchboard to connect a line to his wife in Berlin. He poured a vodka whilst clicks, buzzes and static crackled through the earpiece. After nearly ten minutes Otto was becoming frustrated when suddenly there was his wife.

"Hello, Frau Sieglinde Lieper speaking."

"Ziggy my dear, how are you?" "Otto....ohhh, Otto, it's wonderful to hear your voice. I haven't heard from you for so long I was beginning to get worried. Are you alright? Uncle Heinrich said not to worry but it's not the same as speaking to you in person."

"Of course I am. I told you I would be travelling and probably too busy to write but I'm here now and that's all that matters."

"Thank you Otto dear. I know, and I do appreciate you taking time out of your busy schedule to call me."

"I'll be home as soon as I can but it won't be for the next few months I'm afraid. Look....I'm going to have to hang up Ziggy because I'm tying up a military phone line.

"I understand Otto. Lots of love and thank you for calling it was so sweet of you. Can't wait to make a baby when we next meet. Goodbye darling."

"Goodbye Ziggy."

* * * * *

What was becoming clear was that most of the big city ghettos were almost clear of Jews, Gypsies and Slavs and that the camps were now receiving thousands of Jews from across the whole of conquered Europe as far south as Italy and Greece. On the military front Otto recorded that 1943 had been disappointing for German militarism. It began with the fall of Stalingrad in January and the annihilation of the sixth army. The tank battle at Kursk during the summer was decisive in consolidating Russian ascendancy and the year ended with the Russians taking Belgorod, Briansk, Kharkov and Kiev, the German army falling back to the River Dnepr.

Otto suspected that Himmler was well aware of the true situation in the east but to protect his own position and ambitions he was determined to hide the facts from Hitler and not contradict his tactical decisions which were proving disastrous for Wehrmacht generals in the field. With this in mind Otto was very careful to put a gloss on his reporting so as not to put himself in a position of laying himself open to charges of defeatism and disloyalty to Hitler and thereby suffering the obvious consequences.

Fearing that the Russian remorseless advance would uncover the genocide taking place in the east and fuel their lust for revenge Himmler sent orders that the camps were to be dismantled and the evidence erased and Otto was to report on progress.

* * * * *

Uprisings in various camps convinced Himmler that Jews anywhere were a real security risk. Orders were dispatched that Operation Harvest Festival should be put into immediate effect and Otto was to supervise the successful elimination of the remaining Jewish population of Majdanek camp.

The operation was a huge success and the camp was immediately grassed over and planted with flowers and bushes whilst bricks from the gas chambers were recycled to build a farm.

It was a fine summer morning with a bright pellucid sky. Otto inspected the finishing touches being made to the transformed former camp. Pleased with what he saw he walked along the line of camp labourers shaking their hands. He turned and walked away without looking back. A murder of crows squawked and flapped fracturing the quiet stillness whilst brains exploded as each of the workers was shot in the back of the head by the few remaining SS guards.

Having supervised Operation Harvest Festival to a satisfactory conclusion Otto was pleased to be back in Warsaw where he learned with some satisfaction that he had been awarded the Iron Cross, Second Class and also recommended for promotion to SS Obersturmbannfuhrer, Lieutenant Colonel. Collecting a bottle of vodka from the mess he retired to his room and flopped into an easy chair with a grateful sigh of relief. The first glass of the fiery liquid was thrown down his throat as was the second and the third. Gradually the soporific effect of the vodka numbed Otto. His morose staring into the fire was taking on a mesmeric influence drawing him in deeper and deeper the dancing orange and yellow flames creating visions and shapes. They formed, perished, reformed and mocked in grotesque parodies of human shapes. Sweat was breaking out on Otto's forehead and he flicked his left cheek before burying his head in his hands yelling, "*Nein, nein, nein.*"

Staggering to bed and kicking off his boots Otto lay down and tried to sleep whilst the room wheeled round and round. The boundary between consciousness, sleep and alcoholic stupor was blurred as the revolving ceiling morphed into a whirling pit where naked skeletal bodies on the periphery were continually being pushed into the abyss by ranks following on from behind and sucked into oblivion. Some decomposing bodies struggled to climb out of the pit but were held fast by elastic-like putrefied tendrils. As Otto stared into the abyss a giant hand reached out to drag him down to be saved only by falling off the bed onto the floor retching, vomiting and gasping for air.

CHAPTER 20

Grace/Annette – 1944

The Lysander throttled back and just skimmed the trees before dropping down into a field somewhere south-east of Rouen. Annie had waited anxiously all week and finally got the go-ahead on the last Thursday in March. Thin clouds dusted the night sky playing hide and seek with a new moon. Waiting for take-off she checked her papers and clothes over and over again as a way of calming her nerves. She opened and closed her small battered suitcase more than once moving her clothes around and sniffing inside. A change of clothes had been carefully washed without soap as the smell of this luxury in France would have been conspicuous enough to arouse suspicion. She thumbed the wallet belonging to the body lying on the floor beside her to make sure that everything was there as expected.

The flight had been monotonous and Annie was pleased to feel the bumps and thumps as the wheels skipped over the grass and the plane swung round ready for a quick take-off. No sooner had she flung open the door and climbed down the steps than the reception party of resistance members was already dragging containers of armaments, ammunition and food out of the plane as well as the corpse dressed in full flying gear with a parachute and harness attached. During the flight the body had been covered by a tarpaulin and Annie had not seen the torn clothes stained with blood where shrapnel had entered and accomplished its evil intent. The poor pilot's face was unrecognisable.

"Pierre, Bernard, David it's good to see you all again."

"Grace, welcome back to France. Quick, we must hurry, what do you want us to do with this?" Pierre asked pointing at the corpse.

"First let's get him away from this field. Tyre tracks possibly left by the plane will alert any German search party."

Keeping to the hedgerows they quickly carried the body to the other side of the field. "*Merde,*" cursed Pierre under his breath as the intransigent parachute silk kept slipping and sliding onto the ground tripping him up. They hauled the corpse into the wood and carried it far enough away from the landing field so that the two would not be connected. Eventually they stopped at a narrow pathway wending its way through the trees and which eventually opened out onto a country lane. It was important that they were not detected but it was also imperative that the body was found as soon as possible, in the morning preferably.

"We've got to make it look as if he's bailed out and been unlucky to land in a tree. We'll need to haul the chute up into the higher branches not forgetting to rip the silk and make it look as if he's snapped a few branches off as he's crashed through the top of the tree."

Taking the top off a flask that Grace had in her suitcase she sprinkled fresh blood at the wound sites and on the unfortunate pilot's face.

"Grab this," Pierre said to Bernard, handing him some of the parachute silk, "and follow me."

The two of them climbed quickly up a tree dragging the parachute canopy behind them.

"Go over to that side Bernard whilst I haul some of this through the branches. You do the same over there."

Having tangled the chute in the top reaches of the tree they hauled the corpse up by the chute harness and arranged the straps so that the body dangled convincingly above the ground.

"Here," Grace whispered as she threw the flask up to Pierre. "Put some of this on the bark so that it looks as if he's swung and smashed his face into the trunk."

Grace dribbled the last of the blood down his legs and onto the grass directly underneath where the pilot dangled. Satisfied with their work the four made their way through the wood to the fields on the other side, stopped and crouched down, waited and listened before removing camouflaged branches from four bicycles.

"Where did you get your volunteer?" Bernard whispered.

"He died this afternoon after a raid last night. The blood in the flask was his. We've waited to make sure that every detail is perfect. This has got to look authentic. Don't ask me why, but this mission is vital and just has to work. Not only does my life depend on its success but probably the lives of thousands of allied soldiers to say nothing of civilians. Tell me, did a Mosquito bomber fly overhead minutes before I landed?"

"As a matter of fact one did," David replied, "It sounded in trouble and was leaving a trail of smoke behind it, poor bastard. But how did you know?"

"That was a decoy. Hopefully it will convince the Germans that our guy in the tree was one of the crew and that will give credibility to my story."

Satisfied that there was no other movement in the neighbourhood they mounted their bicycles and set off for the farm and its safe room under the barn floor. Having lived in the Lyons-la-Foret area all his life Pierre knew how to travel across country using the terrain to avoid been observed from roads.

The light of a watery dawn sun was captured by high streaks of fluffy clouds transforming them quickly from a cold white to yellow then red rippling across the sky in layers like sand on a beach after the tide has turned as they finally entered the farmyard.

After some hot soup and home-made bread Grace settled down for a few hours' sleep in the safe room in the barn.

It was imperative that the authorities knew about the dead pilot sooner rather than later so that they would link him to the decoy Mosquito which had flown over the area the previous night. After breakfast Pierre showed Grace on a map the wood and path where they had left the corpse swinging in a tree and the route they had taken from the site to the farm. It was too risky to leave the discovery of the pilot to chance so taking one of the bicycles Grace set off for the nearest village of Etrepagny on the pretext of doing some shopping but in reality to try to make contact with any Germans with whom she might run into.

"Do you want me to come with you?" Pierre asked.

"No, that's quite alright Pierre. I just need to make sure that the Germans are made aware of our friend in the trees and I'll be right back. It's not a problem, don't worry. I'll see you soon."

It was a bright spring morning and Grace set off feeling pleased with progress so far. The countryside had shaken off the grip of winter and was making progress towards summer with renewed vigour and confidence. It was easy to forget that there was a war on as she cycled along peaceful country roads with nothing but song birds for company and the rhythmic squeak of the pedals as she pushed them round and round. But Grace knew that she must remain focused for it was all too easy to relax, become careless and be caught off guard. There was no sign of life until she reached the edge of the small country town of Etrepagny. But even here there were not many souls about. Those people she passed were mainly old women carrying shopping baskets hoping to buy some bread or other scarce staples of life. The old bicycle rattled and shook over the cobbles as Grace cycled on towards the town square where she knew she would find the Marie, Town Hall. It was unmistakable with two Nazi banners hanging one each side of the entrance. There were two guard boxes occupied by two Wehrmacht soldiers. An army lorry was parked nearby with three further soldiers, laughing, joking, smoking and lounging against the engine bonnet one with his foot up on the front bumper. At the other side of the entrance was a motorcycle and side-car on which was mounted a machine-gun. The occupant of the side car was leaning back with both his legs outstretched and dangling over each side of the gun mount. He was also smoking and joking with his motorcycle comrade.

It didn't take long for the assembled soldiers to catch sight of Grace approaching and hail her with wolf whistles and crude comments. Nearing the motorcycle the very young looking rider shouted, "Does your mother know you're out?" Accompanied by much hilarity amongst his comrades. The laughter grew even louder when Grace replied, "Does yours?" The mood changed to one of uncertainty when Grace continued and asked, "Where is your officer?"

"Inside," one of the soldiers leaning on the lorry said pointing his thumb over his shoulder towards the town hall entrance. They all looked sheepishly at one another as Grace propped her bike up against the town hall wall.

"Will you please go inside and tell him that I have something important to say to him." Grace asked in a manner that suggested she expected the soldier to carry out her request. The soldier who had pointed took a last drag on his cigarette and flicked it into the street. Checking his uniform he disappeared inside the building. A few minutes later he emerged with a Wehrmacht lieutenant beside him.

"Is this the girl?"

"Yes sir," the young private replied.

"I understand you have something to tell me mademoiselle." The lieutenant asked in slow but perfectly good French.

"Yes sir, I have seen a body in the wood. A pilot I think."

"Where is this body?" the lieutenant responded with interest.

"There," Grace pointed the way she'd entered the town. "I can show you."

There was immediate activity as the lieutenant shouted orders and soldiers appearing from nowhere began to climb into the back of the lorry and the motorcyclist kicked his bike into life. Grace's cycle was thrown into the back of the lorry and she was directed to climb into the front cab alongside the lieutenant and driver.

She guided the driver to a single narrow lane snaking its way between woods separated by open fields and then asked him to stop when they reached the entrance to the pathway leading into the wood where she had left the body the night before. Fearing an ambush the lieutenant took instant control and barked out orders for his troops to immediately evacuate the lorry and spread out taking cover.

Crouching behind the lorry the lieutenant asked Grace, "Where is this body?"

"About two hundred metres up that path."

"If this is an ambush mademoiselle you will be the first to die because I will shoot you myself," the lieutenant said menacingly.

"If there is an ambush it's none of my making," Grace responded. "I just saw a glimpse of parachute as I cycled into town this morning and when I went to investigate there was a pilot hanging in the tree. I thought it my duty to report it to the authorities."

The lieutenant waited in silence for a few minutes then waved his men forward using hand signals to direct them in a wide encircling manoeuvre. When he was convinced that there were no resistance fighters in the area the lieutenant visibly relaxed and asked Grace, "Where is this pilot of yours then?"

She walked to the entrance of the path through the wood and pointed.

"Come with me." The lieutenant said turning towards Grace.

They walked the two hundred metres into the wood and Grace guided the lieutenant to the parachute captured in the tree.

The lieutenant inspected the site and turning to his corporal said, "Cut him down and put him in the back of the lorry. We'll take him back to Etrepagny and inform the SS in Rouen. Not that there's much to interest them."

They retraced their steps back to the lane. "Pass down mademoiselle's bicycle," the lieutenant ordered one of the soldiers who'd just climbed back into lorry after. "Or would you like to be dropped off somewhere more convenient?" the officer continued in a more friendly manner.

"No this is good," Grace answered.

"I'll need your name and address for my report," he persisted.

Not wishing to draw any attention to the farm where she was staying and remembering her training that, it was always the best policy to tell the truth as far as possible as one lie leads to another to cover it up until you become trapped in your own web. Taking out her SS sponsored identification Annette handed it to the lieutenant whose demeanour changed immediately. The assembled soldiers looked on with bemused interest as the lieutenant straightened up, clicked his heels and saluted Grace.

"That will be all mademoiselle," he said efficiently, "And enjoy the rest of your day."

* * * * *

Her small bed-sitting room in Paris was just as she had left it three months ago but there was a musty, unlived-in smell about the place. Annette hauled the duvet over the backs of two chairs switched on the small electric fire and left it there to warm through. Fresh air permeated the room once the window was opened and it was not too long before the place was habitable again. After a supper of soup made from indeterminate ingredients at a local café Annette returned home and slept fitfully her plans for the next day playing over and over in her mind.

It was lunchtime and the bread and cheese was filling. The sun felt warm on her face and clumps of daffodils and tulips imparted a colourful air of optimism. Annette sat in the Jardin des Plantes next to the River Seine, waiting. Eventually she was relieved as she recognised the figure of Collette approaching. She stood up and they kissed each other on both cheeks.

"It's good to see you again Collette."

"Welcome back to Paris Annette, it's so good to see you safe and well. Although there's not much to come back to. Food is scarce and even more expensive. The Germans are as jumpy as fleas but worst of all the Gestapo have penetrated the Prosper network and arrested the whole inner circle. I think the problem was that it had grown too large, too many agents making too many mistakes. There's even a rumour that the Gestapo have managed to get hold of some radios and codes and is communicating with London as a subterfuge. Paris is a very dangerous place at the moment Annette. I would lie low for a while or get out altogether."

"I have one more important mission to complete before I do anything else. Give my love to the girls at the office. It's been lovely to see you again Collette and thanks for the warning."

"Take care Annette, au revoir."

They kissed again and left in opposite directions. Annette traced the familiar route towards Avenue Foch where the SS Headquarters was situated, showed her papers and entered the building.

"I'd like to speak with SS Hauptsturmfuhrer Otto von Lieper's successor please," Annette asked the desk corporal with an air of authority.

"Who shall I say you are?" The corporal replied with a bored lack of interest.

"Mademoiselle Annette Hugot, Hauptsturmfuhrer von Lieper's private assistant."

The corporal spoke into the telephone on his desk for a few minutes and then turning to Annette said, "SS Sturmbannfuhrer Lindemann will see you straight away. It's up the........."

Annette turned to leave and interrupted saying, "I know where it is."

Memories came flooding back as she climbed the marble stairs and made her way along the corridor to Otto's old office. She knocked on the door and waited for a reply.

"Come."

Annette entered and immediately opened the conversation. "Good afternoon Sturmbannfuhrer it's very good of you to see my straight away."

He was older than Otto with a round face and ruddy complexion. His stomach was beginning to bulge imparting a cuddly appearance but his eyes were deeply set, dark, alert and piercing.

"Good afternoon mademoiselle it's good to meet you at last. Otto has told me so much about you and how you've helped the Party. I hope that you have had a refreshing break......where was it you were going to again?" he enquired.

"To visit my cousins in Rouen and Clermont." Annette replied with the feeling that he already knew the answer.

"Ah yes....Otto did mention it. He also mentioned to me that you might like to continue to work here on a part-time basis as an interpreter, secretary and general assistant. Is that right?"

"If you think that I could be of help and that there is a position for me then I would be pleased to be of assistance."

"I think that you could be of great help. Your German is excellent.... where did you learn to speak so fluently?"

"At the Sorbonne but I spent a wonderful year at Heidelberg University just before the war."

"An admirer of our Wagner so I believe, with introductions to Reichsfuhrer Himmler and even the Fuhrer himself. You seem to have adapted to our German culture without too much trouble mademoiselle."

"There is so much to admire," Annette replied but she was on her guard for Lindemann seemed to know a little too much about her and his probing felt more like an interrogation. "Before we get down to the details of my employment Sturmbannfuhrer, I know it's very presumptuous of me but, I have a big favour to ask you."

"Ask away, but if we're to work together then I'll call you Annette if you're comfortable with that and when we're not meeting formally then please call me Ernst. Now what is this favour?"

"It's rather urgent actually. I have come across some vital informa-tion which must be communicated to Reichsfuhrer Himmler in person immediately. This is so important that it could save the lives of thousands of German soldiers and even shorten the war. I mean no disrespect to yourself Sturmba.......Ernst but I must contact Heinrich directly."

Ernst looked straight into her eyes as he picked up the phone on his desk and dialled the switchboard. When he'd established contact he handed the phone over to Annette.

"Put me through immediately to Reichsfuhrer Himmler, SS Headquarters Berlin, this is urgent and I must speak to him in person." The wait seemed interminable and Annette was relieved when at last someone spoke on the other end of the line.

"SS Headquarters who's speaking please?"

"This is Mademoiselle Annette Hugo personal assistant to Hauptsturmfuhrer Otto von Lieper calling from SS Headquarters in Paris I must speak to the Reichsfuhrer immediately on a matter of vital security. I have met the Reichsfuhrer and he knows me. I must speak to him personally."

"I'll see what I can do mademoiselle. Hold the line."

Annette's heart sank when the message came back, "I'm afraid the Reichsfuhrer is not in the building but he might be at the Reich Chancellery. If you wait I'll try to make contact and patch you through."

Annette became more and more agitated and frustrated as all she could hear in the earpiece were clicks, squawks and static. She was also aware of Ernst sitting still behind his desk staring at her with his penetrating, searching eyes.

At long last to Annette's relief the phone coughed and crackled into life, "Reichsfuhrer Himmler here, who's speaking?"

"Thank you for coming to the phone Reichsfuhrer, its Mademoiselle Annette Hugo....you remember.....we met at Bayreuth last year. I was with Otto von Lieper."

"Ah yes, I remember you well, I understand you have something of importance for me."

"The information that has come into my possession is so vital for the future of Germany that I cannot pass it on over the phone. If it is possible Reichsfuhrer I must meet you as soon as possible and then you can draw your own conclusion, and it is your decision, but I believe that the Fuhrer must be informed."

"If it is as important as you say mademoiselle then you had better come to Berlin. Rail travel is not as rapid as it used to be so I will see you at the Reich Chancellery in two days' time in the afternoon. There will be reservations made for you at The Adlon Hotel. Is there someone with you at the moment?"

"Yes, Otto's successor, Sturmbannfuhrer Ernst Lindemann."

"Put him on the line."

"Reichsfuhrer."

"I want you to arrange for Mademoiselle Hugo to have a travel warrant for Berlin and issue her with all the necessary paperwork to allow her to travel unimpeded. Is that clear?"

"Certainly Reichsfuhrer. I'll attend to it right away."

"Put the mademoiselle back on the line."

"Yes, Reichsfuhrer."

"You will be expected in two days, Goodbye." The phone clicked and the line went dead.

"Well," Ernst said, "I didn't know you were quite so well connected. I'd better be on my best behaviour when you're around."

"Have no fear Ernst, I only follow orders just like you."

* * * * *

After a reasonably comfortable night on the sleeper train Annette exited the Anhalter Bahnhof and was shocked at the destruction visible in all directions. It was common in London to see a bombed out space like a missing tooth in a terrace where someone's home had been but here in Berlin whole blocks were damaged. There was a taste of dust in the air and a thick atmosphere which seemed to adhere to her hair, face and hands. Everywhere, civilians and prisoners alike were scrambling like ants and using spades, brushes and buckets endeavouring to pile up debris and clear the streets. Traffic was moving freely and the S-Bahn trains, packed with passengers, clattered and screeched their way along the tracks. Military vehicles and personnel were everywhere as were red flags and banners with the black and white swastika in the middle. Colourless clad pedestrians weaved their way along the debris strewn pavements avoiding eye contact with each other. She walked towards the Brandenburg Gate transfixed by its neoclassical, overpowering, solid grandeur with bright Nazi banners hanging full length between the twelve grey solid Doric columns designed to form the five passageways through the arch. For a moment Annette couldn't help but stop and look up at the Quadriga triumphant statue of Victoria, the Roman Goddess of Victory riding in her chariot drawn by four horses. In her hand was a Nazi flag fluttering in the breeze. Turning into Unter den Linden she could see the Adlon Hotel in Pariser Platz on the right.

The clock in the lobby showed five 'o' clock as she approached the reception desk. In spite of the debris and destruction outside the Adlon interior lived up to its reputation as one of the most luxurious hotels in the world which boasted among its past clientèle European royalty as well as world renowned entertainment stars such as Greta Garbo, Charlie Chaplin and Enrico Caruso. However the clientele now looked more formidable in their black uniforms. The Adlon was now used by the SS for their dinners, balls and festivities. The lobby was a hive of activity as individuals and twos and threes made purposeful progress in all directions weaving in and out of groups of SS officers standing around talking and laughing.

"Good afternoon, can I help you?"

"Yes, thank you," Annette answered, "I believe that there should be a reservation for me, Annette Hugo, Mademoiselle Annette Hugo."

On hearing this two of the nearest SS officers stopped talking and looked in her direction with puzzlement.

The receptionist hesitated just a moment longer than usual before consulting the register. At the same time Annette was conscious of movement off to the side and she was sure that one of the officers was about to approach her.

"Ah yes mademoiselle I have it here. The Reichsfuhrer's office has made the reservation and Reichsfuhrer Himmler has left instructions that your bill will be paid by his office and that you are to enjoy all our facilities whilst you remain here."

Annette smiled inwardly as the officer stopped in his tracks and retreated to his companions who commenced to indulge in animated conversation whilst trying to surreptitiously glance in her direction.

"Room 125, through the lobby, up the stairs to the first floor and on the right. Would you like someone to take your suitcase?"

"That won't be necessary," Annette responded, "I'm only staying two nights and I haven't brought much with me."

She could feel four pairs of eyes following her progress as she walked towards the stairs.

The room was luxurious enough to be obscene in these times of deprivation and Annette felt both anger and guilt. How can people isolate themselves from their fellow countrymen to this extent which allows them to revel in this sort opulence whilst others are suffering the direst effects of the war she considered? The self-indulgent arrogance displayed in the dining room later filled her with disgust as countless bottles of champagne and the finest of foods were quaffed in whichever direction she looked. She felt sure that she looked conspicuous dining on her own but her confidence projected an entitlement which many observed but no one challenged.

The next morning Annette took the opportunity for a little sightseeing in the immediate neighbourhood. In spite of bomb damage the historical splendour and confidence of Berlin was still there below the surface. The chic tree lined avenue of Unter den Linden. The magnificent façade of the Reichstag although now just a burnt out shell and the oasis of the Tiergarten where Berlin families had once enjoyed weekend picnics in the faux countryside but were now in the process of deforesting the park searching for firewood.

After lunch back at the hotel Annette made her way anxiously down Wilhelmstrasse towards the Reich Chancellery and her appointment with Himmler. From outside the Chancellery had a stern, authoritarian appearance. She showed her papers to the guards and entered through the great gates. Crossing the Court of Honour she approached the main entrance which was flanked by two bronze statues, one representing the Wehrmacht and the other, The Party. Once inside Annette announced her appointment with Himmler and when the details were checked she was introduced to a guide to take her to his office. From the reception room Annette was shown through huge imposing double doors which opened into a large hall clad in mosaic. Following her guide she ascended several steps and passed through a series of magnificent rooms which took her breath away. At last the guide stopped outside an office and knocked on the door.

"Come in."

"Mademoiselle Annette Hugo," the guide announced.

"Come in mademoiselle," Himmler said informally getting up from behind a huge walnut desk and inviting her to sit in a large leather easy chair, "I don't wish to appear ill-mannered and brusque but time is short and if your information is as important as you say it is then we mustn't waste what little of it we have."

Annette had forgotten what an un-Aryan appearance Himmler presented. Considering the strict criteria for membership of his SS his receding dark hair, thick lensed spectacles and weak receding chin were anything but the blonde, athletic German ideal. But she didn't allow his appearance to let her forget what a powerful and evil man he was.

"To get to the point, tell me what you know."

"Whilst staying with my cousins near Rouen four days ago I went for a cycle ride in the country. I spotted a parachute tangled high in a tree and when I went to investigate I found a dead RAF flyer dangling by his harness. I looked in his pockets for some identification and I found this." Annette removed the wallet from her handbag and handed it to Himmler who emptied the contents onto the low table between them. He picked up a return rail ticket stub from Cambridge to Dover via London. There were also two cinema tickets for the Odeon in Dover and an invoice and receipt for a double room for two nights at the Sea View guest house in Dover. Throwing these back onto the table Himmler picked up the three photographs. The first one obviously the flyer taken with his mother and father and the other two pictures were of a pretty young brunette leaning on a beached boat. The sort of pictures of girlfriends that all soldiers carried with them.

Himmler threw the photos back onto the table in disgust saying with impatience," How are these important to the future of the Reich mademoiselle?"

"That was my reaction when I first saw them as well. Do you have a magnifying glass Reichsfuhrer?"

Himmler got up and went over to his desk opening one of the drawers. Returning to his seat opposite Annette, she continued, "Look closely at the background behind the girl in both photos. The young flyer mustn't have realised when he took these snaps of his girlfriend but he has unknowingly captured the unmistakable figure of Churchill and the other person is a high ranking USA officer who looks remarkably like Eisenhower. You can also just make out a convoy of escort Jeeps and a staff car on the promenade with pennants fastened to the front wings. Unfortunately there isn't a wind blowing so we can't see what's on the pennants but I would guess that they signify high ranking personnel. But what is also interesting Reichsfuhrer," and Annette leaned over to emphasise her point, "Are these landing craft you can just make out in the harbour and on the beach hidden under camouflage nets. The harbour is obviously Dover because you can see the white cliffs disappearing down into the sea in the far distance but you can also make out Dover painted on the boat the girl is leaning on and beside the name of the boat even though the weather has faded the paint." Seeing that she had now captured Himmler's interest Annette continued, "I know that there is indecision as to where the allies will mount their coming sea-borne invasion of Europe but I think that these photos, showing Churchill and Eisenhower inspecting preparations for the invasion offer irrefutable evidence that Dover/Calais is going to be the route."

"*Mein Gott,*" Himmler exploded, "This is incredible. The Fuhrer has always insisted that Calais would be the landing place. He has an uncanny instinct where military matters are concerned but he has been trying to assemble intelligence to convince the Wehrmacht High Command. I must get these to him immediately. Once again Annette you have shown your loyalty to the Reich and the Fuhrer. Leave these with me and wait at the Hotel until I contact you, probably tomorrow. I know that you understand the significance of what you have discovered and I appreciate your secrecy and confidence as I'm sure will the Fuhrer."

Himmler stood up signalling that the meeting was at an end but Annette couldn't resist missing the opportunity and asked, "Have you heard from Otto? How is he? I haven't had any communication from him since he left for the east."

"Otto and his new wife are in the best of health." Himmler replied with the merest hint of a smirk.

Annette's training had not prepared her for this sort of circumstance. It was as if a cold dagger had pierced her solar plexus. She hid her reaction as best she could but she knew that Himmler had caught her tell-tale eye movement.

He had sensed Annette's feelings for Otto the first time they met and he was sure that they were reciprocated. His response to Annette's inquiry had been deliberate and calculating taking delight in the fact that he had saved Otto from the political suicide which would have resulted from his marrying a non-Aryan.

"You didn't know that he had married my niece, Sieglinde? A fine German couple who will produce a pure Aryan blood future generation to carry on the work of The Reich."

"I'm very happy for him and your niece." Annette managed to say although she knew that Himmler sensed her insincerity.

"Now I really must see the Fuhrer as you'll understand. I cannot thank you enough for your devotion to The Fatherland and I'll be in touch tomorrow. I'll have someone show you the way out."

Annette walked back to the hotel seeing everything through blurred, tear-filled eyes. Why hadn't he told her? How could he have been such a deceiving bastard after everything they had said and meant to each other? Disappointment and self-pity were replaced by anger which in turn was displaced by despair. Without making a deliberate decision to do so, she automatically steered her way into the hotel lounge bar and in defiance of all her instincts for self-preservation ordered an expensive bottle of Château Laville Haut-Brion Blanc. If The Party was going to steal her lover then the least it could do was pay for an expensive bottle of wine. She chose a comfortable arm chair positioned where she could look out of the window into the street, which did little to cheer her up, as well as see what was going on inside the room. The waiter half-filled her wine glass and deposited the bottle in an ice bucket on the low table in front of her chair. Annette watched the condensation forming on the outside of the glass before running her finger down the side and picking the glass up by the stem. The pale golden liquid awakened her taste buds bringing back memories of hot, carefree summer days sitting by the River Loire with friends during her vacations from the Sorbonne.

Looking round the room at animated groups of SS officers and their lady friends she wondered how she had ended up here, in this situation. With half the bottle consumed Annette began to mellow. Of course Otto loved her. She appreciated how ambitious he was and how under the patronage of Himmler he must have found it impossible to back out of what must have been an arranged marriage. To have thwarted Himmler would have been to consign himself to Party oblivion. Otherwise how could the marriage have taken place so quickly when Otto had been constantly with her in Paris? She convinced herself that it was a loveless marriage of convenience and that eventually Otto would come back to her just as he'd promised.

Her mood lightened and sticking the empty bottle upside down in the ice bucket she made her way into the dining room. The evening was early and the head waiter guided Annette to one of the many, as yet, empty tables. She ordered another bottle of Château Laville, made her selection from the very expensive and varied menu and smiled at other guests, male and female as they passed her table.

An hour and a half later as the dining room began to fill up and the noise level increased accordingly Annette made her unsteady way to her room. She found it necessary to sit on the bed in order to undress without stumbling and discarding her clothes on the floor she curled up in the soft luxurious king size bed and was soon fast asleep.

* * * * *

She was ushered into the same room she had been in the previous afternoon to find Himmler once again at his desk.

"Good afternoon Mademoiselle Hugo, I trust you slept well. At least the RAF had a night off for you. To get to the point....I have spoken to the Fuhrer and he is absolutely delighted with your loyalty. Especially so as I've run a check with the Rouen SS Office and they corroborate your story confirming that a British aircraft was spotted in difficulty after a raid on Dieppe and that without doubt your flyer must have been one of the crew. They found no wreckage and presume that the aircraft must have come down over the channel." Getting up from behind his desk Himmler extended his arm and continued, "Come, you're very privileged, the Fuhrer wants to meet you to thank you in person. I think you have made a very big impression."

Walking along the corridor Himmler continued, "This is Hitler's reception gallery. The office I'm using is only temporary, as you can appreciate my main office is at the SS Headquarters in Prinz-Albrecht Strasse." He stopped outside one of the rooms and knocked on the door before entering the large sumptuously decorated reception room. The opulence was overpowering as indeed was the intention. The furniture was solid and highly lacquered. The brocade upholstered seats were rich in gold and texture and a large painting of the Fuhrer himself hung on the wall behind the largest desk Annette had ever seen. A group of men turned towards them as Himmler and Annette entered the room.

At the centre of the group stood Hitler, his hands behind his back. Also present and introduced to Annette were Joachim von Ribbentrop,

Martin Bormann, Goebbels, Albert Speer, Field-Marshall Gunther von Kluge, and Hermann Göring who was lounging asleep in a large wing-backed chair.

Hitler stepped forward and took Annette's hand in both of his. Her smile managed to hide the shock at how much he had changed since their meeting at Bayreuth the previous year. His eyes, although still staring were dull and lifeless. The penetrating, unnerving probing and underlying threat was no longer there. His halitosis was overpowering and she detected a slight tremor in his left hand as it rested on top of hers.

"Welcome to Berlin Mademoiselle Hugo, are you still enjoying our Wagner?"

"Indeed I am Mein Fuhrer but I seem to have so little time to indulge myself these days."

"Ahh yes.....the war is our lives now but I am delighted that your loyalty to me and the Party is still beyond doubt. I wish I could say the same for some of my Generals. Your recent intelligence is a magnificent piece of detective work and it has given me the additional solid evidence I have been waiting for to back up my instincts. Rommel insists that the landing will take place in Normandy and we have had a number of disagreements about it and especially his proposed plans to deploy his troops. But now, thanks to you, perhaps he will listen to reason. Your news mademoiselle has clarified a difficult decision for me and left me extremely optimistic that we will throw the allies into the sea to swim back to their irritating little island."

Knowing Hitler's penchant for responding positively to flattery Annette risked, "With your permission Fuhrer, on the evidence of the photographs and your proven instinct in matters military I think your assessment of the situation makes excellent sense Mein Fuhrer and your strategy to meet the invasion the only possible one to adopt in the circumstances."

Annette allowed herself to relax slightly as the hint of a smile played around Hitler's lips. Reaching round to his desk Hitler picked up a small, slim black box and turning back to Annette said, "A token of the Third Reich's appreciation for your work and continuing loyalty. I haven't forgotten your part and efficiency in rounding up the Jews in France and now this major breakthrough in confirming the site of the invasion which will allow us to give the allies the bloodiest nose of the war so far." Annette raised her hand to receive the gift from Hitler as he continued to say, "It gives me great pleasure to present you with the Iron Cross, Second Class."

The assembled group applauded politely.

Annette took the medal with its red, white and black ribbon in her hand. "Thank you, I didn't expect this. My reward is to have the honour to continue to serve you Mein Fuhrer but I shall wear this with love and pride."

Hitler nodded to Himmler as a sign that the meeting was over. Annette saluted, "*Heil Hitler,*" and turned to leave the room accompanied by the Reichsfuhrer.

"What will you do now?" Himmler asked once they were outside in the corridor.

"I'm going back to Paris to work for Sturmbannfhurer Lindemann and be ready to be of service to the Party in any way that I can."

"You know....you should consider joining the SS. I would sponsor you myself so there would not be any problem."

Caught off guard Annette hoped that her reply managed to hide her confusion. "You do me a great honour Reichsfuhrer. I've never thought about it but I shall give it serious consideration when I get back to Paris. Thank you for your confidence."

Two corporal guards standing outside the Fuhrer's office stiffened to attention when one of them was addressed by Himmler. "Show Mademoiselle Hugo out corporal." Turning to Annette and extending his hand he continued, "May I add my thanks to the Fuhrer's for your trust and loyalty. I'm sure you will continue your good work and perhaps we will meet again. *Auf Wiedersehen mademoiselle,* have a safe journey home."

Back at the swish Adlon hotel Annette allowed herself the indulgence of relaxing once again in the sumptuous lounge bar. She sat down in the same seat as the previous evening and was immediately approached by the same waiter.

"Would Miss like a bottle of her favourite Chateau Laville?"

"Yes thank you.......er no, on second thoughts......make it a bottle of champagne.....I think I deserve it."

"Certainly," The waiter responded enthusiastically, "Are you celebrating?"

"Indeed I am," Annette said putting the Iron Cross down on the table.

"Congratulations, I am very impressed."

"I am too..... Presented by the Fuhrer himself, and I think I might get a little drunk." Removing the medal from its case Annette turned it over to read an inscription. '*Annette Hugo–1944.* There was also a small, printed card in the box which Annette translated as 'For loyalty and services to the Reich' and signed in Hitler's own writing. The waiter returned quickly with the champagne and made a great show of popping the cork attracting the attention of people at nearby tables. Rummaging in her bag Annette found a pin and carefully pushing it through the medal ribbon fastened the Iron Cross to her jacket left breast. Three SS officers at the nearest table smiled and applauded and Annette smiled back partly in response to the scowls of jealousy on the faces of the officers' female companions. The Iron Cross, First Class was only awarded to Wehrmacht and SS troops. Classified Second Class medals could be awarded to civilians in exceptional circumstances but this was very rare and Annette surprised herself by taking a perverse pride in flaunting her celebrity.

The champagne bottle dead in the ice bucket Annette got up carefully in order to make her way towards the dining room. Each cluster of officers she passed on her way towards the lounge exit having guessed what was going on applauded her as she passed. Annette couldn't disguise the huge smile on her face as she turned and applauded each group in turn whispering under her breath, "Fuck you, and you, and you, and you."

* * * * *

The taxi only just made it to Anhalter Station in time for Annette to catch the sleeper for Paris. Coming down from her alcoholic high she was now the victim of a headache and decided to climb into her couchette straight away. The events of the day refused to vacate her mind. But a trained pragmatism gained precedence and Annette considered her options as the train slipped out of the station. She was hurt and felt betrayed by the news of Otto's marriage to Himmler's niece and reconciled herself to believing that the marriage had been forced on Otto.

There were matters of greater urgency to concern her. She must let London know of the successful outcome of their planned subterfuge as soon as possible. Her life would be compromised as soon as the allies' invasion hit the beaches. Once Normandy was confirmed as the main beach-head her double-cross would be exposed and the fallout from the explosion of Hitler's anger would be felt all over Europe. There would be a price on her head for sure. Should she desert Paris straight away? But to suddenly disappear would immediately throw suspicion on her and expose her as an agent compromising her intelligence report to Berlin and every Gestapo officer in Europe would be on the lookout for her. The best plan she convinced herself was for her to maintain the status quo and return to her part-time work at SS Headquarters in Paris until such time as she could slip away without arousing the suspicion which would alert Berlin to her double-cross. But in order to slip away and re-join the 'Salesman' circuit at Rouen at the last moment she would need to know the invasion date. Feeling confident about her immediate plans Annette allowed the rhythmic click clacking of the wheels and swaying of the carriage to usher her gently towards a light sleep.

The journey was long and tedious and when the train was shunted into a siding for the umpteenth time Annette was grateful that at least she could pull the blanket around her and relax in relative warmth and comfort. Conscious that the train was now moving slowly she lifted the window blind and peered out through sleepy, half-closed eyes. Columns of black smoke reached up to embrace the low, dark, heavy clouds trying their best to hold back a watery, silver dawn. A name plate attached at one end only hung at a drunken angle on the wall of a signal box as it glided slowly past and Annette could just make out the name Mannheim. The carriage lurched and wheels shrieked resistance to a change in direction causing Annette to bang her head on the window surround. She watched transfixed as the train picked its delicate way along a single track where brown sprouting rust evidenced that it had not supported transport for a very long while. From time to time she could have reached out to touch claustrophobia inducing crumbling retaining walls and perimeter walls of industrial workshops. The more open spaces were littered with railway and manufacturing junk. There was little evidence of residential buildings as a procession of gantries, bridges and dirty, derelict looking buildings advanced and receded as the train swayed along its precarious route points switching it onto other single tracks a frequent intervals. As the train negotiated a long curve Annette could see a pall of black smoke arching overhead as if the city had erected a giant black umbrella against some huge malevolent storm. Buildings without roofs and some with walls blown down were now becoming more frequent as were smouldering ruins glowing red and orange. The train slowed to a crawl as it negotiated its way along the track close to a building silhouetted by a raging inferno the flames of which were licking their way upwards through shattered windows. Annette gave a start as falling debris rattled onto the track and roof of her carriage. Orange, red and yellow flames shooting sparks 150 feet into the air flared fiercely the heat forcing Annette momentarily away from the window. The devastation of the city became ever more apparent as the train continued to negotiate its way along tracks long neglected and others more familiar with industrial traffic than the night express from Berlin to Paris. Annette continued to stare out of the window watching trance-like as the cityscape of hell became no more than a receding red glow dropping off the edge of the world.

Annette's first priority was to have something to eat at the station buffet when she finally arrived in Paris. Later that evening she powered up her radio and quickly transmitted 'Dover Sole', twice, which was the pre-arranged code word to signal the success of her mission. What she didn't know was that somewhere in Paris a detector van was picking up her transmission.

"Our little pigeon is back on the wing again Heinz." The operator pressed the phones to his ears and delicately manipulated the wheel turning the directional radio aerial on the roof of the van.

"He's been absent for long time. I wonder where he's been and what he's been up to for the past few months?"

"Damn, he's signed off. At least we know he's back in the air. It won't be long before we clip his wings and bring him to roost."

CHAPTER 21

Otto 1944 – 1945

Whistles shrill, steam hissing, boilers panting, smoke belching from funnels and clanging carriage doors echoed around those vaults of the station roof which had not yet been blown in by the Allies' bombs. Otto could see Ziggy at the gate straining to pick him out from amongst the human wave of service personnel shuffling down the platform. Wearing a long, summer, floral patterned dress and with a small veiled hat pinned to her hair at a jaunty angle she looked incongruous in the drab surroundings of the damaged station. Her right arm, sheathed up to the elbow in an elegant silk glove, shot up into the air waving her cream leather handbag as she shouted, "Otto....over here, Otto."

As soon as he was through the gate she was in his arms her warm wet lips on his, sucking, her tongue searching. Breathless she caught his hand, "You look tired Otto. Come, I've got the car waiting. I'm living in Uncle Heinrich's house. He's always either at the Reich Chancellery or SS headquarters these days so we've got the place to ourselves."

"I only have 72 hour's leave and I really must see the Reichsfuhrer tomorrow" Otto replied.

"Well we'd better hurry up and make the most of the time we have then hadn't we?" Ziggy answered laughing, seemingly oblivious to the alien cityscape around them.

The noise of Ziggy's idle chatter faded into the background whilst Otto surveyed a Berlin showing even more scars of total warfare than the last time he visited. Ziggy steered the car quickly and skilfully towards the Dahlem district where even here damage was now more evident than previously. The occasional bombed out homes of rich industrialists and party members looked all the more shocking beside those mansions which still stood in defiance, their gardens in full summer bloom offering a pretence that what was happening was just an irritation, a fly to be swatted then forgotten.

Ziggy led Otto into the house and straight up the stairs to their bedroom.

"Let me bathe first," Otto said, "I stink of sweat, railways, and death."

"I don't care, I need you now," Ziggy replied quickly unbuttoning his jacket her fingers trembling.

Otto offered no resistance and was content to allow himself to be enfolded, cocooned by her warm soft flesh. Given his current physical and emotional exhaustion he was surprised at how quickly and easily she could arouse him. He had no love for her, not like Annette, but a primeval lust always seemed to take over and drive him towards a combative sex that left him physically satisfied and replete but hating himself afterwards for his male weakness and betrayal. Lying beside Ziggy Otto felt alone, lost and empty. This was not the two bodies, one soul experience that he shared with Annette. The warmth, the fulfilment, the joy of reaching out, risking and fusing with the essence of another human being. The contrast left him trapped by circumstances and depressed. Would he, could he, did he want to change these circumstances or would time do that for him without him having to force a decision himself?

After a hot bath Otto lay down beside Ziggy who cradled his head on her breasts. The heat from the afternoon sun reached down and the heady smell of roses and Ziggy's sweet perfume had a soporific effect which seduced him into a deep sleep.

Later the golden yellow sun gradually turned to red, bleeding its potency into the sky leaving the cotton-wool clouds to soak up its spilled, life-giving energy and change to fuzzy pink whilst bidding a light breeze into life teasing the curtains hanging by the bedroom open window to sway and dance in attendance. A warm swirling gust suddenly tugged at the drapes sending cosmetic bottles on the dressing table crashing to the floor. Otto woke with a start and quickly realising where he was settled back and nuzzled Ziggy's breasts until she stirred. They made love again and afterwards, on his way to the toilet, Otto said over his shoulder, "Get ready, we're going to the Adlon Hotel for dinner and after that we're going to dance the night away if the RAF will allow. I feel I deserve pampering so put on your most revealing dress, let's enjoy ourselves."

*****

"Come in Otto my boy, what a pleasure to see you after all this time."

"*Heil Hitler, Reichsfuhrer,*" Otto replied.

"Two coffees," Himmler shouted through the door. "Sit here Otto, I've read all of your reports and followed your work with great interest. You're a credit to the Reich and especially the SS, as I knew you would be, I'm proud of you and you deserve your short leave with your new wife."

"Thank you Reichsfuhrer, but there is much to do. The war in the east is a mess. Army Group Centre has collapsed and the Russians have reached the river Vistula opposite Warsaw. Fortunately they've exhausted themselves for the time being but they're only waiting for their second breath before they advance again and I fear there is going to be more trouble in Warsaw in the near future."

"When you return I want you to report to General Erich von dem Bach who is in command of the whole eastern area. I'm sure that under Bach you and Heinz together will be able to deal with Warsaw once and for all," Himmler dismissed. "As for the Red Army, Hitler has contingency to send reinforcements, but I've told you to call me Heinrich now that you're part of the family."

"It feels strange sir, perhaps I should call you uncle Heinrich like Ziggy," and they both broke out into laughter.

Taking a sip of his coffee and waiting until they were alone again Himmler continued more earnestly, "The SS needs to be strong Otto, now more than ever the Fuhrer relies on our loyalty. He can no longer trust the Wehrmacht generals and indeed some of the most senior staff openly question his military conduct of the war. Can you believe that? They owe everything to him and seem to have forgotten their sworn oath. You've probably heard that there was even another attempt on the Fuhrer's life at his field headquarters at Rastenburg last month. We arrested Count von Stauffenberg and he was executed immediately on 21st July. We've penetrated his 'Valkyrie' resistance operation but his band of conspirators have tentacles reaching throughout the army and even now the Gestapo is rooting out the traitors. There is more for the SS to do and there will be more opportunities for you Otto. Get a grip in the east and we will send Russia back to the middle ages with us as their overlords. But for now your immediate orders are to help settle this Warsaw business as soon as possible and close down and clear the last major camp in the east at Auschwitz before the Russians get the opportunity to overrun the site. It would offer them a great propaganda opportunity to the world."

"Consider it done Heinrich. With your permission sir, if there are no more orders for the present I must get back to my post and I need to see Ziggy again before I leave. Thank you for your trust in me and I won't let you down."

"I know that Otto. Unlike that French tart of yours in Paris."

"What do you mean?" Otto shot back in disbelief. "I haven't seen her in a long time but she was always loyal to the Party."

"Maybe, but she fed us false information about the proposed landing site for the Allies' invasion in the west and we suspect that she was a double agent. Anyway we have her photo on file and she's now on the Gestapo most wanted list and it shouldn't be too long before she's picked up."

"I'm shocked," was all that Otto could think of saying.

"It just proves that we can only trust our own Otto and even then we have to be ever vigilant. Give my love to Ziggy and I'll keep in touch."

"I'll keep you informed of progress sir and now with your permission I must leave if I'm to catch my train for Warsaw."

"Good bye Otto and good luck."

"Good bye sir."

Otto left the Reich Chancellery and made his way to the nearest 'S' Bahn stop. The tram rattled past Tiergarten on its way towards Grunewald and the Dahlem district. News of Annette had numbed him and all he could think of was that there must be another explanation. She loved him. There was no way that she could have deceived him without him suspecting. He would have known, he would have sensed it. Their togetherness, their lovemaking was real. There was a connection that no deceit could disguise. No...He could not accept it. Without knowing how he arrived he opened the front door to Himmler's house and walked in. Hearing an internal door slam caused by the through draught Ziggy, assuming correctly that it would be Otto returning shouted, "I'm in the garden darling. Come and have a glass of wine you must be exhausted."

Otto sank down beside her on the garden swing seat. "You poor darling, you haven't really had a restful leave have you. You work so hard and Uncle Heinrich is forever singing your praises but that doesn't compensate us for the time we have apart. Still I'm grateful to have you by my side whenever I can."

They finished the bottle and Otto began to feel his body collapsing in on itself. Could this be a metaphor for Germany he thought. In spite of Himmler's optimism Otto knew that the Reich was crumbling from within as well as on the eastern and now the western fronts.

"You seem as if you have the cares of the world on your shoulders Otto." Ziggy said soothingly as she stroked his hand. "Are things as bad as people are saying? People no longer seem to have an enthusiasm or will for the war and I have even heard dissenting voices in the streets. Are we losing the war Otto?"

"Don't worry," Otto replied trying to sound positive. "The SS will stiffen the Wehrmacht and the Russians will soon run out of steam then we will counter-attack and push them all the way back to Siberia where they are happiest with snow on their boots." He hoped that he had sounded convincing but he knew that Ziggy was no fool.

She opened another bottle of cold, sweet Mosel Riesling and refilled their glasses. "Come....let me take your mind off this damned war for a while and give you something to remember on your journey back to Warsaw."

She led him upstairs where they made love. Otto was content to go where Ziggy led but his mind was elsewhere. He responded physically but felt remote, as if he was in someone else's body, in a parallel existence.

Ziggy sensed his distance, "You poor darling, you really are giving your all for the Fuhrer. Leave some part of yourself for me, for us and for little Siegfried. I know...," she continued quickly placing her finger over his lips, "...I said I was pregnant before but this time the timing is right and you must return for the sake of our son, our little Siegfried."

* * * * *

Having reported to General von dem Bach's Polish Headquarters to discuss the situation and imminent military action Otto returned to the SS Headquarters in search of his old friend Heinz. Together they sat in armchairs in the familiar SS office suite in Warsaw each with a glass of vodka in his hand. Otto with a pensive look on his face. The war seemed to have developed an unpredictable life of its own. It was feeding on itself and growing more and more ravenous, out of control, determining events, dictating human involvement rather than responding to it. Otto felt that his involvement was now impotent and that all of his decisions were now reactions to the unpredictable vicissitudes of the war. Heinz leant forward and poured them both another vodka.

"You do know that we're losing this war Otto don't you? Against all the odds the Allies established a foothold in Normandy in June and even now are at the gates of Paris and we're running away like rabbits. It's like the first war all over again. We're fighting a war on two fronts and the outcome will be the same. But....you know the worst of it Otto...... we're fighting amongst ourselves. Like a wolf caught in a trap we're gnawing away at our own limbs in an effort to avoid the inevitable."

"I fear you might be right Heinz," Otto replied with a heavy heart, "But we swore an oath and still have our honour and duty to the Fuhrer."

"Do you really intend to go down with him Otto? He has alienated the whole of the German army officer corps and even the civilians who once adored him. The Wehrmacht despises the SS and we no longer talk to the Wehrmacht. What way is that to run a war? It's a disaster waiting to happen Otto."

"You need to be very careful who you say these things to Heinz."

"Are you threatening me Otto?"

"No I'm not.....of course not Heinz. You know that I know you're loyal to the Reich but there are others who might denounce you as a defeatist in order to further their own advancement. Especially now."

"Why especially now?"

"Since last month's assassination attempt Hitler has appointed Himmler as Commander-in-Chief of the Home and Reserve Armies and with the help of the Gestapo's new powers he has the army and population of Germany in the grip of his hand. He thinks I don't know but all strategy and decisions made by each of the members of Hitler's inner circle are made with the purpose of retaining the Fuhrer's influence rather than furthering the positive direction of the war. I think they all know that the war is lost and they're each manoeuvring to oust the others in their lust for power by taking over Germany when the Fuhrer's gone."

"That's heady stuff Otto. If what you say is true then we are indeed lost......but we have more immediate and urgent business to attend to here in Warsaw. Over the past few days whilst you've been away we've intercepted a lot of radio traffic and managed to gain valuable intelligence from captured resistance fighters."

"I know, von Bach has just informed me."

"With the Russians opposite Warsaw on the eastern bank of the Vistula we need to take the initiative. We know for certain that the remaining Jews are planning an imminent uprising. They've contacted the Polish Home Army and nationalist organisations and even now members of these resistance units are infiltrating into the city and we estimate something like 49,000 Home Army and resistance fighters are already in Warsaw. Stalin is stirring things up by calling on the Poles to rise up against us with the expectation that Soviet forces will shortly enter the city. The Jews are expecting Soviet support and this is giving them encouragement. However what they don't know and what we have found out is that the Russian Army has no intention of offering support to the Polish Home Army which is anti-communist. I think that Stalin will sit it out watching us slug it out amongst ourselves then walk right in."

"My God, what a mess," Otto said holding out his glass for another shot of Vodka flicking his left cheek with his left hand. "Von Bach agrees there's only one solution Heinz, we must surround and attack the Jewish camp and old ghetto area immediately and try to catch them off guard."

"I agree, General Bach has contacted me and suggested we get all unit commanders here this afternoon for a briefing and make a pre-emptive attack within twenty-four hours."

To Jews and resistance fighters hidden in their secret bunkers the rumble and vibration of tanks and lorries could not disguise an imminent attack. Otto sat in his kubelwagen constantly checking the time on his wristwatch. Eventually the sun peeped nervously over the horizon and was immediately assailed and blotted out by the smoke, debris and dust created by a massive coordinated artillery bombardment. Otto looked on with impulsive excitement as gouts of earth and masonry were thrown into the air and the smell of cordite filled his lungs.

He had never experienced combat but had always been aware that he wanted to test himself against the rigours and dangers of close contact with the enemy. Throughout his time in the Hitler Youth and SS officer training this had always been his fantasy. He felt exhilarated, alive in a way that he hadn't experienced for a long time. His car seat vibrated as panzers lumbered forward closely followed by troops bent over to make themselves smaller targets.

The tanks fanned out into the maze of urban streets. Otto jumped down from his kubelwagen closely followed by is two bodyguards and joined a section of troops close up behind the nearest tiger tank. It crossed an area of open ground leftover from the destruction of the uprising the previous year and entered the nearest street. The buildings looked dark, menacing and impregnable even though they displayed evidence of previous shell damage where rendering had been blasted away exposing the red brick walls beneath like scabbed ulcers. The tank creaked and clanked as one track slowed and the other continued in order to steer the monster down the street which appeared deserted. With his machine pistol at the ready Otto followed looking to right and left for the slightest sign of the enemy in building windows and doorways. Suddenly without warning the tank came under immediate attack as a Molotov cocktail was lobbed from an upper story window and crashed down onto the turret spreading a sheet of bright blue and yellow flames. Small arms fire and machine-guns from windows and roofs pinged and cracked into the walls dislodging chunks of brick and tearing wood splinters from doors and window frames. Ricocheting bullets zinged off the street setts spouting granite particles and dust up into the air. Troops scattered into doorways. Those who had not already pitched forward or crumpled dead or wounded pressed themselves against building walls trying to insinuate themselves into the very fabric of the masonry. Otto's reaction was immediate and instinctive and he was thrilled that his recent sedentary lifestyle had not taken the edge off his physical

abilities. Crouched panting in a doorway he yelled out, "Give cover.....
fire across the street." Troops responded immediately offering their
comrades protection by firing at buildings opposite. Still burning, the
turret traversed left and the tank rocked sideways from the recoil as the
shell punched its way into the ground floor of the building and was
answered by smoke and flames exploding out of windows, doors and the
gaping hole in the wall sending debris scattering across the street. Otto
quickly followed up urging troops into the building. Dust and falling
debris restricted their vision as Otto and his two comrades inched along
keeping close to the once beautiful oak panelled wall. On reaching the
first room Otto threw a grenade through the door and after the explosion
darted inside spraying his machine pistol in all directions. Using hand
signals he directed those troops who had accompanied him to clear out
the other rooms and make their way up the stairs floor by floor. Slowly
Otto made his way down to the cellar. As he turned at the first flight of
steps a hand suddenly appeared from round the corner holding an
automatic weapon which was spitting bullets in his direction. Otto
responded immediately with a burst from his own machine pistol and in
one leap jumped to the bottom of the steps and threw another grenade
round the corner following it up with automatic fire. Screams and groans
told him that he had found his mark and he carefully entered the room
where the atmosphere was almost solid and Otto could feel the grit
layered on his teeth.

A cool draught gradually cleared the air and in the gloom Otto
counted three dead men, two women and a teenage boy also dead.
Exploring the cellar he discovered a hole through into another room and
another beyond that creating a hidden passageway for defenders to move
from building to building without being seen. Confident that this part of
the block had been cleared they made their way back up to street level
where the fierce fire-fight was still in progress. The tank turret had now
traversed to the other side of the street and the recent operation was
repeated. Otto risked breaking cover and glanced down the street. A
youth no more than sixteen ran out from a building dropped to one knee
and raised a grenade launching panzerfaust releasing the projectile which
exploded against the front of the tank blowing the left track off its
driving wheels and suspension. He turned to run back to the safety of the
building but was caught in a hail of bullets and dropped to the ground
the panzerfaust skidding into the gutter. The hatch on the top of the tank
turret was thrown open from inside and one of the crew tried to climb
out but was immediately shot from an upper story window of an
apartment further down the street. He collapsed back into the body of
the tank and was immediately followed by another well aimed petrol
bomb. The screams of the remaining crew members could be heard

above the general noise of the battle just before the ammunition in the tank exploded sending the turret up into the air suspended on a column of noise and flames before it crashed down again into the street.

The distinctive whoosh and roar of flame throwers could be discerned as Wehrmacht soldiers tried to root out defenders from cellars and upper floors. The first block was eventually cleared as the last few defenders on the top floor were thrown alive crashing through the windows to crumple up amongst shards of glass in the street below and Otto allowed himself the luxury of a swig from his water bottle. The fighting was fierce and brutal but little real progress had been made. The Jews and Poles fought with a fanaticism which surprised Otto. Their positions only discerned by the muzzle flashes from rifles and automatic weapons.

The sun had seen enough and as if in sorrow gradually extinguished its bright summer warmth to those still able to feel it and a black silent shroud covered the city broken only by an occasional gunshot shattering the silence. Otto left orders for the troops to remain in their present positions. Finding his driver he withdrew to his kubelwagen. "Take me back to headquarters," He said as he sank into his seat and splashed his face with what water remained in his bottle.

Heinz was already slouched in an armchair after his day of observation from the other side of the city when Otto arrived and General Bach was standing looking out of the window. A large glass of vodka was extended and Otto downed it in one reaching for another.

"Well.....what's your assessment Otto?" the general asked. "You look as if you've been enjoying yourself. You shouldn't be on the front line Otto, your too important."

Otto couldn't remain still the adrenalin still coursing through his body and he paced with exaggerated nervous excitement around the room. "I know Herr General but I couldn't just sit there and observe. I knew I had to get involved and I haven't felt so good in a long while. But I think we have a difficult task ahead of us. It's not going to be the walk in the park that we expected."

"I agree Otto. For God's sake come and sit down, you're like a dog searching for a bitch on heat."

"We're spread too thin," Heinz interjected. "We've underestimated the strength and tenacity of the bastards. Every building, every room, every cellar is a fortress. It's going to take us a long time to winkle them all out."

"Unless......."

"Unless what Otto?" The general asked.

"We haven't got enough resources to blanket the whole of the city."

"Agreed."

"What I suggest is that we approach this systematically block by block, street by street. They're moving around the city underground through the sewers and they've blown holes through the walls to interconnect cellars. As we clear one building and move on they infiltrate back in behind us."

"So how do you suggest we deal with the situation?"

"We change tactics. Instead of a blanket artillery bombardment like today we concentrate our fire-power by a methodical boxing in of small areas. Within these areas we clear a few blocks and immediately instruct our sappers to demolish the buildings. That way they will block off the cellars and if they also blow in the sewers that will seal off their secret rat runs. Then we move on to the next area. I also suggest that we request as many large mortars as we can get. Our tanks are vulnerable in urban fighting especially if we deploy them singly down the centre of a street. I suggest we send them in pairs, one each side of the street with their guns trained on the opposite side of the road. That way each tank is protecting the other."

Looking at a street plan, Heinz and Otto broke the city into logical areas assigned to particular units ready for the renewed assault. The following day was relatively quiet as guns were registered anew, tanks re-assigned and lieutenants given new orders.

Forty-eight hours later the area where Otto had previously been fighting erupted as if a giant fist had been thrust upwards from the earth below. Eighty-eight millimetre anti-aircraft guns which had been adapted to anti-tank warfare were brought forward and fired into buildings over open sights. Walls crumbled but many buildings still remained stubbornly defiant. Once again Otto rushed forward and darted into the ground floor of one building. The interior was a pile of collapsed debris from the floors above and Otto stood silently listening for any movement. He jerked his head to one side.....there....he heard something.....there it was again. The sound of moaning. It was coming from below and lying down on a pile of bricks and plaster Otto put his ear to a small gap which had been blown through the floor into the cellar below. Arming the fuse on a grenade he dropped it through the hole and retreated a safe distance. A few seconds later there was a muffled thrump and a puff of dust rising through the hole like a mini volcano. The silence in the cellar was overtaken by the noise of battle outside in the street.

By the end of the day sappers had laid their demolition charges and Otto looked on with satisfaction as a roar like thunder and smoke, dust and debris blasted hundreds of feet into the air. As the dust settled where once had existed a neoclassical solid apartment block only a huge pile of bricks, plaster and smouldering timbers remained.

"Let's see you climb out of that you bastards," Otto said under his breath flicking his left cheek and taking a gulp of vodka from his hip flask.

"I think our tactics are bringing results," Heinz said with satisfaction one evening at the end of September. "But we've been at it for four weeks now and although were making some progress there's no immediate sign of the resistance flagging."

Otto poured himself and Heinz a glass of wine. "At least your intelligence about the Russians was good. We'd be in real trouble if the Reds had decided to join the Jews and Poles."

Their conversation was interrupted by the shrill insistence of the telephone on Heinz's desk. Otto was the nearest and he reached over lifting the phone to his ear.

"Reichsmarshal Himmler for Sturmbannfurher von Lieper," the cold efficient voice said on the other end of the line.

"Speaking," Otto answered.

"What the hell is going on over there Sturmbannfuhrer?" Otto moved the phone away from his ear as Himmler's tirade thundered through the earpiece. That his mentor was displeased was an understatement and Otto replied with equal formality guessing correctly that to rely on family connection would in this instance prove unhelpful.

"What do you mean Reichsmarshal?" Otto replied as calmly as possible.

"This bloody uprising in Warsaw. It's been a month now and the Fuhrer is raging about the lack of progress. I don't want to hear any excuses Otto just get the job done. I'm sending some reinforcements and one further order, which has been relayed to General Bach, the Fuhrer wants Warsaw razed to the ground. You're to wipe out any last evidence of a Polish cultural existence, museums, monuments libraries; the lot. Do you understand? You are to wipe Warsaw off the face of the earth. Don't let me down Otto, your future depends on this." Without waiting for an answer Otto heard the click which signalled that the conversation was at an end.

"My God what was that all about? You look quite pale Otto."

Otto relayed the gist of the one sided conversation and Heinz simply shook his head in resignation. "It's just as I've said Otto....the Nazi Party officials back in Berlin have absolutely no idea what it's like on the front line. They draw their lines on the map and without any understanding of terrain, enemy deployment, or even our own deployment for God's sake, and they think that by giving an order it will be accomplished without delay."

Otto looked shell-shocked. "All we can do is obey orders and keep our thoughts to ourselves otherwise we'll end up on the wrong side of the wire Otto."

When the fighting was eventually reduced to mopping up odd pockets of resistance by the end of October the systematic destruction of the city gathered momentum. Large mortars lobbed heavy shells which crashed through to the foundations of even the largest apartment blocks collapsing them under the force of the explosions. Hitler's order to reduce Warsaw to rubble was being fulfilled.

Otto was pleased with Himmler's response when he telephoned Berlin and finally caught up with him at his house in Dahlem to give him the good news that eighty-five percent of Warsaw had been levelled and 225,000 civilians killed as well as most of the insurgents. "Hitler will be delighted, but it's a pity that it took General Bach nearly two months to deal with the problem."

"To be honest Reichsmarshal we initially only had a garrison force of 15,000 and we were not only fighting Ghetto Jews but the Polish Home Army of 49,000 thousand hardened partisans. At least the reinforcements made a difference and there is not one Jew left in Warsaw. In fact there is very little that is left of Warsaw be it the Polish Resistance, civilians or buildings."

"Excellent...excellent. Listen Otto. As you know, *Obersturmbann fuhrer* Adolf Eichmann Head of Jewish Affairs has been coordinating the work of all the camps and the final solution in the East. He is aware of the work you have been doing for me and I have told him that I want you to go back to Auschwitz as soon as possible. As you know it's a huge complex and I want all evidence of its existence to be obliterated. Can you imagine the propaganda coo it would provide in order to turn the whole world against us if the Russians got there and found it in tact? I want you to assist Rudolf Höss in the decommission process."

"But I thought that Höss had been dismissed after the fraud investigations?"

"Yes, yes but with his vast experience he is still useful to the Party and he has been reinstated. You're to leave Warsaw straight away. Goodbye Otto but don't hang up just yet there's someone here dying to speak to you."

The unmistakable voice of Ziggy crackled through the earpiece. "Otto, Otto is it really you? I've heard about all the fighting in Warsaw and I've been so worried for you....are you really alright?"

"Of course I am Ziggy, I'm the cat that's got nine lives. How are you in Berlin?"

"The bombing's terrible but we're surviving. I'm just bursting to tell you Otto, I'm pregnant. I told you didn't I? I knew it and it is going to be our little Siegfried in mid-April next year. Isn't it exciting? Uncle Heinrich has already booked my confinement for the second week in April at the Haus Dahlem Maternity Clinic.

"Fantastic news darling," Otto replied trying to match Ziggies excitement. "You look after yourself and if not before I'll try to be there with you for the birth."

"You're wonderful Otto. I love you so much. Take care and don't take any risks. Our Siegfried will need a strong father to look up to. Hope to see you soon, Goodbye Otto dear."

"Goodbye Ziggy."

* * * * *

The formalities dealt with, Otto accompanied Rudolf Höss to the far end of the camp where the crematoria were being dismantled. One had already been blown up in a recent prisoner revolt which Höss was pleased to recount had been brutally repressed, Remaining prisoners were being rushed through the gas chambers or shot and the bodies disposed of by being burnt on pyres. The gravity of what was taking place was not lost on Otto and it was a race against time to return Auschwitz-Birkenau to a rural landscape as had been accomplished at Treblinka and Sobibor but Auschwitz with its satellite labour camps was akin to a small city. The Russians were not too far away and a general feeling of panic was in the air. It was inevitable, only a matter of time before the Red hoards overran the site.

That evening as Otto sat in his room morosely drinking vodka his mind worked overtime assessing the current situation and his place in it. The war was lost and he could only conclude that its ultimate denouement would be cataclysmic for Germany, its army and civilian population and especially members of the SS. With the Fuhrer becoming more and more paranoid and psychotic, the higher echelons of the Party more interested in scheming and protecting their way to power rather than continuing the war on the Aryan ideals that originally brought them to power Otto could no longer see that this was a cause worth dying for. The state was devouring itself and everyone associated with it but his love for his country was beyond doubt and it was painful to contemplate rejecting the ideals and beliefs which had become part of him and had defined his value of self, his very persona and reason for existence. Not to mention his willingness to reject the woman he loved to be seduced into a marriage of convenience designed to support and perpetuate the power of selfish, deluded bigots. At that moment, with the smell of smoke and burning flesh still clinging to his clothes and polluting the air around him he made a decision, formulated a plan which was contrary to everything he had ever lived for. He still believed in Germany and fighting for his comrades but he needed an insurance policy.

First thing the next morning Otto visited the depository for clothes discarded by all prisoners on entry to the camp. Making sure that no one was looking he collected a shirt and brown woollen jacket and trousers and made his way back to his accommodation. He removed the top part of his uniform and put on the shirt and jacket then tousled his carefully groomed hair. Setting up his Leica camera and putting the shutter on self-timing Otto took a number of portrait photographs of himself. Removing the film from his camera he made his way to the motor-pool and booked out a kubelwagen. He edged the vehicle out of the compound and made his way into the nearby town of Oswiecim. Without too much trouble he found a dingy photography shop in a narrow side street and was surprised but pleased to find it was open. The street was deserted and Otto switched the engine off and sat for a few minutes. Layers of dirt had rendered the shop windows opaque and there was a further layer of thick mud up to waist height on all the buildings in the street where passing traffic had splashed dirt up from the blocked gutter drains. There would be little call for its services from the local population and Otto surmised that most of its business would be from the occupying forces sending photographs to their families back home.

A bell tinkled as Otto pushed the dirty, paint-peeling, scuffed door open. There was little hardware stock and most of the shelves were dusty and empty. A shabbily dressed Polish old man with a pronounced stoop shuffled into the shop from a back room.

"How can I help you sir?" He asked quietly but politely.

"I'd like you to develop this film for me and print me some passport size photographs of the portrait photos."

"Come back tomorrow," the old Pole replied.

"I'd prefer to have them straight away," Otto insisted. "I'll wait."

Assessing Otto's demeanour the shop owner knew better than to argue and taking the roll of film disappeared into the back room. Otto locked the front door and turned the shop sign round to read 'closed' and followed the owner into the dark room. He watched carefully in the red gloom as the owner with a deftness that belied his dishevelled, aged appearance manipulated the film into a developing tank and applied chemicals and water as required. Inspecting the results the old man slotted the film into a printer, enlarger where he adjusted distances, masking, focussing and exposures to produce Otto's requirements. Otto inspected the snaps of himself with colleagues together with the innocent pictures of places visited, the sort of snaps that any tourist might make but it was the passport pictures that he was interested in. The others he would post to Ziggy. More than pleased with the results Otto left his payment on the counter and when the old photographer was occupied putting the money in the till Otto calmly drew his Luger and shot him in the head. Leaving the 'closed' sign in the window he stepped out into the street and whilst getting back into his vehicle ignored the shrill scream emanating from the shop he'd just vacated.

Driving back to Auschwitz Camp1 Otto immediately made his way to the administration building and the room where files on all the prisoners were kept. A single *SS Sturmmann*, private, glanced in his direction but because of his rank was not challenged. In a business-like, official manner Otto confidently thumbed through a number of files until he found one that suited his purposes. A Pole, Henryk Harmanecki, about his age and height. Checking that no one was paying him any attention Otto pushed the file into his field uniform jacket and walked out. Back in his room Otto scrutinized the file assimilating the personal details, removed a passport and identity card and burned the rest in the open fire grate. So far so good he thought.

The following afternoon Otto had a scheduled meeting with Rudolf Höss to discuss a proposed programme for the closure of the camp and the disposal of those prisoners who might still remain in the camp when the final evacuation occurred. After the meeting he returned to Camp1 and on arrival made his way to the print room where he was greeted by an SS corporal.

"Can I help you sir?"

Looking round nonchalantly Otto could see a number of prisoners engaged in producing and printing various documents, leaflets, notices and camp newsletter. "Yes thanks," Otto replied. I'm looking for an engraver. Do you have one working in here?"

"I'm not sure," the corporal replied, "I'm just here to make sure that they keep their heads down and that there's no trouble, the officer in charge is out at the moment." He turned and said something to the nearest prisoner who pointed to a man of indeterminate age with thinning lank hair. His prison uniform appeared many sizes too big and hung limply from his skinny body. Although looking weak and undernourished Otto watched the man working efficiently with the economy of movement only a skilled craftsman can display. He walked up to the prisoner and spoke quietly. "Are you an engraver?"

"I used to be." The prisoner replied with resignation.

"Come outside." Otto replied.

With apprehension registering on what was otherwise an expressionless face the prisoner followed Otto outside onto one of the camp's cobbled roadways.

"If I wanted you to make a copy of an official stamp and apply it to a replacement passport photograph could you do it?"

"If I had the equipment sir, I could do it."

"Are the equipment and materials you need available inside the print shop?"

"Yes sir, I think so."

"I will take you into the print shop stores and you are to point out what you require. Tomorrow a kapo will accompany you and I will take you to my rooms, you will be well fed there. On the table you will find a passport and identity card. You are to substitute the photos for ones I will leave for you and you will frank the photos with your forged stamp. Is that clear?"

"Yes sir." The prisoner replied quietly.

Once in the stock room Otto placed in his pockets the required tools and materials as directed by the prisoner.

The next morning Otto met the Ukranian camp kapo and engraver as previous arranged and drove them to his rooms.

"You will be locked in here until I return. There is bread, cheese and some meat and I have left some coffee for you both. Don't take advantage of my good will." Turning to the engraver Otto continued, "You are here to work. If you escape you will be hunted down and burnt alive." Looking directly at the kapo Otto continued, "You are to stay with this man while he works. If you attempt to escape you also will be hunted down and I personally will cut you into little pieces and force you to feed them to the dogs. I hope I make myself clear to both of you. Carry out my wishes and you will be rewarded. You may take a break and eat when you like but the work must be done."

The arrangements were repeated the next day and late in the afternoon Otto returned to his rooms to check on progress. He unlocked the door and walked in to find the engraver and kapo sitting at the table each with a chunk of bread and cheese in one hand and a cup of hot coffee in the other. They both stood up as Otto made his way towards them. Spread across the table were the tools of the engraver's trade and beside them the passport and identity card. Otto picked them and looked inside. Seeing his photographs stuck down in each of the documents and artificially weathered to give an authentic appearance a smile spread across his face.

"You are indeed an engraver," Otto said to the prisoner. "This is excellent work. Thank you so much, but sit down and finish your food, you deserve it. Otto made himself a cup of coffee and sat by the window. He ignored the tense atmosphere in the room and waited patiently until the engraver and kapo had finished their food.

"Take the remaining food with you," Otto said, "I'm sure you can use it. Come....time to return to camp."

On leaving the outskirts of the little town of Oswiecim Otto slowed down and pulled the kubelwagen off the road. He killed the engine and stepped out onto the grass verge. With his back to the vehicle he stared across the flat landscape towards Birkenau Auschwitz. He removed his hip flask and took a large gulp of the fiery vodka. Glancing at the inscription there was a split second of conscience as he slowly removed his Luger from its holster and turning round shot the engraver and kapo in the head in quick succession. Replacing the gun Otto took another slug of vodka and flicked his left cheek with his left hand. There must be no loose ends

Later that evening Otto sat in his room picking away at the lining of his battle jacket. Placing the passport and identity card inside the gap he commenced re-stitching the jacket back together.

CHAPTER 22

Annette/Grace/Annie 1944

Annette walked down Avenue Foch in the Paris spring bright sunshine rejoicing in the contrast with what she had seen in Berlin and entered SS headquarters. She flashed her pass at the corporal sitting behind a reception desk and made her way into the ladies toilet room. She looked in an ancient mirror where the copper had eroded away from the rear of the glass which now reflected back a distorted face of disparate images each separated by jagged brown streaks. 'What the hell' she thought and continued to rummage in her bag for her Iron Cross. Removing the medal from its box Annette held it up to her chest and examined the effect. Pinning it onto her jacket she scrutinised the surrealistic, fractured reflection with a conspiratorial smile. The effect was even more pronounced than Annette had ever expected. Even though she was in civilian clothes, lower ranks saluted her and senior officers stared in confounded amazement. At last Annette reached Sturmbannfuhrer Ernst Lindemann's outer office, knocked on the door and walked in without waiting. Major Lindemann was standing by the reception desk and turned to see who had entered. For a split second he was confused but quickly recognised Annette who noticed his eyes focussing on the Iron Cross.

"Annette, it's good to have you back." And with a beaming smile he continued, "I can see that your trip to Berlin was a success, come and tell me all about it". Then turning back to the desk ordered, "Two coffees corporal."

Once in the privacy of Lindemann's office Annette continued the conversation, "It's good to be back sir."

"Ernst…its Ernst, have you forgotten already or has your short trip to Berlin gone to your head? Tell me, what's that bauble on your chest," he teased. "But more importantly what did you do to earn it?"

"It was wonderful," Annette exploded. "I met the Reichsfuhrer who took me to see the Fuhrer. Apparently the Fuhrer was impressed and delighted with the information I'd passed on and when I was finally introduced to him he shook my hand, thanked me for my loyalty to the Reich and awarded me this Iron Cross for services to the Fatherland. Much as I'd like to, I can't tell you what intelligence I had but let's just say that it was the confirmation of events that had been seriously concerning Herr Hitler for some time."

"Well....all I can say is that this is truly remarkable. You must be the only non-German, and a civilian at that, to receive such an honour. You must be very proud and I'm going to show you off at dinner tonight to celebrate."

They sat quietly for a while drinking their real coffee whilst Annette filled in the details of her trip to Berlin and the damage caused by the RAF.

"Right then," Ernst said in a business-like fashion, "Let's get back to the mundane and do some work eh, if it's not beneath such a celebrity? There are some statements to be translated and other documents to be sorted and filed. There has also been a further development in the last twenty-four hours for which I'll need your translation assistance over the next few weeks. We are to hold a number of meetings with the various Paris public services committees, the police, transport, telecommunications, radio, medical, in fact the whole damned infra-structure. You possibly know even more about this than I do with your new friends in high places but, the Party and army general staff are getting concerned about the coming Allies invasion of Europe. These proposed meetings are to discuss contingency plans for our defence and/or evacuation of Paris if the unthinkable happens and the Allies manage to establish and build on a bridgehead. We have enough forces between here and Calais but....better to be prepared. I'll post you later about which meetings and where and when."

Cheese was a luxury Parisians could no longer afford even if it had been readily available in the shops. In fact all dairy products had been unavailable for some time. Butter, eggs and milk to say nothing of pork or beef were just a distant memory. The Germans commandeered all produce but astute farmers passed on produce to the black market and grew rich on the proceeds. Collette didn't enquire as to where or how Annette had acquired her fresh cheese but she gratefully accepted half the chunk offered to her. They sat in the Jardin des Plantes enjoying the warmth of the mid-day sun eating their al fresco lunch and sipping a thin bodied red wine. The last of the spring tulips and daffodils were dying off and there were too many weeds in the flower beds.

"What are your plans?" Collette asked quietly, almost whispering.

"Since I last saw you I've successfully completed my special mission. I have some information to pass back to London but too much for a transmission and I suspect that the Gestapo have my bearing and are just waiting for me to transmit one more time."

"I think you might be right," Collette answered. "During the past few weeks since you've returned I've heard that German radio traffic has increased and there is a fragile nervousness about the place. More agents are being rounded up and even the ordinary soldiers in the street are tense and jumpy. I can only suspect it's to do with the Allies proposed invasion."

"It is," Annette answered. "The German authorities are putting in place contingency plans for the evacuation of Paris. I don't yet know if they plan to destroy the place or will leave it as an open city but they are certainly worried about any Allied advance."

"That's the best news I've heard in a long time," Collette replied tearing off a piece of bread, pressing a hole into it with her fingers and pushing some cheese into it. "I'll pass that down the line, but what are you going to do now?"

"I don't know the date of any seaborne invasion but I know that it's imminent and the Germans think so too. I need to leave Paris Collette. I can't tell you why but I know that when the invasion comes I'll be top of the Gestapo wanted list. Even if I leave too soon their suspicions will be aroused and that could have horrendous consequences for the Allies."

"What have you got yourself into?" Collette asked with concern. "No don't tell me I don't want to know."

"I'm going back to Rouen and join in the resistance sabotage attacks until the Allies get here. Be careful Collette. You don't want to be caught this close to the liberation." "You too Annette. By the way, thanks for the cheese."

Two weeks passed since Annette last talked with Collette. In the meantime the meetings she attended with Ernst were becoming more and more frenetic and Annette was ill at ease. She couldn't put her finger on it but there was a feeling that wouldn't go away. A feeling that if the Allies were going to have a summer campaign then they couldn't possibly delay their invasion for much longer.

At their final meeting Annette was told by Collette that the resistance networks were reporting that coded radio traffic from London to resistance groups was more now prolific and urgent and that she guessed the invasion was imminent. "Be careful and I'll see you here after Paris is liberated."

Annette decided she would take a chance and tell Ernst that she wanted to visit her cousins in Clermont Ferrand for a long weekend and trust to luck.

Gathering in the radio aerial Annette folded it into place in the radio carrying case. Everything was laid out on the bed waiting to be packed into her small, battered suitcase. There wasn't much but she pondered long about what to do with her Iron Cross and the photos of Otto she had kept. These would be difficult to explain if they fell into the wrong hands at the wrong time, but for all the risk she couldn't bear to be separated from the photos. The Iron Cross was more problematic. There was more than a frisson of pleasure in knowing that at great risk to herself she had deceived Hitler and got away with it. With hindsight Annette reasoned that the thrill of a mission accomplished was in direct proportion to the anxiety and danger she had experienced whilst in Berlin. For her the medal was a symbol of her patriotism not loyalty to the German Reich. A significant reminder of a defining moment. Taking a small pair of scissors Annette unpicked some of the stitching on the lining of her suitcase and pushed the items inside. She stitched the slit up again as carefully as she could then packed the rest of her belongings into the case. Annette left her little bedsit for the last time on Saturday 3rd. June 1944 and made her way to the station to catch her train for Rouen.

The journey to Rouen passed without incident. Annette just caught the one daily bus to the small town of Etrepagny from where previously she had directed the Wehrmacht Lieutenant to the dead parachute airman in the woods. She alighted from the battered rickety bus in the town square and made her way carefully across the block pave road to a small, scruffy corner café. Conversations stopped and four local men eyed her with suspicion as she ordered an ersatz coffee and asked to use the telephone. Speaking quietly she phoned the farm and arranged to for Pierre to pick her up outside the café in half an hour.

"Am I pleased to see you," Pierre said kissing Grace on both cheeks. "All hell's broken out here but I'll fill you in on the details later. He put her radio and battered suitcase in the boot whilst Grace opened the passenger door a slid into the seat. Later she felt at home as she sat in the farmhouse kitchen spooning thick, wholesome broth up to her mouth where she blew on it so that it didn't burn her lips or tongue. The four of them sat round the table and Pierre's wife withdrew discretely as a gentle knock on the door invaded Grace's relaxed mood. Pierre went to the door and invited a man she had never seen before into the kitchen.

"Grace this is Philippe Liewer, you probably know him as Clemont, founder of our 'Salesman' resistance circuit."

"Extending her hand Grace said, "It's taken a long time for us to meet up."

"In the circumstances that's probably no bad thing," Liewer replied. Adopting a lower, more urgent voice he continued addressing the small group. "It's as we've suspected, the Salesman group has been compromised. I've heard from Rouen and Le Havre that a number of operatives have been arrested and tortured. There are 'wanted' posters on walls everywhere and as yet we don't know where the leak is."

"Our small group is secure," Bernard offered, "But that's probably because we have stayed small and local, we trust one another."

"That's why I'm here, I know I can trust you," Liewer continued. "I need your help. I'm being picked up tonight to go back to London to give them up-to-date details on the situation. Apart from that I have important information about a Nazi project, 'Cherry Stone'."

"I've heard 'Cherry Stone' mentioned in SS Headquarters in Paris," "Grace volunteered. "It's Hitler's code name for a new wonder weapon. A flying bomb without a pilot. The talk in Paris is that they will obliterate London. Sites are being designated all along the channel coast, some static some mobile."

"I've gathered a number of map references where launch sites have already been erected, one not too far from here. Bomber Command can deal with most of them."

"I knew there was something going on in the forest," Bernard said. "There's been so much transport and movement recently and a large perimeter fence has been erected. We can investigate tomorrow."

"I was going to transmit some information about my last mission," Grace interjected turning towards Liewer, "But it will be safer if you can deliver it in person. It's vital. As a matter of urgency you must let the authorities know the full implications of my recent 'Dover Sole' operation. I have already transmitted the code 'Dover Sole' to London so they know that the operation was a success but what they may not know is that, to the despair of his commanders, Hitler has taken full control of the German Wehrmacht and their deployment in the Normandy and Pas de Calais regions. There is an armoured reserve in front of Paris ready to be dispatched to either the Calais or Normandy areas depending on where the invasion takes place. But, and this is vital, you must on no account reveal this to anyone except your contacts in London. This must reach the highest level as soon as possible....immediately in fact. When the invasion eventually comes Hitler is convinced that the main attack will be at Calais and that any attempt to land at Normandy will be a diversion. When the Allies are sighted off the coast of Normandy he will assume that it's a diversionary tactic and as a result he will delay for approximately two days the deployment of his reserve keeping it back for what he believes will be the main event in the north. This will give the Allies vital time to establish a beachhead against known numbers and positions."

"Phew...that's dynamite. I won't ask how you came by this information but I can see your need for urgency. Consider it done Grace."

"You can also add my intelligence about 'Cherry Stone' to support your own report."

* * * * *

The Lysander swung one hundred and eighty degrees and was airborne within seconds, Liewer safely on board. Later in the safe room under the barn floor Annette curled up into a foetal position and was soon fast asleep.

Fortified by the luxury of bacon and an egg each, Pierre, Bernard, David and Grace cleared away the breakfast things and spread a large scale map of the area on the table. "If the invasion is to be in Normandy then there is much that we can do to upset the German defensive efforts." Bernard said, drawing his finger round the area in a large circle.

"The Allies will make slow progress in this area," Pierre offered. "This is not good offensive territory. The bocage is ambush country. The arable agriculture is all in small fields separated by high hedge rows and sunken roads. One camouflaged German tank could hold up a whole armoured column. You never know what's round the corner."

"We can't do anything about that and I'm sure that the Allies are aware of the countryside so let's see where and what we can do in our area." Grace said. "I'm sure we can be a nuisance by disrupting communications and transport. Let's mark a few places on the map and take it from there."

Using the standardised resistance colour code the group studied the map looking for suitable installations to attack some of which had already received their attention in the past. Opening a box of coloured crayons and marking sites that they thought within their capability, Pierre traced railways with his fingers.

"Here," he said, using the green crayon, "And here and here." The process was repeated over and over again. Blue for power installations and electricity sub-stations, purple for telecommunication sites, red for ammunition dumps and black for fuel dumps.

Tracing two fingers, one down and one across the map to a particular grid reference point Grace added, "Don't forget the launch site for these flying bombs here in the forest between Lyons-la-Forêt and Charleval. As Bernard said yesterday we need to do a reconnaissance.

Pierre and I can do that whilst you two remain here checking explosives detonators and whatever else we may need for a raid tonight."

"This planned raid isn't going to help the liberation," David said rather fractiously.

"Perhaps not this time," Grace answered but it will delay the death of hundreds of people in London. I promise that after this sortie we'll concentrate on those installations we've highlighted on the map."

With bread, cheese and a bottle of wine in their bicycle baskets plus Grace's well-thumbed French Birds recognition book they headed south out of the farm yard. Keeping to narrow tracks through trees and undergrowth they made slow progress. After an hour Pierre signalled Grace to stop and get off her bicycle.

"We'll leave these here," he whispered pushing his bicycle into a ditch and dragging branches over it. Grace did the same. Crouching down Pierre continued, "If you listen carefully you can hear wagon engines and the noise of construction and voices shouting. I've only been this far once before but I think the fence is just through this coppice."

Trying to be as quiet as they could when brambles reached out to snag their clothes and scratch their hands Pierre and Grace crawled forward the last hundred yards to the edge of the coppice. There was no visible security other than a four metre high wire mesh fence. There were no watch towers but there was clear dead ground for twenty metres between the end of the coppice and the fence. The compound was laid out in a geometric pattern with concrete roadways edged by neat hedges and grassed areas between various buildings with occasional trees. Grace guessed that from the air the complex would look like farm buildings.

"There," Pierre pointed, "That structure over there, the one that looks like a mini ski slope....that must be a launch ramp. Strange, but lucky for us it's situated towards the outer edge of the site"

"That's probably a safety precaution, away from storage facilities and personnel in the event of accidental miss-launches and possible explosions."

Their concentration on the size, construction and position of the ramp within the complex was suddenly arrested by the sound of voices approaching. In their desire to memorise the layout they had not seen two German guards approaching along the inside of the wire. Heads down they waited until the voices receded.

"We'll need to know how many patrols there are and how long they take to pass a given point. That'll give us how long we have to get in lay the charges and get out again." Grace whispered.

They waited and watched for half an hour familiarising themselves with the positions of delivery and storage depots, personnel quarters, workshops and what they guessed was the launch control centre next to the ramp.

"I calculate that we'll need four charges for the ramp," Grace whispered. "One for each of the tall stanchions at the front and two more further back to take out a whole section of the runway. I suggest that if we can get close enough we also put charges against the control building although it looks a pretty substantial concrete construction to me. We'll need to use timed detonators in order to give us time to get away before the balloon goes up. Is that all do you think?"

"Yes, let's get back to the farm and put the others in the picture."

It seemed only a short while ago that Grace had been riding her bicycle through the woods on her reconnaissance to the rocket launching site that afternoon. Perhaps it was the adrenaline coursing through her but even in the dark she seemed to be crouching down at the edge of the tree-line surveying the perimeter wire much sooner than anticipated. They waited in silence until a guard patrol past them then all four crawled forward. Bernard and David had their sub-machine guns at the ready whilst Pierre cut the wire in such a way that they could crawl through but leaving it looking intact. In normal circumstances they would have been cursing the weather and although crawling through sodden grass in drizzling rain was extremely uncomfortable they hoped that it would dissuade German personnel from venturing outside. They reached a low hedge bordering the perimeter road and were grateful for its protection. Bernard and David stayed under cover whilst Grace and Pierre rolled over the hedge and continued to crawl towards the ramp. Suddenly, for a couple of seconds, a yellow light streaked across the grass and fearing that they might have been spotted they pressed themselves into the ground and lay deathly still. Seconds later Grace slowly turned her head attracted by the laughter of two technicians standing in the control room doorway joking and smoking cigarettes. Agonising minutes later the door closed with a solid clunk and the darkness swallowed them once again.

Lying on their sides Grace and Pierre reached inside their bags for explosives, tape and detonators. Even though fingers were wet and cold the charges were taped to the front stanchions and they made their way further down the length of the ramp and taped the second set of charges to the ramp supports. Staying under the ramp for protection they crawled towards the control room and taped two large charges to the shuttered windows. There was no way that they would be able to damage the concrete construction of the building but with a bit of luck the explosions would penetrate the interior space through the windows and cause damage to instruments and technicians delaying any launch programme. Resisting the temptation to get up and run they crawled their way back towards the waiting David and Bernard. They retraced their way back to the wire without incident and were well on the way back to the farm when they had the satisfaction of hearing distinct separate explosions indicating that their sabotage had been a success.

Klaxons immediately filled the air with their insistent brain numbing screeching. The quartet of saboteurs knew that any Wehrmacht search would initially have to use the country lanes with their lorries. A cross country sweep would take a little while to organise and they didn't have enough men to search in every direction. Full of confidence they pedalled rapidly along narrow, hidden tracks towards the farm and were grateful once the straw bales were pushed over the hidden cellar entrance.

Pierre was in his pyjamas and in bed when the expected bang and clatter of a lorry tailboard being dropped signalled the arrival of the Wehrmacht in the farm yard. With much noise and shouting and little care for farm buildings or equipment they tore the place apart.

"What's the matter, what do you want?" Pierre enquired, to be answered by a rifle butt to the face.

"Where have you been this evening?" The question was shouted over and over again. "Where are your comrades hidden?" With rifle blows to head and body Pierre couldn't have answered even if he'd wanted to. Below the barn floor, Grace, David and Bernard looked upwards each saying a silent prayer.

Eventually Pierre's wife helped him indoors as the army lorry left the farm empty handed.

The next day the three remained underground living off the rations which were always stored there for just such an eventuality. The sound of the farm tractor moving the straw bales covering their hideaway on the morning of the 6th. June was a nerve-racking moment until they heard Pierre's voice above shouting, "Come on up. Its' safe."

Grace was shocked when she saw Pierre's bruised and battered face. His lips were split and had been stitched by the local vet she learned later. Both eyes were swollen and closed, his whole face looking like a joint of beef ready for the oven. "My God!" Grace gushed, "The bastards."

"Don't worry," Pierre managed to whisper through his remaining clenched teeth. "At least I'm still here in one piece."

"Give it a few days and we'll make the bastards pay for this?" David promised.

"Listen.....did you hear that?" Bernard said expectantly cocking his head to one side. "There....there it is again....you can just hear it on the wind."

"My God, yes," Grace answered with excitement. "It's a bombardment. It sounds like seriously heavy armament to me...navel guns....my God, it's the invasion. The Allies are here at last. Vive La France." Grace shouted and grabbing the others' hands they commenced dancing round and round in the farm yard.

*****

The German Army fought with its usual fanatical, ferocious tenacity and the Allies' advance towards Paris ebbed and flowed. Grace and her small group of partisans were just one of many groups harassing the Germans behind their lines. Other partisans rushed to swell the ranks of the Free French Forces of the Interior (FFI) and slowly but surely after three months of heavy fighting Paris was liberated. Against strict orders from the Fuhrer, The Military Governor of Paris, General Dietrich von Choltitz had refused to reduce the city to ruins. General Leclerc and General Charles de Gaulle led the victory parade down the Champs-Elysees towards Notre Dame but the whole of Paris was not yet safe though and for some weeks after pockets of strong German resistance persisted and snipers continued to be active.

Whilst Paris was being liberated, that same week Grace received an unexpected radio message from Vera Atkins requesting that they meet at her newly established base in the Hotel Cecil in the Rue Beaunier in the Montparnasse area on the Rive Gauche in Paris. Annette knew the district well.

She put her battered suitcase down in the farm yard and embraced David and Bernard.

"It's been a pleasure working with you both," She said with tears in her eyes. "It's been a privilege to know you, I'll never forget you. What will you do now in the evenings? I expect you'll have to go home to your wives, if they still remember who you are that is."

Her joke released some of the morbid tension surrounding her departure.

"And we'll never forget your courage and love for our country," Bernard replied.

"That goes for me too," added David.

"You'll have some stories to tell your grandchildren. God bless you both." After one final embrace and kissing them both on each cheek, Grace threw her suitcase and radio into the boot of the old Citroen and climbed in beside Pierre.

Approaching the railway station in Rouen Pierre finally gave up and said, "I can't get any further, the streets are too crowded."

"Don't worry," Grace replied, "Just drop me off, I can see the station from here. It looks like the whole city's turned out."

"Are you sure?" Pierre asked.

"Of course," Grace replied opening the car door and stepping round to open the boot. Just as she put her hand on the handle Pierre's was there at the same time and he accidentally put his hand on top of hers. Their heads turned to face each other, each with tears in their eyes. Standing up they embraced for what must have seemed like hours, each not wanting to be the first to let go.

"Thank you for looking after me Pierre. I'll never ever forget you."

"No....it's me who should be thanking you Grace. This isn't your country yet you put your life on the line for us. I'll never forget your bravery and comradeship. God bless you in your next assignments. You will always be welcome in my house. I can never thank you enough."

"Your lasting friendship is good enough for me. Goodbye Pierre and God bless you." Grace replied.

"*Au revoir. Dieu peut s'occuper de vous.* Goodbye, may God look after you."

Annette picked up her suitcases and walked towards the station. Pierre stood with tears streaming down his face watching until Annette was lost from view amongst the milling crowd.

The crowd grew denser the closer Annette got to the station. She was pushed and buffeted and her arms almost wrenched from their sockets as her suitcases got tangled up in the forest of legs. In front of the station a wooden platform had been erected for some civic dignitaries' speeches Annette assumed being as five chairs were placed there each an even distance from the one next to it. She manoeuvred round the platform in order to access the station entrance but was forcefully pushed sideways as the crowd rocked one way then the other and the swell of voices shouting filled the air. Above the incoherent roar and as the noise approached Annette began to distinguish individual voices shouting louder and above the rest.

"Whores. Traitors."

"German Whores."

"German tarts."

"Collaborators."

"Horizontal collaborators."

Arms were raised, fists punched the air and fingers pointed accusingly as everyone surged forwards. Annette almost fell to the ground as the crowd suddenly parted like the Red Sea to reveal five women, their arms tied behind their backs, being pushed and dragged over to the platform where they were hauled up to face the anger of their tormentors. Three of the girls were in their early twenties Annette guessed whilst the other two were in their thirties and forties respectively. The younger women struggled and fought their captors whilst the elder women looked on with defiant resignation. Held firmly by groups of men others began ripping the clothes off the women who kicked out to defend their modesty. Off to the side Annette noticed gendarmes and a few Allied soldiers standing around with cold indifference. Once naked the women were forced onto the chairs and were immediately set upon by men with large pairs of scissors. A huge cheer erupted as the first clumps of hair were held aloft like trophies.

"This is what happens to traitors and collaborators," one of the men shouted inciting the crowd to more cheering and jeering.

"We've done nothing wrong," one of the young girls shouted sobbing.

"You slept with German pigs, you whore that's enough," came a response from the crowd.

The eldest of the women shouted in a clear defiant voice, "My heart belongs to France but my vagina belongs to me to do with what I want."

"And any passing German swine as well," some wag shouted bringing much hilarity to the crowd. "If you don't shut up we'll shave your German bush as well."

Once the platform was covered in hair the women had their heads held firmly whilst cut- throat razors were used, none too carefully, to give them a dry shave resulting in cuts which bled down their faces. As a last humiliation they were forced to stand up whilst black swastikas were daubed onto their breasts. Eventually the women were released and quickly picked up their clothes to protect whatever modesty remained. Clutching their clothes close to their bodies they helped one another down from the platform. The crowd parted and they ran the gauntlet suffering more verbal abuse and loud jeering. The excitement over, the gathering quickly dispersed and in shocked sadness Annette looked at the now vacant platform, the remaining tangled clumps of shame tumbling along the timbers and down into the street where they floated in the gutters and disappeared into the drains.

The atmosphere on the Paris train was in complete contrast to the last time Annette had travelled from Rouen to the capital. Where once dower, silent suspicion was evident now everyone was everyone else's friend and bottles of wine passed up and down the carriage together with much infectious laughter. Annette tried her best not to be inhospitable but sitting looking at the landscape flashing past she found it difficult to ignore what she had just witnessed. Perhaps it was the thought that she too could have been one of those poor women. Had she done anything less terrible than those frightened young girls? Was sleeping with the enemy on behalf of king and country a better excuse than sleeping with a German for food, survival or even love? The women had broken no law by sleeping with a German but it was obvious to Annette that no matter that their excuses had nothing to do with politics, in the eyes of their community sex with a German was political. The faces in the crowd distorted in anger and vengeance belonged to both men and women but the thought crept into Annette's mind that those perpetrating the vengeance were men only. Could it be that the men of France, so long publicly humiliated and robbed of their pride, were trying to reaffirm their masculinity and reclaim their womenfolk as an unconscious metaphor for *Marianne.....La France.*

* * * * *

Vera extended her hand, "Come in Annie, it's wonderful to see you again....come....come and sit down. I don't need to tell you that we're absolutely delighted with your work here in France. Especially the satisfactory conclusion of your 'Dover Sole' mission. That must have been very stressful for you."

"I can't deny that the anxiety of maintaining my subterfuge in the presence of Hitler and all his henchman was frightening I have to say," Annie replied. "To be introduced to Hitler again in the Berlin Chancellery of all places was truly threatening. But I think that Hitler was more concerned about hiding the tremor in his hand to notice the tremor in mine. Or knowing the arrogance of the man he probably thought that I was shaking because I was in awe of his presence, which I suppose, in one sense I was." Annie continued to give Vera a full account of her Berlin assignment and her work within the 'Salesman' Circuit. "And of course I have this in remembrance of my efforts on behalf of the German Reich," Annie continued as she held up her Iron Cross for Vera's scrutiny.

"You're kidding me," Vera replied unable to suppress a smile. And turning the medal over to read the inscription on the back she continued, "You're not telling me that you were awarded the Iron Cross for delivering those photographs." The irony not escaping either of them.

Annie finished her report by relating the presentation of her medal by Hitler and the effect her wearing of the medal had at her place of work in the SS Headquarters.

"What a story.....it's truly amazing Annie, but I don't need to suggest that wearing it now won't endear you to the British Army."

"I guess not," Annie replied laughing.

"But this might," Vera continued, "I've recommended you for the George Cross Annie. What you did was incredible, to carry out a bluff face to face with Hitler and his henchman in his own sanctum was an amazing piece of work which really affected the confidence of Churchill and Eisenhower before the 'D' Day landings."

"What can I say," Annie responded, "It was my job."

"Don't be modest Annie, what you did was truly heroic, Captain Charlton."

"A promotion as well, it's all too much Vera, there are a lot of people out there putting their lives on the line."

"Which brings me to the second point on my agenda. I'm here to track down what's happened to other 'F' Section agents who have gone missing. What information I have is vague and confused and of course my mission is not being helped by that bombastic Frenchman Charles de Gaulle who is trying to ignore and even erase any references to the SOE's involvement in the liberation and spread the myth that the liberation is all down to the French alone. What a horrible man. I thought that being as you'd infiltrated the SS here in Paris you might know of or be able to search for documents or use your contacts to gather information. In their haste to leave of course the SS has either taken with them or destroyed a lot of files but you never know there might be something left behind."

"I did hear SS officers talking about captured agents from time to time but I never had any opportunity to contact them or help them unfortunately. Besides they were quickly moved on to concentration camps, the women to Ravensbruck and the men were sent to Buchenwald and Bergen-Belsen to name two. Yolande Beekman was one person I do know was tortured downstairs in the Avenue Foch. Others I heard mentioned were Diana Rowden and Nora Baker and Cecily Lefort who I know did end up in Ravensbruck. There may be some names scratched into the walls in the cells. I recall seeing some when I was there as a guest of the Gestapo for twenty-four hours before being rescued by my SS contact and employer. I'll talk to Collette, one of my contacts here in Paris and get her to meet you. She knew a lot about the Nazi infiltration of the 'Prosper' Circuit. She may be able to give you some information but I guess that until we penetrate further into Germany the paper trail will end here in Paris for the time being. I'll write everything down for you that comes to mind."

"That would be very helpful Annie. You're right about the paper trail coming to an end for now but we can still make contacts and gather information and pick up the trail from here which brings me to the third thing I want to talk to you about. There is no doubt that Germany is going to lose this war and when the end comes Europe is going to be in one hell of a mess. Apart from all the damage to the infra-structure of all the major cities between here and Moscow it's the human cost which is going to be the biggest challenge. Millions of people will be on the move to who knows where? There'll be no food, shelter or transport and revenge will be uppermost in a lot of people's minds. There'll be POWs from here to Russia and from Latvia down to Greece. Refugees, displaced persons, concentration camp inmates, slave labourers all wanting to get home. And what will remain of home once they get there? The whole of Europe is going to be a heaving mass of starved peoples wandering around but as far as we're concerned the major focus will be in Germany. The Allied governments accept that the initial responsibility for these people will fall on the military because they will already be there on the ground but since 1943 the United Nations Relief and Rehabilitation Administration (UNRRA) has been making plans for the distribution of food and medical aid. One of the greatest logistical challenges will be to coordinate this welfare amongst refugees and displaced persons in camps. Not forgetting that Nazis and members of the SS may well disguise themselves as refugees to escape retribution for their war crimes and brutality. These will need to be weeded out and de-Nazified. It will take years before we get back to anything like normal whatever that will mean in the years to come. Annie, I've consulted with the big wigs in London and we were wondering if you would like to consider being seconded to UNRRA. With your gift in languages, empathy and people skills you would be invaluable in front-line administration and delivery of this humanitarian effort. It's a big step for you to consider, I know, so take your time. Finish up here with your report and information about missing agents and you can transfer direct to London to familiarize yourself with the organisation and make preparations for your role when the war ends."

Annie was overwhelmed by this proposed change in her status and there was a long silence whilst she tried to gather her thoughts. Realistically her work in France was at an end and after her complete involvement in the war effort for the past three years the thought of working in a NAAFI or boring war department office didn't really appeal. Here was another chance to make a real difference, to do something positive, to help reconstruct the lives of thousands of people who had suffered for years at the hands of the most brutal, evil regime the world had ever known. How could she refuse?

"I'll do it," She answered with enthusiasm.

CHAPTER 23

Otto 1944 – 1945

(I)

They sat beside the pot-bellied stove which was radiating overpowering heat into the office. Commandant Höss read out the most recent communication from Himmler via Eichmann '......make sure that not one single prisoner from the concentration camp falls alive into the hands of the enemy...'. The Russians were rapidly approaching Auschwitz and fearing retribution the SS was desperate to ensure that evidence of their mass killings would be dismantled and erased before the whole world learned of their systematic and industrial scale genocide. Otto drew his hands back from the stove, rubbed them together and sat up straight.

"My God, this camp complex is huge. Does the Reichsfuhrer expect us to wipe this lot off the face of the earth in just a few weeks?"

"We can only do what we can do," Höss replied with resignation staring at sparks dancing free from the hole in the top of the stove. "The sooner we start the better."

"As I see it there are two problems. One, the prisoners themselves and two the actual structure of the camp."

"Agreed," Höss replied. "But it's as you say, a huge logistical problem. I'll take on responsibility for the destruction of any physical evidence here in the camp if you'll organise and coordinate the various departments for the evacuation and transport of the prisoners."

Otto watched impassively as the prisoners to leave the camp were forced out of their barrack huts by Ukrainian guards and SS personnel and lined up in rows of five across. Some of the women and children were loaded onto lorries but the rest prepared as best they could for the long walk. The rumour was that they were going to be marched to a field where they would be shot. Snow was beginning to fall and Otto never gave a thought as to how members of the camp orchestra were able to play their instruments with freezing fingers. A brazier made from an old oil drum which had been punched full of holes burned in a space at the centre of the assembled musicians but its effect was more visual than practical as the frost laden mist wrapped the heat in its chilled shroud and spirited it away. Thousands of prisoners shuffled and stumbled through the camp gates to begin their walk towards Gliwice and Wodzislaw where they were to be loaded onto trains destined for camps in Germany. Unmoved, hypnotic almost, Otto supervised from the comfort of his kubelwagen. The procession was endless and monotonous. Without being aware of when or how it happened he was staring, unseeing, trance-like, except that somewhere within his brain the scene before him was being mixed and montaged with images of Annette. The emotional, arching, interwoven violin themes of Wagner's Siegfried Idyll infiltrated themselves into his subconscious and transported him to the banks of a slow flowing, clear river where he lay naked together with Annette, entwined in her arms and bathed in the golden glow of the hot summer sun. A sudden loud bang beside him shocked Otto back to the present. He jerked round to see a bundle of tattered prison-striped clothes lying in a heap at the side of the road. Otto had seen death in many guises but on this occasion he stared mesmerised, numb, as each new virginal snowflake passed on the red stain to the next and the next and the next creeping ever closer to where he sat.

Flicking his left cheek Otto thrust the kubelwagen into gear and flooring the accelerator caused the vehicle to jump forwards throwing pebbles and dirt from the rear tyres in its wake. He drove towards the far end of the camp where the strongest and fittest of the inmates were busy dismantling various buildings. Some of the burial areas had already been filled in and were in the process of being turfed over. Pipework and ventilation systems of the gas chambers were being stripped out and the buildings converted to air-raid bunkers. The work was progressing slowly and Otto knew that the deadline set by Himmler would never be accomplished before the Russians arrived. With the cold now seeping into his bones Otto took a swig of vodka from his flask, turned his vehicle round and headed towards the camp gate. Just before passing through the gate his vehicle lurched and he heard a crunching sound. Braking hard he stepped out and walked to the rear. Looking round the vehicle all seemed to be in order but glancing back at the tyre tracks left in the light dusting of snow was something that he guessed he must have run over. Otto walked slowly towards the object and realised that what he had crushed was a violin case. The case was split open and shaped pieces of varnished Maple and Spruce lay fractured and tortured in the snow. Where one end of the shattered bow with its slack gut strings dangling loose and black ebony fret board had been forced into a soft spot in the earth the other ends stuck up in the air with sad, silent impotence. Otto swung his leg and kicked the pieces off the roadway.

Over the next few weeks Crematorium I was turned into an air-raid shelter and Crematoria II, III and IV were dismantled and dynamited. 1944 morphed into 1945 unnoticed as urgency turned to panic. Tons of paperwork and files were loaded onto lorries but even the logistics of this operation were too much and Otto ordered any remaining records to be burnt. News filtered through that the next Russian assault was imminent.

Hitler received a report that the Red Army was about to launch a massive attack from the line of the Vistula on or about the 12th. January. Russian sappers were already clearing mine fields and tank corps were being brought forward into the bridgeheads.

"We must move our panzer reserves forward before the Russians can consolidate their positions," Hitler said, sweeping his hand across the map in a grand gesture without any consideration as to his army's manpower strength, artillery support, deployment or potential battlefield topography.

"We mustn't do that *Mein Fuhrer,*" Guderian replied trying not too hard to hide his frustration.

Hitler flew into an immediate rage, "I'll not listen to defeatist talk from the Wehrmacht," he bellowed.

"But if we send the panzers forward unsupported they will come within range of the Soviet artillery before they can even be deployed," Guderian persisted wearily.

"I agree with you *Mein Fuhrer,*" Himmler offered obsequiously much to Guderian's disgust. "We must attack."

On the 12th. January Marshal Konev's 1st Ukrainian Front attacked in snow and nil visibility. As predicted by Guderian the German defenders were shattered by the scale and ferocity of the Russian artillery bombardment.

Constant radio communication breakdowns meant that information was frequently out of date by the time it reached Hitler's headquarters and the animosity and mistrust was now such that commanders in the field were operationally paralysed being as they were afraid to make decisions without Hitler's agreement. Meanwhile the Russians were making rapid progress. Heavy artillery and Katyusha rockets fired from the backs of lorries continued to harass the Germans. In the front line the hard-frozen ground made the shell bursts even more lethal and the snow covered landscape erupted in craters leaving black and yellow scorch marks like syphilitic ulcers on a pale skin. The danger of leaving the door wide open to Berlin was obvious to everyone except Hitler.

* * * * *

Höss and Otto agreed that they were never ever, in the time remaining, going to be able to obliterate all evidence of the camp's existence. News of the Russian successes fuelled the panic even more and spurred final preparations for the remaining prisoners to be evacuated. Six days after the Russians had begun their offensive 58,000 Auschwitz inmates began their march towards Gliwice and Wodzislaw whilst 7,000 who were categorised as too incapable to walk and hence of no value to the German labour market were left behind. The rail heads were thirty kilometres away.

Landmarks were rendered invisible by an hypnotic, falling curtain of snow. Otto followed the road in the direction of Gliwice and soon discovered that there was no need for landmarks or a road map. At frequent intervals, bodies at the side of the road buried at varying depths in the snow indicated how long they had been there. Those from the first march, before Christmas, were recognized as simple mounds of snow where black, frozen limbs reached upwards at grotesque angles like torn branches from trees in the gutter. Stiff, brittle fingers pointed accusingly at those who were bothered enough to look at the evidence.

Nearing the town of Gliwice the road on both sides was lined by hundreds and hundreds of prisoners some sitting huddled together others lying in the snow either dead or alive or dying, it didn't matter which. The railhead and station and the surrounding fields and church graveyards were choked with prisoners their frozen breaths hanging suspended above their heads. Otto drove straight up to the station, stopped and stood up in his vehicle looking for someone who might be in charge of the chaos. Spotting an SS Lieutenant, Otto jumped down and made his way to where the lieutenant stood looking harassed and bewildered.

"What the fuck is going on here lieutenant?" Otto yelled.

Seeing Otto's rank the lieutenant stiffened to attention, *"Heil Hitler.* We're overwhelmed sir. If you'd care to follow me sir," the lieutenant continued, gesturing Otto towards the rail lines.

At the platforms there were two trains standing made up of both open coal trucks and closed cattle trucks. Some of the open trucks had had a second level floor constructed half way down the depth of the truck thereby doubling its capacity whilst at the same time offering little protection from the elements where the temperature had now plummeted to 30 degrees below freezing. The whole area was crammed with thousands of people some standing others supported by neighbours still others unable to fall because of the crush. Where the trucks were not being filled quickly enough SS officers encouraged the guards to push and throw prisoners onto the train.

"We haven't got enough transport sir," the lieutenant continued. "And we've no idea when or ever if there are going to be any more trains."

"Assume the worst lieutenant," Otto replied. "Is there any sort of command headquarters here or is it all just a fucking complete mess?"

"There are some officers in the station master's office sir, down the platform."

Otto pushed his way through the crowds and burst into the warm office. Chairs fell over and table legs scraped on the floor as the officers present jumped to attention under Otto's verbal onslaught.

"What the fuck are you lot doing here warming your arses whilst there is utter mayhem and chaos out there?" Otto bellowed. "If there are not enough trains get these prisoners on their feet immediately and walk them to Germany. It's that way gentlemen.....to the west. If you don't get this lot on the move I'll have you all thrown into your own open truck and you can freeze your balls off all the way to Dachau. Divide them up any way you please, some for Dachau, as well as yourselves if you don't get a fucking move on, others to Buchenwald, Sachenhausen and Belsen. Now get the fuck out of here and get on with it."

Slowly but surely the crush began to ease as the river of human flotsam began to sway its slow progress westward. Otto billeted himself in a nice comfortable middle class home in the town and planned to follow the march the next day to check on progress.

The next afternoon Otto followed a trail of dead bodies through small hamlets and villages until night was approaching and the column appeared to have come to a halt. Once again thousands of prisoners were left in open fields to fend for themselves. There was no food or shelter in schools, barns or farm outhouses as these were already occupied by thousands of German refugees. In the wake of the German army's sweep eastward through Poland towards Russia four years previously thousands of Poles had been evicted from their homes and businesses in urban and rural areas. These were reallocated free to ethnic Germans from all over Eastern Europe. These same Germans were now fleeing towards Germany knowing that the barbaric treatment meted out to the Poles and Russians at the hands of both the SS and the Wehrmacht would be visited on them without mercy by the advancing

Russians and local Poles. A week later the Russians walked into Auschwitz.

When news of the collapse of the Vistula front reached Hitler he was incandescent. "Is there no one I can rely on? These Wehrmacht generals are all defeatist and treacherous," he ranted.

"I'm willing to serve you *Mein Fuhrer* in any capacity you wish."

Within days Himmler was travelling east towards Schneidemuhl to take up his new command.

Otto returned to Gliwice with a view to making a report to Himmler. He telephoned Berlin and was directed to different departments and offices before eventually being given the number of his new headquarters.

"Hello Otto my boy, how are you and where are you?"

"I'm well, thank you sir. I'm in Gliwice and I'm ringing to give you an update on the evacuation of the prisoners from Auschwitz."

"Don't worry about that Otto, I'm sure that you and Rudolph have got everything in hand. Listen........ I'm pleased that you've contacted me because I want you to come and work with me here at new Army Group Vistula. I need a good staff officer and after your experience in Warsaw I know that you would be invaluable to me. Oh!...... and there's a promotion with the appointment. Congratulations Colonel, and there's an Iron Cross First Class waiting for you as well. Drop whatever you're doing and get here as soon as you can."

Events did not bode well. As Otto made his way to join Himmler no one in the area seemed to have heard of the new Army Group Vistula. After wearily driving around the neighbourhood for hours he eventually found the whereabouts of the headquarters.

Stepping out from his kubelwagen Otto was confronted by a train consisting of smart-looking sleeping cars interspersed with flat anti-aircraft wagons. SS guards stood ram-rod straight at intervals along the platform. He showed his papers and was permitted on board where he was welcomed by a young Leutnant and taken to meet Himmler who greeted him with a hearty handshake. "At last. Welcome my boy, I'm pleased to have you on board. Come, let me give you a guided tour."

They passed through an elegant dining car looking more like an Orient Express carriage than a military headquarters and entered the operations room where lying on the map table was a single map of the area. Otto studied the map and could see at once that the information pencilled there was already 24 hours out of date. Not wishing to upset Himmler or indicate any serious doubts about his military capability Otto proceeded warily. "Have we any further information or maps of the area?"

"This is all we have and pleased I am to have it taking into consideration the panic and rush to get here." Himmler replied.

Otto was far from impressed and was overtaken by a fateful sinking feeling. Further probing revealed that there were few trained staff officers, no transport or supply organisation and worst of all no organised communications centre, the only line of communication being through Himmler's own personal telephone. Otto fought hard to conceal his anger at the pure amateurishness of the whole structure. When he could bring himself to speak Otto asked, "What is our objective?"

"I'm expecting Colonel Hans Eismann from the general staff here any minute. He's going to be my chief of operations."

Eismann looked at the map and shook his head. "What have we got to close this gap and establish a new front?"

Himmler, unsuspecting such a frank, direct question fell back on the typical Fuhrer headquarters' tactic of obfuscation and blustered, "Why we must counter-attack immediately." Waving his hand in a generalised direction over the map he continued, "Smash in their flank." The fact that he had no idea where their flank was didn't seem to occur to him and it was sadly obvious to Otto that his mentor had no idea of any basic military knowledge.

"What battle-worthy formations do we have available?" Eismann persisted.

"Well.....I'm not too sure," Himmler stuttered, "I haven't had time to assimilate the situation," he responded lamely. Eventually Eismann was able to throw together a number of odd regiments and battalions but predictably the operation was a complete disaster. Himmler was forced to withdraw his headquarters.

Otto sat alone in his compartment in the headquarters train turning the events of the last few days over and over in his mind. The further the level of vodka in his bottle descended the more depressed and morose he became. Whilst in Warsaw he had suspected and discussed with Heinz the military incompetence which Hitler exhibited and which his henchmen declined to dispute because of their own personal ambition which hinged on Hitler's sponsorship. But to experience at first hand the abject and arrogant incompetence of his erstwhile idol added fuel to the realisation that he must now accept that the Nazi party was leading Germany to utter destruction. It was not just the fact that Germany was going to lose the war but that the party henchmen were prepared to allow the German people to pay the ultimate price for them to hold on to their delusions and propaganda in spite of knowing that the war was lost. Distraught and angry, Otto questioned and began to regret the indoctrination of his lost youth, the comfort and love of a mother he rejected. His whole existence was predicated on deceit. His whole persona, his life, his very reason for living were a lie. Annette had tried to warn him. Annette had been right all along. 'Sweet Annette, how I miss you now. Will I ever see you again? Will I ever be able to achieve atonement for what I've done, what I've become?'

With Zhukov's Army now within striking distance of the River Oder it was with trepidation that Himmler answered the urgent buzz of his telephone. "What.....are you sure?"

Otto had always been frustrated by only being able to hear one side of a telephone conversation and he strained to catch what was being said over the ear-piece.

To mask his uncertainty and give himself time to think Himmler continued, "I'll send further orders shortly."

"What's happened?" Otto asked.

"Soviet tanks are heading this way. We must order our battalion of Tiger tanks to meet them immediately."

Otto was horrified. "You can't do that sir. You can't send tanks unsupported into the line. You need to bring the artillery forward as well, register the guns and transport infantry in support. Besides, it's still too far away, we don't have the fuel to send the tanks that distance and then expect them to engage the enemy."

"They're not going to drive forward Otto, they're going to be loaded onto flat cars and transported forward by rail. Besides one Tiger is worth ten Russian T34s. See that it's done."

Otto and the other few staff officers present couldn't believe what they were hearing.

Otto insisted on accompanying the battalion. With the tanks loaded and their crews on board eventually he climbed onto the engine footplate and gave the order for the train set off towards the east. The Russians were making rapid progress and with Himmler's communications command being non-existent Otto had no way of knowing exactly where Zhukov's tanks were at any given moment. One hour later the uncertainty was removed from Otto's calculations. Slowing for a sharp bend the train came under heavy fire from four Soviet tanks. It was obvious to Otto that they must have known the train was coming and that the ambush was well concealed.

"Stop......reverse....quickly man," Otto shouted to the driver above the noise of steam, and explosions too close for comfort. Once the train came to a stop and the wheels screamed for friction on the rails the Soviet tanks got their range and numerous rail carriages and Tiger tanks were hit. Fortunately, although damaged, none of the tanks slipped their chains and remained fastened to the flat cars. With the clank of buffers adding to the general cacophony of tank and small arms fire the engine gradually picked up speed and accelerated out of range, luckily without being hit.

Back at headquarters Otto's report was interrupted by Himmler who screamed, "I want the tank commander court-marshalled. He should be shot for incompetence."

It took Otto some time to persuade Himmler that being chained to a rail flat car was not the best deployment for a tank battle, even for a Tiger.

"You have a point Otto," Himmler continued reluctantly and then ranted, "But we must stiffen the army Otto, no defeatism, death and punishment for failure to carry out one's duty. That's the order of the day."

For all his bluster and rants, Himmler's tactical incompetence enabled the Red Army to cross the River Oder over the ice in darkness and fan out establishing a solid bridgehead at Oderbruch. Otto watched with increasing anger and bitterness as Himmler gradually disintegrated into a nervous wreck as a consequence of his lack of experience and damaging decisions which had disastrous effects on his forces.

Himmler now presided over a complete disaster. The Second Army on the left flank was being cut off, the Army Group Vistula was in retreat and on the right flank the Ninth Army was so badly mauled as to be of little use.

Himmler invited Otto to accompany him to his next conference with Hitler.

Appraising the situation in an instant and pointing at the map on a large table in Hitler's office Guderian said, "We need a pincer movement here to cut off Zhukov and release those troops which are trapped in Courland. They're useless where they are, we need them to defend Berlin. At the same time it will enable us to keep a corridor open towards the border."

"There will be no retreat," Hitler screamed.

"If you don't agree with my analyses of the situation Fuhrer," Guderian persisted, "The Second Army will be cut off completely."

"Why must you always contradict me?" Hitler shouted uncontrollably. "I don't know why I keep you in command."

Otto looked on in despair. He couldn't believe what he was witnessing. The future of the army, Berlin, Germany even were at risk and the strategy as presented by Guderian was obvious but here were the people responsible for the direction of the war almost coming to blows.

The argument raged until eventually Hitler relented and an action agreed.

* * * * *

Otto carefully negotiated Himmler's Mercedes through the streets of Berlin where every building had suffered bomb damage from the RAF by night and the USAF by day. Typical of the uncoordinated, unilateral, ill-considered decisions which were the hallmark of the Party henchmen, Goebbels had ordered tens of thousands of mostly starving women civilians to build barricades and tank ditches around Berlin. Otto cursed him under his breath as it was obvious that these barriers were causing havoc with military traffic going east towards the Seelow Heights and the thousands of refugees trying to enter the city. Apart from the fact that no Russian T34 tank was ever going to be stopped by the ditches. Himmler sat beside Otto in brooding silence until such time as they had cleared the city suburbs and were in the countryside heading towards Himmler's new headquarters near Hassleben, fifty miles north of Berlin.

"I believe Ziggy's expecting your baby in a few weeks."

Otto was thrown by this unexpected topic of conversation after what had just transpired during the past few hours at Hitler's state-of-the-war conference.

"Err, yes, she is," he replied, "Why?"

"I've taken the liberty of reserving a private room for her in the Haus Dahlem Maternity Clinic so that when the time comes everything is organised."

"That's very thoughtful of you Heinrich," Otto replied, "Especially as you've so much on your mind these days."

"Think nothing of it Otto, remember family is everything. There's nothing more important in a man's life than his family. Just as the Party is your family as well."

The strained silence in the vehicle induced a heavy atmosphere which was only alleviated on approaching the gates through a high barbed-wire perimeter fence which surrounded the headquarters. Otto switched off the engine and got out of the large black Mercedes. There were a series of wooden barrack blocks on the site and he followed Himmler up the steps of the largest Reichsfuhrerbaracke. The barrack was finished to a profligate high specification and the entrance, at one level impressed Otto but at another disgusted him by its incongruous opulence and ostentatious decoration. Over the next few days Otto was further disgusted by Himmler's attitude and routine. Work never commenced until mid-morning after his bath, massage and breakfast. He left orders never to be disturbed once he was asleep. Having witnessed his particularly inadequate performance at the Reich Chancellery situation conference only served to reinforce Otto's increasing loathing of Himmler. The irony was not lost on Otto when the supposed stress of command proved too much for Himmler and he took time out in a sanatorium and was replaced by Colonel General Gotthardt Heinrici.

* * * * *

The Seelow Heights was the last barrier between the advancing Soviet armies and Berlin. The natural feature represented a formidable defensive escarpment which offered excellent observation across the Russian River Oder bridgeheads. Reinforcements promised by Hitler were little more than training units some so young that with their iron rations they were issued with sweets instead of tobacco. German artillery was so short of ammunition that the batteries were limited to two shells per gun per day and as a result could not waste them on ranging in order to engage in counter battery fire. Consequently the Russians were left to range their guns in peace in preparation for the major offensive on the Seelow Heights.

(II)

"Tell your NCOs to move the men back from the front line," Otto ordered his officers at a briefing. General Heinrici had given him command of part of the northern section of the Heights and he knew the devastating affect the Russian preliminary artillery barrage would have on the forward areas.

At 3.00am the bombardment commenced and was so ferocious that it was heard and felt in Berlin sixty kilometres away to the west. Otto could feel the earth trembling and vibrating under the onslaught of nine thousand artillery pieces of all calibres with Katyusha rockets also ripping their criss-cross trajectories through the heavy, dark night sky like knives slashing through black velvet drapes. Conscious that many of the troops under his command were raw and inexperienced Otto ran from section to section doing all he could to maintain nerve and morale.

"What's the situation here corporal?" Otto shouted above the maelstrom of crashing trees, gouts of earth and hot shrapnel flying through the air as he jumped down into one of the second line trenches.

"We're doing okay colonel sir," the young corporal answered shrinking under his helmet as another shell burst too close for comfort and clods of earth descended with heavy thumps all around them. "Some of the younger ones are a bit jumpy sir."

"Pass the word along to sit tight. This bombardment will last some time and I want them ready when the Ivans start to move forward."

"Yes sir and thank you sir for coming forward. The men will appreciate it."

"Keep up the good work corporal and good luck."

Within minutes Otto was up and out of the trench and running on to the next section.

After interminable hours of bombardment, those soldiers who had not been pulled back from the front line began to wander back towards the rear. Otto was enraged at the wastage as disorientated, dazed troops shattered emotionally and psychologically staggered towards his trenches with wide, staring eyes, white, frozen visages and blood trickling from their perforated ear drums.

Even though the sky was overcast and the cold drizzle persisted the Russian flares signalling the advance were just visible. Zhukov had expected no resistance as a result of his unprecedented artillery bombardment. However, not realising that many of the forward trenches were unoccupied his bombardment had been expended ineffectually.

Otto was experienced enough to know that war is a series of unintended consequences and the resulting engagement proceeded in chaos. Visibility on the Heights was still severely restricted. The whole escarpment erupting like a volcano awakening from lying dormant for hundreds of years. Smoke and earth from shell bursts combined with the rain and mist to render visibility almost nil. With the coming of dawn the Russians deployed heavy bombers and ground attack Shturmovik aircraft but with their targets invisible the affect was haphazard and diluted but still deadly for those on the receiving end.

In the meantime Otto had stayed with his men in the second line trenches. Amid the now deafening noise of drum-fire Otto thought that he could discern a distinctive sound. "Can you hear that?" He asked a lieutenant standing beside him in a trench whilst putting his hand up to his ear. "Listen, there it is again.......Fuck....tanks." The squeak, screech and clank of tank tracks was now clearly discernible. "Get on the radio to the eighty eight millimetre gun battery and give them a bearing... quick." The lieutenant shouted into the mouth piece whilst the drifting smoke cleared just for a fraction giving them both a fleeting view of Soviet infantry running in front of a corps of approaching T34s. The 88mm was a proven tank busting weapon and Otto was relieved when he heard the battery shells whooshing overhead. Creeping forward and putting his Carl Zeiss binoculars to his eyes Otto observed the tanks struggling to move forward. It was almost a scene from the Great War as even the wide tracks of the T34 tanks slithered and skidded trying to find grip in the churning up mud of the shell shattered landscape. Some of the tanks bogged down, others succumbed to the 88s whilst those who made it through found the gradient of the Heights at this point too steep and Otto allowed himself a wry smile as they turned to find alternative routes only to run into an SS Heavy Panzer Battalion of Tiger tanks which inflicted heavy casualties.

The battle ebbed and flowed with attack and counter-attack and because of the poor visibility much of the infantry fighting was at close quarters the Russians inflicting casualties on their own troops in the confusion. The bitter fighting continued during the day and throughout the night and into the next day. The weather improved and Russian bombers and Shturmoviks with clear visibility were now able to inflicted heavy casualties on the remaining German positions. Russian tanks continued to probe forward but once again came under heavy fire from 88s and came to a halt as the result of another counter-attack by Panther tanks.

In the confusion and increasing casualties Otto had managed to keep his battalion in good formation but it was obvious to him that he was not going to be able to hold his position. He could see that in spite of ferocious infantry and armoured defence the Soviet tanks were gradually surrounding the Heights.

"This position is hopeless now," Otto shouted above the noise of the battle to a captain and lieutenant with him.

"What do you suggest sir?" The captain yelled holding on to his helmet as the blast from a shell too close for comfort buffeted them.

"We'll make an organised withdrawal. Each section covering for the others as we leapfrog back to a new defensive line."

The order was given and the two sections nearest to Otto took up defensive positions and engaged the advancing Russian infantry whilst their comrades withdrew. Once these troops were in position behind the defensive line the front line soldiers pulled back and so on. The tactic was a complete success and the men although driven back by superior numbers managed to reach the divisional artillery batteries only to find that the gunners were firing their last shells and preparing for a gunner's saddest moment, blowing up their own gun so that it doesn't fall into enemy hands. The gunners retreated leaving Otto and his men to face the rapidly advancing Soviet armour. They quickly dug fox holes and waited.

Water bottles and stomachs were now empty and time ceased to register in any meaningful way. It could have been minutes or hours when a forward observation soldier on point rushed back through the trees shouting, "Tank....tank." and dived headlong into a ditch. The distinctive metallic, clattering, squeaking sound of tank tracks set nerves jangling as turret-gunfire and machine-gun fire grew louder and louder and trees splintered to the ground like matchwood when the tank eventually burst through the tree-line into a clearing in front of Otto and his troops. The tank machine-gun raked their positions with devastating effect.

"Withdraw," Otto yelled above the din. "Fall back through the wood."

Otto ran at a crouch but being caught in the blast of a tank shell was blown off his feet. Dazed but still in one piece he spotted a discarded panzerfaust and picking it up on the run he dived into a shallow slit trench and pressed himself to the earth like a little boy pressing his thumb into a lump of plasticine. The T34 ground on towards his barely adequate refuge and he could feel the heat from the engine inches above his face as the tank passed right over his prone body. With the tank now moving away from him Otto quickly turned onto his stomach, aimed the panzerfaust and pressed the trigger. The explosion told Otto that he had scored a hit and as the smoke cleared he could see the T34 shedding its left track like a snake sloughing off its skin. Before the Russian infantry support could arrive Otto ran to the tank and climbed up onto the turret. Opening the hatch he dropped a grenade inside, jumped down and followed his comrades into the trees.

The situation was now desperate and field hospitals were being combed for lightly wounded men who were sent forward as reinforcements. Otto was left fuming as Himmler's latest order reached him declaring that ...'no German town will be declared an open city or position surrendered under threat of execution...'. It was obvious to him that Himmler didn't know or worse didn't care that the artillery was out of ammunition and that tanks were being abandoned through lack of fuel. The next day pockets of Germans still held positions on the Seelow Heights but they were now hopelessly marooned behind enemy lines.

Exhausted troops pulled back and officers, Otto included, did their best to organise improvised battle groups. There was no longer a defensive line and these disparate groups fought isolated engagements whenever they came into contact with the advancing enemy without any overall strategy to guide them.

Otto and his worn out comrades staggered westward along the Reichsstrasse Route 1 where they were joined by troops from other battalions and mingled with thousands of refugees whose farm carts, prams, bicycles, donkeys and horses clogged the road. To add to their misery they were constantly being strafed by Russian ground attack aircraft, the Luftwaffe having ceased to exist as a fighting unit. With each strafe they dived into the ditches and civilians, refugees and soldiers ran into the fields looking for what little cover was available and a few more bloodied and shattered corpses and wounded were left behind. But it was another sight which fed Otto's mounting despair and anger.

They approached a small town and Otto was horrified to see the bodies of Wehrmacht soldiers hanging from lamp posts with notices either hung from their necks or nailed to the lamp posts saying 'traitor', 'deserter', or 'coward'. There were more than twelve Stations of the Cross on this road to Calvary.

"Stop, where do you think you're going you cowards? Turn round and face the enemy of the Reich or you'll be shot by order from the Fuhrer" Three Feldgendarmerie, military police personnel with automatic weapons at the ready faced Otto and the few Wehrmacht and SS soldiers with him in his small group.

"Do you see these?" Otto pointed to the insignia of his rank as a colonel. "Who do you think you're talking to?"

Swinging his automatic machine pistol to emphasise direction the Feldgendarm sergeant answered. "You are walking this way and the enemy is that way. Obey the Fuhrer's orders or pay the consequences."

"These men haven't eaten or hardly slept for the past five days and have been in continual contact with the enemy. How many Russians have you killed this week?" Otto spat at the sergeant.

"Turn around or we open fire," came the reply.

Otto held up his hands in submission and turned away as if to head back east. Slowly he dropped his right hand to his machine pistol and out of the line of sight of the sergeant slid the safety catch off his weapon and in one swift move swung round spraying the three Feldgendarmerie with a full magazine of bullets.

Night fell and with every kilometre the river of human misery seemed to swell ever more claustrophobic and oppressive with the cries and moans of the old, young, sick and wounded filling every empty space. In the confusion Otto became separated from his small group of comrades and he decided to take to the side roads but these too were crammed with refugees. He trudged passed more lines of corpses hanging from lamp posts with the word 'traitor' hung from their necks and vehicles abandoned in ditches as they had been destroyed or run out of fuel. He didn't know it but at the same time as he was making his way direct towards Berlin the remnants of the Ninth and Vistula Armies were being pushed back towards the Berlin. Against Hitler's orders they intended to slip away to the south of the city and head west in the hope of reaching the Allies before being annihilated or captured by the Russians. Lines on a map were of no further use in showing the disposition of Soviet advancing armies or the retreating German forces. The situation was chaotic.

The temperature dropped as darkness fell and Otto looked for somewhere to rest up. Completely separated now from his small band of comrades he took a calculated guess and followed a cart track for about two kilometres which eventually led him to a small hamlet. Making his way to the nearest farm house Otto knocked on the solid wooden door. There was no answer but he thought that he had seen a momentary flicker of light through a downstairs window and heard a noise inside. Raising his machine pistol this time Otto used the butt to hammer on the door and he could hear it echoing inside. "Is there anyone inside?" He called out. He waited a few moments and when there was still no answer he aimed his gun at the door lock and fired a quick burst then kicked the door in with his boot. Using caution learnt during the street fighting in Warsaw Otto edged his way inside the building. Someone was still here or had just vacated as a wood fire burned brightly in a grate in the kitchen. Convinced that the crude, sparsely furnished rooms downstairs were unoccupied Otto crept quietly towards the stairs. He stood still, pressed against the wall, listening to the light wind in the trees outside and the timbers of the house talking to each other. Even though he stepped on the stair treads close to the wall where, he knew they would have maximum support and least movement, the stairs still creaked his progress to the upper storey. He stood still on the landing, quiet, listening like a deer scenting danger in the wild. There......he heard a low, soft, muffled moan which he knew was not the wind in the eaves. Edging into the bedroom he took hold of the bed clothes and in one movement threw them up, thrust his gun under the bed and dropped to his knees. His heart was now pounding and he was relieved that there was an empty space under the bed. The only other pieces of furniture in the room were a wash stand, wooden chair and a large wardrobe. Approaching the wardrobe from the side he reached across and pulled open the doors. The hinges creaked accompanied by an involuntary scream like that of a rabbit caught by a ferret.

Otto stepped back into the middle of the room pointing his machine pistol at the open wardrobe. "Don't shoot, don't shoot, we're not armed." Crouching on the floor half hidden by hanging clothes was what Otto assumed to be a mother with her arms around a small girl perhaps six or seven years old. Sitting beside them with her knees up under her chin was another girl about seventeen or eighteen Otto guessed.

"Is there anyone else in the house?" Otto asked quietly.

The mother took some little comfort in recognizing Otto as a German officer.

"There's only us," came the reply, "They took my husband away to join the Volkssturm, the people's militia."

"Come out," Otto said softly bending forward and extending his hand towards the mother. "I'm sorry if I frightened you. I don't mean you any harm. In fact I'd be grateful if you could spare me some food....I can't remember when I last had something to eat..... and somewhere for me to stay tonight and I'll be on my way in the morning."

The woman lit an oil lamp and Otto could see that she was dressed in serviceable country clothes. The tired look and sallow appearance of her complexion couldn't hide a classical jaw-line and the high cheek-boned symmetry of her face. He guessed that she was in her late 30s and in spite of the effects of her hard country life she was demurely beautiful. "My name is Gudrun Dietrich," said the mother smoothing down her apron, "And this is little Heidi and my elder daughter Helga."

"Pleased to meet you Frau Dietrich and you little Heidi and Helga." Clicking his heels he continued, "I'm Standartenfuhrer von Lieper. But that is too much of a mouthful so you can call me Otto."

"You poor boy, you look half dead," Gudrun said softly. "Come down to the kitchen and I'll see what I can find."

It was then that Otto glanced an unrecognisable reflection in a full-length mirror on the wardrobe door. The last time that he'd looked in a mirror was at his wedding when a smart athletic SS officer in his pristine, new black uniform had met his gaze. Now the face was pale and drawn underneath unkempt stubble with deep sunken eyes staring back at him. His shoulders had a pronounced stoop unlike the straight, erect figure of but a few weeks ago. His battle dress was torn and covered in dried blood and his whole person covered in mud stains and dust.

"It's time you girls were in bed," Gudrun said with loving affection. "Go on.... shooo," She continued, clapping her hands and making as if to chase them. Little Heidi shrieked and laughed running towards the bottom of the stairs as Helga, following her mother's lead, clapped her hands and chased Heidi up the stairs.

The loving domesticity seemed out of place and alien in his current circumstances but at the same time reassuring and comforting.

"I'm sorry about your door," Otto said with genuine contrition. "I'll see if I can repair the lock tomorrow morning."

"Thank you, that's very thoughtful of you," Gudrun replied rummaging around in the kitchen cupboards. "I have a little vodka here somewhere if you would like a drink."

"I'd much prefer a glass of water," Otto replied recognizing how hoarse his voice sounded. "My mouth is so parched and I'm so dehydrated. I can't remember when I last had a drink."

Gudrun placed a glass of clear cold water in front of Otto who ran his finger down the outside of the glass before picking it up and downing the refreshing liquid. Gudrun watched with outreaching tenderness.

"Would you like a bath before eating?" Gudrun asked out of the blue.

"Could I?" Otto replied immediately with childish anticipation. "Are you sure that it's no trouble? It's the best offer I've had in weeks."

Gudrun walked through a door to the left of the kitchen range and entered what Otto assumed was some kind of utility, outhouse. There was a crashing of things falling and being knocked over and Gudrun eventually returned carrying a large tin bath. She set it down in front of the fire. Turning on one of the kitchen taps above a deep stone sink she drew hot water down into a large, churn-like jug and poured it into the bath.

"Here, let me do that for you," Otto said getting up from his chair and reaching across touched Gudrun's hand as he relieved her of the jug, "That's too heavy for you."

"Oh I've had to lift heavier objects than this on the farm these last few years," she replied with a nervous laugh.

"How long have you lived here?"

"About four years now. My husband's older than me.....we're ethnic Germans and were living in Lithuania when the authorities offered to relocate us here with the promise of our own house and free farm. It seemed too good a chance to miss. But now I'm worried about the future. We only hear propaganda on the radio but I've seen the streams of refugees shuffling along the roads and more lately soldiers like yourself who, I can only assume are retreating from the Russians."

"I shouldn't be saying this but you're right to be concerned Gudrun. We're going to lose this war and soon. The Russians are not too far away and even now we could be behind some of their forward positions. For your own safety and that of your lovely family I urge you to pack your food and valuables and make your way to the west as soon as you can, immediately in fact."

You've confirmed what I've been thinking," Gudrun replied quietly, "But I've been putting off the decision hoping for good news."

"There is none Gudrun. Leave as soon as you can. Don't stay in Berlin the place is in ruins and chaos and things will get a lot worse if the Russians get there before the Allies. Keep heading west until you reach either the American or British forces."

"Thanks Otto, I'll follow your advice. Now....leave your clothes there beside the door into the living room and I'll see how much of the filth I can remove without washing them. I have a little soap left which I've been saving for a special occasion....and...well....I don't suppose in the circumstances there's going to be a more special occasion than this."

"Thank you. That's so kind and thoughtful of you. You don't know how much I appreciate your help."

"I've left a razor for you. I thought that you might like a shave."

Gudrun withdrew discretely into the living room as Otto took his clothes off and left them in a pile beside the door. He stepped into the bath then sat down and allowed the hot water to soothe away the aches of battle.

Gudrun quietly began to pick up Otto's filthy uniform and she glanced over to where he was luxuriating in the water with his back to her holding up a mirror in one hand and manipulating Gudrun's husband's cut-throat razor in the other. He had not had a haircut for weeks and removing his cap had allowed his hair to spring out in all direction. She stared at the red and yellow flames from the fire beyond him flickered through his unkempt blond curls imparting a golden halo. Her eyes strayed to the well-defined muscles of his back and she allowed herself to feel the prickling, swelling, wet sensations she remembered but hadn't experienced for many years. Just for a split second their eyes made contact in the mirror and although Gudrun looked away immediately the scarce admitted message was potent in its content. Putting the clothes down, she quietly walked towards the bath. Bending down she picked the flannel off the edge of the bath where she had left it and dipping it in the water squeezed the soothing liquid over his back.

Otto bent forward in order to allow Gudrun to wash the filth and sweat from his back and the aching tiredness from his body and she leant forward and kissed him on his shoulder. He stood up and at the same time taking hold of Gudrun's hands pulled her up and drew her to him. Her kiss was gentle and nervous initially but quickly became urgent and demanding, driven by years of physical loving neglect, desperation and accumulated frustration. Taking his hand she led him naked and dripping into the living room and stopped beside a chaise-longue, where the red velvet pile had been scrubbed away along its edges. Otto helped her to undress and she lay down on the cushions pulling Otto down on top of her. Their mutual climax was quick in coming. Otto made to get up but with her arms still around him and her left knee raised and her leg clamped round him Otto sensed that she didn't want him to slip away. They lay comfortably entwined for some minutes each drawing solace and comfort from the close proximity of the other. After many barren years of frustration and the fear of the immediate danger that lay ahead Gudrun allowed her desperate need for the most human of contacts to take control once again. That contact which, if even for just a fleeting moment gives life its meaning, transports body and soul to a higher plane, a moment of connection which communicates and transcends self.

Almost imperceptibly her internal contracting movements were slow and gentle at first. As she felt Otto responding, her body took over in an increasing demanding, uncontrollable, grasping desire for resolution. The animal noises she heard she realized were coming from her and not wanting to disturb her children she clenched her fist in her mouth drawing blood as her body exploded in an involuntary series of spasms of an intensity that left her with but a tenuous hold on consciousness. Descending from this plateau was reassuring and comforting but left her with aching muscles where she had gripped Otto as if her very life depended on not letting go.

Slowly Otto got up and made his way into the kitchen where he finished washing himself. Gudrun dressed silently with her back to him. Picking up Otto's clothes she took them outside and removed as much of the filth as she could. Moments later they were both sitting silently, deep in their own thoughts beside the kitchen fire eating bread and *wurst* and drinking hot ersatz coffee.

At last Gudrun broke the silence, "It would be better if you didn't sleep in the house," She said almost apologetically. "The Feldgendarmerie and local Gauleiters have made periodic checks in the locality and if they find a man of service age the whole household is arrested."

"That's all right, I understand. I can sleep in the barn. I've slept in worse places these past few weeks."

"Thank you Otto, I'll fetch you some blankets. You should be all right in the loft there's plenty of hay and straw up there."

Otto held her in his arms and gently kissing her on the lips said, "Goodnight Gudrun and thank you for everything. I'll never forget you."

"Thank you for reminding me that I'm a women. Good night."

The sound of heavy lorry engines disturbed Otto's deep sleep and insinuated their diesel growl into his consciousness. Immediately alert Otto rushed to a gap in the barn wall where two planks were hanging loose. In the pale light of dawn he recognised a Russian troop carrier turning into the farm yard whilst a second lorry deviated off to the right towards other residential homes and farm buildings. With a stab of brakes the lorry skidded to a halt accompanied by the immediate noise of the tailboard being dropped. Otto held his breath as he counted at least twenty Red Army soldiers some heading towards the house whilst others checked out the surrounding area. He could only watch transfixed whilst they shouted and kicked in the already damaged front door. From his vantage point Otto could see both sides of the house and as the troops rushed in Otto observed Gudrun and her daughters with coats over their night clothes running out of the back door and heading towards the barn. Unfortunately they were spotted by those troops searching the area who shouted and rushed up to the family grabbing hold of them and punching Gudrun and Helga into the barn entrance. From his hiding place in the loft Otto could only stare as almost before Gudrun and Helga had hit the ground one of their assailants had his belt undone and his trousers around his knees. He fell on Helga and punched her viciously in the face. Her screams grew louder and wilder as he forced her legs apart and brutally entered her. "She's a virgin this one," He yelled triumphantly to his comrades, "And I'm the first."

Officers looked on with disinterest as one of the soldiers held little Heidi who was screaming, "Mutti...Mutti," and struggling to break loose whilst, like a pack of rabid dogs, the rest fell on Gudrun and Helga in turn again and again and again until Otto lost count. Helga's screams became soft moans until eventually she lay silent and unmoving as the last Russian soldier climbed off her. Gudrun struggled for as long as she could but fist blows subdued her into unconsciousness.

When they'd finished the soldiers stood around joking and drinking vodka from bottles. In the distance Otto could here other inhuman screams as the rapes he had just witnessed were being repeated in neighbouring houses. He continued looking at the scene below through a crack in the floor boards with tears in his eyes. Otto couldn't remember crying, ever, and the hot, gritty burning was a new sensation for him. Was he crying for this one destroyed innocent family or was he crying for the thousands of other families in every city, town, village and hamlet that the Russian hoards had passed through venting their hatred on everything German. Perhaps they were also tears of frustrating impotence. He had never backed down from a difficulty or confrontation and his instinct was to jump down and fire his machine pistol into the Soviet animals but there were too many of them and he knew that it would only end in his own futile death and he still had a life to live. Was he and others like him to blame for this catastrophe, this descent into the law of the jungle? The idea that the Russians were simply paying in kind for what the Wehrmacht and SS had done to them five years ago in the ruthless execution of their plan to exterminate all Slavs as well as Jews. 'Oh Annette,' he thought, 'Is this what you meant when you said, those who sow the wind will reap the whirlwind? Am I really looking into the abyss?'.

"Shoot me please," Gudrun pleaded through split lips as she regained consciousness. Her nose was obviously broken and bloodied face echoed the blood on her thighs and legs. "Please shoot me."

"What do you think we are?" One of the Red soldiers replied laughing. "We're not SS, we're soldiers of the Soviet Army. We don't shoot women!"

His comrades burst out laughing in appreciation of his humour whilst at the same time they torched the house whose old dry timbers quickly became an inferno. They then turned their attention to the barn and set it on fire too where the straw easily caught alight and quickly spread the flames to the wooden structure. The whole barn was rapidly filled with suffocating smoke and Otto quickly looked round for an escape. Trying desperately not to cough and with his handkerchief over his mouth he spotted at the back of the loft an opening used to haul straw bales up from carts for storage. The solid wooden jib was still in place and Otto was relieved to see that the rope was still tied off and hanging down. Reaching out from the opening he grabbed the rope and quickly slid down to the ground. Without hesitation and keeping the barn between himself and the Soviet soldiers he ran crouching across the track and through a gateway into the adjoining field. Keeping close behind the hedge Otto left a scene which was to be seared into his memory.

(III)

Otto's throat was parched and grit coated his teeth like sandpaper. It was constant and drifting everywhere in the atmosphere. From his hiding place in a bombed out apartment in the Berlin Alexanderplatz he looked across the ruined cityscape where not a single building had escaped either bomb or artillery damage as far as the eye could see. Individual columns of black smoke reached up into the sky and hung suspended before mushrooming out to combine with each other forming a dark layer through which the sun tried in vain to penetrate with any degree of warmth. The Russian long range artillery kept up their nerve tingling bombardment and fires raged in every direction. Against this constant background noise Otto heard the distinctive sound of light field artillery firing and could see the guns being fired over open sights a few blocks away with infantry running in and out of buildings firing their rifles and automatic weapons. The crashes of masonry and resulting clouds of plaster and brick dust billowed up into the air. With destruction and the noise of battle everywhere Otto was surprised when he saw a white bed sheet being pushed slowly out of an upper storey window in the block opposite. Immediately and out of nowhere an SS squad ran across the street and entered the building. Otto waited, watching and listened to the distinctive rattle of automatic pistol fire followed by the screams of the civilians in an action which Otto thought seemed pitiful and pointless. The white sheet quickly disappeared from the window. He couldn't for the life of him reconcile why his erstwhile comrades were killing fellow German citizens in the face of the advancing enemy.

Negotiating piles of rubble, shell craters and unstable walls Otto picked his way through wrecked abandoned buildings towards a bridge over the River Spree leading to Unter dem Linden and the city centre. Streets were barricaded with burnt out vehicles, masonry and furniture from nearby homes and manned by young boys, old men and companies of the city's Wehrmacht Berlin defence army. Otto spared himself a wry smile, cracking the layer of caked dust on his face and eyebrows, thinking that the poor devils had no idea what they were facing and that their inevitable sacrifice was futile and would achieve nothing.

By late afternoon Otto broke cover and approached the barricaded bridge over the River Spree. Recognized as an SS colonel Otto was allowed through the barricade and across the bridge where he was approached by a young lieutenant.

"*Heil Hitler.*" He saluted.

"*Heil Hitler,*" Otto responded with little enthusiasm.

"What's the situation up ahead sir?" The lieutenant asked anxiously.

"The Russians are about half a kilometre up the road lieutenant. They're making slow but steady progress in this direction and will probably be here within twenty four hours, probably less. Is the bridge mined?"

"Yes sir but because the water, electricity, gas and telephonic services use the bridge to cross the river and the canal further down the road I have to wait for special orders if it is to be blown."

"Very good lieutenant, carry on. Those barricades, if they're not blasted out by the artillery they'll be overrun by tanks. Make sure that you've plenty of panzerfausts, they're your best chance."

"Yes sir, thank you sir," the lieutenant replied but Otto was already making his way towards the next bridge over the Spreekanal.

Like Jack Frost slowly creeping up a window pane the Russians closed in on the centre of Berlin from all directions fighting their way towards the Reich Chancellery. In spite of the proximity of soviet troops Otto could see from his hiding place that the early morning food and water pump queues outside the Karstadt Department Store were already long. As he watched, a lone shell whooshed and crashed into the street. The smoke cleared gradually to reveal a gap in the food queue where previously people had been waiting patiently. On his last visit to Berlin Otto had witnessed a similar event and those in the queue and passers-by had willingly helped and rendered first aid. Now, as he watched in silence the queue shuffled forwards to close the gap slowly and callously stepping over dead and wounded in the process. No one wanted to lose their place. Further up the street machine-gun fire could be heard but the Red Army infantry were too busy looting and raping to make much further progress towards Otto and the civilians.

Calculating his chances Otto ran across the road towards the head of a queue at the nearest water stand-pipe. Ignoring the complaints and anger of those already waiting with their jugs and buckets he took his cap off and put his head under the clear stream of water and washed the dirt and dust from his face. He filled his bottle, drank and gargled away the accumulated dust in his mouth and throat spitting the grey coloured spittle onto the ground. He refilled his bottle and intended to head in the direction of the Anhalter railway station but an hundred yards further on he spotted a squad of Red Army soldiers and dived into a building running down the debris strewn stairs into the cellar. He was met by cries of alarm as a group of civilians cowered in the gloom.

"It's all right," Otto said trying to allay their fear, "I'm German."

"You're SS." One of the women shouted pushing him in the chest. "Get out, go away. If the Russians come in and find you here they'll kill the lot of us. Go away, please."

In disbelief Otto left the cellar but instead of going back up the stairs he turned left into another smaller room and stumbled over piles of rubble. Just like in Warsaw a hole had been blasted through the wall in front of him. He climbed through and sat down with his back to the wall whilst he decided what to do next. His deliberation was interrupted by the sound of running feet coming down the cellar steps and Russian voices shouting from the cellar.

"*Du SS, du SS.*"

"*Nein, nein, Ich bin ein zivilist,* no, no I'm a civilian," one of the three men replied.

But a burst of automatic fire told Otto that they had been killed anyway. Immediately there were the inevitable screams coming from each of the two women. Otto slid the safety off his weapon and quietly crept back towards the cellar. The brutal scene taking place was sickening but Otto had to wait his chance if he was to kill the six soviet soldiers without hitting the women in the process. He didn't have to wait long. With both women lying on the ground all six Russians were standing as they changed places. Otto burst into the room and before the surprised Russians could respond Otto sprayed bullets into their bodies. The sound was deafening in the closed environs of the cellar and just before he released the trigger of his gun Otto was knocked to the ground with a severe pain to the left side of his face. At the same moment there was the sound of Russian voices coming from above. With his gift for languages Otto had picked up enough Russian and shouted back up the stairs, "No problems, all is good down here." Then everything went black.

Otto didn't know how long he had been unconscious until his moan alerted the women beside him.

"Are you all right?" the woman who had pushed him away asked with concern.

"I think so." Otto replied putting his hand up to the left-hand side of his throbbing head. "What happened?"

"I'm not sure, but in this confined space I think a ricochet came back and caught you on your temple. Your eye was bleeding so I bathed it using your water bottle and put your field dressing on. Thank you for saving us but I fear it will happen again. The women in the queues say that every night after they've drunk themselves stupid the Ivans go on what they call a Frau hunt, raping anything in a skirt no matter how young or old. Unless I can find a Russian officer who'll offer me some protection by taking me as his campaign wife."

"I suppose we all have to do what we can to survive." Otto replied. "But I'm afraid I'm going to have to leave you. Good luck."

"Before you go, I hope you don't mind me saying but if I was you I'd get rid of that SS uniform. The Ivans hate the SS with a vengeance and will shoot you on sight. You might stand a better chance in civilian clothes. There are escaped foreign, guest workers all over Berlin and you could blend in. You seem to be the same build as my son. If you go up to my apartment, or what's left of it on the first floor you'll find some of his clothes in a wardrobe. You're welcome to take whatever you want."

"Thank you for your help," Otto replied struggling to his feet still groggy and with a severe pain down the left-hand side of his face. With vision in only one eye he stumbled as he misjudged his distance from a pile of rubble on the floor.

"You can't go just yet," the women responded. "Let me bring some things down for you."

Minutes later Otto was standing in a pair black scuffed shoes over-hung by baggy, shapeless trousers, a red check, woollen shirt and grey pullover. The jacket was also made from thick grey wool. He placed a navy blue woollen cap carefully over his bandaged head.

"Will I pass?" Otto asked.

"I think so," she replied, "But in any case better than in an SS uniform. One other thing for you to consider. I'd think about getting rid of that tattoo on your arm. The Ivans are now wise to the fact that SS have their blood group tattooed at the top of their left arm and I've seen them ripping clothes off men to check."

"Thanks once again," Otto replied, "I can't thank you enough."

"You helped us at great risk to yourself so I think we're even. Take care."

Ripping the lining of his uniform jacket Otto removed the false identity documents and put them in the inside pocket of his civilian jacket. He was reluctant to leave his machine pistol but put his Luger in one of the jacket pockets where he could get at it quickly in an emergency. It was now dark and a thunderstorm had put out some of the fires. Otto made his way towards the large air-raid shelter at the Anhalter railway station.

In the city the Russian First Guards Tank Army had breached the Landwehr canal and were heading for the Reich Chancellery. The third Guards Tank Army had penetrated Grunewald and entered Charlottenburg. There was still bitter fighting to come but the end was in sight.

The shelter was crammed to overcapacity and the stench of sweat, unwashed bodies and urine was overpowering. Pushing his way further inside Otto stopped at the entrance to an ante-room and was shocked and angry at the charnel-house before his eyes. The floor was slippery with blood as first-aiders worked in cramped conditions to tend to the wounded with limited resources. Doctors with blood up to their elbows worked on more severely wounded people who were stretched out on flimsy trestle tables. The whole scene was dimly lit by bicycle dynamos kept going by other exhausted Berliners.

Otto knew that the shelter was connected to the Berlin underground rail network and he forced his way down to one of the U-Bahn tunnels and jumped down onto the line. Safety was not a problem as the network had ceased operating weeks before. He calculated that his only chance was to use the tunnels to cross under the Landwehr canal and then negotiate his way through Schoneberg and Steglitz to reach Dahlem and Ziggy. Progress was slow in the dank gloom and was further hindered by the loss of vision in his left eye. More than once he tripped over a rail sleeper and occasional dead body. Dim, yellow emergency lights waxed and waned and the sound of a diesel generator up ahead gave some pretence at normality. There were other people in the tunnel but no one talked each occupied with their own misery and quest for survival. Otto swallowed water from his bottle and plodded on.

Moments later a sudden draught of air rushed passed him closely followed by the muffled sound of an explosion behind him. He stopped and listened and panicked as he recognised the distinctive sound of water rushing towards him. Initially, within minutes the water was up to his knees but was now rising slowly. Otto tried to quicken his steps but it was impossible. The water rose higher still and he tried to maintain his balance whilst pushing away debris, rats and floating bodies. As suddenly as it had begun the volume of water slowed then stopped and settled at chest height.

The screams of others in the tunnel gradually subsided as people realised that the immediate danger had passed. In spite of his headache Otto reasoned that a shell must have landed in the Landwehr canal directly above the tunnel fracturing the roof and allowing the water to flood in. He was not to know that the explosion had been caused by his own SS colleagues who deliberately destroyed the canal bed to flood the tunnel in order to slow any Russian advance. Fortunately there were a number of connecting tunnels and the force and level of the water had been dissipated otherwise he would have been washed away in the torrent and drowned.

The freezing water numbed Otto's limbs as he continued to wade through the flooded tunnel frequently stumbling, plunging below the black turgid water and resurfacing time after time gasping for air. Wreckage, flotsam and floating bodies continued to impede his progress and there was the ever present eerie screech and squeak of rats. There was nothing he could do but press on with dogged determination even as every muscle and sinew resisted each faltering step. Imperceptibly at first, but gradually the water level began to fall and Otto realised that he was now making his way up a gradual incline.

The sun was setting when Otto at last extricated himself from the tunnel and reached the surface. The spasmodic sound of artillery had not abated and palls of smoke continued to hang over the city. With the Reich Chancellery now behind him Otto could see his way clear to the west along Heerstrasse towards Charlottenburg where he knew he would have to turn south in the direction of Dahlem. He waited, shivering in his wet clothes, for nightfall and in spite of the falling rain the systematic destruction of Berlin was evidenced by fires still burning and smouldering in ruined apartment buildings. Knowing that Russian soldiers were probably probing defences ahead of their main front line Otto carefully manoeuvred himself in the dark from damaged building to building and cellar to cellar each one occupied by little groups of ragged humanity huddled together in mutual fear. Eventually tiredness overwhelmed Otto and he looked for somewhere to hole up for a while. Close by was a building which had recently been hit by a shell. The timbers were still burning and Otto decided that any passing Soviet patrol would assume that the occupants would not have survived and that therefore it would be a safe place to hide. He could hear small arms automatic weapons firing but looking to right and left and crouching down Otto ran across the street and dived in to the ruined building. Manoeuvring past fallen masonry and timbers he made his way down to the cellar. Crawling in to a corner behind a door which had been blown off its hinges Otto propped himself up against the wall and surrendered to the void which exhausted sleep brings.

He woke with a start and in the daylight creeping through the ground-level cellar window surveyed the destruction surrounding him. His wet, plaster dust impregnated clothes had dried to the consistency of cardboard and were as stiff as his muscles. Otto stood up, stretched and dusted down his clothes. Sitting down again on a dislodged joist he tipped up his water bottle savouring the last mouthful of the refreshing liquid. Small arms fire at street level insinuated itself into his consciousness and he instantly knew that he was still in danger. The previous warning of the civilian woman about the Russian obsessional hatred of SS soldiers and knowing about the identifying blood group tattoo played on his mind. To cut the tattoo off his arm would leave a tell-tale wound that his civilian clothes and identity papers could not explain away. It was a game of Russian roulette and Otto allowed himself a wry smile of resignation at the pun. He might get through without capture. He might be killed outright. The unthinkable was that he might be captured and tortured before being killed by the Russians or eventually, if he made it to the west, to be put on trial by the Allies for war crimes.

Making his way up the cellar stairs the heat from a still burning timber gave Otto an idea which he immediately dismissed but which wouldn't go away. He was already wounded in his left eye and if somehow he could extend that wound to his left arm then this might disguise his real identity and add credibility to his cover story. Otto slouched down on to the stairs trying to pluck up the courage to carry out his plan. With quickening heart beat and sweat on his brow, Otto removed his jacket and shirt. He stared at the red glowing timber, stuffed his handkerchief in his mouth and quickly reached out with his left arm and embraced the burning joist. The scream gagged in his throat and was muffled as he blacked out and crumpled up on the stairs.

The skin under his arm and on the left side of his chest were already burnt away and blistered by the time Otto finally came to. With great difficulty he managed to put his shirt and jacket back on but the exertion and pain proved too much and he slipped into unconsciousness again. Time passed in a delirium of excruciating pain and before he knew it night was falling. The screams of women unfortunate enough to be caught in the drunken Ivans' nightly Frau Hunt filled the air as Otto managed to drag himself up to street level. With his left arm hanging uselessly Otto dodged from doorway to doorway keeping in the shadows. Eventually dawn approached and he looked for somewhere to hide and stumbled once again in to the nearest cellar.

A sense of movement and the sound of a sharp intake of breath informed Otto that he was not alone. His remaining good eye began to focus in the blackness and he counted at least ten old men, women and children. He could feel the tension subside as the group realised that he was not a Russian soldier. Otto also allowed himself to relax as he sat down on the floor with his back against the wall.

"Have you any news? All we here are rumours which buzz around as thick as blowflies around a corpse." One of the old men ventured, his voice breaking and wheezing.

"Not really," Otto replied with tired resignation. "The Russians are in the centre of Berlin or at least what's left of it. I believe that their plan is to encircle the whole city and seal it off before the Allies get here."

"That would be true." Another of the old men volunteered. "We were trying to make our way west but were forced back here to Dahlem to escape a Russian Tank Army south of here which looked like it was turning north through Grunewald in a flanking manoeuvre."

Otto sat quietly weighing up his options. There would be Soviet troops probing forwards in front of the main battle tanks and he must get to Ziggie before them. He knew that his son's expected birth was now overdue and that his best chance of finding Ziggie was to make for the Nursing Home where her uncle Heinrich had reserved her a private room. Here in the west suburbs there was less evidence of the fierce resistance fighting taking place in the centre of Berlin but time was of the essence and he decided to chance making his way in daylight.

The spacious villas and wide tree-lined streets of the Dahlem district were a world apart from the utter destruction of central Berlin. The occasional crack of a field gun or whoosh of a Katyusha rocket seemed obscenely out of place. Keeping off the street and taking great care when creeping from garden to garden Otto made his way towards the Haus Dahlem Maternity Clinic. Hiding behind a large stone built pillar which had once supported a wrought iron gate, now long ago requisitioned and melted down for armaments, Otto's heart sank at the sight of two large gaps where tanks had blasted holes through the clinic perimeter wall. He watched and waited. Everywhere appeared quiet but he feared the worst. Making sure that the coast was clear he reached the nearest gap in the wall, crept inside the grounds and hid in the nearest bushes. Smashed windows, chairs and cabinets and other items of furniture littered the lawn as well as bodies which had obviously been thrown from upper stories. Black scorch and smoke marks stained the walls indicating that some areas of the building had been set on fire. With one last quick glance Otto ran round to the front of the building and with his luger in his hand rushed in to the entrance reception area. The scene was one of complete devastation with furniture, wall pictures and papers scattered everywhere. Wherever he stepped there was the crunch of broken glass and bullet holes had blasted plaster off the walls leaving open scars. The bodies of nursing staff and civilians littered the waiting area where pools of blood glinted in the light pouring through shattered windows. A crooked sign on the wall indicated 'Maternity' and pointed towards a wide staircase. On the landing a set of double doors had been kicked in and hung at drunken angles. Moving more cautiously Otto entered the long corridor with doors on either side leading to private nursing rooms. The corridor was a repeat of the reception area. Overturned medical trolleys, stretchers, bed linen, mattresses, instruments, enamel bowls and the bodies of nursing staff stretched the whole length of the corridor. Blood was splashed and smeared on every surface. The throbbing pain in his burnt arm and chest were almost unbearable but Otto was determined to search for Ziggie and his son Siegfried. Room by room, Otto made his way slowly down the corridor. Some doors were closed, others ajar and others kicked off their hinges. The same scene of savage carnage, of murder and rape were repeated room after room and Otto was in utter despair as he realised that his worst fears were about to become a reality.

The door to room 12 was slightly open but Otto had to put his good shoulder to it in order to overcome some resistance on the other side. He pushed slowly and the door reluctantly opened accompanied by a metallic crashing sound which echoed incongruously in the silence of the corridor. The vision in front of him assailed Otto like a blast in the chest from a grenade. In spite of cuts and dried, matted blood in her hair the figure of Ziggie was instantly recognisable. Otto clung to the door jam in order to stop himself from collapsing to the ground. The scene was little different from those in the previous rooms he had viewed but this was personal. He retched but being as he hadn't eaten for some time there was only the bitter taste of bile burning the back of his throat. Ziggie was tied cruciform to the bed, her nightdress rumpled up round her waist cruelly exposing her vulnerability to the hate and lust of her attackers. The blood smeared on her thighs and soaked into the mattress left him with no doubt as to how she had died. The horror of the scene in front of him transfixed Otto and he was unable to look away for a long time. Gradually other details in the room crept into his consciousness. Ziggie's Walther handgun was on the floor beside the bodies of two Russian soldiers as testimony that she had succumbed to her degradation by resisting to the end. A cot next to the bed was overturned and empty. Turning to inspect the rest of the room Otto's attention was drawn to a smeared splash of blood on the wall beneath which was the body of a new-born baby. Otto felt his knees give way and he had to hold onto the ironwork at the foot of Ziggie's bed. A puncture wound in the baby's stomach suggested that he had been swung on the point of a bayonet and flung against the wall. Otto crossed the room and sank down beside Siegfried. He placed his hand gently on the cold, pale-blue skin and picking up his son clutched him to his chest sobbing and crying uncontrollably only stopping when utter exhaustion intervened.

Otto sat unable to move, numb. The events of the past few weeks tumbled in and swamped him, the physical, emotional and psychological journey bringing him to this final denouement. The ultimate moment of looking in a mirror and seeing the true self rather than a reflection of the self one wants to project to the outside world and which feeds the destructive ego. The vessel was at last empty. There was a void. A dark, desolate abyss. No longer an arrogant belief in himself or the infallibility of the Nazi State. No longer the surety of the master race destined to rule over Slavic untermenschen. The realisation that his whole world, everything he had lived for and believed in had been a lie left him traumatised. Everything that he had assumed and believed about the Nazi dogma and himself was a lie, imagination, an illusion. Accepting this filled Otto with a fear that he had never experienced before. Realising that his life had been a living fantasy which had collapsed, how was he to find himself now? There was utter despair in the acceptance that his life had been moulded by acts of power which had seduced him, acts of power of which he had not realised had robbed him of the human right to freedom of choice. He had never acted of his own volition, never had a moment of true self-consciousness until now.

At long last Otto struggled to his feet and gently laid Siegfried on Ziggie's breast. Cutting the bonds that tied her hands to the headboard he placed Ziggie's arms around him. Rearranging her nightgown and picking up her hand pistol he stepped over one of the Russian bodies and moved to the doorway. With a last backward look at his previous life Otto walked slowly down the corridor. He was just about to leave the corridor when his attention was drawn to a low soft moan coming from a room he had just passed. Inside the room which was some kind of nurse's station was a young nurse lying on the floor. Her uniform was dishevelled and her face covered in blood. As Otto looked on her hand slowly moved to her head and she moaned again. Otto moved towards a sink and was surprised when the cloth he held under the tap was drenched in clear cold water. He bent down and gently bathed the nurse's face. Her moans became stronger signalling that the cold water was bringing her round.

"It's all right," Otto said quietly. "It's all right, your safe now. They've all gone. Let's see if you can sit up."

With his one good arm Otto struggled to coax the nurse into a sitting position on the floor. It was obvious what had happened and Otto continued to talk quietly to her. "Don't worry, I'm not going to hurt you. The Russians have all gone, you're quite safe now." He continued to bathe the girl's face and waited until the sobbing subsided. Thinking it best not to dwell on what had happened Otto continued, "Is there somewhere where we can make a hot drink? I know that you probably don't feel like it now but something to eat would be good for you."

The nurse lifted her head slowly and replied, "Thank you. There's a kitchen down stairs but.........."

"Don't worry, it's all quiet....they've moved on. What's your name?" Otto asked quietly. "I'm Henryk."

"Marlene."

They made their way towards the kitchen each relying on the other for mutual support. Gas and electricity having been cut off for some time a field kitchen stove was free-standing in one corner of the room with a flue venting out of the window. There was plenty of paper lying around and wood from broken chairs and finding some matches it was not long before Otto had a kettle of hot water boiling on the stove. The Russians had obviously ransacked the cupboards and the floor was littered with broken utensils, cutlery and various split packets. Rummaging round Otto found some ersatz coffee, some pieces of black bread and some powdered egg in one of the ripped packets. A short length of wurst at the back of one cupboard was a welcome find.

Eating proved painful for Marlene who winced every time food passed her split lips but Otto was pleased to see that his makeshift meal and hot coffee had revived her somewhat to say nothing of himself.

"What's wrong with your arm?" Marlene asked Otto quietly.

"It got burnt in a cellar that was shelled by the Russians."

"You have to be careful with burns," Marlene replied. "Let me look at it. Come, there's a surgery next door."

Much to his embarrassment Otto winced as Marlene removed his jacket and shirt bringing skin away in the process.

"This is a serious burn," Marlene said with a slow dull professionalism. "Let me see if I can find a soothing balm, a cream to take the heat and sting out of it and disinfect it. Infection is a danger and you must keep it dry."

Finding some clean lint and makeshift bandages made from bed sheets Marlene dressed Otto's wounds making him a little more comfortable.

"Now," she continued, removing the rags tied round his head and eye, "Let me see what I can do for this." She cleaned the wound on his temple, applied some cream and expertly bandaged his head. "I'm afraid that you will lose the sight in your eye. It looks serious to me but I'm not a doctor. Try to get it seen to as soon as you can."

"Thank you," Otto replied, "Considering the circumstances you're been so kind."

"As you have been to me," Came the flat reply.

"Look.....the war is lost and Berlin will soon be in the hands of the Russians. I'm making my way west. I'd rather end up in the hands of the Allies than the barbarous Russians. Why don't you come with me?"

"That's very kind of you," Marlene replied, "But I have family here nearby. I shall stay and take my chances."

Handing over Ziggie's Walther pistol Otto continued, "Then take this for protection, it's the least I can do after what you've done for me."

"Thank you," Marlene replied placing the small handgun in her apron pocket. "Good luck. I hope you make it to the west."

With a sharp intake of breath, Marlene recoiled as Otto leant forward to kiss her goodbye on the cheek.

"Sorry," Otto said quickly, "Sorry, I didn't think......I didn't mean to........"

"It's all right," Marlene replied quietly. "Go quickly and be careful....I'll be alright. Goodbye and good luck."

Otto exited the treatment room and got no further than two or three steps when a single report from the gun he had left with Marlene filled the air with a deafening finality.

(IV)

Thankfully the spare key was still under the third plant pot to the left of the rear entrance. Otto slid it into the lock and opened the door. Before entering he glanced round. The last time he had seen this garden was on the day of his marriage to Ziggie the previous year. As he passed through the door he was immediately aware of that musty smell of a house which has been shut up and unoccupied for some time. Himmler was otherwise engaged and his family had left Berlin months previously. Fortunately the house had not been looted by either Russians or fellow Germans. Finding a valise upstairs Otto returned to the kitchen and began searching the cupboards for food a commodity which had never been in short supply in the Himmler household. Very soon there was a stack of tinned food on the table, a bottle of schnapps and four cartons of cigarettes, a currency more valuable than gold in an economy which had completely disintegrated. Otto arranged tins of Argentinian corned beef, steak and kidney stew in gravy, different soups, chocolate bars, various tins of fruit and packets of real coffee inside the valise. A knife, fork, spoon, a tin opener, enamel mug and two packets of pain killers were zipped in to a side pocket. Trying to pick it up with one hand he realised that in his condition it was now too heavy to carry any distance.

Choices were made and tins removed one by one Otto checking the weight of the valise each time.

Whilst packing the valise Otto realised that apart from the unappetising powdered egg he'd reconstituted and eaten in the clinic with Marlene he couldn't remember the last time food had passed his lips. Searching the larder revealed that left-overs of bread, fresh meat and dairy products had long since been reduced to mounds of green mould and a smell which was far from pleasant. However in another cupboard he discovered some sealed packets of savoury biscuits. Gas and electricity were cut off so there was little chance of hot food. He opened a tin of corned beef and shook the trapezoidal lump of meat onto a plate and cut it into slices. Inspection of a wine-rack on one of the kitchen work surfaces revealed a nice Bordeaux. Otto sat down at the kitchen table, placed a slice of corned beef between two savoury biscuits and biting off a good mouthful washed it down with a welcome glass of rich red wine.

Wandering through to the large living room Otto helped himself to a generous glass of Himmler's best Napoleon brandy and sank into the soft leather cocoon of a large armchair. Through the window he watched dark clouds tumbling across the sky hastening a melancholy dusk to embrace the nervous solitude of black night. The sounds of gun fire from various calibres drifted on the night breeze coming from the east and experience told Otto that they were far enough away not to be an immediate threat. He knew it was essential that he made his way south and west as quickly as possible but the physical and mental exhaustion of the past few days and the soporific effect of the wine and brandy combined to seduce his body into surrendering consciousness and he fell into a deep sleep.

He awoke with a start and immediately took in his surroundings. His head throbbed and his mouth and tongue were furred thicker than the collar on an overcoat worn by Göring. Somewhat refreshed after a good wash and cleaning his teeth Otto forced himself to breakfast on the last remaining slice of corned beef followed by a bowl of tinned peaches whilst surveying a map of greater Berlin which he had found in Himmler's office. Time was now of the essence if he was to put distance between himself and the rapidly advancing Russians. Remembering that he and Ziggie used to bike ride in the Grunewald forest he went out into one of the garden outhouses and was relieved to find that the bikes were still there albeit tyres needing to be pumped up.

There was no evidence of fighting or Russian presence in the immediate area and taking a calculated risk Otto fastened his valise to the pannier frame and pedalled south away from the Dahlem district of Berlin towards Zehlendorf, Potsdam and Brandenburg. Very soon he realised that he was just one small ripple in a tide of humanity flooding westwards towards the River Elbe and the protection of the Allies.

At the same time the remnant of the 9th. Army was still trying to break out due west through the pine forests south of Berlin. Thousands of fleeing refugees clogged up every road and track. Progress was slow as lorries and tanks pushed aside and crushed broken down military vehicles and refugees' hand carts, wheelbarrows and prams. Military vehicles were abandoned as they ran out of fuel.

The scene was like nothing Otto had ever witnessed before. Thousands of refugees mingled with thousands of Wehrmacht soldiers from two armies the whole countryside a seething mass like ants after their nest has been disturbed by a stick. Otto realised that training and experience were useless in his present circumstance and that lady luck and fate were now his bedfellows. Tanks and other military vehicles forced him onto the verges and into gutters at the side of the road. Doggedly pushing his bicycle along a forest road a new but familiar sound attracted Otto's attention and looking skywards he spotted a squadron of Russian ground attack planes manoeuvring into position for a strafe. Throwing his bike off the road he dived into a ditch whilst others who were capable scattered and ran. The roadway and surrounding forest erupted in columns of earth, flames and crashing trees as bombs fell all around and frightened civilians shouted and screamed in fear. The planes wheeled and climbed ready for their second strike which this time was with their canons and machine guns. The ground vibrated, shook and boiled and rippled like hot soup in a pan whilst the heavens were rent as shells and Katyushka rockets shredding trees sending branches, shards and splinters flying through the air impaling individuals indiscriminately leaving them to bleed to death from horrific wounds. Soon the attack was over as quickly as it had begun but Otto knew that they were simply returning to base to refuel and rearm. The fighting was some of the fiercest Otto had ever experienced, including the Seelow Heights, with huge casualties on both sides. Chaos was everywhere as Russian reinforcements pushed both refugees and the Wehrmacht military deep into the Halbe forest where the tanks' tracks were not able to find purchase on the carpet of slippery pine needles or the sandy soil but remaining on the roads through the forest exposed them to further strafes.

As dusk approached the ferocity of the fighting died down and the cries and moans of the dying and wounded drifted eerily through the trees. Otto was exhausted and hungry. He found a glade which offered some protection from the Russian artillery which continued to lob shells randomly into the forest. The hollow was already occupied by an emaciated woman of indeterminate age and two children of about six or seven years old whom Otto assumed were hers. The children looked inhumanly skinny and reminded Otto of figures he'd seen in the camps, their legs like pieces of string with reef knots where their knees would be. As he dropped to the ground the woman put her arms around the children and drew them to her.

"It's alright," Otto said in a quiet but hoarse voice. "Don't be afraid, I'm not going to hurt you. I'm trying to get to the west just like you. My name's Henryk, Henryk Harmanecki."

"I'm Gertrude and these are my children little Eva and Jurgen."

"I expect you're hungry," Otto continued. "Look after my bike and I'll be back in a minute."

Otto left the slight decline and looked around for a helmet of which there were many littering the ground some still attached to bodies and wounded. Picking one up, he returned to the shelter of the glade. Immediately he arranged some stones in a horseshoe shape and gathering kindling and wood soon had a fire. Releasing the valise from his bike pannier he opened two tins of steak and kidney stew and poured them into the helmet. Adding some water from his bottle he placed the helmet on the fire. The two children with large white eyes bulging in their small thin faces looked on passively.

Otto could feel his saliva glands pricking the inside of his cheeks as the rich smell of the stew assailed his senses.

"Do you have tin mugs?" Otto asked Gertrude.

"Yes we do," She replied rummaging in her rucksack, "But we haven't used them for some time."

The stew continued to bubble as Otto lifted the helmet away from the fire using the canvas chin-strap. "Careful, it will be boiling hot," Otto warned as he tilted the helmet and measured portions plopped into four mugs. He smiled to himself as he watched the family wrap their hands around their mugs then picked up their spoons and blew on each spoonful before savouring the rich nourishing stew. They had second helpings and licking their fingers all four scoured the mugs for every last drop. If it was at all possible the children's eyes grew even wider when Otto poured orange segments and sweet thick juice syrup into their now spotless mugs.

"Thank you and God bless you," Gertrude said later savouring her first taste of real coffee in years. "I didn't think I would experience decent human generosity ever again."

"Just hang on a little longer," Otto replied, "The war will be over very soon. Get some rest I fear that tomorrow is going to be difficult."

When dawn approached the ground erupted as if attempting to bury every last human being. Fear and panic quickly reasserted themselves amongst refugees and soldiers alike. Otto looked on helplessly whilst one young soldier of not more than seventeen or eighteen years old tried unsuccessfully to dig a slit trench with his helmet between the tangled mass of pine tree roots. Engines coughed into life and tanks began to move forwards as the first air attack of the day combined with Russian armoured divisions and artillery to create a maelstrom of hot flying steel that disintegrated trees and flesh indiscriminately.

Ignoring his own advice to Gertrude and her children to keep their heads down Otto peered over the lip of the glade to see Wehrmacht wounded fighting one another to climb up on to the tanks for transportation. Otto lowered his face to the ground in despair after observing one soldier, too exhausted and severely wounded to claim a place, simply collapse in the roadway to be crushed by a passing tank. He never thought that he would see the day when a lightly wounded soldier would drag a more severely wounded comrade from a tank in order to take his place. After two tanks had rolled forward a red stain on the forest road and a flat shredded uniform was the only evidence that a human being had been lying there.

Slipping back down in to the glade Otto opened his valise. He took out two bars of chocolate and reached out towards Gertrude. "Here, take these, they'll help you to keep going. Keep away from the roads, the Russians will be targeting the tanks, artillery and transports."

"Thank you Henryk, you've been so kind. God bless you."

"And you too," Otto replied. "Don't stay in the forest longer than you have to, it's too dangerous, keep moving west and good luck."

He crawled up over the edge of his sanctuary and crouching made his way westwards for a further three days and nights whilst the battle raged unabated in the forest. At last the trees began to thin out and there appeared to be open ground ahead but the River Elbe was still two or three days away. The Russians had already ranged their artillery on the open countryside and as their armour moved towards the Germans' right flank casualties on both sides were appalling. Otto watched from behind a tree, disbelieving when he watched a Tiger tank traversed its gun to engage a Russian T34 the turret sweeping numerous severely wounded soldiers to the ground to be left to their fate. There was no clearly defined front line and tank skirmishes were in progress everywhere. At last, sensing that they were near safety thousands of soldiers and civilians alike dashed for the river crossings at Schonhausen, and Tangermunde and a ferry at Ferchland. American bridgeheads had been established at these crossing points and as Otto observed Wehrmacht envoys negotiating with the Americans news of Hitler's suicide began to circulate. The Americans were completely unprepared for the sheer mass of thousands and thousands of military and civilian personnel desperate to cross the river to safety. Panic spread like wildfire throughout the refugee masses as word filtered back that the Americans were only allowing wounded and unarmed German soldiers across the river. Otto was near enough to make out an American officer with a loud hailer. "Refugees must make their own way back to their original homes. Civilians are not permitted to cross the river. Refugees must go back." Very quickly groups of civilians spread out north and south of the bridge at Schonhausen looking for somewhere to cross out of sight of the Americans.

Moving south along the river bank Otto watched as desperate individuals dived into the wide, fast-flowing river only to be carried downstream never to resurface. Attracted by a group of people shouting Otto joined them to see a young man tie a line round his midriff and dive into the swirling water. In spite of himself Otto couldn't help but cheer encouragement with the rest of the refugees as the swimmer struck out for the other side with strong purposeful strokes. The current carried him down stream so that when eventually he reached the far bank the rope line had been played out diagonally across the water. A loud cheer erupted as the young man clambered up the bank and ran back to tie the line off around a tree opposite to where the rest of the group were standing. People waiting formed an orderly queue and mothers with families tied their children to the rope with safety lines and gingerly entered the water to face the strong current.

Not wanting to get his burn wound wet Otto continued south along the river bank and watched other groups of people making rafts by lashing planks of wood, oil drums and petrol cans together and trying to cross in dinghies which they had obviously stolen from properties they had passed on their way to the river. Surmising that the railway line must cross the river at some point, Otto continued to move southwards whilst at the same time Wehrmacht soldiers were being given priority to cross into the American zone. Their rear-guard perimeter was shrinking rapidly under the Russian assault. Thousands of civilian and military casualties continued to mount because of slow progress at the crossing points as the Americans searched for SS, foreigners and civilians who were trying to infiltrate over the bridges. The Americans began to take casualties as the Russian artillery bombardment intensified and orders were issued to withdraw from the crossing points. This was an opportunity too good to miss for the refugees and they surged forward swamping the bridges not caring whether old, young or infirm were crushed in the stampede.

By now Otto had reached the railway bridge across the Elbe between Stendal and Schonhausen. His heart sank when he saw the twisted, tangled mass of steel girders and railway lines. However, as he drew closer he could see that people were getting across albeit slowly and with care not to slip from the mangled structure to certain death in the dark waters of the River Elbe.

"You go first," Otto said to a mother in front of him who was obviously anxious for the safety of her little girl. "Step across to that sleeper and when you've got a firm grip I'll reach her over to you."

"Thank you," The young mother replied breathlessly. Gingerly she edged her way forward then stretched across eyeing the torrent rushing under her feet.

"Don't look down," Otto shouted. "Have you got a firm grip?"

"Yes, I'm ready," Came the reply.

Otto held the whimpering waif as she reached her skinny arms out towards her mother. They repeated his slow manoeuvre time and again until they were all safely on the far bank. Otto looked back at the mass of lost, displaced and frightened humanity as the fan-shaped queue shuffled forwards to a single file ready to negotiate the damaged bridge to safety.

Relenting in the face of an endless hoard of desperate humanity on the west bank of the river the Americans tried to maintain some semblance of control. G.I.s lined every roadway directing the exhausted civilians and military towards hastily arranged temporary reception areas and camps. The black, turgid river of despair shuffled onwards continuously. Having used the last of his tablets the pain in Otto's arm and chest was becoming unbearable. He allowed himself the luxury of hope as the presence of USA personnel, jeeps and lorries flying about with purpose became more numerous and stockpiles of military materiel and rations appeared to grow ever more skywards as he looked on. To his left coils of barbed wire formed a make-shift perimeter fence behind which thousands of exhausted, ragged remnants of the once invincible Wehrmacht stood or sat on the grass in small groups the fortunate ones smoking a cigarette. A little further on Otto realised that the refugees were also being corralled in barbed wire enclosures with no cover and open to whatever the elements would throw at them. He quickly spotted that there appeared to be some sort of selection or triage system being applied up ahead, the relatively fit and healthy being directed towards enclosures whilst those requiring medical treatment were being directed towards rows of marquees with red crosses painted on their roofs. As the queue moved forward slowly Otto removed his coat and shirt to reveal his blood-stained bandages. Eventually he was confronted by a row of trestle tables manned by American officers. Swaying unsteadily he collapsed to the ground not entirely as a result of his deliberate deception.

The needle was withdrawn quickly and efficiently and under the influence of the morphine Otto surrendered unconditionally to the peaceful embrace of painless unconsciousness whilst at the same time on behalf of the German Reich General Jodl surrendered unconditionally to the Allies in Reims.

CHAPTER 24

Annie & Otto (Henryk) 1945

"Wait in here please Captain Charlton. They won't be very long."

The building, just round the corner from the BBC was drab and nondescript. Annie sat down on a hard wooden bench situated in a short, depressing, scratched and damaged wood-panelled corridor with a window at the far end criss-crossed with sticky tape as protection against flying glass. Although the Luftwaffe had long ceased to present any threat to London and all the V1 rocket launching sites within range of London had been overrun after the 'D' Day landings there were still attacks from Hitler's second terror weapon the V2 rocket.

"If you're ready Captain Charlton; come in please."

The four gentlemen in civilian dress sat behind a huge mahogany desk which itself was in front of a large fireplace. On the mantelpiece were photographs of Prime Minister Churchill and President Roosevelt flanked by the union flag and the stars and stripes which both hung sad and limp. On the chimney breast was a large portrait of the king. The windows were also taped and the drapes hung heavy and shapeless with months of dust giving the whole office a depressing ambience.

"Sit down Captain Charlton, please. I'm Cartwright representing the Director General, Herbert Lehmann, and this is Smithers representing the financial advisor, Critchley from Displaced Persons (DPs) and Public Information and Robinson representing Health and Welfare. We're pleased that you could come along. We're desperate for volunteers of the right calibre and I have to say you come very highly recommended. I understand that you're being seconded from the First Aid Nursing Yeomanry can you tell us something about your experience?"

"Well.....Mr. Cartwright, I've signed the Official Secrets Act so I can't say too much, but suffice to say that for the past two years I've been working in France and Germany. You'll have to use your imagination I'm afraid."

"I believe you're fluent in French and German."

"Yes, and I've enough Polish to get by."

"Excellent, excellent. Tell us, what made you want to be seconded to the United Nations Relief and Rehabilitation Administration (UNRRA)?"

"With the liberation of France my work there is finished. From my experience I can only guess at the scale of chaos, desperation and misery which will become manifest when the war is finally over to say nothing of mass starvation and disease. But I do know that there is going to have to be a huge international humanitarian effort if we are to eradicate the worst affects visited on Europe by Nazi Germany."

"You're right," Mr. Smithers interjected. "We're funded internationally and our primary task will be one of repatriation and resettlement of the millions of displaced persons but in field service all UNRRA personnel will come under the orders of the Supreme Commander of the Allied Expeditionary Force (SCAEF) through military channels."

"This could be a source friction," Robinson added. "In my experience no man can serve two masters but enough of the politics for now. But don't let that put you off. I believe that as a result of their experience in Italy and latterly in France the military now accept that they need us. They were the first on the spot but I think they were overwhelmed by the sheer number of DPs.....Russians, Poles, Czechs, Yugoslavs to be fed, clothed and housed, together with sanitation problems, medical care and to be moved out of the combat area. Supreme Headquarters, Allied Expeditionary Force (SHAEF) has realised that with the defeat of Nazi Germany the Allies will be faced with a staggeringly huge internationally complex problem of repatriating millions of Europeans. We have estimated something like eight million. The primary responsibility will be theirs but clearly they will need outside help. We know that there is enormous opposition to involving UNRAA and both the American and British military are rather contemptuous of our personnel and that their involvement in military matters will create a security hazard but I think their experiences in Italy have shown them that the army has its limitations and cannot get into the relief business nor do welfare."

"It's not all bad news though," Cartwright continued. "Agreement has been reached at the highest level and the military have agreed that UNRRA is to provide 250 teams to look after the DPs in Germany but they've just now increased that number to 450 and we'd like you to lead one of these teams. What do you say? We'd give you training of course and hopefully you should be more than ready by the time the Allies reach Berlin."

"I've no wish to get involved in the politics of the organisation but I'm more than willing to do what I can at the chalk face." "Who knows, your military rank may stand you in good stead. Welcome aboard and we'll be in touch with your training programme."

Annie shook hands with each of the sub-committee. Leaving the building she made her way to number 31, Wilton Place, near Hyde Park where she had secured a residential room in the First Aid Nursing Yeomanry Headquarters.

Annie found the training a bit of a mixed bag. Transport and requisitioning logistics, registration documents, prioritizing welfare and occupational needs in a camp environment, provision for children and the sick, sanitation requirements, nutrition, education. The list was complex and endless. But what Annie found most helpful were the practical exercises in the counselling of traumatised individuals. She found the theory of personality pathology brought about by torture and deprivation fascinating and she could see a real need for these skills. What she found less encouraging was to be lectured on DPs by someone who had never even met one. Something else that disturbed Annie was the knowledge that UNRAA was not to give aid to Germans returning home from outside its frontiers. Many had settled on land vacated by Poles and Jews in the east during the early stages of the war but these settlers were now returning to Germany in their thousands as the Russians advanced westwards. It didn't seem very humanitarian to Annie for the scale of relief to be divorced from need.

By mid-April it was obvious that the war was coming to a rapid conclusion. Annie found herself with a group of other volunteers embarking at Southampton bound for France where she was to meet her team. Cherbourg was heaving with activity, military traffic and personnel. She eventually located the UNRAA office and introduced herself to the area coordinator.

"Hello, I'm Captain Charlton. I've come to assemble my team and prepare to make our way up into the British Zone in northern Germany." Annie said extending her hand.

"Hi bud, I'm Grayson," The coordinator replied with a strong American drawl without offering her hand. "If you're expecting a team of thirteen I'm afraid you're going to be disappointed. You'll be lucky if you get half that. I'm afraid those inept civil servants in London have promised too much and now can't deliver. We're short of personnel and those we've got are of doubtful use. I'll get you a team of six together but I can't guarantee any qualified medical staff."

"How soon can I expect to get under way?" Annie asked.

"Don't ask me honey, I'll be in touch."

It was over a week before Annie was able to assemble her team of six and there was no news on transport or departure date. Annie quickly realised that without a logistic infrastructure of its own UNRAA had to rely on the military for transport, food and supplies. The trouble was that the military authorities, while paying lip service to UNRAA's aims and work were not really prepared, except in exceptional circumstances, to cooperate more than they felt absolutely necessary. Annie used the time to explore the area and she seethed with anger on seeing supplies sitting on the dockside day after day and she decided to approach Mrs. Grayson again. After another four weeks of idle waiting and frustration Annie decided to take matters into her own hands.

"How long am I supposed to stay around here kicking my heels?" Annie said forcefully.

"Listen honey, I can't do nothin' without authorization from the military."

"You're the area coordinator for God's sake, so coordinate." Annie replied letting her temper get the better of her. "Three of my depleted team have already resigned because of this stupid inertia and waste of time and the rest are about as low in morale as it's possible to get."

"You're welcome to try to do better if you want," came the resigned reply. "There are some Limey trucks down in Granville, see if you can use your English charm to get one of those."

Unhelpful, cheeky cow Annie thought whilst she returned to her barrack accommodation in a foul mood but determined to make progress either with or without official authorization.

"Do you fancy a trip to Granville, Perkins?" Annie asked one of her remaining team sitting on his bunk bed smoking a Woodbine. Perkins was a cockney driver who having lost his family in the blitz and been invalided out of the army had since volunteered for UNRAA.

"Yeah, it'll be something to do other than sitting here on me arse week after week. I didn't sign up for boredom. Why?"

"We're going to commandeer, requisition or steal a couple lorries down there and bring them back here to be loaded up with supplies."

"I'm up for that. When do we go?"

"Right now," Annie replied.

Asking around the base and putting the word out that she was looking for a lift to Granville Annie and Perkins soon found themselves sitting in the front of a Bedford QLD lorry heading south along the coast road. Just as they were about to enter Granville Annie pointed and shouted with excitement, "Look! My God, look at all those lorries parked in those fields. There must be.....oooh at least a thousand standing there."

"That's a good guess Captain," the army driver said. "There are about eleven hundred give or take but out of the whole damned lot there's only about a hundred that's in good running order. They've all seen a lot of service and the bloody French peasants keep cannibalising them for spare parts to keep their own vehicles running. I swear I sometimes think we fought the wrong bloody country."

"Isn't there any security?" Annie asked innocently whilst trying to formulate a plan. Her SOE training was not for nothing.

"Not so's you'd notice," the driver replied. "There's a depot office where all the paper work is done, such as it is, although from what I've heard it's all a bit haphazard, and a couple of guys who wander around when they're a bit bored but apart from that the Frenchies look on it as a free market."

"If you'd drop us at the entrance that would be wonderful," Annie cooed.

"What 'ave you got in mind?" Perkins asked with a smile as the Bedford coughed and rattled its way out of sight. "I could see that you were hatching something."

"You go and have a look round and see if you can spot anything worth driving whilst I go and reconnoitre the office procedures. If you get stopped just say that you're Captain Charlton's corporal and refer them to me."

"Right oh ma'am," Perkins replied with a smart salute.

Annie waited until Perkins had disappeared then she entered the weather-beaten office. A bored lance corporal from the Royal Army Service Corps stood in the front office behind a counter. When he saw Annie he straightened up in a bored, slovenly fashion and saluted.

"Can I be of any assistance captain?" The lance corporal asked with obvious disinterest.

"Yes I hope you can lance corporal and then I won't have to report you for being the sloppy soldier that you are."

At this the lance corporal stiffened and became more attentive.

"I want two lorries. How do I go about getting them?"

"We'll need a counter-signed requisition form ma'am."

Spotting a pad of blank forms in a tray alongside other pro-forma on an extended shelf under the counter and an RASC rubber stamp Annie continued. "Can you provide me with a list of serviceable vehicles in the pound?"

"I have a list somewhere but it'll not be up to date because lorries are being left here all the time. Let me see if I can find it in the back office."

This was the chance Annie had been waiting for and once the lance corporal disappeared from the front office she reached over and taking the requisition pad ripped off a number forms, stamped them and slipped them into her pocket. When the lance corporal returned Annie made a pretence at scrutinizing the lists, then seeing Perkins through a side window slipping back out on to the road she thanked the lance corporal for his help and left.

"Did you find anything Perkins?"

"Yes captain, ma'am.....what should I call you?" Perkins asked quizzically.

"Annie will do, unless I'm in uniform and there are other military around.

"Well....Annie most of them are pieces of junk but there are two Leyland Mk.2 Hippos. They've been knocked about a bit but they're a relatively new model so they can't have seen too much activity. They're ten tonners with a low loading height which should be just the thing for us."

"Excellent, let's walk into town and find ourselves a café so that I can fill in one of these requisition forms whilst we have something to eat and I think we deserve a bottle of wine, don't you?"

After lunch Annie and Perkins returned to the lorry park where Annie handed over the completed RASC requisition form with her signature and a forged, illegible, authorizing counter signature. The lance corporal, now wary of Annie didn't scrutinize the document too closely and was relieved when she left the office holding two sets of keys. Minutes later with full tanks of fuel they were snarling and roaring their way north heading back towards the docks at Cherbourg.

Having used rank, charm, bluff and forged requisition forms Annie and her assembled team of six stood watching as each ten ton truck was loaded with supplies. Blankets, tinned and preserved foodstuffs, coffee, tea, sugar, cigarettes, clothes, shoes, stationary materials, basic medical supplies and much more.

"It's about time some of this stuff was moved by the people it's intended for," one of the dock workers volunteered. "You wouldn't believe the amount of stuff that just vanishes into thin air and turns up on the black market. Especially cigarettes. The French would steal your eyeballs if you weren't looking. It's reached the stage where the black market is now organised racketeering.

"In that case then, the sooner we get under way the better," Annie said. "Thanks for your help, and if you can squeeze some extra supplies on board we'd be more than grateful. Better that it's used for the refugees than to put money in the pockets of French criminals."

"I'll see what I can do ma'am, wink, wink, nudge, nudge, know what I mean?"

* * * * *

At the same time as Annie was embarking for Cherbourg the brigadier's Jeep was approached Bergen-Belsen concentration camp somewhere near Hanover in Northern Germany. His handkerchief was already covering his mouth and nostrils by the time he passed through the gates.

"Stop," he yelled at his driver. Slowly he stood up in the Jeep with one hand on the top of the windscreen to steady himself. "Dear God.....," he said quietly as he stood looking transfixed at the scene. Brigadier Llewellyn Glyn-Hughes was sickened and shocked at the sight which greeted him. He had heard reports of the American liberation of Buchenwald concentration camp but this didn't prepare him for the sheer scale of inhuman brutality witnessed all around him. In front of his Jeep he watched despondently as a small boy of about four years old and dressed in rags sat on his hunkers engrossed in playing with some pebbles next to a pile of naked, rotting corpses. Piles of corpses were everywhere and blocking gutters by the sides of the roads. Skeletal individuals were lying on the ground everywhere and propped up against barrack walls but it was impossible to distinguish the dead from those still alive.

"Get the regimental Medical Officer on the radio," he shouted at the communications corporal in the following Jeep. "He's to stop whatever he's doing and get himself here immediately, do I make myself clear corporal, I mean immediately."

It was not long before the brigadier and M.O. explored further into the camp complex.

"Jesus, Mary and Joseph," the M.O. whispered almost to himself as they passed pile after pile of rotting corpses and thousands of other inmates barely alive. "Stop, I need to inspect one of these barrack blocks," the M.O. said anxiously.

The brigadier sat in the Jeep for some minutes. When eventually Doctor Jenkins staggered back out through the door he put his hand up on the wall for support, bent over and vomited violently.

"Are you all right Doctor?" the brigadier asked concerned.

"Sweet Jesus....... I've seen some sights in my medical career during this bloody war but I never expected in a thousand years to see anything like what's inside there." The M.O. heaved again. Taking deep breaths to compose himself Doctor Jenkins continued. "There are live skeletons in there covered in excrement lying beside rotting corpses. I believe that we've got typhoid, typhus and tuberculosis epidemics on our hands as well as mass starvation. God knows what state their minds must be in."

"Okay doctor, time is of the essence here. What needs to be done now?"

Doctor Jenkins snapped back into professional mode and answered pragmatically. "The first thing is to get as many field kitchens up here as we can. We also need the engineers and their equipment immediately to dig a series of pits and get rid of these bodies lying around. The louse that carries typhus is still infectious even after a body's been dead a few days. As a matter of utter urgency we must contact the Americans for a delivery of DDT to fumigate those who are still alive otherwise this epidemic will spread to our forces. And I've seen no evidence of running water, we'll need the engineers to connect a supply immediately."

"Let's get things moving doctor. Back to headquarters driver..... Stop," the brigadier countermanded just as they were about to leave the camp. The Jeep shuddered to a halt and Brigadier Glyn-Hughes stepped down and approached a lieutenant who saluted smartly. "What have we here?" lieutenant he enquired.

"They're SS guards sir. We captured them trying to escape in the immediate area outside the camp as well as some hiding inside." The assembled group, male and female, sat and lounged around on the grass smoking cigarettes. The brigadier scrutinized them and became incensed by their surly, dumb insolent and arrogant expressions. Overcome with emotion and anger he shouted, "Get these bastards on their feet lieutenant and set them to work clearing up the mess they created. I want the dead cleared out of these huts. Bodies in the gutters and spread around the camp are to be assembled in piles. They're to load the bodies onto lorries and trailers and accompany them to the pits the engineers are going to dig and then place them in the mass graves. No gloves, no protective clothing, just as they are lieutenant. We'll see if that knocks the supercilious smirks off their fucking faces."

Within a few weeks the place was transformed. Communal graves, each containing five thousand dead were filled in. However, the military did not fully understand that the metabolism of people who had suffered starvation would not be able to cope with immediate quantities of rich food and many camp survivors continued to die even after their liberation. The final tally subsequently indicated that overall 28,000 of the 35,800 in the camp died from neglect, starvation and disease. Ex Western European prisoners who were fit enough were repatriated as quickly as possible leaving the camp comprising of mainly Jews and Poles. Camp 1 was razed to the ground and burnt, cleared and all previous inmates de-loused bringing the epidemics under control. Camp 2 had once been the German Tank Training School. The barrack blocks were well built, four-story buildings grouped around thirty parade grounds with broad avenues and leafy gardens. With impressive efficiency a hospital was established as well as a bakery, canteen, theatre, recreation areas, administrative and living quarters.

In the aftermath of Germany's surrender the country was organised into zones of occupation and for the fleeing refugees and DPs from Berlin and the Russian occupation, the British zone was their first Allies contact. Thousands were transported to Bergen Belsen which was now designated a reception DP camp. But these latest inmates of Belsen were not all survivors of the death camps, many were relatively healthy Jews who had fled to the east in 1939 and 1940 and were now fleeing westwards to escape the Soviet Communist State.

* * * * *

The journey from Cherbourg to Belsen was long, tedious and frustrating. Many detours were negotiated because bridges had been destroyed either by Allied bombing or retreating German demolition. Annie had to rely on all of her resources to coax fuel from the military depots they passed. It was a very tired and weary crew who pulled up outside the administration block at Belsen at the end of May, weeks after they'd left Southampton.

Annie led her team into reception and presented her documentation.

"Wait here please," the corporal at the reception desk requested and he returned a few minutes later with an officer.

"Major Hargreaves. What can I do for you?"

"I'm Captain Charlton seconded to UNRRA, you must be familiar with the organisation. My team are here to work with you on the resettlement and welfare of the DPs."

"We've had no notification about your arrival," Major Hargreaves said rather dismissively.

"That doesn't surprise me," replied Annie. "It's just typical of the cock-ups in communication between the military and UNRRA." And not being in the mood to be messed about Annie continued, "Well, we're here now Major so if you could show us to some quarters we'll get settled in ready to start work in the morning. Perhaps some of your men would be good enough to help unload and store our supplies in a secure depot. We don't want them to find their way on to the black market do we?"

Taken aback somewhat under Annie's polite but forceful opening gambit the young Major Hargreaves felt unsure and found himself instructing the corporal to organise quarters for Annie and her team.

"After we've settled in captain perhaps you'd be good enough to show me round the camp then we can discuss our respective responsibilities. We don't want to stand on each other's toes or find ourselves duplicating our efforts, that would be a waste of your time and resources and ours, don't you think?" Annie was determined that her team was not going to under-perform as a result of lack of support from the military. She knew that any shortcomings would be laid at the door of UNRRA staff and she was not prepared to see the morale of her team being undermined.

"Er......yes of course. I'll see what I can organise."

On their tour of the camp Annie was quick to assess the situation.

"The Jews and Poles appear to be segregating themselves." She commented.

"You're right," the Major replied much impressed by Annie's astute and immediate analysis. "They're giving us a right headache. We want to repatriate as many of the Jews as quickly as we can back to their country of origin where possible but many of them now see themselves as one nation rather than Polish, Russian, German or Czech or whatever. "Well, I suppose that's one for the British Government to solve."

"We're also having problems with Polish crime and lawlessness," Major Hargreaves volunteered, "We've managed to secure work for some Poles outside the camp but the locals complain about looting and rape. So we need to be strict. You know," he continued more reflectively. "We assumed that they would all be grateful for their liberation and our help but we find the DPs apathetic and paranoid. They physically refuse to work or carry out any tasks assigned to them even if it's for their own good and my men are fed up with their incessant complaints and demands."

"Perhaps this is where we can help Major," Annie replied quietly. "These people have been brutalised, dehumanised and degraded by people in uniforms. There is nothing you can do to them that hasn't already been meted out to them a thousand times worse. Is it any wonder that they resent orders or requests from you? I don't think they even consider what the different uniforms mean. As they see it they're still in a camp, and this was a concentration camp don't forget, with uniforms ordering them about. It also seems to me that much of the squalor and grim conditions evident in parts of the camp are derived from the demoralisation and hopelessness. We need a structure to help them rebuild their view of self-worth and value".

"We're also having great difficulty in trying to repatriate those Poles who want to go home. The Russians are refusing to transport them as long as there are still Russians in the west and they're being difficult about access to the autobahn network. A recent convoy of lorries carrying returning refugees across the Russian frontier was stopped and the Poles were raped and looted whilst British officers were forced to look on and ordered not to interfere. As I understand the situation now, the Polish Government in exile in London is telling their countrymen not to return to Communist dominated Poland so we're stuck with them. So you see Captain Charlton there are major political forces at work outside and we have to deal with the backwash here in the camp."

The tour was informative and productive and Annie and Major Hargreaves established a working partnership. The military accepted its responsibility for the logistics, supplies and security whilst Annie's team met with Jewish and Polish leaders to discuss setting up democratically elected DP camp councils. Giving them back responsibility for themselves, Annie reasoned, was a way of restoring their self-esteem and human dignity. The various team members, with the help of the camp councils quickly established community services, counselling, and education for children in the first instance and recreation activities. Contact with the Red Cross was established to help DPs trace missing family members and boosted morale. Involvement in the camp welfare and community was encouraged to raise fallen spirits and keep the DPs away from mischief and crime. Annie's weekly review meetings indicated that the ambience and routine of the camp was slowly being transformed.

(II)

The canvas walls of the rehabilitation marquee were rolled up to allow a warm spring zephyr to air the interior. With a cup of coffee in his hand Henryk sat beside his bed watching the feverish activity everywhere with interest.

"What's going on?" He asked a passing medical orderly in his excellent English.

"We're moving out." Came the reply. "The scuttle bug says it's something to do with the US of A, Limey and Frenchie Governments dividing Germany up into different occupation zones and this area now belongs to the Brits so we've been ordered to get on our bikes."

"Where does that leave me?" Henryk asked.

"Don't ask me bud, I just does as I'm told, but I would guess that you're now the responsibility of the British Military."

Henryk eased back into the collapsible director's chair and took a sip of his coffee. The healing process on the inside of his chest and arm had been remarkable. The burns had stopped weeping and new tissue was beginning to grow over the damaged area. The scar on his left temple would eventually be barely noticeable but he was wearing a black patch over the unseeing eye. The American M.O. had suggested that cosmetically with a glass eye no one would know the difference.

It was pointless to speculate he thought. Wherever he was going to end up was out of his control so best just to enjoy the good food, peace, and safety of the moment and wait and see.

He didn't have long to wait and ponder as two days later a long convoy of British Military trucks groaned and whined their way, amidst a self-generated dust storm, into the American temporary camp complex. Those still seriously wounded were stretchered on to ambulances whilst as many refugees and DPs as the trucks would hold were quickly helped on board. The whole process was conducted quickly and efficiently and before lunch Henryk, together with others was being jostled, swayed and bumped in the back of a lorry heading further westwards.

After a tiring, strength-sapping journey the trucks eventually slowed and turning off the narrow country road passed through some large gates. Although reading the letters from the reverse side out of the back of his truck Henryk was able to make out the name Bergen-Belsen and was immediately confused. He knew this had been a concentration camp and whilst it was not one of the deliberately designated death camps he also knew the treatment the prisoners would have had to endure at the hands of his SS colleagues.

Henryk jumped down from the truck and was immediately surprised by the normality and order of the place. DPs were observed walking calmly about the place whilst children were laughing, playing and chasing one another frequently bumping into adults. Whilst there were a few British soldiers to be seen lounging about they looked bored and disinterested as he walked in line behind a civilian towards a building with a sign above the door saying canteen. At the same time the ambulances were disgorging stretchers and personnel carried them into the hospital.

The meal was hot, welcome and nourishing and when everyone had finished a captain accompanied by two aides entered the hall and stepped up on to a small platform at the opposite end of the hall to the serving hatches.

"Quiet please, silence." One of the aides shouted.

"I'm Major Hargreaves in charge of this camp for the British Military. May I welcome you and hope that you will be able to use your time here to adjust and plan for your future when you eventually leave us. It is not our intention to keep you here longer than we have to and it is our job to see you all repatriated or resettled as soon as possible." He stopped talking and looked towards one of his aides who translated what he'd said into German and the second aide who continued in Polish. "You're free to come and go as you please. You're to report to the assembly hall after breakfast for registration in the morning. Settle in and make yourselves at home. You can buy extra rations and almost anything else you want but I have to tell you that the German Mark is virtually worthless. Your best bet will be to barter cigarettes. There isn't anything that you can't have for a few cigarettes. With your cooperation we'll try to find you work outside the camp and you will be paid the German rate for your labour. Try to make the most of your time here. In the circumstances we're doing our best for you. Good luck."

Henryk and the rest were then conducted to a nearby barrack building and allocated into separate rooms each with four single beds, clean linen and blankets and a locker.

He dumped his valise on top of his locker and lay down on top of his bed. 'Well. So far so good' he thought. But as he began to relax he considered how he was going to carry off his new identity as a Pole. His major problem was that whilst he had learnt enough Polish to get by during his last three years on the eastern front he was not fluent and certainly not in a position to fool a native Polish speaker. Whilst his identity card showed that he had a Warsaw address he decided that he would bluff by saying that he had been born and brought up in western Poland near the Prussian border where many people were German speakers. He would just have to be careful.

After breakfast Henryk queued with hundreds of other new arrivals outside the assembly hall. Once he'd shuffled through into the hall the queue divided into five separate lines each one with a desk at the front manned by a civilian. The individual registration process seemed to take an age and as each one was completed Henryk pushed his valise forward with his feet. The tinned food he'd taken from Himmler's house had been consumed a long time ago but he still had remaining some real coffee and he was determined to protect his precious cartons of cigarettes.

When at last it was his turn to register he walked slowly across the yellow line towards a chair set in front of the desk with his head slightly bowed so as not to draw too much attention. The woman behind the desk pulled a form from the top of a large pile and taking a rubber stamp thumped it into an ink pad and stamped the top of the form.

"Name please?"

"Henryk Harmanecki."

"Nationality?"

"Polish."

"Have you any identification please?"

Henryk hesitated. There was something familiar about the woman's voice, a memory dredged from deep down, long buried in a past life, something known but intangible, he couldn't put his finger on it.

"Have you any identification please?" The voice repeated bringing Henryk back to the present. He lifted his head slightly and noticed the name plate on the front of the desk, Captain Annie Charlton, UNRAA Team Leader. 'Charlton' – hadn't he seen that name somewhere before."

"Have you any identification please?" The voice repeated again. "A simple yes or no will do," Annie continued trying not to get impatient.

Henryk reached into his jacket pocket and taking out his documents extended his hand and chanced a look at his interviewer. Recognition was instant and he froze, in disbelief and utter confusion.

"*Mein Gott!*" The words forming slowly and quietly.

Annie immediately looked up and searched the face with its black eye patch in front of her for some minutes.

"*Mein Gott!*........It is you isn't it?......Annette?" The questions tumbled from Henryk in quick nervous succession. "How did you get here? What are you doing? I thought I'd never see you again. I'd given up all hope. I meant all those promises I made to you what seems like a lifetime ago now."

Whilst Henryk continued his now animated questions Annie sat transfixed, staring at him. Her fountain pen dropped from her hand and rolled on to the floor. "Otto?.......My God is it really you Otto? I didn't recognize you. I'd given you up for dead." And she immediately looked round nervously in case anyone was listening to them. "We can't talk, not here, not now. I'll meet you after lunch." She bent down and picked up her pen and had to use her other hand to steady the pen as she continued, "I must finish your registration."

He watched Annie approaching. She had discarded her rather severe two piece suit and white blouse for a red, floral summer dress. Henryk too had at last changed out of the clothes he'd been given by the woman in a cellar in Berlin. He had bartered some cigarettes for a bar of scented soap and taken his first shower, albeit in cold water, since he couldn't remember when. The suit he'd been issued with fitted, almost, but it was clean, dark blue and made from a good quality wool. Waiting to see Annette seemed interminable and gave his mind the opportunity to become more anxious and confused. When he spotted her coming towards him she was as beautiful as he remembered.

Annie too was uncharacteristically uncertain and since registration she had played different scenarios over and over in her mind all with unsatisfactory conclusions.

"Shall we walk?" Annie said quietly.

They left the barrack block and once through the camp gates turned into a country lane leaving the perimeter fence behind. The sun was warm and a lone cabbage white butterfly danced and fluttered amongst the early meadow wild flowers. The atmosphere between them was heavy and tense and Annie eventually said, "Where do we start?.........I loved you."

"Past tense!" Henryk responded. "I've never stopped loving you."

"I don't know who you are. You never told me that you were going to marry someone else. How do you think I felt when....with a sneer on his face, ...that obsequious little man Himmler informed me with great pleasure that you were going to marry his niece? After all that you said to me at the station when you left Paris for the east. It was all lies. You deceived me."

"I deceived YOU." Henryk emphasised slowly with a cynical laugh, swinging his arm in the direction of the camp. "Do I call you Annette or Annie?" He continued sadly, slowly and quietly "Should we talk in German, French or English perhaps? I don't even know for sure whether you're English or French or what you are. I think I could learn a lot from you about deceit."

"What about you," Annie continued more viciously his time, "Was I just a bit of the rest and recuperation package for SS officers.....the Eiffel Tower....the Louvre....the wine and a free fuck?"

"As I recall," Henryk answered calmly and with resignation, "You were more than willing to be picked up. That's it isn't it! You played me. Reeled me in like a salmon, and I fell for it......hook line and sinker....I think you say in English. Deliberately.....you used me....how cruel is that? Don't try to take the moral high ground Annette, I mean Annie or whatever it is you're calling yourself today."

"If it's an accusation of cruelty you want to make then tell me about your SS service in Poland Otto....did cruelty feature just a little bit in Auschwitz?" Then more cynically, "Or do I call you Henryk?"

The initial hurt that they both felt having been vented in anger they fell silent again, each reflecting on accusations and counter-accusations. It was the war that had brought them together and the war which had forced them apart. Circumstances beyond which they had no control, or had they? Annie had known exactly what Otto was and yet she had allowed herself to fall in love with him. As if by telepathy Henryk asked quietly, "You said that you'd loved me. Was that true or was that just part of your resistance cover story? You knew what I stood for."

Annie reflected quietly as if trying to clarify things in her own mind. "Yes......I allowed myself to be picked up.....in the beginning. You were a useful contact for information for the Allies. But.....and this is true..... in spite of everything, I did fall in love with you Otto."

Conscious of his Damascene conversion, his acceptance that his life had been a fantasy and fearful that he might be now in jeopardy of ruining a second chance, of losing the one good thing that remained, Henryk plucked up his courage and risked his next question.

"Why did you fall in love with me Annie? Please tell me, it's important to me."

"You were handsome, witty, intelligent, and fun to be with but I fell in love with that part of you which you yourself were unaware of or suppressed, I was never quite sure. That sensitive part of you which you allowed to be buried beneath layer upon layer of Nazi propaganda. That sensitive part which you dare not admit to the Party or even yourself."

"Annie.....Annie........" Henryk could not continue the sentence, tears welling up in his eyes. He fell to his knees crying uncontrollably then fell forwards his head buried in his hands his whole body wracked with heaving sobs.

In spite of herself, Annie looked on with compassion.

"I....I....cannot even begin to tell you about my life these past two years." Henryk managed to say between gulping for breath and wiping his eyes and nose on his jacket sleeve. "It's too painful, my nightmares too vivid and sickening." He flicked his cheek and continued, "Things which I'm not proud of. Things which dragged me down into an abyss. I often thought about the advice you gave me." He put his hand inside his jacket pocket. "Look I still have the brandy flask you gave me as a present in Paris. It has been with me every single day. I read your message every time I took a drink. It helped me think of you."

"What about your wife?" Annie asked quietly but coldly.

"She's dead, and the few days old baby Siegfried. Killed in Berlin by the Russians. I never loved her. You must believe me. It was a marriage of convenience. I was only ever with her for a few days. It was made clear to me that if I wanted my career to progress I must marry a good German Fraulein. I didn't want to tell you because I knew that it would hurt you unnecessarily and none of us knew how the war would end. Believe me Annie I regret it. I regret my whole existence. Do you understand......I want to......I'm trying to reconstruct my life anew? Looking for forgiveness, even trying to forgive myself. This is the hardest thing I have ever done in my life. I want to work towards....*Sühne*.

"*Atonement*." Annie said quietly.

"Yes...atonement....that's the word. I meant what I said earlier, I've never ever stopped loving you. After what we've both been through these past two years why do you think we've met again, here, now? Do you believe in kismet? It was meant to be Annie. I believe that against all the odds we were meant to be together. The only thing that has been real in this whole insane fantasy is our love for one another. I can't believe that the love you had for me has died."

"I haven't come to terms with the shock Ot......Henryk. You'll have to give me time."

They didn't see each other for some days each nursing their bruised emotions. Annie's days were filled with work but her re-acquaintance with Henryk was always in the forefront of her thoughts. She knew that deep down she still loved him. Was she prepared to let the unpredictable consequences of the war destroy that?

As the days passed she observed Henryk from a distance gaining the confidence of the children in the camp. It started with one or two kicking a football but as the children gained in health and strength graduated into a sports club with Henryk organising other athletic activities drawing in help from other camp members. He also began teaching lessons in English. Gone was the superior air of arrogance to be replaced by an empathic understanding and patience which gave him an authority based on trust rather than fear and power. These she knew were the latent qualities that had attracted her to him in Paris three years ago.

Weary days of administration, politics, arbitration, counselling and red tape dragged on and occupied Annie consistently until one day during her morning coffee break, even though Henryk had been on her mind constantly, she suddenly realised that it was weeks since they had been alone together on the bombshell-day that they had been re-acquainted. She had seen him during her rounds of the camp and his observed visits to the hospital intrigued her enough for her to make enquiries. She was informed by the M.O. that Henryk had lost the sight in his left eye and that he was badly burnt on the left side of his chest and under his left arm. The circumstances of these injuries fuelled her imagination and curiosity and she decided to use this as an excuse to contrive to meet him during one of his medical appointments.

"Oops! I'm sorry," Annie exclaimed bumping accidentally on purpose into Henryk in the hospital entrance. "Oh! It's you Henryk," She said feigning surprise.

"Hello Annie," Henryk replied diffidently. "I've been wanting to meet up with you again but I fear you have been avoiding me."

"No....not at all," she squirmed, ".......well...yes...maybe. Not deliberately Henryk. My duties here keep me busy especially the endless politicking." And then more intimately she continued, "You have been on my mind every minute of every day. I have thought of nothing else but what you said when we last spoke. Come on....let's walk a while....I could do with a break."

It was late morning and the mid-summer sun was already enticing the air to dance and shimmer creating an out-of focus landscape where greens, yellows, browns and blues bled into each other like a surrealistic painting. Leaving the camp they turned south along a single roadway arrowing straight between tall pine trees.

"There's a little hamlet down here, Walle. We can get a cup of coffee although I expect it'll be black market price." Taking a risk Annie continued, "I've noticed you coming out of the hospital on a few occasions. Is your eye giving you trouble?"

"No... no," Henryk replied positively. "Apart from the fact that I've lost the sight in my left eye the wound has cleared up. I expect at some stage I'll get a glass eye which will restore my handsome features and I'll be able to throw this black patch away. Does it make me look like a pirate?"

"No it doesn't. Not to me anyway." Annie replied thoughtfully. "But it does give you a passing resemblance to Wagner's Wotan. Has it given you the same inward power of self-knowledge though? The power to look inside yourself with self-understanding."

Henryk laughed self-consciously. "It would cost more than one eye for that I'm afraid. But...yes....I suppose losing the eye was just another small step along a painful path of making sense of what I was....what I'd become."

"How did it happen?" Annie asked cautiously. "It doesn't matter if it's too painful for you."

"No...it's all right." Henryk replied positively and he proceeded to relate how he'd killed the Russian soldiers raping innocent women in a cellar in Berlin and being caught by the ricochet of his own bullets.

"And what about your burn. I've heard that it's quite severe. Is it troubling you?"

Henryk hesitated before answering. Dare he tell her the truth? The deliberate way he had burned himself to escape retribution and probably death for war crimes. He was afraid that this revelation would not be the way to help resurrect their relationship. He was trying to cauterise all memories of his life in the east and there would be little gain by revealing the real circumstances of his injury. Would he ever be able to tell her the truth? Was he even now trying to build a relationship on lies and secrets? Would the past ever really let him go? "It happened when I was hiding in a burning cellar in Berlin whilst trying to make my way to the west. It has been quite debilitating and painful but it's almost completely healed over although there will be quite a scar. And what about you Annie? What happened to you after I left for the eastern front?"

"Not much really....." She didn't want Henryk to know that in using him she had been able to access Himmler and the German High Command to perpetrate the biggest double-cross of the war. Knowing this would really feed his doubt that she had only pretended to fall in love with him for his usefulness to the Allies. Could her love really transcend the lies and deceit the SOE role had forced on her? Would any future relationship be forever built on a foundation of sand? "....I joined a resistance group near Rouen and took part in some sabotage of railway lines and telecommunications buildings...that sort of thing. And then after the liberation of Paris my work was done so I returned to England and volunteered to help clear the mess up in Europe and here I am. Look...there's the café."

The tiny village was deserted and they crossed the central square with its uneven block pave surface where tree shadows carpeted the blue/grey granite setts. The café was little more than a conversion of the front room of a small residential house with four unoccupied tables and chairs outside on the pavement. Inside there was only room for four small tables each with four chairs and a small counter/bar facing them. Seated at a table in one corner were two old men who looked at them with obvious disdain and huddled together in quiet conversation obviously discussing the new customers. Just as they sat down the proprietor appeared. "Yes....what can I get you?"

Annie looked at Henryk and said in German, "It's been a long time since breakfast and that walk has given me quite an appetite. I could really fancy some bacon an egg and coffee."

The proprietor shuffled uncomfortably. "I'm sorry that is not on the menu," he grunted.

Knowing that there was always food to be had in the countryside, at a price, Henryk slipped his hand into his pocket and withdrew two full packets of cigarettes. He slid them across the table and said, "Make that bacon and egg for two, no doubt at your market price, and keep these as a gratuity for your first class service, all right."

The sun hammered down fuelling a hot exotic intensity as they made their way back towards the camp. Wood pigeons flapped and cooed through the trees unseen whilst blackbirds sang to mark out their territory. Their hands touched accidentally and instantly Annie could feel the hot tingling nerves travelling through her body.

"What are you going to do when you eventually leave the camp?" Annie asked forcing the issue that was uppermost in both their minds whilst trying to control the tremor in her voice.

Henryk replied thoughtfully. "You know that I've got a Polish identity now...for obvious reasons...but a repatriation to Poland was never in my plans. I suppose I could try to rebuild my life here in Germany but I would always be looking over my shoulder. So...I suppose it all depends...."

"Depends on what?" Annie probed knowing full well their situation.

Each was reluctant to make the first commitment, to risk, and the longer the issue remained unacknowledged between them like a ticking bomb the more the tension mounted.

"What about you?" Henryk enquired. "Are you going to devoted yourself to the wandering displaced of Europe for the rest of your life?"

"Probably not....I don't really know....I suppose like you it depends.....on how things turn out. I guess we both know from recent experience that life has a habit of throwing up the unexpected."

Without warning Henryk pulled Annie into his arms and kissed her full on the lips. The frustration inside her was immediately released in a cascade of familiar sensations and feelings and she pressed, moulding herself to his body craving the closest of all human physical contact that they had once shared. When at last they separated, without hesitation, and in one mind they pulled and dragged each other over the small bank at the edge of the road and into the pine wood. Henryk immediately found a small hollow hidden from the roadway and threw his jacket down on the soft green moss and slippery carpet of pine needles. The jacket had scarce time to hit the ground before Annie was on her back pulling him into the yearning void. She clung to him, legs wrapped around him straining up to meet him, she needed to enclose him, to hold him within her. She felt alive, powerful, drawing strength and vitality from their oneness and knew in her heart that this was her destiny. It was over very quickly and they both cried out as they abandoned themselves to the explosive release of long dormant emotions.

They lay entwined allowing their gasping breaths to slowly return to normal.

"You have no idea," Henryk whispered into her ear, "how many empty, self-doubting, freezing nights I have dreamed of this moment. I have never stopped loving you Annie and now that both Germany and I have each reached our *Götterdämmerung* I want nothing more than the chance to build a new life with you. For you to be the last thing I see each night and the first thing in the morning."

"Oh Henryk.......I want nothing more than to put the last two years behind us. To start again, to discover each other all over again. There must be no mention of the past, we cannot change it. It is a mirage. It was unreal, it's gone. It will only live in our minds if we allow ourselves to play it over and over again like a movie. What we project onto the world's screen is what we see back. Our lives are in this moment, in the here and now, this instant. The past is dead and the future is unknown. We can only reach towards the love inside us second by second."

They fell silent for a few moments and Annie became conscious of the soft almost imperceptible sensation of Henryk slipping away from her like a sea anemone withdrawing into itself. Deliberately she slowly and gently contracted her pelvic muscles and again and again. Feeling Henryk respond and swelling once more to fill her void she began to respond in return with more urgency raising both Henryk and herself to a new plateau from where they both plunged into a mutual oblivion.

"Why don't you come to England with me?" Annie asked expectantly as they resumed their walk back towards the camp.

(III)

At one of their review and planning meetings Major Hargreaves raised the issue of food rations, fuel for the winter and the black market dealings within the camp.

"Food is going to be a problem this winter Annie. I expect the natives will become restless but there's nothing we can do about it. Perhaps you can try to put them in the picture as it were. The situation is beyond our control. It's just our luck that this part of Germany is not productive arable land. They always relied upon wheat from the east, from land now occupied by the Russians and there's little chance of them exporting foodstuffs. The American zone is the productive one and they have little enough for themselves without having any to spare for us. So it's up to our government to send us supplies which they have to import from around the world as well as from America. There's also the problem of fuel for the winter. God knows, there's enough to worry about without this."

"I know," Annie replied with resignation. "Leave it with me and I'll mention it."

"There's a matter I need to discuss with you Mr. Rosensaft." Annie mentioned during their next progress meeting. "Winter will soon be on us and there's the question of stockpiling wood."

"So we're also to be forced into slave labour as lumberjacks as well. We had enough of that during the war and don't have to accept it anymore."

Months of placating, pleading, supporting, counselling, negotiating, organising and battling with the military authorities over supplies apart from the emotional chaos of her own private life finally erupted in complete exasperation. "Good God man it's for your own good. For Christ's sake," she yelled at him. "Either you organize wood cutting or you fucking freeze to death….the choice is yours," she yelled over her shoulder as she stormed out of the door determined not to let Rosensaft see her crying.

Walking towards their pre-arranged rendezvous Henryk scrutinized Annie from a distance. He walked towards the car she was leaning against noting the long tweed, fitted overcoat tied with a knotted belt of the same material which emphasized her elegant height and confident stance. On her head was a kind of dark red trilby hat, the brim of which was turned up at the back transforming to a downward curve at the sides and front and set at a jaunty angle slanting over her right eye. He thought she looked chic and sophisticated, exotic even in the drab surroundings of the camp.

Annie watched him approaching and waved enthusiastically. "My word, don't you look dapper." She said with her right arm in the air and her left arm diagonally pointing to the ground. "Ta Daaaaa!"

"It's amazing what you can buy with a few cigarettes. I got a Jewish tailor to nip and tuck the baggy suit I was issued with and now it fits better than......Saville Row I think is the street?"

"Yes, Saville Row. Perhaps you'll buy a suit there one day. Jump in," she continued holding open the passenger door.

Without a second thought Henryk jumped into the car and was immediately confused. "Where's the steering wheel? The steering wheel's on the wrong side."

"I'm driving. You haven't got a licence....and the steering wheel is on the right side because we won the war."

Henryk looked at Annie with a puzzled expression on his face but when he saw that she was smiling they both burst out laughing.

"Come on let's get this engine started and put the heater on this October weather is getting colder and colder. It looks like Jews, Poles and Germans are not the only thing the Russians are sending us from the east."

Henryk turned round and threw his valise onto the back seat beside Annie's small travel case. "Where are we going?" He asked with anticipation.

Annie steered the camouflage green W.D. Humber saloon through the camp gates and headed south. "A surprise........I've booked us two nights at the Hotel Saxony in Celle. I'm ready for a break and I get to be alone with you. It's called killing two birds with one stone."

"You English and your idioms," he replied laughing. "Why the town Celle by the way?"

"Because it would be nice to see a city centre that hasn't been totally destroyed by bomb or shell and we can wrap up warm and enjoy walking through the old medieval town centre, the gardens, castle park and along the banks of the River Aller."

Annie continued driving through woods and green fields and the thickening, brooding sky tried its best to darken their joyous mood but failed miserably. Eventually a weak sun disappeared behind buildings and the late afternoon was giving way to early evening as Annie drove through the historic old town and parked in the courtyard of an old coaching inn, The Saxony Hotel.

"Identification." A suspicious and seemingly resentful receptionist asked.

Annie slipped her G.B. Passport and army officer identification papers across the desk and Henryk did the same with his Polish identity card and DP registration card. The uniformed receptionist made an issue of scrutinizing in turn Henryk's face and his papers through his thick lensed spectacles and it took all of Henryk's forbearance and control to stop himself from slipping into SS mode and scaring the shit out of this insignificant little control freak.

Knowing the German predilection for respecting authority and obeying orders Annie said in strident, perfect German, "I hope there isn't a problem." Her eyes boring straight into those of the hotel employee. "Otherwise I might have to close this establishment down for infringing the law on black market trading. I don't think your employer would be very pleased. Do you?"

"All is in order Captain Charlton" the receptionist responded bowing his head. If there is anything I can do for you during your stay with us."

"Thank you. That is so kind of you." Annie replied with cynical formally.

"Pheeew! Remind me never to fall out with you." Henryk said.

Annie pushed him playfully once they'd turned the corner away from the reception desk and they chased each other up the stairs whooping and shrieking like school kids. Annie sagged against the wall in the corridor whilst Henryk put the key in the lock. They tumbled through the door and collapsed on the bed with riotous laughter.

After freshening up they entered the dining room and looked at each other knowingly as the head waiter seemed almost over attentive. Like the rest of the building the room was timber framed with large baulks of old oak decorated with animal carvings. The plasterwork between was painted with hunting and Hanseatic scenes and mounted stags' heads and antlers hung from picture hooks. They were conducted towards a discrete table considerately not too close to the burning logs crackling and sparking in the large open fire grate.

"Would sir and madam like something to drink whilst looking at the menu?"

"Yes please," Henryk replied. "Bring us a bottle of Riesling Auslese."

"I'm sorry sir but our wine cellar stock is virtually non-existent. All I can offer you is a drinkable house white."

"That will have to do then," replied Henryk

The menu was limited and they chose vegetable soup, meat of unknown provenance with potatoes and vegetables and cheese and biscuits.

"What should we drink to?" Henryk asked lifting his glass.

"Oh! I think you know," Annie replied impishly. "Why don't we drink tooo....us?"

"To us."

"Can you remember what you said about German wines when we first met in Paris? You said that German wines were superficial, obvious and pretentious. Did you really mean that or were you just being provocative?"

"That's for me to know and you to find out," Annie replied giggling.

Their soup arrived and they fell silent for the moment.

"I'm really finding that work at the camp is draining me Henryk," Annie said unexpectedly between courses. "I'm thirty next year and I've given a lot for King and Country during the past five years. I'm really thinking that I deserve a life of my own. The in-fighting and politics both within and between UNRRA and the military is just too tiresome and wasteful. You know......I get most satisfaction in counselling individuals one-to-one. The Jews especially are overtaken by their experiences in the camps and preoccupied almost to the point of morbidity. As long as they stay here in the DP camp their pathology will continue. They need normal surroundings to help them move on to something like normal psychological health."

Henryk listened intently, staring at the face of this beautiful woman who loved him and was impassioned by idealistic altruism.

"Good God, Henryk. This war has turned a lot of things on their heads."

"The Poles are also showing psychological reactions to their collective experience," Henryk volunteered. "But things are improving. Their quarters are not now so squalid as a result of their own indolence. There is still drunkenness, dishonesty, crime and even cruelty but there is also culture, laughter and honour and artistic expression." He paused. "Enough of this navel gazing," Henryk said determined to lighten the serious atmosphere which had descended on them both. "Now that we've finished this pitcher of barely adequate wine why don't we take a bottle up to our room?"

"At this price you'd better declare it the best wine in the world," Annie ventured smiling. "Well, what do you think?"

"Ummmm! Very mature." Henryk answered knowledgeably looking at his glass and swirling the liquid round. "A clean after-taste, with a hint of long lasting love and an impish teasing on the tongue.

324

A beautiful bouquet with a hint of pleasure to come. I think this will be a very good vintage year which will be remembered long into the future."

"You devil," Annie exploded. "You're pulling my leg," she continued bursting out laughing.

"Ahaaa!" Henryk responded, "How do you like being teased. Taking your pun about legs, I think the boot is on the other foot," he continued smiling. "Do you think I'm getting used to these English idioms for every occasion?"

They made love slowly, teasingly, delighting in the familiarity and nuances of each other's bodies. Annie ran her finger tips lightly over Henryk's burn scar.

"Does it hurt too much?" She asked quietly.

"Not now," he replied. "It just feels as if the skin is stretched and tight sometimes."

"Let me see if I can help you relax again then."

Afterwards they lay side by side on the bed.

"Marry me and come and live in England with me?" Annie asked straight out.

"You mean you want me to make an honest woman of you?"

"No....not really." She replied smiling, and putting her hands on her tummy continued, "I mean that I don't want our son to grow up without his father."

CHAPTER 25

Annie, Henryk (Henry) and Saskia 1946 – 1967

(I)

"First Aid and Nursing Yeomanry. May I ask who's calling please?"

"Captain Annie Charlton."

"How may I help you Captain?" The young female voice asked efficiently.

"I'd like to speak to Vera Atkins if she's available please. It's a matter of some importance so I'd be grateful if you could track her down for me."

"You might be in luck Captain, I believe she's just returned from France and Germany. If you hang on I'll see if I can find her for you."

"Try to be quick because I'm calling long distance from Germany."

Annie waited for what seemed like ages before the crackling and clicks on the other end of the line indicated that the receiver was being picked up again.

"Annie....my giddy aunt, it's wonderful to hear from you, although I've been hearing plenty about you. Seems like you've made a big impression with UNRRA over there in Belsen."

"Thank you Vera. But listen, I hope I won't disappoint you after that big build up but I really, really need you to do a massive favour for me if you can. I'd be forever in your debt."

"Goodness...this sounds serious....shoot."

"I'll come straight to the point. I've married a Polish D.P. who registered here at the camp." Annie could hear the loud silence on the other end of the line. "I need to resign my commission. Could you possibly arrange for me to be demobbed ASAP? Of course I'll be resigning my position at UNRRA as well. I'm pregnant. I expect this is a bit of a bombshell for you."

"Oh I've dealt with worse than this Annie since the war finished. I'll see what I can do."

"There's more Vera. I'm conscious that this is an imposition what with all your other investigative work and reports to write."

"You've more than earned any help I can offer Annie. And this country doesn't know how much it owes to you. What do you want me to do for you?"

"Being as Henryk and I were married by a Padre in the military chapel out here I expect he'll be entitled to British citizenship but he'll need a passport etc. Could you forward the relevant documents and forms for me and Henryk to complete and if you could use your contacts in the Home Office to arrange for these to be dealt with speedily that would be a great help. Henryk's surname is Harmanecki so obviously I'm now Mrs. Harmanecki but we'd like to apply for a name change by deed poll. People might still be a little....how shall I put this.....a little sensitive what with the war and the current privations and rationing so we think that Henry Harman sounds much more acceptable."

"Leave it with me Annie and I'll get on it right away. We'll be sorry to lose you. We had you marked down for a high flying career in the military. You'll be greatly missed. I can't persuade you to stay on can I?"

"Thanks. That's very kind of you Vera but I'm afraid my work in Belsen has left me absolutely drained and of course I have the baby to think of now, so thank you for the vote of confidence but I've decided my life lies elsewhere now."

"Well good luck to you whatever you decide to do and please stay in touch. I'll get the stuff sent to you in a diplomatic bag so everything should be with you shortly and if you return the relevant information to me I'll see that there's a smooth passage through all the red tape. God bless you Annie. Goodbye."

"I can't thank you enough Vera. Goodbye."

* * * * *

"I've written to mum and dad so they're fully in the picture. We'll fly to London then get the train up to Newcastle. All we need to do now is send a telegram letting them know when to expect us. Let me think....."

Arrive Central Station Nc/le STOP
Thurs. 14th. March. 17.54 STOP
Please pick us up under the portico. STOP

"I hope your parents will like me." Henryk replied with some concern.

"Don't be silly, of course they will. How could they not. I like you. You'll see, you're one of the family now and you'll soon have your feet under the table."

The privations of post-war England were to be seen everywhere. There was much evidence of bomb damage in London. People were dressed in dowdy, shapeless clothes which, because of rationing would have to last a little bit longer and shop windows showed little to offer. But Henryk was eager to face his new life even though the journey turned into a miserable odyssey because of the non-functioning heater in the railway carriage.

"Wow! Look at that view," Henryk uttered with amazement rubbing the condensation away from the carriage window with his sleeve to get a wider vista.

"Yeah, I always feel that I'm nearly home when I see Durham Cathedral and castle from up here on the viaduct. It's strange. Our farm is just on the Durham side of the border with Northumberland so Durham is our county city but we all still think of Newcastle as home."

Twenty minutes later the train slowed to cross the King Edward VII Bridge over the River Tyne. Once again the elevated position opened up a panoramic view of Newcastle quayside with its numerous bridges of various design and colliers and cargo vessels tied up or sailing on the tide under the watchful eye of the medieval keep.

"The keep there was built by Henry II in 1172 so you're both ancient monuments with the same name."

"Oh no...... I can see that our marriage is going to be one big, hilarious laugh."

"Come on you old ruin, get your things together we're home."

They left the main body of the station and entered the huge, solid stone, neoclassical entrance portico. Annie stopped and looked round. Spotting her dad she dropped her suitcase and ran into his arms.

"Oh daddy, I've missed you so much."

"Welcome home Annie we've all missed you too."

By now Henryk was struggling towards them dragging Annie's luggage as well as his own.

"Here. Let me help you," Robert said taking the largest case from Henryk and putting it in the boot of the car.

"Daddy, this is Henry. Henry Daddy." They shook hands vigorously and warmly.

"Welcome Henry, I hope you'll make yourself right at home." Robert said in his rusty Polish.

Henry flicked his left cheek hoping that he'd managed to hide his surprise and turning to Annie said jovially in perfect English, "You little devil, you didn't tell me that your father spoke Polish."

Annie laughed and Robert continued, "Well, Annie forgot to mention whether you spoke English or not. Its twenty five years since I spoke any Polish so I'm pleased your English is much better than my

Polish. Come on you must be dog tired. Get in the car and we'll head for home."

The car had scarce time to shudder to a halt before Rhoda and Annie's younger sister Rowena were crossing the farm yard heading towards them.

"She's been on tenter hooks ever since we got your telegram," Robert laughed.

"Welcome home pet. It's wonderful to see you again after all this time." After giving Annie a huge hug she turned her attention to Annie's new husband. "And this must be Henry....welcome to Hill Top Farm Henry. I hope you'll think of it as home from now on."

"Thank you for your warm welcome Mrs. Charlton......."

"No, no, no, son, its Rhoda and Robert...you're family. Ha'way in your dinner's just about ready. You must be famished after travelling all that way."

Annie and Rowena hugged. "I've missed you so much Weenie," Annie said whilst they were still in a clinch.

Weenie whispered in Annie's ear, "He's gorgeous, you lucky so and so. What a dish. That patch over his eye makes him look sooo..... exotic and mysterious. Has he got a brother?"

"You're wicked and incorrigible Weenie. Come on inside."

The atmosphere was intoxicating as everyone had so many questions and so much to say. So much lost time to catch up on. So many plans to discuss. And the first grandchild to look forward to.

"Dump your things upstairs. There's plenty of room. You can have the second big bedroom with the double bed. Freshen up, come back down and I'll dish up.

"You've gone quiet," Annie ventured when they were alone in the bedroom, "Is everything all right?"

"Of course," Henry responded as light heartedly as he could muster. "It's all so overwhelming. Your mum and dad are wonderful. Come on let's go and have something to eat before we turn in I'm really tired."

At the bottom of the stairs Annie heard her mum whispering, "Here they come."

Entering the large farmhouse kitchen a loud pop resulted in a champagne cork flying across the room and nearly putting out Henry's other eye accompanied by ooohs and ahhhs.

"A toast I think," Robert said. "To the future."

"The future," everybody repeated and they sat down round the table.

"I've been dying to ask pet...when's the baby due?"

"The back end of June." Annie replied....as far as I can make out."

"So much to catch up on," Rhoda added. "I didn't tell you in my last letter," she talked without drawing breath, "but the latest news is that Rupert's down in London. At the London College of Music." Turning to Henry she continued, "Annie's brother wanted to be a mining engineer but he was wounded at Monte Cassino in Italy. Not too badly but enough to stop him from going underground. So he's turned his hobby singing in a male voice choir into an opportunity for a different career."

"I am pleased he was not too badly wounded," Henry replied. "Too many young men have not returned to their loved ones."

"Aye, that's true," Robert added, "Just like the last time."

"Our Libby's away too, that's Annie's sister," Rhoda pointed out to Henry. "At teacher training college in Newcastle. She wants to teach infants. So there's only our Rowena, or Weenie as we call her because she's the youngest, at home now and she's training to be a secretary in Newcastle. So it'll be lovely to have the house alive with family again."

The meal finished Rhoda shoooed Annie and Henry up the stairs. "I'll clear up down here. You two must be dead beat. Get a good night's sleep and we'll have a good old chin wag in the morning. Good night..... and it's wonderful to have you both here with us."

Undressing for bed Annie looked at Henry, "Are you sure you're okay? You were very quiet over dinner."

"Yes, of course, just tired as I said before and it's overwhelming to be with such a loving family." How could he share with her his suspicions? They were probably just coincidence anyway he hoped, but he was far from convinced. He thought of what Annie had said back in Celle, that they should live in the here and now and let the past go. But would the past ever let him go?

Next morning after breakfast Robert asked breezily, "Have you two any plans for today? It's still cold out, or do you just want to rest up after all the travelling yesterday?"

"No...it's okay dad, we slept like logs. Why? What do you have in mind?"

"Well I know that your mother's dying to know every little detail of what you've been up to and what your future plans are. You know what she's like. And whilst you two are getting up to date I thought that me and Henry could get to know one another a bit better whilst I show him round the Charlton empire."

"What do you think Henry? Would you like to explore our vast estates?" Annie asked Henry enquiringly.

"Yes I would find that very interesting," Henry replied. "My father and grandfather......" In that instant he was just about to say 'owned land in Germany before the war' but managed to continue at the last moment, ".....always wanted to work on the land." He had relaxed and let his guard down in the warm, friendly loving atmosphere. He would have to be more alert in future.

Robert walked Henry up to the highest point of his land and proudly pointed to the wide sweep of the Derwent Valley. "When I came home from the last war I vowed I would never ever go away from here again...and I haven't. I love this place."

"It's really beautiful," Henry agreed.

"Once the Ministry of Food and Agriculture relax their war rationing regulations I can start to build this place up again with beef and dairy herds as well as the arable side. I need to mechanize more as well."

"You obviously have big plans Robert. It must be wonderful to have a vocation and love what you're doing. It makes all the hard work worthwhile I guess."

"This is only part of the empire. Come on back down to the car and I'll give you a conducted tour of our other enterprises."

They spent the rest of the day visiting Robert's haulage and transport depot in Scotswood Road, Newcastle and the fruit and vegetable warehouse on the quayside. "This side of the business was a nightmare during the war." Robert volunteered. "The U-boat blockade stopped a lot of fruit getting through from overseas but business is picking up again now."

There was the fruit and veg shop in Westgate Road and the large Victorian terraced house in Jesmond to visit. "What do you think?" Robert asked with not a little pride. "We've also got a shop in Consett and still do markets and street hawking."

"Very impressive," Henry replied. "But why are the transport and warehouse businesses called Hadleigh Holdings when your name is Charlton?"

"Ahhh! I was very fortunate and was left them in a will, but that's a long story for another day. Changing the subject, I know it's early days and you must feel disorientated in a new country etcetera but have you and Annie had time to think ahead....about what you want to do I mean? I don't want to press you or impose on you. You're free to do whatever suites you and Annie best but there can be a position somewhere within the family businesses for you if you want it."

"That's very kind and thoughtful of you Robert, I'm overwhelmed by your welcome and generosity."

"Not at all; family is the most important thing in our lives."

Henry had an immediate unwelcome flashback and remembered Himmler saying exactly the same words in a different context. "After my experiences in Germany and the DP camp working with Annie I thought that I might like to be a teacher. Try to give something to the next generation so that we can avoid another conflict like the one that's just ended."

"I want you to know that Rhoda and I will support you and Annie in any way, whatever you decide to do. Education isn't cheap and if that's what you want to do then perhaps you might like to work here part-time to help out with your finances. And of course there's the little nipper to consider as well."

"Nipper......?" Henry enquired with puzzlement.

"Sorry Henry, you're English is so perfect that I forgot you might not know some of our slang words. Nipper means baby or small child."

The whole family finished the evening meal early and whilst clearing things away Rhoda suggested, "Why don't you round the day off and take Henry for a drink at the hotel down in Chepfield?"

"Aye, I could do with a pint. What do you think Henry, do you fancy seeing the night life in a northern pit village?"

Robert drove the car up the track and out onto the road leading down into the village. Just before passing under the mineral track railway bridge the sky lit up with a red glow and heat could be felt through the car windows.

"What's that?" Henry asked startled.

"Oh...that's just the ovens," Robert replied, "You get used to them."

Henry flicked his left cheek then gripped his knees to steady the tremor in his hands.

"Are you all right?" Robert asked.

"What ovens?" Henry asked his mouth dry.

"Coke ovens. This pit produces some of the best coking coal in the country. They must be emptying the ovens into trucks. Are you sure you're okay.... you look like you've seen a ghost. Like someone's walked over your grave."

"Not one but thousands," Henry whispered cryptically almost to himself.

By now Robert had pulled up outside the hotel. "Come on let's away in for a pint. Do you drink beer?"

"Yes, I enjoy a good beer."

"Good, then we'll start you off with a bottle of good old Newcastle Brown Ale. The best beer in the world and I've drunk some of your Polish beer too."

"Two bottles of broon please Mary."

The hotel bar was busy and Robert acknowledged a number of friends. They sat at a cast iron table near the coal fire burning in an open grate.

"There's a nip of frost in the air," Robert said pointing at the fire. "See how the flames are drawing yellow. Sooo what do you think of our local brew?"

"It's delicious, lovely thick, sweet, nutty flavour....I like it......." Putting the glass down Henry ventured, "Charlton......is that a common name in England?"

"Well....not in England exactly but it's a fairly well known historical name in these parts. Goes back to the fifteenth and sixteenth centuries when there was constant fighting and raiding across the Northumberland border with Scotland. The Robsons are another ancient family name."

"You're a long way from Poland and it's not a place English people visit so how do you come to speak our language?"

"That's another long story but to keep it short in 1916 I was taken a POW in the Battle of the Somme. "What regiment were you in?"

"The DLI...everyone, well almost everyone, from here joined the Durham Light Infantry."

Henry felt his stomach rise up to his throat and as if his heart was going to burst out of his chest.

"Anyway, I was sent to a camp called Wahn near Cologne then a strange thing happened. A high ranking German officer....von Lieper.... Albrecht I think I remember his name was....asked an assembly of prisoners if anyone was a farmer so I volunteered reckoning that working on a farm would have to be better than breaking stones in a quarry. It transpired that he had a huge estate in Poland....near a place called Ciechanow, north of Warsaw, do you know it?

Henry's mouth was so dry he could hardly speak. He lifted his glass and gulped down some beer giving himself time to calm his growing panic. "No, but I've heard of it."

"Apparently his wife, Katharina was having trouble managing the estate whilst her husband was away at the western front and he wanted someone with experience to help out. She lived in the large country house and I lived in a converted stable across the yard. In two years I picked up a lot of rough Polish from her servants and the old men in the little village where I used to drink on parole. Anyway, eventually the war ended. Albrecht von Lieper returned in 1919 and I made my way back home via Danzig where I hopped on a ship bound for Edinburgh. Are you sure you're all right Henry...you're sweating?"

"Yes...yes...it must be the fire...sitting so close."

That night Annie's breathing was slow and quiet. Henry lay beside her his mind in a turmoil with thoughts like crisp, brittle leaves swirling round in an autumn storm. There was no longer any doubt in his mind. The facts were too obvious to be coincidental. Ciechanow, the large country house, the pen knife name and DLI carving on the window sill in the converted stable. He had even known his father and mother's names. His mother's parting words burned within him, "You're a half-breed.....your father was English." It had to be...there couldn't be any other explanation. '*Mein Gott,* what am I going to do with this information now' he asked himself. Then his brain exploded as the unthinkable flashed into his mind. Oh my God, have I married my own sister? This can't be happening, it's unbelievable. The nightmare was becoming an unbearable catastrophe.

Robert too had a disturbed night. He had managed to put Katharina's letter informing him that they had had a son together in 1919 to the back of his mind these past few years but his conversation with Henry had brought it all back to him. At least he hadn't revealed this part of his history to Henry or anyone else in the family for that matter. Let sleeping dogs lie was his motto.

At breakfast, Henry hoped that his inner tension would not transmit itself to the rest of the household but he had to come to terms with his fears as soon as possible and try to verify the truth. Difficult though it would be he resolved that he would have to cope by himself with the knowledge that Robert was his father. He couldn't possibly resurrect this particular skeleton. There were enough in his life already and it might destroy the whole family and his chance of a settled future. But the burning question was that he really needed to know where he stood with Annie one way or the other. But how to do that without giving the game away or arousing suspicion.

"Did you and your mother discussed possible names for our son yesterday? We haven't had time to give it any thought but I know that some families like to keep continuity." Henry asked Annie casually whilst eating his bacon and eggs and fried bread and trying to keep it down.

"How do you know it's going to be a boy?" Rhoda asked cracking another fresh egg into the frying pan.

"Oh..it is...we just know don't we Henry? But no we didn't. Now you come to mention it I think I'd like to name him after my dad. How do you feel about that mum?"

"I think your father would be very proud. What do you say Robert?"

Henry was more confused than ever and listened intently.

"Aye, John James was the best pal anyone could ever have and I think it would be a good way to remember him Annie, he'd love it."

Henry's mood lightened immediately and he asked rather too excitedly, "But I thought that you were Annie's father, Robert."

"Nay lad, Annie's father, John James Horton was killed in 1916 in the same action where I was taken prisoner. He was married to Rhoda and Annie was theirs although he was killed before Annie was born. After the war Rhoda and I got married and I adopted Annie as my own and a wonderful daughter she has been too."

So Annie was his half-sister with no blood connection. The relief Henry felt was pure joy. Perhaps now he really could get on with the rest of his life.

(II)

John James Harman was born 7lbs 6ozs on June 4th 1946 and the family settled into a routine dictated by the needs and wants of a new born baby. After the initial excitement of coming home to Hill Top Farm and the birth of their son Annie and Henry had had time to discuss their options and what they wanted for the future. Pieces of the jigsaw had been identified and it was only a matter of putting them in the right places at the right time.

* * * * *

Annie was nursing John James and she looked up when the kitchen door opened. "How'd the interview go?" she asked in eager anticipation.

"Good.....I think. But you can never tell, can you." Henry replied taking his coat off and going to hang it up on a peg in the hall. "They were obviously impressed by my determination to commit to the university. They said that they always had a few places for mature students and although I didn't have any educational records or documents, because of my fluency in French, German and Polish they were prepared to believe that I had graduated from Warsaw University. And being as Russia is going to be a political force in the future my interest in studying Russian also seemed to gain nodding approval. They accepted that all my records had been lost in the destruction of Warsaw during the war. The fact that I was married and had a British passport was significant as was having a permanent local address."

"So where does that leave us?" Annie asked moving John James from her left breast to her right.

"Well...Durham University's Kings College in Newcastle is mainly an engineering, medical and dentistry college but they do have a small modern languages department which is keen to expand so we'll just have to wait and see. They said they'd let me know but it does raise the possible issue of where we live. We can't keep relying on your mother and father."

"I know. I've been thinking about it. It's wonderful having mum's support but I want us to make our own way and have our own lives together. I know she loves having the baby here and I don't want to hurt her feelings but I'll bring it up with her when the time's right."

A fortnight later the post lady rapped on the back door with her smooth round pebble as she did at all the houses on her delivery round. Few families had letter boxes. She opened the door and threw in the post. Durham University was printed on one of the envelopes. Henry picked up a knife from the kitchen table and with nervous anticipation slit it open. He withdrew the letter and opened it slowly. Robert, Rhoda and Annie held their collective breaths and watched Henry with fingers crossed behind their backs.

"They've accepted me," He voiced excitedly and he pulled Annie out of her chair giving her a breath expelling hug. "I start in October at Kings College."

This deserves a celebration drink," Robert suggested making his way over to the large pine welsh dresser and taking down a bottle of whisky. "Let's drink to success," He suggested.

"To success," Everyone repeated lifting up their glasses.

"Well done darling," Annie said coughing as the spirit hit the back of her throat. Taking the timely opportunity she continued, "We'll need to consider our living accommodation and arrangements."

"Why?" Rhoda answered quickly, "You can stay here and Henry can travel in to Newcastle every day."

"Thanks mum, I knew you'd say that.....and we don't want to hurt your feelings.....but we really need to establish our own home and family. We can't keep depending on you and daddy, it's not fair."

"She's right Rhoda love. Remember how we enjoyed making our own routine when we were first married. They need to be on their own." Turning to Henry and Annie, Robert continued, "If you're determined to move to Newcastle then can I run this by you. My old mate Tommy.....he lost a leg on the Somme and he's never really been a well man since....has just retired. He was my manager at the haulage yard and I let him live in the house in Jesmond. He's back in Chepfield now so why don't you take over the house in Eslington Terrace, just off Osborne Road in Jesmond. You know the place Henry I showed it to you a few weeks ago when we toured the Charlton empire."

"Yes, of course," Henry replied. "It's a fine house."

"It's the ideal solution. The university is in the Haymarket, just five minutes' walk away and you can live there rent free. The house is really owned by the company Hadleigh Holdings but I'm seriously thinking of buying it off the books before property prices go through the roof. That way it'll be a family asset rather than be lost to us if we ever sell the business. What do you say?"

"Thank you daddy that would be wonderful. Henry and I can't thank you enough. It would be the perfect start. I've got some money saved up from my army salary which I banked because I didn't need it in France. And I expect that Henry can get a part-time job to help out. We'll also have to apply to Durham County Council Education Department to see if we can get a grant."

"That's not a problem, I also mentioned this to Henry when we were out together. He can help in the office at the Scotswood Road depot checking delivery schedules and time sheets etc. I'll have a word with the new manager and you can arrange to fit your hours in around your lectures Henry."

"Thank you Robert. What can I say? It's perfect." And moving over towards Robert, Henry shook his hand vigorously.

Henry had never been so happy. He couldn't believe that life could be this good. He managed his studies during the first year without any difficulty although he did find learning Russian taxing but fascinating. Work at the depot was repetitive but a welcome diversion from his studies as well as providing a needed income and his new glass eye was a complete cosmetic success.

Graduation in 1950 presented another piece of the jigsaw to be meshed in to the family picture although it now seemed to Henry that pieces were beginning to tumble uncontrollably out of the box. John James now attending the local primary school. Henry completed a Master's Degree and commenced a Ph.D. and was offered a post at the university teaching undergraduates. Annie secured a job teaching languages at the Girls' High School two minutes' walk from where they lived and their joint income was sufficient to employ a child minder to collect John James from school and look after him until Annie could get home. Henry found a literary agent, who, whilst suggesting that his Ph.D. theses was a bit specialised, was prepared to take a chance on publishing "Wagner's Ring Cycle – A Study of Political Power." which was an instant success amongst serious music lovers, politicians and academics.

The modern languages department was gaining a reputation for academic excellence and as a consequence was expanding whilst at the same time relations between the Newcastle Kings College campus and the main university authorities in Durham were becoming strained to the extent that eventually in 1963 they separated and the University of Newcastle established an identity and constitution in its own right.

On the back of his well-publicised research Henry was appointed Head of the Languages Faculty in the new university.

(III)

Saskia closed the heavy front door to the large Victorian house in Claremont Road just off the Haymarket where she shared a flat with two other girl students. She had gone over it a hundred times in her mind but the tension she felt was palpable. Her thoughts raced as she tried to reconcile the vicissitudes by which her short life had delivered her to this monumental decision. Instead of making directly towards Eslington Terrace in Jesmond she turned into Exhibition Park hoping that the walk through this green oasis in the centre of the city would give her time to calm her nerves.

* * * * *

Although born in England, Saskias's parents were Polish. As a little girl she grew up speaking both English and Polish at home and was left in no doubt as to her heritage by the stories of the old country her father and mother would proudly tell her. They had both been members of the Polish resistance movement and spent the latter part of the war living in secret camps in the forests but they had fled Poland as the Russians had advanced westward at the close of the Second World War and made their way to the British Sector in Germany from where they were given permission to emigrate to England.

Life had been hard Saskia remembered for the Polish exiles and her mother and father had been willing to take on any menial jobs in the east end of London in order to eke out a decent living. Saskia's one enduring memory of those days was that she never ever seemed to see her father without his old battered camera in his hands. He was always taking photographs and with the little money he saved he managed to buy some second hand equipment and set up a dark room in the kitchen of their tiny flat. Friends and neighbours were delighted with the photos her father produced of their babies and children and eventually he would present these images mounted in tasteful frames which he sold at a profit. Gradually his reputation spread until such time as he was able to set himself up as a full time photographer progressing from a back street premises to something more upmarket with the opportunity for a greater profit margin from the retail sale of photographic equipment as well as his portraiture business. Saskia was aware that their quality of life improved and that luxuries were now readily available but she was never allowed to become blasé and spoilt or forget her roots. And this did

338

cause her some tension in her early teenage years when developmentally she was struggling with establishing her own identity. But there was one enduring element of the family history which burned in her and was never allowed to fade.

Saskia excelled at school and at the age of eighteen found herself faced with having to make a choice of university where she was determined to study modern European languages. She filled in her application forms and was delighted when she was given an offer by the University of Newcastle. She had researched the courses offered by various universities and the reputation Newcastle had established persuaded her to put it down as one of her choices.

* * * * *

Saskia joined a group of other animated undergraduates as they made their way into the lecture theatre. There was a buzz of anticipation and excitement which eventually subsided as three members of the university staff dressed in academic robes mounted the platform. The welcome address was delivered by Professor Henry Harman. Whilst still overwhelmed by the whole atmosphere, Saskia listened politely to the morale boosting speech which outlined the privilege presented by the university to those who were prepared to engage with the work ethic and seize the opportunities which the university degree would open up. When he had finished, another member of the trio delivered information about the various university domestic arrangements but Saskia's attention had wandered. From her seat high up in the tiered lecture room she found herself drawn to Professor Harman. She sensed an unbidden curiosity within herself. A sense that there was somehow a connection that she couldn't put her finger on.

During her three year course, Saskia's contact with Prof. Henry Harman was limited to passing him sometimes in the department corridors, his lecturing responsibilities being directed towards post graduate students. But in the final term of her degree he was offering a module on how German music composers reflected or influenced German culture and Saskia signed up.

The close contact during lectures, group and individual tutorials, sometimes at his house in Jesmond, gradually firmed up her initial suspicions. Henry had noticed Saskia staring at him on a number of occasions when she thought that he was otherwise occupied and the experiences left him uneasy and cautious to the extent that he looked up her initial application documents. On this occasion during a tutorial their eyes made that sort of contact which, for a fleeting moment conveys the hint of secret, hidden elements and leaves each feeling naked and vulnerable. Henry flicked his left cheek and asked tentatively, "Saskia Wiedza's Polish isn't it?"

"Yes," Saskia replied, "but I was born in London."

"There must be a story there," Henry probed.

"Nothing unique," Saskia replied in a non-committal tone. "My parents came to England from Poland after the war like hundreds, possibly thousands of other east European exiles." And then with deliberate intent she continued, "From Oswiecim," and immediately in his one good eye she recognized the involuntary reaction to this information which confirmed for her that he knew that she knew. "Do you know it?" She continued as if nothing had happened. "It's a little town north of Krakow. Perhaps you know it better as Auschwitz."

"I've heard of it of course," Henry replied with caution trying to mask his anxiety. "But other than reading Holocaust literature I have no personal knowledge of the place. I've never had a reason or opportunity to visit it."

The conversation resumed its academic content and the subject of Saskia's family history was never mentioned again.

* * * * *

Saskia walked slowly past the band-stand in Exhibition Park and tried to calm herself with the knowledge that she had planned meticulously for every eventuality. The warm, bright late May sunshine had brought a number of students as well as city office workers out into the park to enjoy their al fresco, packed lunches. She passed little groups of people sitting and lounging on the grass chatting and was distracted by the excited shrieks and laughter coming from the large boating lake. Diverting round the perimeter where oars dipped and splashed into the lake showering the boat occupants with water Saskia stopped beside the Science Museum building for a moment to watch retired gents and ladies in white trousers, skirts, blazers and Panama hats playing bowls before she eventually exited the park and crossed over the Great North Road.

Clayton Road was deserted and Saskia looked right and left before turning into the lane that ran behind the houses of Eslington Terrace.

Marking was ever the blight of any teacher's work load. It was time consuming and never ending. Henry sat at the kitchen table with a pile of assignments to assess. It was term time so John James was at school and Annie was teaching at the Girls' High School. He had just finished a cheese and chutney sandwich for lunch and dumped the plate in the sink when there was a knock on the back door. He could see through the net curtains that it was one of his students. This was not unusual, for Henry often conducted group and individual tutorials in his home as well as the odd social gathering. The students had free rein and it was always an excuse for a booze up. A policy he decided on long ago as a way of offering personal support for his students whilst helping him to get to know them as individuals and understand their hopes, ambitions, anxieties and worries.

He opened the back door to find Saskia standing on the door step. She was of medium height and slim, dressed in a yellow, orange and pink psychedelic mini-skirt with skin-tight, white pvc, knee length boots. She had the latest black mascara false eyelashes, long, straight brushed blonde hair and wore a tight, white, skinny ribbed sweater emphasizing her conical breasts and had a canvas bag slung over her left shoulder.

"Saskia...come in." Henry said trying his best to hide his anxiety and growing tension. "You've come just at the right time to give me an excuse not to spend the afternoon marking these papers. To what do I owe this pleasure? Pull up a chair and sit down."

Saskia clunked her bag on to the work top beside the sink and on removing a ring binder a bottle of red wine rolled out. "I thought that if we were going to have a heavy conversation then a glass or three of wine might oil the wheels so to speak," she said standing the bottle upright. "Don't get up I know where you keep the glasses." She opened one of the wall cupboards her mini-skirt riding up exhibiting what was left of her not too covered modesty as she stretched up for two glasses. With her back to him she poured two generous helpings and turned placing them on the table.

During his German music/composer/culture module Henry had inspired her, he thought, with his love of Wagner's music and was now in the process of discussing with her her proposals for a thesis for her Master's Degree. 'Wagner's Ring – A Journey of Personal Discovery.' It had the makings for a fascinating piece of research, completely different from his own political perspective but it had dredged up unbidden memories of Annie's interpretation which she had touched on in her brief conversation with Hitler at Bayreuth a life-time ago. Saskia's proposed thesis was that each of the characters in the Ring Cycle operas represented a facet of an individual's personal psychological make-up. And that the whole four operas were a journey of self-discovery. A quest to grow away from our collective unconscious primeval ego which thrives on chaos towards a harmonious, conscious understanding of mature love and self, to find a way of becoming the individual who really is himself.

"I presume you want to discuss some aspect of your research." Henry asked taking a long drink from his glass.

"Yes...I need you to be a sounding board...to see whether what I want to say.....strikes some truth with you.... shall we say."

"Okay, where do you want to start?" Henry invited.

"I want to endeavour to establish that all the characters in the four operas are archetypal representations of different aspects of human personality and that as such Wotan represents the core psyche and that the self is discovered only when man recognises his inner experience. In the opera, Wotan's striving for mastery of the world is not a deliberate attempt at political power as you argue in your book but is, I'm suggesting, an allegory for the ego's efforts to retain absolute power and authority within the personality."

"But isn't the end result the same," Henry suggested. "Power fades whether political or egotistical and empires eventually crumble and fall as indeed does Wotan's Valhalla castle in *Götterdämmerung*.

"Indeed......but it's no good securing authority, personal or political, against all possible attacks from outside. The real danger, I'll argue, comes from within Henry. Surely you of all people should know that. My central theme is individual personality....and....in this context if the ego wins the personality will be undeveloped and in the worst case scenario be damaged. Just like Valhalla. Buuut.....if the ego is unable to maintain control and can accept defeat freely then the whole personality will flourish. If man stays in his primeval, unconscious state then he is abdicating his human responsibility for himself and is heading not for reality but towards illusion and ultimately chaos and personality disintegration. It is not possible for man to enjoy a fulfilling existence without empathy and love in its widest meaning of joy in life itself....I think we need another glass of wine don't you?" Saskia suggested turning to the bottle on the work top. She refilled the glasses with her back to Henry then turned back and placed them on the table.

"To continue," she said looking at her notes. "You can't understand Wagner's tale without giving importance to his dependence on symbolism. Wotan roams the world searching for wisdom which he acquires by drinking from the fountain of wisdom and pays the price of an eye, turning his sight half inwards." Her voice hardening Saskia looked directly at Henry and continued, "Have you roamed the world looking for wisdom and personal salvation Otto? How did you end up here? Was the payment of your left eye sufficient to give *you* psychological insight into your actions?"

"Wohhha, wait a minute Saskia, I...I feel a bit woozy," Henry said with a moan. "I'm feeling a bit weak and you're becoming fuzzy.....I think that wine's gone straight to my head. Who...who...who's this Otto by the way? I....I don't know what you're talking about."

Saskia ignore Henry and continued, "Wotan carries a spear on which all his double-crossing dealings, scams and bargains are carved and is a metaphor for his will to defend, not his person, but his ego against being deflected from its purpose. It is the projection of his inner image of authority. What was your totem Otto von Lieper? What was the symbol of your destructive ego authority? Was it your SS ceremonial dagger or your Nazi banner with its ancient rune swastika at the centre? Or perhaps it was your aptly coloured black SS uniform with its death's head insignia and implied fear, cruelty and terror?"

"I...I...don't know what you're talking about....I've never felt like this before after only a couple of glasses of wine. Saskia....I feel so weak....Wh...wh...what's wrong with me?"

Saskia once again ignored Henry's questions and continued, "If you think about your own life and your own experience I'm convinced that there have been times when you've tried all sorts of deals, tricks, bargains and deceits even, to gain extrovert achievement, to get what you want, to keep control, to maintain your authority. The danger is Otto that if we continue to adhere to this illusory authority we build a huge wall around ourselves which blocks out the love, wisdom and those unconditional qualities which give meaning to our lives and humanity."

"Help Saskia...I...I'm not well."

"Here, take another sip of wine," Saskia suggested handing the glass to Henry.

"Did you deliberately decide to stay in your primeval state Otto or were you never given the opportunity to question your reason for living. Never allowed to explore those aspects of being which separates humans from animals, good from evil. Is that why you did what you did Otto?"

"I...I...don't know what you mean. Who is this Otto you keep mentioning?" Henry was now slouching on to the table for support. "I...I...don't understand what's happening to me."

"Chloral hydrate.....in the wine....courtesy of a boyfriend reading pharmacy. That's what's happening to you Otto. But don't worry, you won't feel anything, unlike your thousands of victims during the war. The chloral hydrate will only make you unconscious. It won't kill you. At least I hope not if I've got the dose right."

Realising that bluff was no longer an option Henry gasped, "How did you find me?"

"Sheer chance Otto or perhaps Devine providence whichever option you choose." Reaching behind her Saskia took a book from her bag. "Look...your photograph on the back of your book." And then opening her purse she produced two dog-eared, creased photographs one of a man wearing a rough woollen jacket the other of a young SS officer. "Recognise this man Otto?" She asked holding them next to the book back cover. "They're the photographs of a younger man but placed next to your book photograph it's unmistakeably the same person don't you think Otto?"

"Wh...wh...where did you get those photographs?" Henry asked with halting difficulty and trying to stretch out his hand.

"Remember the little photographer's shop in Oswiecim Otto, or rather Auschwitz as you Germans called it. You had some film taken there to be developed and printed in 1944 and then to cover your tracks you murdered the old photographer. Then you returned the next day and murdered his wife. But what you don't know is that it was all in vain Otto. You see Otto, my grandmother had made copies from the negatives she had cut from the strips and which you returned to claim the next day. But she had already given copies of these photographs as possible future evidence to their son, my father, who was fighting as a member of the Polish partisans."

"But I changed Saskia.....I realised what I was...what I had become.....I've *lived* it a thousand times in my mind Saskia....I repented and changed my life around.......I have lived the last twenty years towards atonement."

"That's the whole point Otto......YOU LIVED......How can you ever expect forgiveness for what you did Otto? It's time you paid for those thousands of lives with your own." Saskia spat out with venom. "There is no redemption for the likes of you Otto von Lieper."

Henry collapsed knocking his wine glass over and fell to the floor. His chair skittered across the kitchen. Saskia moved quickly whilst Henry was still unconscious. She pulled the gas cooker oven door down and dragged Henry towards it. Using all her hate, anger and adrenalin enhanced strength she hauled the upper half of Henry's body up onto the horizontal oven door placing his head as far inside the oven as she could muttering to herself, "It's not Zyclon 'B' Otto but at least you can have your own personal mini gas chamber." Using tea towels she blocked the bottom of the doors leading into the dining room and the garden then turned on the gas for the oven and all the hobs. On leaving the kitchen to enter hall she spotted the gas fire and turned that tap on too. It would get the job done quicker.

From inside the hallway Saskia pushed the mat up against the kitchen door to stop any gas leaking out. Then she made her way into the lounge. It was a large room with a high ceiling decorated with intricate plaster coving and central light surround. A black cast iron fireplace against the opposite wall was framed by original Victorian tiles and a heavy mahogany surround and mantle. Either side of the chimney breast in two alcoves were well stocked built-in book shelves. Saskia crossed to look at the books and spotted a Hi Fi turntable and two shelves crammed with L.Ps. She thumbed through the family collections and slid out one or two records to look at their covers before placing her choice on the turntable. She sank into one of the womb-like leather armchairs which was part of a three piece leather suite and closed her eyes as the opening River Rhine leitmotif 'E' flat major chords of Das Rheingold swelled and gradually flooded the room submerging Saskia in a world of Gods, giants, dragons and dwarfs.

The rasping of the stylus clicking through the speakers brought Saskia back to the present. She got up with a jerk, switched off the player and replaced the record making sure to wipe all the surfaces she'd touched. She crossed the hall and kicked the mat at the bottom of the kitchen door aside. She took a deep breath and placing her handkerchief against her mouth she moved quickly into the kitchen, switched off all the gas taps and opened the back door and the window above the sink to clear the air although it was important that for her plan some presence of gas remained. She moved with urgency and bending over Henry put her fingers to his carotid artery to confirm that there was no pulse. The chair Henry had been sitting on was still up ended on the floor and Saskia dragged Henry's body in to a position that looked like he'd collapsed off the chair by accident. Closing the oven door she moved to the sink where she washed and dried her wine glass and replaced it in the cupboard. She wiped the wine bottle and Henry's glass clean of her prints before pressed them into his hand a number of times making sure that his finger prints would be found. More wine was poured into the glass then the glass deliberately knocked over spilling the contents across the table top. Ensuring that all the surfaces she'd touched were wiped clear Saskia filled the kettle with water and put it on one of the hobs. She turned the gas on but didn't ignite the ring. One last look around the kitchen and Saskia was convinced that it was the scene of a dreadful accident. She left by the kitchen door and making sure that there was no one about walked down the empty Clayton Road to the corner of Osborne Road where she got on a trolley bus heading towards the Haymarket and the university campus.

Two weeks later the Newcastle Evening Chronicle reported the coroner's verdict as death by misadventure.

CHAPTER 26

Hazel 2010

I felt a tinge of guilt as I stood slightly apart observing the pathetically small gathering. I suppose it's the result of living so long. Old friends and contemporary relatives have already gone. It's not that we're unhappy, uninteresting people, quite the reverse actually. But here, on a cold autumn morning with a grey, backdrop water-filled sky, imparting a flat featureless monochrome landscape in whichever direction you look, it's difficult not to absorb the melancholy of the surroundings. The mist was seeping into my soul whilst at the same time imparting an atmosphere that descended on everything and everybody like a shroud. Rainwater cascaded from ill-fitting guttering and spouted out from the down-flow pipes flooding across the driveway. At least we're sheltered by a grey concrete roof which is supported by black metal pipes blistered where rust has burst through the paint like a lanced boil. The last of the summer flowers are discarded in a bedraggled, soggy pile waiting to be carted away to a compost heap I presume. As I edged back towards the small group of people individual wood-chips in the borders glistened where they caught the light from electric safety lamps in the roof over the walkway. I watched the hearse glide off into the gloom bearing with it the last memories of my Gran. My dad, John James, looks uncomfortable as he always does in group situations. He was not an unsociable person by any means but he always seemed to find it difficult to make small talk. I suppose it comes from years of being absorbed in textbooks and reading his non-fiction histories of the First World War. As a child it was ages before I discovered that his legs and head were joined together by a torso rather than a newspaper. The family in-joke was always that, 'He doesn't say much does he?' Mother on the other hand is her usual chatty self. How father and she have managed to stay together for almost 50 years is beyond me but they have a mutual love that's obvious for all to see. My husband, Simon, who's an even less sociable animal than dad, stands slightly aside trying to morph into the background. A great aunt whom I only know by name is in animated conversation with mum, but then mum could chat to anyone about anything. Members of the family who are missing included my brother Marcus, who because of work commitments had been unable to travel from Southampton and my great uncle Rupert and his wife Elspeth. Rupert was her step-brother and was in a nursing home in Suffolk suffering from Parkinson's. His wife Elspeth who, because of her own infirmities, couldn't possibly make the long journey north by herself. Another great aunt, Libby was visiting her daughter in Dublin. So here we are, husband Simon and me, mum Beth, dad John, and great aunt Rowena, two village friends of Annie's and two representatives from the nursing home gathered at the crematorium to give Gran not much of a big send off.

Gran suffered a stroke in 2003 and as a result had spent the last eight years in a nursing home. I suppose it's easy to criticise but the whole responsibility for Gran's financial affairs and visiting fell on mum and dad in particular who was her only son. Towards the end Gran's mind went and she could no longer recognise anyone or hold a coherent conversation. She was blind as a bat and deaf as a post so I guess that dad's visits must have been quite traumatic. Shortly after her massive stroke mum and dad had responsibility for clearing her house and putting it on the market to help pay for her nursing home care. No bequests or death duties there then. Simon and I live in Prague because of Simon's work and we just happened to be on a home visit when Gran passed away.

"This rain and mist is chilling my bones, I vote we go to a pub for something to eat. At least we'll be in the warm. The Miners' Arms is just up the road," ventured dad, interrupting my thoughts.

"It is lunchtime," mum added in her usual pragmatic way.

"Come on then," I said.

"I'll follow you. They do some nice food in The Miners' Arms," Rowena said knowingly being as she lived just four or five miles down the road in the other direction.

The pub was no more than half a mile away situated at the top of a hill with beautiful views over the River Derwent and Chepfield Forest on the other side of the valley, when it wasn't raining that is. It was just opening for the lunchtime trade as our cars pulled into the car park. As we entered the heat wrapped itself round us like a comfort blanket. The tables were already laid in the dining area and a welcoming wood fire crackled, smoked and spit in the hearth. Nineteenth and twentieth century black and white photographs of various local pits festooned the walls. Groups of miners with black faces peered out into the room through large, round, vacant white eyes. Pictures showing all aspects of life underground including pit ponies hard at work made fascinating viewing. Other sepia, cracked and scratched photographs recalled daily life in a mining village with shabbily dressed women hanging out washing, shopping or just sitting on wooden chairs or three-legged crackets gossiping to neighbours and scruffy kids playing football and marbles or spinning tops and chasing hoops down the road. A well-fingered ordnance survey map indicated the sites of dozens of local collieries. I found this very poignant being as there's now no longer any physical indication as to their previous existence. Except perhaps an occasional huge winding pulley set in concrete where the shaft used to be. Since the industry was decimated by successive governments the sites have been landscaped over but the villages and people left to wither away. Miners' lamps of different designs and vintage hung from the beams and various tools of the trade and pit pony harnesses were secured to what wall space was left.

"Well, what's everyone having to drink?" dad asked rubbing his hands together and eyeing up the choice of real ales lined up along the bar. Simon helped dad with the drinks whilst mum, Rowena and me took our coats off and sat down at a table nearest the fire. We scrutinised the large and varied menu, gave our orders to a pleasant young waitress and sat back waiting for the food to arrive.

"She'll be a big miss," Rowena said sipping her tonic water.

"Aye," dad replied, "She was a tough old bird. I really did expect her to get a telegram from the queen. Still, ninety-four's a bloody good innings. For someone who was interested in history she certainly lived through some momentous events. You know, she never had a day's illness in her life. What is it that they say; a creaking gate hangs the longest?"

"I don't really know much about her life dad," I said.

"I don't think any of us do pet," dad replied as the waitress put our food on the table. "Enjoy your meal," she said, flashing a big smile.

"She only gave away what she wanted to and as for the rest, well, it's a family mystery. As you know I've traced my side of the family history back to 1798 and a cousin of mine has gone back as far as 1646 but that's not our direct blood-line. Basically the family tree's just a list of dates, births, deaths, marriages and occupations. But with a bit of imagination and background reading I suppose you can flesh out your ancestors' existences, sort of bring them alive if you like. Are you really wanting to finding out about Gran's life?"

"It could be an interesting project if that T.V. programme is anything to go by. What's it called again? …. 'Who Do You Think You Are'".

"Yes, but they have loads of professionals to help and easy access to records not to mention unlimited funds to jet all over the world following up leads. On your own it could take ages."

"Maybe, but I'd still like to give it a try......it's just something I'd like to do."

The conversation continued to flow during the meal.

"Your dad and I spent a week in East Anglia researching my side of the family," mum added, "visiting towns and addresses we'd accessed from nineteenth century census forms on the computer. It was fascinating and gave me a kind of connection, an understanding of who I am and where I'm from. It's difficult to describe but I really, somehow, wanted my ancestors to understand that their lives had a purpose and that I owed my existence to them."

"Yeah, that's it, I want to connect, God knows the old bat was difficult enough to understand or get close to when she was alive so maybe I think I owe it to her now she's gone."

"I guess knowing where to start's the main problem. All I really know is that she was born in the November of 1916 two months after her father John James Horton...who I'm named after... your great grandfather, was killed in the battle of The Somme. Rhoda, your great grandmother married again to Robert Charlton and he brought up Annie as his own as well as having three other children with Rhoda, Libby, Rupert and Rowena here. By all accounts Robert was in the trench with John James when he was shot dead and Robert was taken prisoner in the same action that saw your great grandfather killed. He must have had quite an adventure in Germany because when he came back he could speak both German and Polish. That must account for Gran's early interest in languages and she went to Durham University with spells at The Sorbonne in Paris and Heidelberg University just before the Second World War. After graduating, for whatever reason, she joined the army but no one really knows what she actually did in the war, she never talked about it. Anyway, she met this Polish refugee in Germany after the war and they got married and here I am and there you are."

"There's bound to be some records of war service," Simon volunteered having served in the navy during the Falklands war.

"I seem to remember that Annie was in Germany for some time after the war ended working either for the war department, the government or something but what she was doing I've no idea," Rowena said. "Anyway, it caused quite a stir in the village when she arrived back home with a Polish husband. At least the gossip died down a bit because they'd changed their name from Harmanecki to Harman."

The waitress came to clear the table and asked, "Any more drinks?"

"Not for me thanks, I'm driving," dad replied.

"Me neither," Rowena added, "I'm absolutely full, it was lovely, it'll keep me going till supper time. Well, I'd better be on my way and remember John, don't be a stranger. At least next time we meet it won't be at two 'o' clock in the morning at the Queen Elisabeth Hospital."

"No indeed.... God I hope not..... but thanks for all your support over the past few weeks, it hasn't been easy."

"That's true but your mum was special you know John and after all, she was a mum to me too when Rhoda was too busy with the business. She brought Rupert and Libby up as well you know before she went off to university. I do think that our Libby could have made the effort to be here. You can fly direct from Dublin to Newcastle and Annie was her sister after all. Anyway let's not get into that." Rowena put her coat on and kissed mum and dad. "Stay in touch, and don't forget. Nice to meet you Simon and good luck with your project Hazel. Let me know if there's any skeletons to rattle. Bye."

"Bye."

Rowena pulled her coat tight against the rain, got into her little blue VW Polo and turned right out of the car park.

"I suppose we'd better be getting back as well. Here's the keys, you lot get into the car and I'll follow you after I've paid the bill."

We made our way back to Sunderland in the gloom the windscreen wipers swishing to and fro, now slow, now speeding up in the slipstream spray of lorries as they rumbled past on the other side of the road.

"There's that old tin box full of papers and letters we collected when we cleared out your mother's house. I've asked you a dozen times to sort through it but typical you, you just stuck it up in the loft and never got round to it." Mum said out of the blue.

I looked at Simon and smiled as dad said, "Is this going to be a five minute argument or a five hour one?"

"No it isn't going to be an argument at all unless you make it one. I was only just saying that there might be some information buried amongst all the rubbish which Annie hoarded all these years."

"Right I'll see if I can find it when we get back."

I looked at mum's tight-lipped, stony expression and as she caught my eye we both burst out laughing as bangs, crashes and curses assailed our ears coming down from the loft. It seemed ages before there was a loud thump and a profanity as dad fell from the loft ladder and yelled, "I've found it."

The four of us sat at the dining table as dad opened the rusty, battered old Huntley and Palmer's biscuit tin. He turned it upside down and papers, bills, receipts, identity cards, ration cards, post cards, an old purse, scruffy wallet and dozens of photographs and letters cascaded across the table and falling onto the carpet.

"It's going to take ages to read all of these," I said.

"Well, if you're serious about this project of yours you'd better take the box with you and then you can go through it in your own time," dad suggested.

"Maybe we should save some time and sort them into separate piles now which we can prioritise," Simon suggested.

"Good idea."

Hands skimmed and shuffled across the table from all directions gathering together photos in one pile, letters in another and miscellaneous papers in another but my attention was drawn to one letter in front of me and I couldn't resist reading it there and then. "Wow, listen to this. It's dated October 1914 and it's addressed to great grandma Rhoda.

Dear Rhoda,

Only a line hoping you are in the best of health as it leaves me the same and there is one thing I want to ask you and I hope you will not be vexed. The Sunday night I was at Chepfield I saw you and you would not speak to me. What have I done to you? You left me and went to the one you loved best and I stood out of the way and said nothing. I was very down hearted but I stood it all. But I know John James had more right to you than I had, but Rhoda dear, you might always give me a smile and a cheering word if you did not love me. I love you but I need not say any more. You said you would not marry a Catholic. But Rhoda dear I always thought you would give me a kind word and I think many times of the walks we had and the tears I lost, but by the way Rhoda I gave you a choice and I am a fellow that reasons on anything and Rhoda I thought it over and it was best for you to do what you did by giving me up and I will say no more and Rhoda dear, don't go past without speaking.

Sincerely Yours, Harry.

"Grief, how sad is that? Poor Harry has the hots for great grandma who won't marry a Catholic and gives her heart to great granddad John James. It's very Mills and Boon isn't it but it does feel a bit spooky prying into someone else's private life even though it was nearly a hundred years ago?

"I suppose it just proves that affairs of the heart never change, except for marrying Catholics that is," dad chuckled. "Although it was still a big issue in the village even when I was a lad."

"There's dozens of letters here all written with dip pen and ink in spidery copper plate writing. This is going to be more fun than I thought. I can't wait to really get started," I said idly picking up a dog-eared, creased, stained post card. The writing in pencil was faded but still legible – just. It was addressed to Rhoda Horton, Mersey Street, Chepfield, Newcastle-upon-Tyne, England. On the other side at the top was printed in a gothic script, **Wahn Kriegegefangerlarge.** As I tried to decipher the message written below the heading I could scarce contain my excitement and shrieked out loud.

"What's the matter?" Mum yelled.

"You're never going to believe this but this is a post card from Robert to Rhoda written in 1916. It's been sent from a Prisoner of War Camp in Germany. Just a minute and I'll try to read it out to you." Where the pencil had faded beyond legibility I tilted the card against the light where the indentations of the words were still discernible.

Dear Rhoda, I expect by now you have heard the sad news about J. J. I am so sorry. I was with him & you can rest assured that he did not suffer. I am well & in a P.O.W. camp in Germany. Good luck & I'll see you after the war. All my love, Robert.

"My God, you don't think that they were having an affair behind great granddad's back do you?"

"Who can tell? But I don't think so," dad replied. "As far as I'm aware J. J. and Robert were the best of marras but more importantly this is your first real piece of evidence from the period and must be a good starting point for you."

Unlike Gran, languages was never my strong point but I did know that *Krieg* was German for war and that a *'large'* was a camp so it didn't take a detective to work out that Robert's P.O.W. camp was at a place called Wahn. I was one jump ahead and already had my Blackberry in my hand googling 'Wahn'. "Apparently Wahn was a big POW camp just south of Cologne." I said.

"Why don't we stop off there on our drive back to Prague," Simon offered.

"Could we?" I replied scarcely containing my excitement.

"No problem. We have to drive across Germany anyway and we can stop over at Cologne instead of Frankfurt. It's not really out of our way. We can ask around and find out what we can."

CHAPTER 27

Hazel 2010

Parked in the queue of cars at the terminal in Newcastle waiting to board the DFDS Seaways ferry for Amsterdam I turned to Simon laughing and said, "Dad's a cynical bugger but he's right you know, old farts who drive Volvos do all have beards, thick rimmed glasses and wear Jesus sandals, not forgetting their wives with Laura Ashley shapeless dresses." I think the couple standing beside their Volvo in front of us knew that we were talking about them because they stared with disdain just that little bit too long before sniffing and turning away to point at something on the other side of the river. "Yeah, motor home drivers and caravanners, the blight of the universe, all wear cheap, crumpled Sports Direct tee shirts and Bermuda shorts and display varicose veins on their fat little legs. And that's just the women. At least 'Volvo Man' wears tasteful socks with his sandals if he wears them at all." Simon added making a good imitation of dad's northern accent. By the time we'd stopped laughing the queue had started moving forward and it wasn't long before we were up on deck looking down at a dark, choppy River Tyne making its turgid way out to sea on the turn of the tide.

Where once ocean-going liners and battleships had been built we glided past derelict slipways and sad-looking shipyards eking out an existence by repairing and renovating damaged North Sea oil-rigs. The fish quay at North Shields, once a thriving industry with hundreds of fishing vessels looked empty and neglected due to EU regulations and was overlooked by a yuppie housing development on the other side of the river. South Shields with its maritime history now just an ancient memory slipped silently by whilst the huge statue of Lord Collingwood of Trafalgar fame high on the northern river bank stared out blankly, seemingly in confusion and despair. As we sailed over the bar the ancient monument of Tynemouth Priory slowly receded and the coastline quickly mutated into a grey slash across the horizon.

We had a pleasant enough but very expensive dinner, for what it was, and then retired to the Commodore lounge away from the Geordie trippers who were determined to drink the bar dry and party the night away. After an unsettled night we were up early, washed, dressed and finished breakfast just as the ferry was approaching Ijmuiden, the port for Amsterdam. Simon and I had lived in Amsterdam for a while because of Simon's work but this was a part of the city with which we were unfamiliar. When we'd finally disembarked I parked up on the quay and Simon set the sat-nav for Wahn. I enjoy driving and fortunately Simon was quite happy to sit back and let me get on with it. Dad taught me to drive and I think that I've inherited more than a little of his impatience with other less competent drivers. His little helpful sayings have stayed with me all this time, like 'slow car, fast wheel' in a three point turn and his favourite 'wherever there's a bus there's always a bus stop' as idiots following too close to the bus in front would hold up a whole queue of traffic when the bus pulled in to drop off or collect passengers. By 10.30 we were striking out on the A1 and heading for Cologne. The traffic was heavy and speed limits rigorously enforced. The German autobahns were also busy and contrary to popular myth are only de-restricted in certain sections so that it was late afternoon before we finally reached Wahn, south of Cologne. "I'm, really feeling tired now. Can we find an hotel and do some ferreting around in the morning?" I said.

"Everywhere will be closed by now anyway," Simon answered fiddling with the Tom Tom trying to locate the nearest decent hotel.

The next morning, refreshed by a good night's sleep and a hearty breakfast we climbed into our BMW, X5 and eased our way out into the morning traffic. "From what I've seen on Google Earth and read on the internet I think that the best idea might be just to drive generally round the area getting our bearings and suss out the general lie of the land. What do you think?"

"I agree," Simon replied, "being as the POW camp was based on or near today's airport maybe we should circle the airport perimeter and take it from there. Turn off right at the next intersection into Grengeler Mauspfad and follow the L284."

"Shit!"

"What's the matter?" Simon quickly replied with concern.

"A bloody Porsche right up my backside, that's what. We all want to get past the bloody lorry you idiot," I shouted. "Wait your turn, sitting on my chuff isn't going to get you there any quicker."

We circled clockwise on to the K20 Rambusch and finally into Alte Kolner Strasse. "It's a busy airport isn't it?" I volunteered.

"Yeah, but not too built up around here though," Simon replied. "Surprisingly there's a lot of trees and open countryside. Look there's a guy in uniform up ahead pull in and we'll ask him for some directions or information."

"*Guten tag,*" I ventured in my best GCSE German, "*Wie geht's? Können Sie mir helfen? Sprechen Sie Englisch?* Hello, how are you, can you help me please?"

"*Guten tag, danke, es geht mir gut. Ja Ich kan ein bisschen Englisch sprechen.* Good day, I'm okay thank you. Yes I can speak a little English. How can I help you?"

"I hope so," I replied. "My great grandfather was taken prisoner during the First World War and was kept here at Wahn prisoner of war camp. Do you know where the camp was?"

"Well....yes....in a way I do," the uniform replied thoughtfully. "It was a very long time ago of course and there have been many changes. I am based here at Cologne – Wahn Luftwaffe Barracks in those buildings over there and they are part of the old place but all of the camp and most of the old prisoner barracks have been destroyed. When the war ended, the camp was taken over by the Luftwaffe and then after the next war it was occupied by the RAF for a time. Now we have it back."

"Do you know if there are any written records?"

"I do not know but if anything survives you will probably find it in the Cologne Archive but I have to tell you that the building collapsed in 2009 and many records were lost. We do have a memorial to the prisoners but it is inside the camp and is....how do you say in English.... out of bounds to civilians. I would like to take you there but it is forbidden. But I will say to you that we have a parade there every year, like your remembrance day, where we remember the dead. We Germans remember our past enemies and honour them in a military ceremony. You have a camera, perhaps?"

"Yes I do," I replied opening the car door and taking the digital compact out of the glove box.

"I have a few minutes. If you can wait I will go back into the barracks and take a picture of the memorial for you if you like."

"Oooh! Would you? That would be great...that would be very kind of you."

"Wait here and I'll be five minutes."

The uniform turned round and quickly disappeared through the large wrought iron barracks gateway.

"Wow, how lucky is that," I said giving Simon a big squeeze.

"Yeah...well you're certainly on a mission now aren't you?" Simon replied with a smile.

As promised the uniform returned within five minutes and handed over the camera. "I hope these are good for you," he said.

With childlike enthusiasm I exclaimed, "Wow, they're great," as I studied each image showing different views of the dark granite, austere memorial with the imperial eagle carved in relief and an inscription in old Gothic script. Then I noticed the scattered, weathered wreaths and frayed national flags which instead of being in remembrance seemed a metaphor emphasising a sad, forgotten generation and lent a sombre ambience to the pictures. Suddenly I became aware of a voice punctuating my thoughts,

"There is something else I can do for you?" The uniform asked.

"Errr No. You've been very kind and helpful and we don't want to take up any more of your time. We can't thank you enough and once again you've been very helpful. We're ever so grateful. *Vielen Dank und Auf wiedersehen"*

"Auf wiedersehen und viel Glück.
Goodbye and good luck"

"Interesting…. but it looks like a trip into Cologne," I said as I clipped my seat belt up.

"Let's see if we can park up near the Archive and have some lunch before we get our hands dirty on dusty book shelves in the dungeons." Simon suggested with fake coughing and spluttering.

"Can I help you?" a large, official, middle aged lady asked from behind a long reception counter which displayed various European national flags presumably indicating the languages spoken. "My name's Frau Krantz"

"Yes, I hope so," I said, "Do you have any records from the First World War? I'm interested in the prisoner of war camp that was at Wahn just south of here but I expect that any records were probably all destroyed during the Second World War."

"Well….actually," Frau Krantz replied sounding quite miffed, "Most of the district records survived the bombing because they were taken away into safe keeping. As you can appreciate we are very short of storage space and some of the records have been outsourced. Others have been transferred to microfilm and are stored at the Barbarastollen caves in Oberried in the Black Forest. Take a seat and give me a moment to find out where your record interest might be."

We sat down and I turned to Simon, "Do you believe in national stereotypes?" I asked.

"Don't even go there," he replied diplomatically.

Frau Krantz returned ten minutes later and waved us over to the counter. "I think that you might be lucky," she said. "Follow me."

After negotiating lifts, stairs and endless corridors we entered a large room furnished with rows and rows of steel shelving and storage cabinets on rollers manoeuvred by large black wheels on the end of each row. "What exactly are you looking for?" Our guide asked.

I told her and after consulting a computer screen she led us to one of the archive shelves and took down a cardboard box containing a collection of musty files. She carried the box into an ante- room and placed it on a table. "Obviously for security reasons I cannot allow you to stay in the archive room by yourselves but you are welcome to stay in here and look through the files for as long as you like. Would you like to me to stay and help you with translation?"

"That would be very kind," I replied, "My German is not very good and certainly not good enough to understand the old Gothic script."

"Where do you want me to start," Frau Krantz asked more softly or perhaps it was just me beginning to warm to her.

"Well….I know that my step great grandfather was captured in November 1916. I have a post card dated just before Christmas 1916 sent to England from Wahn Kriegegefangerlarge."

"Okay, I presume your great grandfather was English because I know that Wahn was a vast camp housing mainly French, Polish and Russian prisoners as well as English and other nationalities. At least that will narrow the search down. We can search the camp registrations from November onwards until hopefully we come across your ancestor."

I watched as she rummaged through the box for a few minutes before lifting out two dirty, creased files containing hundreds of paper records. "What was your ancestor's name?"

"Robert Charlton," I replied, "In the Durham Light Infantry if that's any help."

I could feel myself becoming tense with excitement as she turned endless pages of dog-eared yellowing record papers. Her fingers ran down lists of names, sheet after sheet until finally slowing and stopping at one entry in particular. In that instant my heart skipped a beat and I crossed my fingers. There in a faded, spidery, almost unintelligible scrawl was the name Robert Charlton. "Wow! He's here Simon," I shouted, "Oops! Sorry Frau Krantz," I said putting my hand to my lips.

"That's Okay," she replied, "I can imagine that this is quite exciting for you. Let me see," she continued. "Ah ha! He was a farmer, your great grandfather yes?"

"Yes," I replied, "Well actually he's my step great grandfather because my real great grandfather was killed in the same action that

Robert Charlton was captured. He later married my real great grandmother and brought up my grandmother as his own child. Sounds complicated doesn't it?"

Frau Krantz ignored my last remark and continued to scrutinize the records. She seemed to capture my intoxication when she let her formality slip and shouted, "Look, here….in December 1916 he was released from the camp and given into the custody of a Generalleutnant Albrecht von Lieper and here is a record of a travel warrant issued for a train journey to Ciechanow in Poland."

"My God," I whispered in absolute amazement. "So it's true, that's how he managed to speak Polish as well as German."

"Well I can't help you with that," Frau Krantz said, "That's all the information that we have here. I think that you have been very fortunate."

"Yes, I think we have. Thank you so much. You have been so helpful I can't thank you enough. It's absolutely amazing."

"I'm pleased to have been of help. Good luck with the rest of your search. I expect that you will have to continue your journey to Poland but if I can offer you some more advice you can go to Berlin where you might find out some information about von Lieper. With a 'von' and his high army rank it sounds as if he might have been a land owning Junker originating from Prussia."

"Slow down," Simon said, as the adrenaline was pumping and I dragged him back to the BMW. "If you think we're going to Berlin now you've got another think coming. I've got to go to work tomorrow and you'll just have to hold your horses until my next holiday."

We set the sat-nav and left Cologne on the E32 heading for Zahrebska, Prague via Frankfurt and Nuremburg.

CHAPTER 28

Hazel 2011

This was not going to be as easy as I'd first thought. I admitted to myself that we'd been very fortunate with our initial information from Cologne. Now that we'd returned home to Prague I was back at work lecturing and setting up a post-graduate psychology course for New York University Outreach College for American students in Prague. When not engaged in my university work there was my voluntary counselling commitment to fulfil at the student health centre as well as my paid professional counselling at a medical practice in Prague city centre.

The summer heat in Prague can be very debilitating for those of us who were brought up with chilly winds blowing off the North Sea at 'sunny' Roker even in the hottest of summers. I was lounging on the balcony of our penthouse apartment never tiring of looking out over the hills that made up the Prague skyline, laptop open, when I heard Simon come in from work. I heard him kick off his shoes, drop his rucksack and go up to the bathroom for a shower.

"I'll be with you soon when I smell a bit sweeter," he yelled down.

Within a few minutes I could hear his flip-flops slapping their way down the wooden stairs.

"Had a good day?"

"Oh…the usual. I wish these Czech workers didn't have to be told what to do all the time. They'll do exactly what's asked of them but then they'll down tools and wait to be told what to do next instead of using their initiative."

"I expect that's the left-overs from the communist system."

"Yeah….maybe but some of them'll be out of a job if they don't buck up."

"Look, it's too hot to cook why don't we go up to the Zanzibar restaurant and have something al fresco?"

"Good idea, come on, let's go."

We lived in the residential district of Prague 2 and the Zanzibar, a popular restaurant with the locals, was situated in a square at the top of our street. Being outside the tourist areas the roads were not busy. It wasn't so much a square in the usual sense but was a large junction where five cobbled roads met with a large fountain roundabout in the centre. Sitting at a table outside the restaurant the spray from the fountain seemed to have a cooling effect on the atmosphere but it might just have been my imagination. Nevertheless it was certainly calming to hear the water spouting from dolphins' mouths with their soporific splashes. The only downside was the constant cigarette smoking that afflicted both young and old Czechs and which was one of the reasons why Simon and I always sat outside. We were regulars by now and were greeted with smiles and shown to a table. We ordered a cold white wine each and waited for our food.

"I've been giving our quest some thought," I said.

"Oh yes," Simon replied with suspicion, "Your quest....and what have you decided?"

"Well, I've looked on the net and there appear to be dozens of different archives in Berlin. I suppose I could telephone or email each one but that's going to take up a lot of time and besides half the fun of this project is to go and visit in person." "Yeah....go on," Simon said suspiciously.

"It appears that almost all the important German archives have been re- housed in a new building at Koblenz."

"Yeeees......" Simon replied knowing what was coming next.

"Can we go......to Koblenz. It's on the Rhine and you know that you've always wanted to do a Rhine cruise," I wheedled.

"As it happens.....as if you didn't know....I've got a few days holiday owing so if you can organise your schedule I'll fix it up with my boss and we can go next week.....hopefully. How's that sound?"

We left the suburbs of Prague on the E50 and pointed the X5 west in the direction of Plzen. It never ceases to amaze me how many miles you can crunch travelling on the dual carriageways sweeping over the vast forested landscape of east Europe. We drive straight through the old border crossing between the Communist Czech Republic and East Germany, a vast concrete area where nature, in the form of grass and weeds, is doing its best to erase the follies of human distrust and misunderstanding. The large number of customs and passport lanes and guardhouses like rows of huge starting gates at a horse race are still delineated by bent rusting steel bars set in cracked concrete. We sweep on towards Nuremberg, the X5 revelling in stretching its limbs on the autobahn. Even on these almost empty motorways you need to keep an eye on your rear view mirror because no matter how fast you're going there's always someone much faster coming up behind you. The German driver is used to this and you're never held up or blocked. I find myself agreeing with dad who always says that every British driver should experience travel on an autobahn in a seriously fast motor just to appreciate what it's like then perhaps we wouldn't get the little Englander attitude where lane discipline is unheard of or the 'you're not getting past me you flash git in your BMW' attitude which is frustratingly all too prevalent on our motorways. Eventually we skirt Frankfurt and head for Koblenz where we find an hotel for the night.

We leave the car in the hotel car park and walk to the Bundesarchiv which is situated not far away on Potsdammer Strasse. It's an impressively large, modern glass and aluminium structure glinting in the morning sun. We walk up to the long reception counter in the entrance hall and introduce ourselves to a smartly dressed young woman.

"*Guten Tag.*"

"*Guten Tag.....*I hope you can help me?"

"We can try," Petra replied in perfect English pointing to her name badge.

"I'm trying to find some information on a First World War German officer, Prussian we think, called Generalleutnant Albrecht von Lieper."

"Hummmm! I'm afraid I'm going to have to disappoint you already. Virtually all Prussian military records dating back to the middle of the nineteenth century were destroyed in Potsdam, Berlin during a USA bombing attack in 1945. There were only a few records that survived but these have never been cross referenced or recorded. It's an impossibility I'm afraid. In any case you would need to know his regiment."

Petra could see the disappointment in my body language. "I'm sorry not to be able to be of more help. Is the officer a relative?"

"Not exactly," I reply, "But he is very closely connected with my family."

"Just a minute and I'll see if one of the older and more experienced archivists can offer a suggestion. Take a seat and I'll be back in a moment."

"Well at least we've got the Rhine cruise to look forward to so it's not going to be a complete waste of time."

"Don't be too disappointed," Simon said in consolation, "I always thought that it was a long shot and when you see those old photographs of flattened German cities after the war it's surprising that anything at all has survived."

I watched the constant stream of people entering and leaving the building wondering if they were all on a fruitless mission like me. I saw

Petra coming back to the counter, nudged Simon and we walked over to where she was waiting.

"You might just be in luck," she said with a smile. "At least it might provide another little piece in the jigsaw for you, *Ja!*"

"Anything," I begged, "Anything at all would be fantastic."

Petra continued, "Apparently....and I didn't know about this... there are a series of books, registers called 'Rangliste der Königlich Preussischen Armee.' The entries are not originals but are limited copies which have been updated over the years. There is a good chance that your von Lieper, provided that he was, as you say, a Prussian officer, might be there. Again unfortunately the registers are not alphabetical and you really need to know his regiment, place or district of enlistment and dates of service."

Once again Petra witnessed my disappointment.

"But there are still some avenues open to you. Once you find out his regiment you can try to access the Regimentskirchenbucher, the regimental church register or the Garnisianskirchenbucher, the Garrison church register which probably will list birth, marriage and death..... This might be, how do you say, clutching at straws," she continued, "but all officer wounds were recorded. If von Lieper was wounded, and there's probably a good chance that he was, you can research in that direction. The records are held at," Petra scanned the piece of paper she was holding, "Ah! Yes, here it is, Deutsches Bundesarchiv, Militararchiv, Wiesental Strasse, 10, D-85356, Freiburg. His military pension records could be there as well. If you write or email with all the information you already have they may be able to trace him and fill in the missing details for you. I think in the circumstances this is probably your best way forward. I'm sorry I couldn't be of any more help to you." Petra said genuinely.

"No, thank you very much...at least we haven't come to a complete dead end yet. Thank you for your time and help."

"My pleasure *und Viel Glück* with your search."

Feeling a bit shell-shocked we dodged into a little café for a snack whilst we tried to absorb all that Petra had told us. Feeling refreshed after a cold meat and cheese salad and a glass of Rhine white wine, we left the café and took a taxi to the Rhine ferry pier and bought a return trip to Rudesheim am Rhine. It was a sensible system where you could travel in one direction on the boat and back on a train or vice versa. We scrambled on board and managed to find a seat on a bench at a table where a crowd of Germans were already half way to being happily paralytic. Simon moved off to buy two steins of beer just as the boat slipped its moorings. The Rhine valley is a super highway of trade with roads and railways flanking both sides of the river which is confined in a steep gorge. We passed barge after barge carrying minerals, cars and other industrial produce. Pleasure boats speeded past with much good-natured waving and shouting. As the ferry made its way up river the steep green banks were covered with ranks of grape vines. Ruins of medieval castles perched high up on precarious rock outcrops lent belief in the Twilight of the Gods. We knew the mythology of the Lorelei maidens whose hypnotic singing lured Rhine sailors to their deaths on the rocks but we were not prepared for what happened as the ferry manoeuvred its precarious way round the sharp bend in the river which negotiated the Lorelei rocks. Instantaneously our drunken German companions and many more on other benches at other tables on our deck broke out in the Lorelei song swaying side to side with their steins and wine glasses threatening to spill their contents over everyone. There was nothing to do but join in or be pushed off the end of our bench. It was great fun. It was difficult not to be sucked into the history and mystery of Germany's Teutonic past and the whole trip was a magical experience.

We stepped off the ferry at Rudesheim, and walked round the old town and market with all the other tourists. The buildings and streets were pristine and very pretty but a little too twee in a chocolate box way for my liking. But it did bring back memories and I showed Simon where I'd played my flute in the school orchestra whilst on an exchange visit twenty-three years ago.

Having seen more castles in one day than we'd seen in a lifetime we climbed wearily on to the train for Koblenz and were more than pleased when we eventually opened the door to our hotel bedroom.

Back home I rushed to the door and scrutinised the post for weeks after we returned from Koblenz. On those days when I left for work before the post had arrived I'd rush into the apartment to extricating envelopes which had become jammed under the door as I entered. Just when I was about to give up, one day the letter box rattled as usual but this time an A4 brown envelope with German postage stamps fluttered on to the wooden floor in the hallway. My hands were shaking so much I could hardly hold the envelope to open it. I ripped it open without ceremony and inspected the enclosed papers. Initially scanning the documents I couldn't help whooping out loud with delight as I took in the information. Generalleutnant Albrecht von Lieper was indeed wounded. The records showed that he had been wounded in the shoulder by shrapnel at Brigade headquarters behind the lines on 15 November 1916, the same day that Robert Charlton had been taken POW and John James my real great grandfather had been killed. It was all here. What a fantastic coincidence, they all must have been in the same action but on opposite sides. Albrecht von Lieper was born in April 1871 on his father's estate at Schwersez near Poznan. His next of kin was his wife, Katharina von Lieper née Klaus and at the time of his wound his address was given as Chrzanowo Estate, Chrzanowek, near Ciechanow, Poland. As a General Lieutenant, von Lieper was in command of the 2nd Guards Infantry Division. The jigsaw pieces were beginning to come together. Now that I had more detailed information I could refine my internet searching. I couldn't wait for Simon to come home from work to tell him the good news. I virtually jumped on him as he came through the door that evening.

"This is getting more like Dan Brown's Da Vinci Code every week," he said in response to my enthusiasm.

"I've been on the net again and apparently in Poland records are kept in civic registers, Urzad Stanu Cywilnego located in the Town Halls. That's the good news, the bad news is that many civic registers from Western Prussia have been removed by the Russians. I think I'll email details to the Civic Centre in Ciechanow requesting any information at all on the von Lieper family and see what we get back."

"You're like a terrier with a rat. I can sense a trip to Poland coming on. At least here in Prague we're pretty well central for gadding about Europe."

This was just too good to be true. Two weeks later I opened my emails and there was one from Poland with a number of attachments. I almost spilled my laptop onto the floor in my excitement. The first attachment was a death certificate for a Heinrich von Lieper aged 18 years killed on the River Marne 1914. The second attachment was also a death certificate, this time for a Walther von Lieper also aged 18 years killed near Amiens in 1918. These could only have been Katharina's two sons both lost in the war. The third attachment was a copy of Albrecht von Lieper's death certificate which registered he had been shot in 1919 in Berlin but the body had been sent back to Prussia by his wife Katharina and this time her address was given as Simsee Farm, Riedering, Rosenheim, Near Munich, Bavaria. Poor woman, she lost her husband and two sons all within just over four years. What was intriguing was the address given on Albrecht's death certificate. The two sons were registered at Ciechanow where Katharina was living during the war. I could only make an educated guess that being as all of her family was dead there was nothing left for her but to return to her own parents' house in Bavaria. Assuming that, as in England, weddings take place in the parish of the bride a search of parish records in Bavaria might confirm my suspicions. Another garden path.

Here at least was my first real positive lead since Wahn definitely linking Robert with Albrecht von Lieper and Poland. I just had to check this out. Katharina and Bavaria would have to wait their turn. Simon came back home at his usual time and I bounced into the hall to greet him.

"Okay, where are we off to now," he said with little real enthusiasm.

I suppose it was rather selfish of me to spring it on him after a hard day at work in 33 degrees temperature.

"Sorry...I should at least let you get your feet through the door and have a shower before bouncing on you but this latest info is amazing."

When we'd settled on the balcony with a cold beer we started to plan a trip to Ciechanow in Poland to try to establish exactly where the von Lieper estate was. Maybe there would be someone local who could tell us something. It was another long shot but so far they all seemed to have hit their targets. I had a good feeling about this trip as well.

Simon hardly ever took time off from work so fortunately he had accrued quite a few holiday days owing. The route to Ciechanow looked pretty straight forward and once again we found ourselves leaving Prague on another adventure but heading east this time. Considering that it's only twenty years since the communists left Czechoslovakia the new investment in the infrastructure can be seen everywhere but nowhere more than in the number of new wide dual carriageways spreading out into the country in all directions. Our journey was about 350 miles passing through Lodz and Warsaw, a little more than from Newcastle to London. Traffic was light so once again I just set the cruise control on the X5 and sat back relaxing in the ease with which we swallowed up the miles.

It was late afternoon by the time we parked up outside the Town Hall in Ciechanow. It was a beautiful neo-gothic white and cream building with a clock tower rising from the centre of the front elevation. We entered and approached a desk manned by a man in a uniform. I was pleased to see that the man was young because there would be a good chance that he would have some understanding of English. The older generation I suspected, as in the Czech Republic, probably learnt Russian in school as their second language.

"Hello, do you speak English?"

"Yes, I have a little....can I help you?"

"I want to find an estate, a large farm at Chrzanowo, it was owned by a German called Albrecht von Lieper during the First World War."

"I show you on map," the young man said and he disappeared into an office behind his desk. Unfolding the map he pointed with his finger and continued, "You leave Ciechanow, this road, Pultuska and go to Chrzanowek Topolowa, here. You find Chrzanowo to south. Big estates were made smaller farms for many farmers by communists after war. Nazis take farms from Russians and Poles and give to Germans. No big farms left. Be difficult for you I think."

"Thank you very much, you have been very helpful," I said turning to leave the building but the young man stopped me and handed me a tourist folder.

"You take guide to city, very interesting. You find name of roads here," and he drew with a biro our route out of the city. "I hope you enjoy our city."

"Thank you, you've been very kind."

We sat in the car looking through the brochures and Simon, pragmatic as usual, suggested, "You've driven a long way, why don't we book in at an hotel now?" And pointing to one in the brochure, the Hotel Baron, he continued, "This one looks okay and it's just round the corner. We can have an early dinner and then, if you're up for it we can walk round the main tourist spots leaving all tomorrow to look for this farm and then drive back to Prague."

There was still plenty of warm summer evening sun left as we made our way to the Jewish cemetery. According to the tourist guide, in 1939, just before the German invasion of Poland, the population of Ciechanow was 20,000 and 45% were Jews. Of course I knew that there were Jewish areas in most cities in Europe but it seemed incredible to consider that half the town was made up of Jews. Needless to say that this percentage didn't last long once the Nazi death squads started work. The cemetery was simply an open field now. Headstones were removed after the war for building development and were retrieved along with some remains and these were placed inside a monument in what had been the centre of the cemetery. The monument looked sad and neglected surrounded as it was with a rusty wrought iron fence sections of which were leaning in different directions, weeds curling round the iron posts as if trying to drag themselves up out of the sadness in which they were rooted. Even more depressing were the soviet flats that ringed the field and probably still had bodies under them. Grey, ugly, architecturally featureless concrete domestic buildings that blight every former Russian occupied city. We walked on towards the Castle Mazovia which was built in the fourteenth century. It looked massively solid and impregnable standing on the riverbank. It was a large square plan with four high, thick red brick walls. At two corners were massive round towers with slit windows. The roof had collapsed and been looted for timber ages ago so that all that remained was the square shell. The guide brochure informed us that during the war the city's Jews had been rounded up here before being transported to Treblinka and Auschwitz concentration camps and Polish partisans had been hanged inside the castle. I turned to Simon saying, "It seems that wherever you go in Eastern Europe the hand of Nazi Germany appears to cast a depressingly black shadow."

"Maybe that's just because of the quest you're on," Simon replied. "You're following the trail of a soldier so it's probably no surprise that you're been directed towards areas where soldiers have left their footprints."

"You're probably right, but I hope this journey doesn't become too depressing. I suppose we're really a very lucky generation. My great grandfather and grandfather both took part in a world war each and I haven't been touched by war. Except for you of course who was involved in the Falklands but I didn't know you then."

Simon didn't reply and I didn't press him.

There was already heat in the morning sun as Simon set the satnav for Topolowa. The device directed us down Pultuska Street as the official in the Town Hall had suggested and steered us towards Chrzanowek. We were not sure where to go next and decided to drive around in the countryside near Chrzanowo and Topolowa to see if we could locate anything that looked like an estate house or farm. It seemed an impossible task as we circled round and round making frequent diversions down single cart tracks and I was grateful for our 4 wheel drive.

I sensed his frustration as Simon said, "We're getting nowhere fast here. Topolowa's a real one horse village but I spotted a little bar in the main street, well, I mean, only street, why don't we stop in there for a drink and ask for help?"

"Okay," I agreed.

It was nearly lunchtime as we ducked our heads and stepped down into the little bar. It was a leaning, warped wooden building from a bygone age with a low wooden beamed ceiling, barrels for tables and a ceramic tiled stove and flue in one corner. Through smarting eyes, because of the cigarette smoke, I could make out two old men playing draughts with a third looking on. An empty bottle of Polish vodka stood sentinel beside three small glasses. Two other old men were sitting smoking beside the unlit stove and a further old man sitting on a high stool in the corner beside the small bar. As we walked in they all stopped what they were doing and gave us a look of suspicion like cowboys in a western film as strangers, spurs jangling, entered the saloon.

Simon pointed at a beer tap on the bar and held up two fingers. The barman, younger than his clients, filled two glasses with cold lager.

"Do you speak English please," I asked.

He didn't reply but pointed and nodded his head towards the draughts spectator.

"Excuse me please, but do you speak English?"

"I have a little," he replied with a thick accent. "I help you?"

"Yes please...I want to find a farm near here that belonged to a German officer in 1918." I wrote this down on a piece of paper and continued, "His name was Albrecht von Lieper and his wife was called Katharina I think."

"You are German," the man asked in what I thought was a threatening manner.

"No, English," I replied and I saw his face muscles relax.

He turned to his companions and conversed in Polish for a while before turning back towards me. Picking up the empty bottle he turned it upside down and shaking it over one of the empty glasses gave me a knowing look and smiled."

I nudged Simon and he went to the bar and bought another bottle of the same brand vodka. The Pole said something to the barman and he gave Simon two more glasses. Two stools were made available and we were motioned to sit down. The old Pole pointed to his chest and said, "My name Stanislav."

"I'm Hazel and this is my husband Simon."

We shook hands all round and Stanislav poured out five glasses of vodka. I could guess what was coming as we all chinked glasses and the Poles downed their drinks in one.

"I learn to speak English in shipyards at Gdansk but I too old and come home now. Long time ago my grandmother tell me about her mother Maria and father Tamas working at the big house. The German officer was a bastard but his wife was very kind to my great grandmother."

"Did she ever say anything about an English prisoner of war?" I asked trying to contain my excited curiosity.

"Yes she did. He was good man my grandmother says and in love with the German woman Katharina I think."

I was certainly not ready for this bombshell and wondered if he was not stringing us along.

"Can you take us to the big house?" I asked.

He said something to his companions and then replied, "I will take you but it is old and dangerous now. The Russians and Germans make little farms for their people over the years. Come, not far, I take you."

We drove around in open country for some time and eventually diverted off the road and down a track that Simon and I thought we'd passed earlier that morning. As the high hedgerows opened out we could see a large building, invisible from the road, at the end of the track. We entered a courtyard and stopped. It had obviously been a magnificent country mansion but was now a derelict empty shell, a skeleton which had once supported the confident, extrovert expression of a proud, flamboyant body. The stucco plaster decoration had long ago fallen off the walls leaving areas of bare brick. Any colour had bleached out long ago. The roof had fallen in probably as a result of a fire. Evidence of neglect and decay were everywhere. Simon walked through a stone archway, surprisingly still standing, and made his way towards what would have been the formal garden and grand entrance to the manor but the garden was long overgrown with neglect and the wide steps leading up to the entrance were now either dislodged or broken and covered with green moss and lichen. Where once had been proud Doric columns stood two broken stumps like rotting teeth in a skull. Pane-less windows gazed out, lifeless across the landscape and fire-blackened eyebrows reached up to the non-existent hairline. Some outhouses on my left took my attention and I wandered through one of the doors hanging at a precarious angle on one large rusty hinge. The room had once obviously been a byre but at some time had been converted into a living space. There was a metal stove with ash and twigs spilling out and the flue pip disconnected and dangerously hanging from the roof. Next to the stove was a dresser also leaning at an angle, with some drawers missing and others hanging out covered with cobwebs and the dust of years. A cracked and broken stone sink filled with rubbish and topped by an old-fashioned hand pump stood beside the dresser. An upturned table with one leg broken off and a broken dining chair were in the middle of the floor together with an easy armchair with straw and horsehair escaping from a myriad slashes in the leather cover. At the far end of the room was what remained of a massive double bed. The mattress, disinterred of its stuffing, was folded, damp, stained and stank and the once magnificent headboard and footboard of solid carved walnut leaned inwards almost touching in the centre. I moved over to the window where what was left of the window glass was so smeared with layers of dirt that it was impossible to see through. The shutters had long ago fallen off. I turned away and dragged my finger through the dust on the windowsill. It was a silly thing to do and I involuntarily exhaled an 'ouch' as a splinter lodged under my skin. I looked down at the rough area where the splinter had detached itself and noticed what looked like carved letters. Taking more care this time I brushed some more and blowing away the excess dust and dirt couldn't help but shriek at the top of my voice in unbounded excitement.

Simon and Stanislav, hearing my scream came running into the courtyard with Simon shouting, "Hazel...are you alright...where are you?"

"I'm in here Simon, I'm okay, come here, quick, you're never going to believe this."

"Are you sure you're alright?" Simon gasped breathless on entering the doorway.

"Yes, yes, look at this, I can't believe it, my God it can't be...."

Simon looked at the windowsill and read out what was carved there. '*Robert Charlton 9th. DLI 1916/17/18/19.*' My God, you've really hit the jackpot this time. It's unbelievable, after all this time.

Stanislav looked puzzled and I said, "This is my great grandfather. He is the English prisoner of war who was here with your great grandparents."

"So it was all true," he replied sagely.

Leaving the outhouse we made our way to where the once formal garden and the cultivated fields rubbed up against each other. The golden wheat was ready for harvesting, full heavy heads swaying gently in the light zephyr and the heat haze shimmering, dancing and blurring. I imagine Robert must have stood here almost a hundred years ago casting a contented eye over his labours. Remembering what Stanislav had told us a little earlier I also wondered whether or not Katharina had been at his side. Three years together, anything is possible, especially if her husband was indeed a bastard and she was lonely. Was it just an interlude, a moment in time? What lasting affect would this have on each of their future lives I wondered? We are what our past has made of us and our life choices are sometimes tinged with regret. I wonder if Robert carried this moment with him into his future relationship with Rhoda. Are we all doomed to a life of sadness, regret, moments left unresolved irretrievably frozen in our consciousness?

Stanislav pointed way into the distance and said, "See woods. Nazi Concentration Camp down there for Jews in war. Gone now but many die. Not many people remember it now."

"Ooooh! I don't want to get into that now," I said I'm too excited about what we've discovered." I took Stanislav's hand and shook it saying, "Thank you so much Stanislav, we would never have found this place without you. Another stroke of good fortune so once again, thank you so much."

"I pleased to help make you happy," Stanislav replied beaming. "I tell my friends at bar. They not believe me."

"If you're finished here Hazel, come on, we'll take Stanislav back to the bar, see if they can give us a spot of lunch, and no vodka this time, and then hit the road for Prague.

Sitting on our balcony enjoying the sun one late summer afternoon I mused that my family research has taken almost a year and has cost a lot of money. Not just on the trips to Cologne, Koblenz and Ciechanow but also the cost of paying for various archivists' time and the cost of copied documents. It's just as well that Simon doesn't know about these hidden expenses. He's been such a dear but I just had to satisfy my curiosity one more time in order to finish this part of the jigsaw. My laptop was open, as ever, and I was desperate for an email back from the Archiv des Erzbistums München und Freising. A couple of days ago I had sent them an email giving as much data as I had about Albrecht and Katharina and asked them if they could provide me with any further information. I went into the kitchen to get myself an iced drink when a ping, you've got mail, sent me rushing back through the lounge. It was silly to be in such a hurry as I receive dozens of emails every day but I was so hyped up and in such a hurry that I nearly knocked my laptop over the balcony down on to the tram tracks far below. "Yeeeesss," I shouted, there it was, they had found some relevant information which they would post to me on receipt of their fees.

A week later there they were on the table. All was confirmed. Albrecht had married Katharina Klaus on 10th. March 1896 at Riedering Catholic Church. Her father Werner and mother Helga signed as witnesses and the home address was given as Simsee Farm, Riedering, Rosenheim, München. The second document stunned me and it took me some time to gather my thoughts and consider its implications. It was a birth certificate for a boy, Otto, born on 5th. December 1919, mother Katharina von Lieper, father Albrecht von Lieper. I lined up the three remaining documents. They were all death certificates, one for Katharina and the others for her father and mother all killed on the same day 15th. October 1944 in an allied bombing raid on Munich. Apparently one of the bombers overshot the target and a stray bomb hit the farmhouse.

CHAPTER 29

Hazel 2012

Sitting on the balcony enjoying the heat of the Prague summer sun I could hear Simon in the living room speaking into his 'Blackberry'. Another problem at work I guessed and which was confirmed when the tap, tap, tap of his computer keyboard drifted through the French windows. I took another sip of chilled, cheap Czech white wine and continued surfing the net.

"What on earth are you looking at now? You're forever up in 'The Cloud' roaming the ether on that laptop. I think I'll drop it over the balcony one of these days."

"It's this family tree thing. I'm just trying to get a feel, a flavour for the period through which Gran lived. She was born during the First World War, lived through the General Strike and the Great Depression, the rise of Nazi Germany, the Second World War and the rise of the Welfare State as well as many other monumental events in history."

"Yeah, you haven't done anything about that for a while have you?" "I've been working, or haven't you noticed?"

"Okay, okay, don't get shirty, I was just saying."

"I think I'll get that old biscuit tin out again and see if I've missed anything."

A few minutes later and I was beginning to wish I hadn't. The piles of paper, letters, photographs and much more besides was as daunting as ever. I found it at the back of the wardrobe and brought it down stairs. I took the lid off and tipped it upside down. All the papers and photographs and the two scratched, well-worn, brown leather wallets dropped out. I picked each up in turn and although it was obvious that there was nothing inside I turned them upside down and shook them. The silk lining inside the largest wallet crackled, or at least something underneath the silk crackled and it was then that I noticed that a short length of stitching attaching the lining to the leather had come undone.

372

I squeezed the leather to open up the gap and peered inside. There, in the space between the leather and the lining I could see a piece of folded paper. I ripped the stitching a bit more as I put my finger and thumb through the gap to retrieve the paper. Unfolding it, it was obvious that it was a letter.

"Eeeeeeeh!" I screamed.

Simon came rushing into the living room, "Are you alright? What's the matter?"

"It's a letter," I blurted out, "There's a letter hidden in this old wallet."

"Get on with it then, read it out."

Although written in English the writing was beautifully executed but in that old German script which made reading it slow and ponderous.

Simsee Farm, Lake Simsee, Riedering, Nahe Rosenheim, München. December 1940.

Mein Liebster Liebling Robert,

I don't know whether or not you are reading this letter but if you are holding it in your hands then for the sake of the love we once had please read what I have to say. It is impossible for me to send a letter to England from Germany so I am giving it to a Jewish friend who is making his way to Palestine and he has promised to post the letter from Switzerland. If you are reading this then I am doubly blessed in so far as my friend has escaped to safety and I can feel close to you.

This letter is as painful for me to write as it must be for you to read but I hope that you will understand and that your anger will not end in hatred for I have loved you with all my heart and have never stopped doing so. You are probably wondering why I have decided to contact you after twenty years. I have wanted to many, many times and have lived to regret my decision not to accompany you to England after the war in 1919. I knew that once back home you would make your own life on your farm and that it would have been selfish and impossibly cruel of me to complicate any new relationship you had made.

Much has happened since we parted. The day after you left Chrzanowo in Poland, Albrecht and me travelled to Berlin where he was accidentally shot dead outside the railway station in one of the many violent street battles between the Communists and Social Democrats which were happening all over Germany at that time. Left on my own I went to live with my parents at the above address. In December the same year I gave birth to a baby boy, Otto. May God forgive me Robert I should have let you know but as I've said you would have your new life to build. Albrecht's name is on the birth certificate but he is yours Robert. We made a beautiful baby son together.'

"Oohh......my....God," I blurted out, "Step great-granddad Robert really did have a love affair with Frau Katharina von Lieper, Generalleutnant Albrecht's wife when he was a prisoner in Poland. How romantic is that?"

"And dangerous as well I suppose," Simon added. "Well you did wonder when we visited Chrzanowo a few months ago so now you know."

"This begs a very big question though. I wonder if Robert told Rhoda about this letter."

"I somehow doubt it," Simon considered, "Especially as it's been secreted away in this wallet. What purpose would it have achieved even if he had told her? No, I think the poor guy had to carry the burden of his past all by himself."

"Not necessarily," I responded thoughtfully. "Robert died before Rhoda and I expect she did what we're doing now, that is, go through all his private papers, photographs etc. etc. as you do when someone dies. She must have found the letter. Okay, Robert didn't tell her when he was alive but the letter was left there to be found later. So Robert is dead, we know that Katharina died in an air raid in 1944 so poor Rhoda as the last member of the triangle was left to carry the guilt and anger for both of them. The other question is; why didn't Rhoda destroy the letter? She could have done so in anger, she could have done it to protect the memory of their relationship and marriage or she could have done it so that future generations, i.e. us, wouldn't find out about our dodgy German connection. So why did she leave the letter there? More fascinating is the question, did Grannie Annie know about the letter? Did she read it and if so, when did she find out about her step-father's, German, SS son? Good God, her step-brother a Nazi."

I read on with difficulty as the words jumped around on the page because my hand was shaking.

'I know this will be a shock to you and I understand that you may even hate me for not informing you that you were a daddy at the time and that I have robbed you of the chance to know and love your son.

Our two nations are at war again and it is to my shame that Germans have supported Adolf Hitler who has brought us to this terrible conflict. It is with a heavy heart that I have to tell you that our beautiful innocent son succumbed to continuous Nazi indoctrination and propaganda and in spite of all my arguments and persuasion, to my eternal sorrow, he is a member of the Waffen SS and seems to delight in carrying out the Nazi doctrine of hatred for all people and things not German. On one occasion he even denounced his own mother to the Gestapo. I told him in 1940 that he was not a pure Aryan. That he was only half German because his father was English. He left the house in a temper fuelled by anger and hatred and I have not seen him since then. I suppose the news must have undermined his whole perception of self and the reason for his present and future existence. I fear that he will resolved this inner conflict and doubt by over compensating and lashing out and directing his hurt and anger at the innocent.

Oh how I have dreamed of the life we could have had in England bringing up our son together on your farm, but it was not to be. How I hate a Catholic doctrine which has been the cause of so much misery and denial of love. I think that my life was destined to be one of sorrow except for a tiny window in time when I loved and was loved in return and my soul soared. I do not know how I can ever ask, or expect, you to forgive me when I cannot even forgive myself.

Have you joined the army again, I wonder, to fight against Germany in this our second world war? I have a fantasy of you and Otto meeting on the field of battle and perhaps being drawn together by some mystical blood tie but in my heart I know this can never happen. Perhaps when this war is over there can be some reconciliation but coward that I am I will leave that decision to you dear Robert. I will understand if I hear nothing from you and it will never diminish my love for you.

Ich verlasse Sie mit meiner unsterblichen Liebe. Auf Wedersehen und Gott segnet Sie mein Liebling Robert. I leave you with my undying love. Goodbye and God remain with you my Darling Robert.

"Poor woman, how sad is that? Still I suppose we all have to live with the choices we make and she has certainly lived to regret hers."

"I suppose after all that time the guilt was just too much for her and she had to involve.... off-load onto Robert." Picking up the second wallet and looking inside Simon continued, "She was right in the letter, it was probably a cowardly thing to do after twenty years but hey, were only human." Automatically he did what I had done earlier and turned the second wallet upside down and shook it. He inspected it closely and in animated excitement shouted, "There's something inside this one as well, between the lining and the leather just like the first one."

Simon rummaged around with his index finger and eventually pulled out another piece of paper. "It... looks....to me...like a.... yes it is...it's a birth certificate."

I couldn't wait and rather rudely snatched the paper from Simon. It was a copy of the self-same birth certificate for Otto that we had collected a few months previous except that under, NAME OF FATHER where Generalleutnant Albrecht von Lieper was written it had been crossed out and replaced above it by Robert Charlton. The handwriting looked very suspiciously like that of the letter. We both sat in silence for a couple of minutes trying to take all this in. Taking another sip of wine, eventually I said. "Soooo.....let's recap on what we know. My great-grandfather John James married my great-grandmother, Rhoda in 1916. He died on The Somme in the September of the same year and Annie was born in the November. John James' friend, Robert was taken prisoner during the same action in which John James was killed. Because of the intervention of a high-ranking German Officer, Generalleutnant Albrecht von Lieper, Robert was shipped to Poland where he worked on a farm as a P.O.W. He was there for nearly three years during which time he had an affair with von Lieper's wife, Katharina. Katharina who lost both of her sons, Heinrich, 18 years old in 1914 and Walther also 18 years old in 1918 at Amiens. Von Lieper was on the other side of no-man's-land in command of the 2nd. Guards Infantry Division and was wounded in the same action that killed John James. When the war ended, Robert returned to England alone because Katharina, still being married to Albrecht would not go with him. She must have known that she was pregnant at the time but she didn't tell him. What a tumultuous decision that must have been for her, she must have been so torn apart. Robert comes back to Chepfield where eventually he marries John James' widow, Rhoda. He adopts Annie as his own and has three other children with Rhoda Elspeth, Rupert and Rowena. Meanwhile, Katharina and Albrecht leave Poland the day after Robert and Albrecht is accidentally shot during a political street battle in Berlin. Katharina returns to her former home near Munich to live with her parents. She gives birth to Robert's son, Otto, in December 1919 but registers Albrecht as the father. I suppose I can see the logic in her doing that because of her situation and her son's inheritance from the von Lieper family estate. Otto grows up during the Weimar Republic and the rise of Adolf Hitler and is seduced by Nazi political doctrine. Eventually when war comes he joins the Waffen SS. Meanwhile, in England, Annie grows up in quite a privileged household because of Robert's good fortune, and when war comes she too joins the army, doing what exactly, we don't know. Right... sooo... that leaves us with three loose ends. What did Annie get up to and what happened after the war and what happened to Otto?

CHAPTER 30

Hazel 2012

I watched dad as he opened the envelope that I'd just given to him. He looked at me with a sly hint of conspiratorial suspicion and slowly withdrew the card inside. His face instantly beamed and he pointed a finger at me. I'd also given mum an envelope and we both looked over at her to see her reaction. Her face was a picture. She looked at the card and stared uncomprehending. Dad's reaction was immediate and he held up two fingers before rushing over to give me a big hug and shake Simon's hand. Mum still had a blank stare, completely oblivious to what was unfolding. We all looked at her and burst out laughing as the cards were obviously scan photographs of an in-uterine foetus, well, twins actually. Eventually the penny dropped and the new Granny broke into a smile at last.

"I can't believe it," she said, "This was the last thing I expected. It was the farthest thing from my mind."

Even then she hadn't twigged that the two scans were of different babies. Mum's not normally slow on the uptake but her uncertainty and confusion were so funny and uncharacteristic. For the second time in a matter of few minutes the revelation that she was going to be the Granny of twins resulted in a shriek of excitement and a flood of tears.

"I was just not on this wavelength," mum said. "You always told us never to expect being grandparents. You were always going to be a career girl and babies were never on your horizon."

"Well, I suppose it's all this delving into the family tree. It's made me reassess my priorities and made me realise that families are the most important things in our lives."

"When are they due?" Mum asked.

"October."

"We'll have to clear our diary and come over to Prague then."

"Okay.....so now that we're all up to speed with what's happening," dad said smiling and looking at mum, "I'll disappear to Sainsbury's and get a bottle of champagne."

"That's okay dad," I said, "We came over from Prague to tell you in person rather than tell you over the phone and we've brought a bottle with us."

"Then we'll have two," dad replied never being one to pass up the chance of a few glasses rather than one.

Later when we were all a bit merry I plucked up my courage, rummaged in my bag and handed over Katharina's letter to Robert to my dad uncertain as to how he would react. We waited quietly whilst he read the letter through. He raised his head slowly and said, "Oh my God.....you really have opened up a can of worms haven't you."

"What is it?" mum asked with some evidence of trepidation.

"Well...." I said, "You know that step great grandfather Robert was a prisoner of war on a farm estate in Poland from 1916 to early 1919. The letter dad's got in his hand proves that he had an affair with Albrecht von Lieper's wife, Katharina, whilst the Generalleutnant was away at the western front. Not only that, and this is the biggy, they had a son together which great grandfather Robert knew nothing about when he came home to England after the war. That's not the worst of it. Apparently this son, Otto, grew up to become an SS Officer during the Second World War."

Dad looked at me and said slowly, "So this means that my mother, Annie, your grandmother, had a half-brother who was a Nazi during the last war. Bloody hell! So where is this Otto now? Do you know anything about him?"

"Not at the moment," I replied. "I seem to have come to a dead end. As you know thousands of records must have been destroyed during the war but I haven't given up yet."

"I'm not sure I want you to find him," dad replied.

During this conversation mum had quietly been reading the letter. "Why did she wait until 1940 to contact Robert? Why then, after all that time? She sat on this knowledge for twenty years. Reading through this letter the poor woman must have been tormented all that time. What an unhappy life she must have had. It appears that the only joy she had in her life was when she was with Robert and even then there must have been a huge cloud hanging over her....poor woman."

"Not only that but she also lost her first two sons in the First World War as well and I don't think that her marriage was a happy one." I added.

"What must Robert have gone through when he received this letter? Here he was in Chepfield bringing up his own family not even knowing that he had a son in Germany. I wonder if he ever told Rhoda about the affair or even told her that he'd received a letter from Katharina. It seems the more we find out the more questions it raises. I suppose all families have their little secrets and we'll never know."

"Not such a little secret I think," dad responded.

"It's fascinating though isn't it, you've got to agree," I said lightly. "We can't change history but it really is all... a bit....Gothic isn't it? I'm inspired all over again to try and track this Otto down."

"Well, all I can say is it's a good job your Granny Annie isn't here to listen to all of this." Dad said with resignation.

"I'm surprised at just how much material and information I've been able to unearth during this...quest. In fact I now know more about the family history than I do about the recent past. Whilst we're on the subject dad can't you fill me in on the rest of the family up to the present?"

"Where do you want me to start? You already know that Robert married your real great grandmother John James' widow Rhoda and adopted Annie as his own. Robert and Rhoda had some good fortune when Robert's previous love, Margaret, left him the business in Newcastle. So between them, Robert and Rhoda looked after the farm here in Chepfield and the haulage and fruit and vegetable businesses in Newcastle. Your great Aunt Libby was born in 1921, your great Uncle Rupert in 1923 and finally your Great Aunt Rowena was born in 1924. You've got all of their photos in the biscuit tin I gave you last time you were here. Libby trained as a primary school teacher and taught during the war. Later she married a local guy, Jim, who had a very successful career as a chemist with a specialist knowledge of metal corrosion in nuclear power stations. They had two sons. One went to Cambridge and the other to Oxford....one lives down south now and the other in Paris I think. Jim died some years ago after suffering from dementia and Libby died just a few weeks after Annie. Rupert served throughout the war in the medical corps, mainly in the Middle East. When he returned he attended Kings College in Newcastle which was part of Durham University in those days to read mining engineering. Unfortunately he was wounded during the war and also had a bad accident underground and had to abandon his studies. He'd always had a good voice and was a member of the chapel male voice choir so he decided to change careers and went to the London School of Music where he met his future wife Elspeth. He became a professional singer and even performed on the BBC. I think he had a bit of a struggle really and eventually after a spell as a pig farmer turned to music teaching in a secondary school in Suffolk. True to his roots though he stood for parliament as a labour candidate but had no chance in rural, Tory Suffolk. He's just died this year too. That leaves Rowena who's still with us and she trained as a secretary. That's about it I think."

"What about your dad?" I asked. "He was polish wasn't he? I don't really remember granddad."

"Yeah…well…there's a bit of mystery about this as well. As far as I know my mum was well educated with a degree in modern languages from Durham University before the war. She was enlisted in to the army but no one seems to know what she actually did during the war. Anyway, when the war finished she worked for the government I think in Germany for a while helping to get the country back on an even keel but even here I'm not sure what she was doing. She married my dad over there, a Polish refugee, Henryk Harmanecki, and then came back to live in the big house belonging to the business in Jesmond. Dad changed his name to Harman and we always called him Henry. Both he and mum ended up teaching languages and here I am. I remember being fascinated by his glass eye. He wouldn't talk about it in any great detail but he lost his eye during the war at the same time as his arm was badly wounded. He didn't like anyone to see the scars all up his chest and left arm. He died in peculiar circumstances in 1967. A tragic accident involving the gas cooker. I was an only child so you don't have any aunts or uncles. I met your mum at Leicester University and she has a sister, Linda who married a farmer and lived on a farm in Suffolk. You remember our summer holidays there when you and Brother Mark used to play with your cousins in the fields and barns. And of course they now live in Kelso. So they are your Aunt Lindy and Uncle Tony who produced your cousins Dick, Ted and Charlotte. There, that should flesh out your family tree a bit more. I'll draw it out and write it all down for you. I know that there are still lots of family secrets and sub-plots not to mention the shenanigans on your mum's side of the family but we'll leave that for another time eh? You can only stand so much excitement in one day, besides your mum's too excited about the next generation to worry about the last.

It had been a flying weekend visit and on Sunday afternoon dad drove us to Newcastle Airport to catch our flight for Prague. We walked into the departure lounge and mum and dad accompanied us as far as the gate. We kissed, hugged and said our goodbyes and mum as usual was in floods of tears as we finally waved and turned the corner out of sight.

Monday morning and I had the apartment to myself. Simon had gone off to work early as usual. In my excitement I was desperately trying not to drop toast crumbs onto my laptop keyboard. It was a pity that I hadn't known about Otto when I was in Koblenz enquiring about Albrecht von Lieper. I didn't think it would be a good idea to ask Simon to visit Koblenz again so an email would have to suffice. I googled the address of the Koblenz Bundesarchiv and sent an email requesting any records or information about SS Officer Otto von Lieper and sat back with my fingers crossed. Two days later I was reading the reply.

Thank you for your enquiry regarding SS Officer Otto von Lieper. I am sorry to inform you that no SchutzStaffel (SS) records remain in Germany. As you will appreciate many records were destroyed during the Second World War.

I could feel my heart plummeting like a lead sinker and I read on.

However at the end of the war whatever SS records were available were confiscated by the American Army and shipped to the USA. You might like to send a request to the National Archives and Records Administration College Park, Maryland, 8601 Adelphi Road, College Park, Maryland, 20740 – 6601. Good luck with your search. Bundesarchiv, Koblenz.

What a roller-coaster ride. I was sure that this wasn't good for my health as once again disappointment quickly changed to excitement and expectation and I could feel my heart thumping. I quickly sent off an email to the USA and sat back staring at the screen almost willing an immediate response.

* * * * *

There was panic at work. Some ship in the Adriatic had dragged an anchor severing a fibre optic cable for the internet service in the whole region. This was within his sphere of responsibility so Shawn had gone to work early to sort the problem out and I decided to stay in bed for an extra forty winks. However a thump on the lobby floor disturbed me so I decided that I might as well get up. My flip-flops slapped on the wooden stairs as I made my way down to the kitchen in the hope that a good dose of caffeine would fire up the synapses. I walked past the lounge door and the sun was already streaming in through the open balcony French windows presaging another blistering day. We generally received a lot of mail so that envelopes of various colours and size littering the floor behind the front door was not unusual. I stooped to pick them up and it took a few seconds to register that the large brown envelope had USA postage stamps. My heart thumping, I rushed into the kitchen and switched on the kettle whilst extracting a knife from a drawer to slit the envelope open. By now I was shaking with excitement. I pulled the documents out of the envelope and spread them out on the kitchen table. Although everything was in German it was obvious that this was a copy of Otto von Lieper's SS service record. What immediately drew my attention and interested me most was his photograph. The person staring out at me was dressed in the familiar black SS uniform with its highly polished peaked cap and prominent death head insignia. The eyes were hypnotic and even though it was only a two dimensional copy of a photograph they had a penetrating, unnerving potency but I had to admit that he was extremely handsome and dashing in that arrogant Aryan fashion. And yet, there was a strange, unsettling hint of something familiar about the face. I immediately dismissed this as familiarity with the historical archetype of young Germanic heroes as depicted in many Second World War history books.

I placed my coffee mug on the table and sat on a chair with one leg up and my knee tucked under my chin. Even though I found the old German Gothic writing difficult to decipher I began to piece together the broad outline of Otto's life and war. The record showed that he was from pure German stock stretching back over two hundred years except that what I knew and the German SS High Command didn't, was that Otto's father was English and not the Prussian Junker Albrecht von Lieper named in the documents and I allowed myself a wry smile.

According to his record Otto served in Poland early in the war before being transferred to Paris. I knew that *Verheiratet* meant married and picking up one of the papers it became obvious that it was a copy of a marriage certificate between Otto and a Sieglinde Himmler. My God! Could that really be THE Himmler I wondered. I would need to read up about Heinrich Himmler and his family but the witness signature at the bottom of the document definitely looked like H i m m l e r. Immediately after getting married Otto was posted again east where he joined Himmler's staff fighting the retreat to Berlin at which point his record ended abruptly. Could he have been killed by the Russians I wondered? I knew that the fighting during the last few months of the war against the Russian advance on Berlin had been fierce and uncompromising and that German casualities had been horrendous. The Germans were meticulous with their record keeping so I could only speculate. Perhaps in the chaos of the final months and weeks of the war the keeping of records was no longer a priority. Perhaps they had been lost or destroyed or perhaps it was Otto who had been destroyed and unaccounted for and I resigned myself to admitting that this was probably the end of the line as far as Otto was concerned. And then the facts hit me again. Otto was my step great grandfather's son, so, through his marriage to my great grandmother Rhoda, Otto, the SS Officer was my great uncle and my father's uncle. I wondered how he would take this latest news.

I had started a folder listing chronologically the information I had so far assembled about my ancestors and I decided to bring it down from our study upstairs so that I could add this recent set of documents. I collected the ring binder and deciding to look once again through my collection of letters, papers and photographs to see if I'd missed anything. I placed the old biscuit tin on top of the binder. Still in my dressing gown and slippers I made my way back down stairs. My feet were sweating and somehow my left foot slipped inside my flip-flop and I lost balance. I reached for the banister to stop myself tumbling down the stairs and in the process the Huntley and Palmer's biscuit tin slipped off the ring binder and crashed down the stairs bouncing off the wooden treads in turn with a loud clatter spilling the contents all over the hallway. "Shit." I hissed. At least I'd kept hold of the folder so I wouldn't have to replace everything in order again.

I put the binder on the kitchen table and getting down on my hands and knees started to shuffle all the old papers, letters and photographs together. I commenced to tidy up by picking up the wallets and replacing them inside the biscuit tin. I was just about to drop them into the tin when I noticed that the inside base was no longer flat but was tilted at an angle. It seemed obvious that it had been dislodged when it bounced down the stairs but a loose base in a mass produced biscuit tin was not something I'd expected. A few biscuit crumbs which had been trapped in the joint escaped onto the floor. Taking a knife from the kitchen drawer I held the tin sideways and inserted the knife into the gap jiggling it trying to dislodge the tight fitting false bottom. Whoever had made the false base had done a good job of disguising it with a perfect tight fit. After a few minutes twisting and manipulation the base came away with a jerk catching me unawares and sending some hidden contents skittering across the floor. There were a few photographs and some small boxes one of which had burst open spilling a medal onto the parquet flooring. By now I was beside myself with excitement and I gathered the contents up and placed them on the kitchen table.

I sat unmoving for some seconds just staring at the objects on the table. Then I slowly reached out and picked up the silver medal with its red, white and blue striped ribbon. It was a 1939/45 War Medal. I quickly reached for the nearest box and being all fingers and thumbs in my haste to open it the lid came away once again spilling the contents out onto the table. This time the medal had a green, black and orange/flame coloured ribbon with the words Defence Medal on the front. There was nothing to identify the owner of these medals but being as these tins had been in Gran's possession it seemed a fair assumption that they were hers. The next box revealed a red, dark blue and light blue ribbon attached to another medal with the words The 1939-1945 Star round the edge. There were four boxes left and I assumed that they too contained medals but nothing could have prepared me for their content. In the next box was a medal in the shape of a silver cross with its white and purple ribbon. On the back was engraved Capt. Annie Charlton 1945. Wow! So they **were** Granny's medals. As always my laptop was within reach and I googled 'Second World War Medals'. Scrolling through the list of military decorations I found the exact picture of Gran's medal. I sat back flabbergasted. She had only gone and won the Military Medal. How special was that I thought. What must she have done to win such a prestigious award? This was becoming to feel like all my Christmases rolled into one. With shaking hands I opened the next box more carefully this time to reveal another medal in the shape of a cross with two swords criss-crossed through the centre. The red and green ribbon had a silver-gilt palm attached to it. Around the centre were the words 'REPUBLIQUE * FRANCAISE' and on the reverse was once again engraved Capt. Annie Charlton 1945. Googling French military Second World War Medals revealed once again a replica of Gran's medal which turned out to be no less than the Croix de Guerre. The penultimate box also revealed a medal in the shape of a white enamelled cross also with the words 'REPUBLIQUE * FRANCAISE' clearly visible. I still had the French medals site open on my laptop and 'My God' the Legionne d' Honneur medal was staring back at me. What an exciting war Granny must have had. It seemed to me that there was little left that she could have been awarded but nothing prepared me for what was inside the final box. Removing the lid, there in the box was the unmistakable, iconic shape of a German, Nazi Iron Cross with its red ribbon flanked by black and white stripes. What on earth is a German Iron Cross doing amongst Second World War Allies medals I wondered as I picked it and turned it over in my hands. On the back was an engraving,

Annette Hugo – 1945

Inside the box was a business card size piece of cream coloured card with a printed inscription which read,

Annette Hugo
Für Treue und Verdienste um die Reich.
Adolf Hitler – 1944

and was signed in his own hand I presumed by Adolf Hitler himself.

'Who the hell was Annette Hugot?' I thought to myself. Not another blind alley. I took a deep breath and tried to calm myself down and think logically. Annette Hugo didn't sound a very Germanic name...more French I thought. Perhaps a friend of Granny. But why would a French woman be awarded a medal by the enemy? Could she have been working for the Germans I wondered, a traitor, a spy perhaps. In which case why was it in Granny's posession? Perhaps they had been friends and Granny had discovered she was a traitor and....Heaven forbid....killed her. My mind was once again going into overdrive.

I googled 'Translation' and then typed in the inscription from the back of the Iron Cross. The translation stared back at me, 'For loyalty and services to the Reich.' My immediate reaction was, what services, how loyal and over what period of time. I sat for some minutes staring at the medals then suddenly I remembered the photographs.

I picked up the black and white snaps. The first picture was of a group of four young women accompanied by Nazi officers. They were sitting at a pavement table outside a French cafe raising their glasses of wine in salute, laughing and generally seeming to be having a good time. On the back of the photo were four names written in the positions in which the four women were sitting. Beatrice, Marianne, Brigit and with excitement I read, Annette. So she was French. I turned the picture over to look again at Annette but she had her glass raised in such a position that it hid the bottom half of her face making recognition difficult. Beneath the names was written Paris – 1942.

The next photograph was a head and shoulders shot of a beautiful blonde young woman together with a handsome SS Officer taken at the same cafe as the first photo. On the back was written Annette and Otto, Paris 1942. Looking at the photo again it became obvious that the young woman had been caught unawares. It was not posed like the group photograph and was taken from the side catching her three-quarters profile. The officer was looking at her intently. The more I looked at the two people in the picture the more I had the feeling that there was something familiar about both their appearances. Nothing specific but just a nagging awareness. The last photograph showed a portrait of the same SS officer. On the back of this snap was written, 'To Annette, All my love.' 'Otto 1943.' Quickly I searched Otto's SS service papers on the table and held up the sheet with his photograph and placed the Paris snap alongside it. I felt relief and excitement and a number of other emotions as it was confirmation that they were both pictures of the same man, Otto von Lieper. But who was Annette?.

Absentmindedly I shuffled the photographs from Granny's biscuit tin and was immediately drawn to one photograph in particular. A picture of Gran as a young woman leaning against a haystack. She was standing with her head turned three quarters towards the camera in a pose almost exactly the same as the photograph taken in Paris. It was as if I'd been hit by a sledge hammer. 'My God' I thought, 'It can't be...... that is Annette.' The blonde hair was a little longer and she was wearing make-up but the same symetrical face with its clearly defined features and unblemished skin was the same woman beside the SS officer. Granny Annie was Annette.

I sorted through the old photographs more intently than I had previously and picked up another photo of Gran with her head resting on the shoulder of a man I presumed to be Granddad Henry. They looked very young and very much in love. I recognized that the photo had been taken standing on the door step of the family home in Jesmond. Once again the rush of recognition exploded in my head. I grabbed the photo of Otto and held it against the photo of Gran and Granddad. My heart skipped more than one beat and I froze staring at the obvious before my eyes but refusing to believe it. Although the two pictures were separated by a few years there was no mistaking the strong chisled facial features of Otto as he bent his head down towards Gran Annie. I could scarce believe what I was looking at. The implications of what I'd discovered were monumental and not a little frightening.

Simon sat quietly whilst I gabbled twenty to the dozen telling him what I'd discovered. The evidence was still spread out on the kitchen table from this morning and Simon shuffled the papers and picked up each medal in turn whilst letting me get it all out of my system.

"So....what conclusions do you draw from your latest discoveries?" he asked infuriatingly unemotional.

"What do you think?" I fired back. "See if your interpretation and conclusions are the same as mine."

"Well....I think you've proved conclusively this Annette's identity. We know that your Granny Annie was in the FANY during the war and that FANY personnel were recruited into the Special Operations Executive the SOE, working as agents in occupied France. We also know that Annie was in France during the war but we never knew in what capacity. It seems to me that your Gran was an agent and that Annette Hugo was her cover name. We don't know what, if any, were her specific orders but it's obvious that she befriended a Nazi SS officer, Otto, whilst in Paris and this may have been her specific mission, to access information and intelligence for the Allies. She must have established herself as a double agent and walked a very dangerous path. I hope that her control back in England knew what she was doing and the information she was feeding Otto because the Germans obviously valued her input and I guess this is why she was awarded the Iron Cross. She obviously fed some vital intelligence to the High Command for Hitler, no less, to present her with the medal."

"I agree...go on." I said with obvious anticipation.

"It seems to me that against all the odds Annie and Otto fell in love. But then we find that he married into the Himmler family. That doesn't surprise me. There's no way that the SS High Command would allow Otto to marry, ostensibly, a French national no matter how helpful she was being with intelligence."

"But then they seem to lose touch," I couldn't help interjecting. He's transferred to the east and then finds himself involved in the defence of Berlin against the Russian advance at the end of the war. It's at this point that the trail seems to go cold and we can only speculate."

"Go on then," Simon said, "speculate away. What's your take on what happened next?"

"Well.....somewhere between the end of the war and twelve months later Annie's working in Germany in some capacity and she marries a Polish refugee, Henryk Harmanecki who changes his name to Henry Harman and my Granny becomes Mrs. Annie Harman. From the photographs it's obvious that this Henryk Harmanecki is really Otto. He's changed his identity and you don't need a degree in psychology to guess why he would do that."

"To escape retribution I'd say," Simon offers. "Being an SS officer in the east we can make an educated guess that he was involved in some capacity in the Slav ethnic cleansing programme and the Jewish holocaust. Once the outcome of the war is beyond doubt Otto, like many other SS personnel, hid his identity to escape either capture by the Russians and certain death or capture by the Allies and prosecution for war crimes. I'd hazard a guess that he escaped through Berlin to the west and was housed in a refugee camp somewhere in northern Germany and that that's where he and Annie met up again by chance."

"Sounds very feasible. If that's what really happened I'd like to have been a fly on the wall when they came face to face again. How emotional and shocking must that have been? BUT......and this is the big shock. If what your saying is true, and I agree with you, then my Granny Annie married an SS officer who was probably a participant in the most horrific and heinous crimes against humanity. How could she do that? Not only that, BUT....MY GOD....he was also her brother. How unbelievable is that? Well.....her step-brother with no blood relation actually but still it's absolutely unbelievable."

"Of course the other big question is," Simon responded, "Did she know who he really was either before or later after they were married? Yes she must have known on meeting him again that Henryk was really Otto. But did she ever really know that he was her brother? We'll never know."

"All of this secrecy and subterfuge now raises doubts in my mind about the circumstances of Granddad's death."

"What do you mean?" Simon asked quizzically.

"Well....he died in 1967. It was a tragic accident when he supposedly left a gas ring on in the kitchen without lighting it. Or perhaps the flame blew out and he didn't notice....but anyway he was gassed and the coroner's verdict was death by misadventure. What if.....and I'm stretching my imagination here.....what if the guilt he'd been carrying all these years was finally too much for him? What if he took his own life? Even scarier is, what if the Jewish Mossad secret service had tracked him down and liquidated him or some descendant of a camp survivor recognized him and took revenge? I suppose we'll never know but these speculations can't be any more fantastic than the truth that we've already unearthed, don't you think?

I sat dazed taking all this in. "What am I going to tell dad? How can I tell him that his father was his mother's brother and the bad news that he was also an SS officer who was probably complicit in the deaths of thousands of innocent people? What should I do Simon?"

"I'm sorry sweetheart but I really think that it's a decision only you can make. But if you want my candid advice I'd let sleeping dogs lie. Perhaps you should tell him about his mother's exploits during the war but there is nothing but heartache to be gained by divulging all the other information about Otto. You're just going to have to accommodate the other stuff and come to terms with it yourself."

"It's just all too unbelievable. It's like a novel. Who would ever believe the pattern of the true events in the lives of these two people? Now that's an idea......."

"Oh noooo....... I don't like the sound of this." Simon moaned. "You don't mean what I think you mean ......do you?"

"Why not? It would make a fascinating novel and in any case I think Gran's life should be remembered for posterity. Just a minute....how does this sound for a beginning?

With a heavy, breaking heart Katharina turned away from the horse and trap bearing Robert away before it had even reached the archway leading out of the courtyard..........She was not sure whether the nausea that was overtaking her was due to her pregnancy or whether it was the realisation that she would never ever see her young English lover again."

****

BIBLIOGRAPHY

The following books helped provide the author with a background and context within which the fictional characters in the story play out their lives.

Beevor Antony   Berlin. (The Downfall 1945). Penguin

Beevor Antony   D-Day. (The Battle for Normandy). Penguin

Burleigh Michael   The Third Reich. (A New History). Pan

Evans Richard J.   **The Coming** of the **Third Reich. Penguin**

Evans Richard J.   The Third Reich in Power. Penguin

Evans Richard J.   The Third Reich at War. Penguin

Koch H. W.   The Hitler Youth. Coopers (Origins & Development 1922-1945). Square Press

Kramer Ann   Women Wartime Spies. Pen & Sword

Lowe Keith   Savage Continent. (Europe in the Aftermath of World War II). Penguin

McDonough Frank   Opposition & Resistance in Nazi Germany Cambridge University

Overy Richard   The Morbid Age. (Britain and the Crisis of Civilization, 1919 – 1939). Penguin

Overy Richard   The Third Reich. (A Chronicle). Quercus

Pugh Martin   We Danced All Night. (A Social History of Britain Between the Wars). Vintage

Robb George   British Culture and the First World War. Palgrave

Shephard Ben   The Long Road Home. (The Aftermath **of the second world war). Vintage**

Weale Adrian   **The SS – A New History Abacus**

Lightning Source UK Ltd.
Milton Keynes UK
UKOW06f2337020616

275518UK00016B/412/P